RICH MAN'S SKY

✦

WIL McCARTHY

RICH MAN'S SKY

This is a work of fiction. All the characters and events portrayed in this book are fictional, and any resemblance to real people or incidents is purely coincidental.

A Baen Books Original

Baen Publishing Enterprises
P.O. Box 1403
Riverdale, NY 10471
www.baen.com

ISBN: 978-1-9821-2604-9

Cover art by Dave Seeley

First printing, April 2021
First mass market printing, April 2022

Distributed by Simon & Schuster
1230 Avenue of the Americas
New York, NY 10020

Library of Congress Control Number: 2020058604

Printed in the United States of America

10 9 8 7 6 5 4 3 2 1

"I CAN DO THAT"

The President of the United States had asked Alice, four months ago: "Do you feel yourself to be expendable in the national interest?"

To which Alice had replied, "Yes, ma'am. Except to the extent it's my duty to remain a functional asset." The Air Force provided structure to Alice's life, and as its Commander in Chief, President Christina "Tina" Tompkins was at the very top of Alice's chain of command. So yeah, it wasn't in her nature to even think it over.

Tompkins had replied: "My *God* that's a good answer."

Something fishy was going on at Esley Shade Station; a rogue trillionaire, far from the reach of Earthly law, had built a structure capable of measurably affecting the Earth's climate, and thus the national security of the United States of America.

"The mission is to secure control, by any means necessary," the President had said.

"Yes, ma'am. I can do that," Alice had answered, with a calm that surprised everyone in the Oval Office, herself included.

"Let me be clear," the President insisted, not quite believing Alice understood her. "We *have* to intervene, and it has to be covert and deniable. Sex, lies, blackmail, pushing people out a goddamn airlock. Are you prepared to do these things for your country?"

Alice had frowned at that, not sure how to answer. "I don't have experience in zero gravity, ma'am. That would be my primary concern."

"Jeee-*zus*," the President had said to the assembled generals. "Cancel the rest of the interviews. I want this woman in orbit by the end of the week."

BOOKS by WIL McCARTHY

Rich Man's Sky
Antediluvian

The Queendom of Sol Series
The Collapsium
The Wellstone
Lost in Transmission
To Crush the Moon

The Waister Series
Aggressor Six
The Fall of Sirius

Flies from the Amber
Murder in the Solid State
Bloom
Once Upon a Galaxy

For Gary. Again.

1.1
16 March 2051

✧

Burning Man, Nevada, USA
Earth Surface

"Mother, you can't be serious."

"Why not? It's all mine in another two years; I can do whatever I want."

Alice Kyeong scoffed, then sighed. "You should sell it and move farther out. You could retire on the profits."

"I'm already retired."

And that was true, in a manner of speaking. The two of them were drinking piña coladas, sitting in hammocks slung above a tasteful arrangement of grass and paving stones, set between two steel cargo containers, in the shade of a palm tree that had done surprisingly well here, all things considered. Under the Revised Homestead Act, Alice's mother Soon-ja (or Sonya) Kyeong had acquired nine hundred square meters of bone-dry desert in the heart of the old Black Rock City, where the original Burning Man festival used to be held every year. One of the two steel containers held living quarters that were actually pretty luxe for just one person, and the other held an Intensive Grow Unit where recycled gray water and pink LED lighting fed a variety of vegetables and meat cultures that could, in theory, keep her fed indefinitely. The containers were painted a glossy white that refused to attract dust, and their roofs were adorned with photovoltaics and water-vapor-harvesting hydropanels and satellite and microwave antennas that (again, in theory) provided all the power and water and Guaranteed Personal Bandwidth, or GPB, a person or small family might require. With eighty percent internal recycling, plus free weekly trash service to pick up the sewer cake, the setup certainly covered the basics of daily life, and the Drip Feed even provided enough cash for her to order occasional clothes and stuff.

But what kind of life was that? What would she do if something *broke*?

"Fuck the vast resources of outer space," Sonya had said when she moved here five years ago. "Fuck cities and self-jamming traffic. Fuck corporate farms and robot waiters, and the wonders of the cruelty-free McDonald's hamburger. I'm going AWAY."

Alice had thought her mother was crazy, but if so she was the leading edge of a quarter-million other crazies. As people started really buying into the new Homestead Act, and as the price of container housing dropped and the quality improved, Burning Man, Nevada, had exploded (so to speak) well beyond the concentric rings and spokes of the once-nomadic Black Rock City, soon filling the canyon end to end with the cargo-container neighborhoods of Gerlach and Sulphur and Granite Peak and Jackson, finally flattening out against the edges of the Pyramid Lake Paiute

Reservation to the south. Like some weirdo Disneyland, where public nudity and intoxication were downright encouraged, it was full of food kiosks and colorful mesh shade canopies and piped music, all connected by a crazytown monorail system. Now there were even firm plans to run a hyperloop junction from Sacramento right through to the town center, connecting them all back to the civilization they had nominally abandoned.

And so, once her seven years of homesteading were up and the property was hers to buy and sell, Sonya Kyeong would be slinging her hammocks over some very pricey real estate indeed. It wasn't the first lucky break Sonya had blundered into through sheer randomness; she was like a car with a flat tire, unable or unwilling to drive in a straight line. Back when they'd lived in San Diego, she had once swapped Alice's bicycle for a set of old dishes, which turned out to be a collector's item, so she'd turned around and sold them for enough money to buy a working car *and* a brand-new bicycle.

"I'm giving it back to the government so there's nothing for you to inherit," Sonya insisted now, sipping from the curved metal straw that protruded from her drink glass. "One-dollar leaseback until I die, and then poof! You're disowned, baby girl. I can't be associated with what you're doing. At all."

Alice sighed again. "Mother, that doesn't even make sense. I don't want your house, or your money. You'd just be hurting yourself."

"Well, it's *my* self, to hurt if I want to. Personal sovereignty, yeah? Why are you even here? Shouldn't you be in flight training or something?"

"I'm finished with that. I finished yesterday, and came straight here to say goodbye."

"Wonderful. I'm so glad to hear it. So this time next month you'll be in the arms of your space pervert? 'Bigballs' or something? The drug addict?"

"His name is Igbal Renz, as you know—as *everyone* knows—and my contract doesn't specify that I'll get pregnant with *his child*. But he's funding a space colony, and I'm a colonist, so damn it, yes, having children is part of the deal."

"Ooh, I'll be such a proud grandmother. How many *men* is he inviting up to his colony, by the way? Hmm? And where exactly is it? Behind the L1 Mirror, a billion miles away? Such a *man's* man, blocking out the sunlight and calling it a gift to the people of Earth! But there's *nothing there*. Literally nothing, not even air. You think *this* is roughing it?" She spread her arms, encompassing her little square of paradise. Her cargo containers protected a fenced-in courtyard, a tiny, private oasis of green in the Black Rock Desert. "There isn't even gravity. Your bones will turn to mush in a week."

Alice paused, momentarily at a loss for words. Nearly everything her mother had just said was wrong in one way or another; the "L1 Mirror" was actually the Earth-Sun-Lagrange-1 Shade, or Esley Shade for short, and it wasn't a *mirror* at all. It was dark gray! And there was quite a lot of human-made stuff out there by deep space standards, and it was less than a *million* miles from Earth—only four times farther away than the Moon. And zero-gee adaptation drugs had a long track record of preventing bone loss and muscle wasting for years at a time, and of course were widely abused by body builders here on Earth. As everyone knew.

But it *was* true that fewer than ten percent of the colonists Igbal Renz had accepted so far were male, and fewer still had been granted flight privileges. It was true that Alice had questioned her mother's choice *to actually live* at Burning Man, full-time and forever. It might even be true that Igbal had a substance abuse problem; persistent rumors to that effect had been circulating for years. But so did Sonya Kyeong! It was half the reason people came out here—to vape and snort and inject their drugs of choice, away from disapproving eyes.

The hammocks creaked in the warm, dry breeze until the silence became uncomfortable. Finally Alice said, "Where do you think I get the impulse? You *should* be proud of me, for believing in something. In a better future. Like mother, like daughter, I'm going away, and I may never set foot on Earth again."

And all of that was true. Alice believed the future of humanity was in outer space, and it sure wasn't the governments of Earth that were making that happen. She'd waited all her life for NASA or ESA or somebody to set up real space stations and moon bases, and they hadn't. Men like Igbal Renz and Lawrence Edgar Killian had. Whatever their flaws, the Horsemen dreamed big.

Sonya sipped her drink in silence for a long moment, and then said, "Okay, fine. When you put it like that, I suppose you're entitled to my blessing, however strange it all seems. I suppose *all this* seems strange to *you*, so yes, I'm aware of the irony. You hear me? I'm aware. But understand this: If things went wrong here in Nevada I could just grab a parasol and *hitchhike* to Winnemucca. Hell, I could *walk* there in three days, with a backpack full of water and a Danielle Steele novel. You can't do that. You're going to really be at this guy's mercy."

"It's not just one guy," Alice told her.

"It is," Sonya insisted. "Hear me, baby girl: it is. I didn't like you going in the Air Force, either, but there was nothing . . . fishy about it. It's not like the male officers go around, you know . . . Yeah. And I know it gave you structure, which you seem to need. But I was glad when you got out. It meant you could finally start living! But oh, baby, *this* is how you do it? My heart breaks. You're breaking your poor mother's heart. But you're going to be thirty years old in a few months, so I suppose I have to start letting go."

Alice couldn't quite suppress a derisive snort at that, because by any reasonable measure Sonya had "let go" when Alice was thirteen. Maybe younger. There were so many more pressing matters to attend to! The drinking, the drugs, the parties, the men. Hadn't poor Sonya, the reluctant parent, waited long enough to start living her own life again? Alice had joined the Air Force not to spite her mother, but to pay for college. To pay for *anything*. To get anywhere at all.

Sonya glared over the rim of her glass for a moment, cold and sweaty in her hand, but then seemed to exhale her ugly thoughts, and relax.

"Can I see it from here?" she asked. "The mirror?"

"It's not a mirror. It's a solar collector. A solar power station."

"Okay, solar collector."

After a pause, and because she didn't want to confirm her mother's opinions about her surliness and ingratitude, Alice said, "You can kind of see it, yes. If you put on eclipse glasses, there's a very faint little circle near the center of the solar disc. That's where I'll be."

"At the center of the circle?"

"Close to the center, yes."

"Then that's where I'll look."

It was a weirdly maternal thing for her to say, and she seemed briefly smug about it. But after that, the two of them swung and sipped for a while without speaking. These were actually Alice's favorite times with her mother: when they sat quietly, with nothing to say. It let her imagine they were two normal people, with some kind of normal relationship. An Air Force colleague had once told her that Sonya Kyeong sounded like a textbook sociopath, and Alice had denied it vehemently. Nope. No way. Sociopaths were manipulative and charming! But over time Alice had come to suspect her mother was simply too lazy to put in the effort. An *incompetent* sociopath, putting on the guise of motherhood from time to time because it suited her ego.

"Are you running away from a boyfriend?" Sonya asked her now.

"No," Alice admitted. "I've been away from that stuff for a while now. From anything serious. You?"

Sonya shrugged. "Whatever. Nothing much. Nothing serious. I had *hopes* for you, Alice, to be different from your old Mommy, but the apple doesn't fall far, does it? Who knows. Maybe Bigballs will treat you nice."

"Mother—"

"Okay, okay. I'll stop. Just be careful out there, all right? I can say that much."

"I will," Alice assured her.

And that *wasn't* true. That wasn't even close to true, because the *President of the United States* her own self had asked Alice, four months ago: "Do you feel yourself to be expendable in the national interest?"

To which Alice had replied, "Yes, ma'am. Except to the extent it's my duty to remain a functional asset." The Air Force provided structure to Alice's life, yes, and as its Commander in Chief, President Christina "Tina" Tompkins was at the very top of Alice's chain of command. So yeah, even if Alice was technically allowed to say no to that question, it wasn't really in her nature to do so. Hell, it wasn't in her nature to even think it over.

Tompkins had replied: "My *God* that's a good answer."

What Sonya Kyeong didn't know—what fewer than fifty people in the whole world knew—was that Alice had not retired from government service at all, but had spent most of the past four months in the Marriott Stars Hotel in low Earth orbit. Delays in opening the hotel had nothing to do with supply lines or contractor difficulties or scaling up the life-support system. In fact, the hotel had been well on track to open three weeks *early*, until the Feds commandeered it as an impromptu command center, conscripting the twelve employees who were on site at the time, slapping uniforms on them and swearing them to life-in-prison secrecy.

Because yes, there *was* something fishy going on at Esley Shade Station; a rogue trillionaire, far from the reach of Earthly law, had built a structure capable of measurably affecting the Earth's climate, and thus the national security of the United States of America. What Sonya Kyeong didn't know was that her baby girl was on her way to Esley to, you know, *do something* about that.

"The mission is to secure control, by any means necessary," the President had said.

"Yes, ma'am. I can do that," Alice had answered, with a calm that surprised everyone in the Oval Office, herself included. After all, she was just a glorified paramedic, never pointed a weapon at a human being who wasn't already pointing one at her.

"Let me be clear," the President insisted, not quite believing Alice understood her. "Space used to belong to everyone, but there are parts of it now that very definitely don't. More and more of it is just some oligarch's private fantasies. Four powerful men, telling the rest of us how it's going to be. We'd be concerned even if Igbal Renz were *just* some sexist, hedonistic . . . person. But that's not the case. Look, he's a very smart man, and he's made himself very, very dangerous. We *have* to intervene, and it has to be covert and deniable. Sex, lies, blackmail, pushing people out a goddamn airlock. Are you prepared to do these things for your country?"

Alice had frowned at that, not sure how to answer. "I don't have experience in zero gravity, ma'am. That would be my primary concern."

"Jeee-*zus*," the President had said to the assembled generals. "Cancel the rest of the interviews. I want this woman in orbit by the end of the week."

1.2
21 March

✦

Paramaribo, Suriname
Earth Surface

"I can't believe how sweet this is," said Dona Obata.

"Agreed," Alice said. They had ordered coffee, and without asking any further questions the (human) waiter had brought it to them iced and black, with something like seventeen sugars mixed in.

They were on the patio of a crumbling stucco café in Paramaribo, Suriname, South America, sweating in the steam-cooker heat. Alice was wearing a white straw hat and flip-flops and a sundress, partly because she was undercover, and partly because the sun was too brutal for anything else. Jesus, one hundred fifty million kilometers away and it was still too damn close for comfort. At Earth-Sun Lagrange Point 1—the balancing point between the gravity of the Sun and Earth—the Sun would be 1.6 million kilometers closer still, and about two percent brighter and hotter. But of course they'd be hiding in a space station, in the shade of the Esley Shade, which was only one percent transparent to

11

visible light. Like a really dark pair of sunglasses—which Alice was also wearing.

Dona Obata—whose skin was the color of dark acorns—was wrapped in an African-print sarong, and wore wedge heels with leather wrappings halfway up to her knee. No hat or glasses for her, but she did pick a seat facing away from the midmorning glare, and was sweating profusely. Dona was also undercover, from someplace called *le Commandement des Opérations Spéciales*. The third member of their undercover party, First Sergeant Bethy Powell of the New Zealand Special Air Service, would be meeting them tomorrow night before the launch.

"I hear sugar is practically free here," Dona added. She was nominally French, though she'd grown up in the Republic of Congo, somewhere near Kinshasa, and still carried the accent. Her cover story was that she was a twenty-eight-year-old tax auditor, no kids, never married. Alice didn't know much about her actual history, or where she'd learned to fight, but knew that she was lethal at zero-gee hand-to-hand combat.

"Hmm," Alice said, touching the cold glass to her forehead for a moment.

They were staying in character, pretending they'd only just met, because Paramaribo was full of spies and reporters and space-industry professionals from all over the world, and the risk of being overheard and ratted out was substantial. The city was also full of scammers and hustlers of various kinds, and ethnically Dutch social climbers looking to get in the graces of whoever was in power. The street beside them was paved with bumpy rectangles of a material a bit like cobblestone and a bit like cinder block, and traveled by everything from autonomous trucks to noisily hovering delivery and surveillance drones and even the occasional donkey cart, and there were cameras on every corner, piped to God-knows-where. From this point forward, literally anyone could be listening.

A woman in a tank top, short shorts, and flip-flops approached them from the street.

"Hello?" she asked tentatively.

"Jeanette? Jeanette Schmidt?" Dona Obata asked, having recognized one of the civilian colonists from her profile pictures.

The woman looked relieved. "Yes. Are you Alice?"

"*She* is." Dona nodded toward Alice.

"Oh. Right. Of course. Vietnamese?"

"Korean American," Alice answered. Some might consider it a rude question, but Alice didn't, and anyway it was too damn hot to worry about anything but the cold beverage in her hand. In return she asked, "German American?"

"*Jawohl*, by way of four generations in Texas. May I sit?" Jeanette looked flustered, or maybe just overheated. She then proceeded to pull up a chair without waiting for an answer. She was surprisingly heavy for a space colonist—almost two meters tall, and thickish through the limbs and middle. Alice couldn't tell how much of it was fat and how much was muscle or skeleton, but right away she knew Jeanette Schmidt must have some skills in seriously short supply up on Esley Shade Station. In most countries on Earth, it was technically illegal to discriminate in hiring based on height or weight, but in the space business every kilogram of matter cost thirteen thousand U.S. dollars just to lift into orbit, so the value of the person herself had better exceed that, or she was most definitely staying on the ground. Alice herself was certainly a smaller-than-average person, and so was Dona Obata.

To Alice, Jeanette said, "I like your hat. I'd buy one if we weren't blasting off in two days. Hell, I still might."

"It's critical life-support equipment," Alice agreed.

She racked her brain for details about Jeanette Schmidt. They were shipping out for Esley with six other women besides Bethy Powell—six innocent civilians who had no idea they were headed into trouble, alongside three undercover soldiers bent on mayhem. Six dossiers were not a lot to memorize, but Alice hadn't done it. All she could dredge up was that Jeanette was the youngest of the group. Maybe twenty-five years old? She looked it, too.

"You're coming from a mining school in Colorado?" Dona asked her.

She smiled. "School of Mines, yes. It's more like a mathematical school, or an economics one, but my master's degree is in Near Earth Asteroid Resource Utilization. So yes."

"Ah," Alice said. That answered that. The Esley Shade and station were made of asteroidal material, and so was everything else they were building up there. Degrees like Jeanette's were rare, and in high demand, so she could probably have carried the mass of four people and still gotten the job.

As if sensing Alice's thoughts, Jeanette looked sideways at her for a moment and then said in her light Texas drawl, "I also want kids, and not necessarily in the framework of a traditional relationship. And I rank very low in claustrophobia and agoraphobia, high in agreeability, and I meet the IQ requirement with room to spare."

It was a challenge of sorts. *I meet the profile, lady. Why are *you* here?*

Dona intervened, saying to Alice, "Aren't you also from Colorado?"

To which Alice said, "Intermittently, yes."

"Ah, that's right. You're in the Air Force."

Alice made a dismissive gesture she hoped did not look calculated. "Not now, but I was, yes. A member of the Pararescuemen, which is an air-drop medical team."

They were far more than that, as Dona knew perfectly well. The Pararescuemen were the silent accompaniment to special forces of nearly every other branch of the U.S. military. When some shot-up Navy Seal screamed "Medical Evac!" into a walkie, from an exposed position on some godforsaken beach, it was someone like Alice Kyeong he was screaming it to. *We couldn't handle it here, so we need *you* to come get us.*

And of course the Special Tactics Rescue Squadrons were elite fighting units in their own right, and the 23rd was first among equals. Alice could pilot a glider, had been through Airborne School and Underwater Combat Training and EMT-paramedic training, and could eat Army Ranger School for breakfast. She'd gone in with a pre–GI Bill associate's degree in aeronautical engineering from the University of Colorado (C-minus average), and always figured when she got out, *if* she got out, she'd take a job with the Flight for Life air ambulance service or something. Some of the Maroon Berets chose medical school instead, but that was not the solid job guarantee it once had been, and anyway it seemed so *dull*. Alice actually had no clear idea what she wanted to do with her life, but prodding the diseased flesh of flabby civilians probably wasn't it. On that basis, even Flight for Life would be a questionable choice.

"I got out last August," Alice said, "when I heard Renz Ventures was recruiting for long-term space colonists. I figured my qualifications would jump me to the front of the line, and I was right."

Of course, the Renz Ventures recruitment team had thought they were speaking with someone in Colorado Springs. Some of the time that was true—especially when they flew out to interview her in person—but most of the time she was up at the Marriott Stars, getting the shit kicked out of her by people like Dona Obata and Bethy Powell, and the U.S. Space Force combat instructors. "Zedo" was the art of hand-to-hand combat in microgravity, and it had literally been pounded into Alice over a period of months. The "physical screening" RzVz had done was trivial by comparison. Ten pushups? Fifty sit-ups? A zero-gee multi-parabola flight totaling less than two minutes of weightlessness? The hardest thing they'd asked her to do was swim out the window of an airplane they'd slid down some cables, into a tank full of water that never even touched the rounded top of the fuselage's ceiling. There wasn't even any glass for her to break through, or parachute to fight her way out of. She'd completed the entire course in a single week, and then gone back "home" to the Marriott Stars.

So the only real cover in Alice's backstory was the fiction that she'd spent the winter living off savings, eating instant ramen in a duplex she'd bought back in the liquidity crunch of 2046. But it really was her house, and she really did spend some time there, living simply, and she really had sold it so she could move to outer space. All that was perfectly true, and it did not leave much for her to memorize or screw up. Which was good, because her life had not given her much reason to practice her acting skills, and she was constantly surprised by how stiff and wooden she appeared in photographs and videos other people had taken of her. Point a camera at her and she froze. So yeah, a deep, convincing cover was not something she was sure she could pull off.

And so, as her own self, she was a little piqued with the chip on Jeanette Schmidt's shoulder. Agreeable? Really? Try a High Altitude Low Opening parachute jump into choppy coastal waters, with cartel bullets rat-a-tat-tatting from the shoreline. But here and now it was too hot to argue—too hot even to maintain her annoyance, so Alice simply, belatedly stuck out her hand and said, "It's nice to meet you."

It was weird, the contrast of this moment with her months in orbital combat training. She remembered Dona Obata landing a roundhouse kick on the side of her head four weeks ago. Even though Dona had been taking it slow, and wearing padded kickboxing boots, Alice had spun away on a trail of blood droplets and hit the Bubble hard, and spent the rest of the shift with an icepack clutched to her temple. How did Dona know how to *move* like that? A lifetime in gravity, a billion years *evolving* in gravity, and Dona somehow took to space like a ballerina. And Bethy! Jesus. Bethy Powell had grown up on a cattle ranch with four brothers, and it showed on the way she could wrestle and punch and knee and gouge and *twist*.

"Go!" the instructor would shout, and even if Alice and Bethy were twenty meters apart, Bethy would launch herself like a ball of pure aggression, and before Alice knew it she'd be snugged against the hotel's smooth, white Bubble wall in a submission hold, struggling for breath. Every goddamn time. Against the instructors she felt a bit more competent, because they were skilled at fighting down to her level, but even so she was not a large woman, nor a particularly strong or agile one. Just very, very determined.

Two of the five initial mission candidates had been weeded out as hopeless, but Alice had been retained for training and then finally selected for the mission, either because she was still the best they had (a distant third place was still better than a distant fourth or fifth), or simply because she'd never complained. Got the shit kicked out of her every day for months and never complained, because she was a goddamn Maroon Beret and they didn't. Not an *Army* Maroon Beret, but a Pararescueman—elitest of the elite.

And surely she'd learned *something* in the process?

"Sorry, Alice," Bethy would say, with her slow down-under twang, then let go and drift away.

The lights in the Bubble were bright, and the windows

were small, and the final three candidates spent most of every day shift in that sphere of off-white blankness, enduring bone-strengthening gravity-replacement exercises to supplement the anti-wasting drugs, and learning various zero-gravity skills. Not just zedo, but how to fieldstrip an XREP stunner dart pistol, how to locate the Sun and Earth when there were no visual references, how to slither silently through inflatable obstacles covered in wind chimes, and of course Alice's favorite: how to tie back your coverall sleeves so they weren't in the fucking way all the time. The one time she'd nearly won a fight against Dona was because Dona's hair got caught in her zipper sleeve and she couldn't bring her arm down to block. She'd brought her knee up instead, trapping Alice's arm and spinning her hard against the Bubble, but not before Alice had landed a solid "practice punch" to the solar plexus. Take that, French Congo.

So many days like that. Ninety of them? It seemed impossible; when she thought back, she could only really account for maybe eighteen or twenty of those. Even harder to remember were the "nights" in the hab modules attached to the Bubble—in what would soon become the luxury suites of the Marriott Stars. From low Earth orbit the actual Sun provided fifty minutes of daylight and forty-six of darkness, over and over until you couldn't stand it anymore, but the hotel simulated a summertime routine of fourteen-hour "days" when the interior lights were at maximum the whole time, and nine-hour "nights" when the shades were closed and the lights were dimmed. Half an hour of twilight in between, when bland, nutritious meals were served.

By convention, the night shift was private in-your-cabin

time, and although most people didn't sleep much in space, Alice sure did. And the rest of the time she was trying (and failing) to meditate, or reading books on a ruggedized tablet she'd dragged through hell and back with the Pararescuemen. But those were just trashy romance novels, not memorable, either. Buxom women getting kidnapped by suspiciously polite pirates, or falling in love with suspiciously intelligent handymen or business moguls with more free time than any real person ever had. Sometimes women falling in love with other women, not because Alice had any leanings in that direction, but just for variety's sake in that monotonous place. Say what you like; she had expected living in outer fucking space to be a *lot* more exciting.

The most memorable thing about the Bubble was its smell: a weirdly antiseptic blend of air conditioners, new-car plastic, gymnasium sweat and Fresh Mountain Pine. The hab modules were the same, minus the sweat—a small mercy for which Marriott was presumably thankful, since they would probably never be able to fully clean that reek out of the Bubble.

Paramaribo also smelled of sweat, but other than that its aroma couldn't be more different—a mélange of rotting salt marshes, food on the edge of spoiling, old-fashioned asphalt and diesel smog, and a million different flowers calling out to the hummingbirds.

Having joined Alice and Dona at the little iron-mesh table, Jeanette Schmidt ordered a margarita (which Alice hadn't even realized was an option), and produced a little paper fan.

"I'd sell my soul if I lived here," she said, with sweat trickling off every part of her. "For a little sphere of cool air to follow me around."

"No buyers," Dona answered. "Trade sanctions."

"Ah, bullshit," Jeanette said. "There are twelve countries under ITAR sanction, doing just fine. *Some*body's buying souls, and refining them into rocket fuel."

"You've sold it already," Alice told her. "To the sperm of Igbal Renz."

That came out sounding darker than she'd intended, and she immediately realized she was going to have to watch that shit, because she was supposed to be just another eager colonist lining up to have space babies of her own. But Jesus, ITAR stood for International Traffic in Arms Regulations, and it meant the little nation of Suriname was illegally importing and assembling rocket parts that could be used to drop a warhead anywhere on Earth. They really could. And those parts were coming from illegal 3D printers in Mauritania and Sudan and rogue bits of the former North Korea, fed by engineering talent parked in international waters, and raw materials coming from all over Africa and South Asia.

Renz Ventures spent a lot of money in places like this. Some would say they *laundered* a lot of money in places like this, but the distinction hardly mattered, because you couldn't extradite a global supply chain and put it on trial, and you couldn't declare war on the economic renaissance these countries were enjoying. Hell, America couldn't even declare war on the drug cartels, not really. Just shoot them up when they really, really, *really* crossed the line on human rights, and wait for the power vacuum to fill again next week. But the Embargo States were different: better organized, less autocratic, with a rising middle class who did not like their shit being meddled with.

And RzVz was only the most public face of the industry. Dan Beseman was up there quietly building his robotic Mars base, and that Orlov guy was . . . running an orbital fuel factory or something? Alice was embarrassingly vague on the details, except that the U.S. government had its eye on him as well, and the people in charge of Alice's recruitment and training had made some veiled references to "additional strategic interventions" in outer space, sometime in the nearish future. And of course there was Lawrence Edgar Killian, who traveled the world in a shiny orange blimp, and controlled assets on the Moon's south pole. *The New Yorker* had once run a cartoon of the Horsemen: caricatures floating in spacesuits and holding up cardboard signs. Dan Beseman's said MARS OR BUST!!!, beneath a face that looked at once vapid and obsessive. Lawrence Killian floated beside him with an overly serene expression, a monk's robe over his spacesuit, and a sort of steel halo riveted to the top of his space helmet. He held a sign that said GOD PUT THE MOON CLOSER. The most insulting caricature was of Igbal Renz, who was drooling, had a hypodermic needle sticking out of his arm, and somehow had an unzipped fly at the crotch of his spacesuit. His sloppily painted message said HEH. SPACE. Upside down from the three of them, a scowling Grigory Orlov, with braided epaulets on his shoulders, held a (right-side-up) sign that said PAY ME TO EXIST.

The caption beneath all of them: *Relax. The future is in good hands.* It had gone viral on various data networks, but even after all the briefings Alice had sat through, that one little cartoon was about eighty percent of what she knew about where she was headed.

"I sold my soul, too," she added, now, trying to sound more cheerful. "It's the price of admission to outer space."

"You're talking about my *eggs*," Jeanette corrected sweatily. "Yes, those are sold, along with the womb space to develop them. Although I hear Iggy's pretty far along with his liquid-phase incubators."

"No EMA slowing him down," Dona said, in seeming approval.

Jeanette blinked. "EMA?"

"Uh, it's like your Food and Drug Administration, I think. Nosy bureaucrats."

"Ah. Well, yes. I imagine that helps, yes. Along with unlimited funding! Anyway, whatever. Thank you for letting me sit with you; you're the only two team members I was able to track down. A lot of people are still in transit or something. Or lying low."

"How long have you been here?" Dona asked.

"In Suriname? Two days. In Paramaribo specifically? Since this morning. I took the bus from Georgetown. I do *not* recommend it."

Georgetown was across the border in Guyana, which was legally accessible via commercial flights from the United States.

"I flew in from Cuba," Dona said, perhaps truthfully. "I *do* recommend that."

Alice kept her trap shut, because she had personally

taken an Air Force cargo jumper to the USS *John Travolta*, parked out past the continental shelf, and rode shotgun on a mismarked civilian helicopter to the outer suburb of Lelydorp, from which she'd used paper currency to hire a series of taxicabs. Chances were, the Surinamese authorities knew the U.S. had inserted *somebody*, but since that happened on a weekly basis, they wouldn't find it particularly remarkable. Still, it had been dumb. American dumb: expensive and complicated and pretty much unnecessary. Immigration control here was a joke; you didn't even need a passport from most ports of entry, and anyway Alice Kyeong was *supposed to be here*.

"It *is* nice to meet you out here in the sunshine," Alice said, to change the subject, "but I think I can just meet everyone else in the Playa Blanca bar."

Dona snorted at that. "Ah, yes. The beach."

The Playa Blanca was a hotel owned by RzVz, and was where colonists and staffers checked in to await their ride to orbit. The name was a bit of a joke, as it meant "White Beach"—something Paramaribo definitely did not have. It was a town of white clapboard and red brick, with colorful metal roofs, and with grass and palm trees sprouting up from everyplace that wasn't freshly paved. With its rusty, sun-faded charm, Paramaribo was the sort of place one might *expect* to find nice beaches. But no, the land seemed mostly to slope down into reeking mangrove swamps, and the occasional shoreline of muddy gravel that reminded Alice of a dozen rough HALO drops she'd made over the course of her six-year career. The hotel bar was nice, though. And cool. Perhaps the name

Playa Blanca simply meant: This is where all the white people wash up. A White Beach indeed.

"Well, I wanted to get out and look at the place," Jeanette said. "I was expecting something a bit more refined, but okay. With all the money flowing through here it should be nice in twenty years."

"It's not so bad here," Alice said. "You want to see real chaos, go to Burning Man sometime. Money flows through there, too, and that hasn't straightened it out."

To which Jeanette replied, "Honey, I sure won't. If things go according to plan, this town might be the last place on Earth any of us ever see. Isn't that a strange thought?"

It was, yes. But Alice and Dona were here to make sure things *didn't* go according to plan, at least in terms of Igbal Renz retaining steering control over the Esley Shade.

"There aren't many left to meet," Dona said. "Three of us are already in orbit."

That surprised Alice and Jeanette both.

"Really?" Jeanette asked. "Which three?"

"Nonna Rostov of the Russian Federation, who is some sort of materials scientist; Saira Batra, who's a mathematician; and then some Argentine engineer whose name I forget."

"Is it Pelu Figueroa?"

"Yes, that's her. The three of them caught a commercial cargo throw up to low Earth orbit yesterday, from Ascension Island, in the South Atlantic. I'm not sure why. Here at *our* launch site, we're meeting Elizabeth Powell, Malagrite Aagesen, and Rachel Lee. That last one is a doctor, I believe."

"What kind of doctor?" Jeanette asked.

Dona shrugged. "No specialty listed, so I'm going to guess tube monitor."

That was another joke, kind of. Over the past decade or so, telerobotic medicine and nanorobotic medicine and AI diagnostics had sort of converged, and now there were more and more things treated in "the tubes" or "the barrels" or "the coffins" by, basically, fully autonomous robotic jellyfish. The economic fallout was hitting certain kinds of doctors very hard, and some of them responded by filling the on-site physician quota at a tube farm. Others met the challenge by quitting or changing careers or committing suicide. Or, perhaps, fleeing to outer space.

"There's a spaceport on Ascension Island?" Alice asked.

"Horizontal takeoff only, but yes. Since July."

"Where are you two getting all this information?" Alice demanded suddenly. "Was there an informatic I was supposed to download or something?"

"You're supposed to be monitoring the online crew manifest," Jeanette told her, not unkindly. "How do you know you're still scheduled to fly?"

"What do you . . . They can remove me from the flight? For what?"

"Of course they can. Somebody higher priority can bump you at any time. Or they could shift the weight allowance. How much stuff are you bringing?"

"Just e-books and personal effects. About six kilograms altogether."

Some rather *interesting* personal effects, courtesy of the Space Force and the Central Intelligence Agency, but all of it could pass through an AI luggage scanner without so much as a blip.

"Really? No candy or booze? What are you going to trade? What are you going to *do*?"

"Hmm. Look stupid?" Alice didn't know if this conversation was helping or hurting her cover, so she shut up again.

"You still have time to buy some of that," Jeanette said. "I'll help you."

"Hmm."

"Really, I think you should."

"Okay." Alice relented, partly because she didn't want to arouse suspicion, partly because Jeanette seemed like a genuinely nice person, partly because there were still thirty hours to kill, and partly because it actually did sound like a good idea. Funny that she hadn't really thought about the personal, practical side of all this: *actually* leaving Earth. *Actually* living on a space colony. Actually blending in by way of actually doing real work up there, and sharing living space with real people, until she and Dona and Bethy figured out when and how they were going to strike.

"This isn't something we want you to rush," President Tompkins had told the three of them in the Oval Office, over mugs of Kona coffee laced hard with Kentucky bourbon. "And it *certainly* isn't something we want you to botch."

Laurent Patenaude, the mustachioed president of France, had added, "Get them to trust you before you slip in the knife. It's the only way, really."

Something changed in Jeanette's face as Alice thought

these thoughts, and Alice worried again that she might just possibly be the worst spy the human race had ever seen. No poker face! None!

But fortunately, Jeanette read something altogether different into Alice's features. She asked: "Honey, are you scared? I know I am."

"I'm not scared," Alice said truthfully. Very little in this world truly frightened her, and some spoiled, sex-crazed trillionaire certainly didn't.

But Jeanette drew a deep breath of the city's stifling air and repeated, "I sure am. You know, when I was twelve years old, my father took me on an amusement park ride called the Slingshot. You had to wait in line for, like, three hours. They strapped you into this ball and cranked it back on giant bungee cords and just shot you up in the air, as high as the tallest buildings in Dallas. You could look down at the giant air conditioners on their roofs! But you know what the worst part was? Waiting in that line. Watching that ball go up in the air, over and over again, trailing screams of terror behind it. Dad and I nearly chickened out a dozen times, but we were also egging each other on, and even then I knew I wanted to be an astronaut. I'd *always* wanted to be an astronaut, and I figured, how am I ever going to strap myself in a rocket ship if I can't ride a damn amusement park ride? That's what settled it for me. That's what kept me in that line, and ultimately I think it's what kept my Dad there as well. The ride itself was really short. Just two seconds of gee force, two seconds of weightlessness, and then several minutes of pointless bouncing and spinning while they cranked the thing back down again. It was anticlimactic. It's the waiting that'll kill you."

Alice *could* see a hint of fear—more than a hint—in Jeanette's eyes. Now she wasn't thinking about her sweaty bus ride across Suriname and into Paramaribo. She wasn't thinking about the margarita in her hand or the night she was going to spend on clean hotel sheets. She was thinking about sitting in a thin tube of, basically, fiberglass, with a million pounds of thrust behind her, flaring out in a three-thousand-degrees-Celsius tower of flame and smoke, and absolute nothingness on the other side of that wall.

And although Alice had made that trip three separate times already, along with the fiery reentries to bring her back down, and fancied she had already mostly gotten over any nervousness and was solidly professional about the whole thing, she realized that attitude wasn't going to sit well with Jeanette Schmidt. To keep up appearances, Alice was going to have to show some (fake) vulnerability here.

"Okay, maybe I'm a little bit scared," she said, dredging up some of her feelings from that first trip to the Marriott Stars. Her first HALO jump was actually a lot scarier, so she thought about that, too. Ten-thousand-meter exit, nine-thousand-meter free fall, a thousand-meter arresting glide on a minimal parafoil chute, and then buckles-off and a ten-meter drop into water. That was broad daylight and clear skies, with a glassy-flat reservoir as the landing target; every step measured and monitored and the drop coach speaking calmly through her headset the whole time. And yet, the fatality rate for first-timers was well north of one percent, and the rate of serious injuries was closer to twenty percent. It was like stepping calmly into a car accident.

"Yes, yes, we're all properly afraid," Dona said dismissively. "But I'm thinking about something else. It occurs to me to wonder why colonists Batra, Figueroa, and Rostov were taken up ahead of schedule, and on a cargo flight. What's the hurry? Unless RizzVizz *are* shifting things around on the manifest."

"What's your point?" Alice asked, with genuine annoyance. Here she was, trying to shore up her cover story, and here Dona was just walking right on over it. Talking *way* too close to the troubling facts.

"My point is, I don't like it," Dona said. "It smells bad. It gives me cause to worry how secure our *own* seats really are, or how professionally this project is being run."

And then Alice realized that Dona was actually trying to share operational insights with her. They were undercover, yes, and could not speak freely, so Dona had to make herself sound like an annoyed tourist rather than a hired assassin. But the distinction was surprisingly moot: *What if our flight is canceled? What if we don't get to go?* Could months of planning go down in flames because an entry in a spreadsheet cell had changed? Esley Shade Station supposedly had enough emergency transports parked in LEO to get everyone back to Earth (though probably hungry and thirsty and bored and stinking to high heaven), but there was only one regular crew ferry, and it held twelve people and came to Earth every ten weeks. So what would happen if, for example, Alice and Dona got bumped to the next mission, and Bethy Powell got to Esley two and a half months ahead of them?

Too much opportunity for someone to screw up, or for someone to get smart and figure out that not all of their colonists were legit. If this mission were an outright *assault*, the Space Force would be handling it. This was something slower and quieter. But no, that didn't mean they had all spring and summer to get it wrapped up. And it opened up an even more serious possibility: that Bethy might secure the Esley Shade on her own, leaving the government of New Zealand in charge of things, with France and the USA forced to deal at arm's length, along with the other four Coalition nations. From the point of view of the President, the Department of Defense and the CIA, that would be nearly as bad as leaving the Shade in Igbal's hands.

"Suriname *is* noted for its stability and high ethical standards," Jeanette offered wryly.

"Mmm." Dona was not amused by that.

"Well, is there anything we can actually do?" Alice asked.

Dona shrugged. "Probably not. But until we're actually on that crew shuttle, spiraling out and away, we're not really secure."

"Hmm. Great."

Changing the subject again, Jeanette asked Alice, "So you've been to Burning Man, huh? Was that the festival or the town?"

"Both, actually," Alice answered. "My mother dragged me to the last three festivals, when I was in grade school. But I was talking about the town, where she's a founding resident."

"Oh. Well, that's kind of neat. Are you and your mother close?"

Alice snorted. "Ah, no. She's crazy."

"Honey, everyone's mother is crazy. Mine was a full-time homemaker with a PhD and a whole shelf of psychiatric medicines. How about you, Dona?"

Still unamused, Dona said, "A seamstress, back when that was still a human job. My father was her postman. Is it crazy that they put three children through college in Europe? I don't know what they were thinking. My mother's a saint. I'm sorry yours isn't."

"Oh, now don't be a buzzkill," Jeanette said, again not unkindly. "We're just making conversation, here. Nothing serious intended."

"They're still in Africa, with no children to look after them. I could get them admitted into France, but they refuse to budge."

"I'm sure they're lovely people."

"Thank you. They are."

"And now you're leaving the *planet*," Jeanette said, her face lighting up with sympathy. "From space, you *really* can't help them. And here I am making jokes."

Alice didn't know how much of what Dona was saying was true and how much was bullshit cover story, and for the moment, she didn't care, because it was, again, treading too close to operationally sensitive areas. Dona wasn't really *moving* to outer space, and chances were her parents didn't even know she was visiting there at all. Did she have fake parents she could make a show of contacting? If not, then this whole subject was problematic, and offhand the only way Alice could think of to derail it was to throw some shade on it.

"Oh, boo-hoo," she said. "We're all leaving people behind."

"Well, that wasn't very nice," Jeanette said after a pause. To Alice's surprise, the look on Jeanette's face actually did make her feel bad. Question: *Why you gotta be like that?* Answer: *Because I'm a hired assassin, not a hired friend.* And like a good assassin she doubled down and pressed onward.

"I'm serious. We're leaving a whole planet behind, all of us, with the intention of not coming back. With the *contractual obligation* of bearing that pervert's children. Or somebody's. It's a big step, yes, and now is not the time to start crying about it."

"He's not a pervert," Dona said, snapping out of it. Getting back into character, where she belonged. "He's a great man."

To which Jeanette replied, "Oh, I think he might be a bit of a pervert."

And then somehow they were laughing, all three of them.

After that they shut up for a while and just drank their cool drinks, and watched the pedestrians and drones and robots and trucks and cars and bicycles go by.

"Such a busy place," Dona said finally.

And that was true: Suriname had started with one tiny spaceport, and then it was three, and then the three had merged into a whole city of airfields and launch pads and offshore platforms, and as of last year this little country was handling forty percent of all the off-Earth traffic. Forty percent! Next year it might be fifty, with the bulk of the growth coming directly out of the hides of the U.S. and Australian and French aerospace industries. That was the amount of traffic that skirted ITAR rules, and every other sort of rule except the rule of money. And the Four Horsemen—Igbal Renz, Dan Beseman, Grigory Orlov, and Lawrence Edgar Killian—controlled the vast majority of that.

The idea made Alice shudder. Even reckless, heedless, emotionally stunted Alice, yes, because that was *way* too much power in *way* too few hands, and there was no telling where it might lead. If absolute power corrupts absolutely, and perverts could buy whole shiploads of willing brides and *blot out the fucking sun*, then yes, Alice was proud to be a part of the governmental response.

Ostensibly, the Esley Shade was about solar energy. ESL1 Shade Station was a giant factory and research laboratory, turning asteroidal material (basically, rocks) into habitat modules and spaceship parts, and that took tremendous amounts of power. Esley Shade Station was also constantly making more material for the Esley Shade, too. The larger it got, the more material it took to add another meter to its diameter, and also the more susceptible it was to getting holes and tears from micrometeoroids, which needed to be patched with additional material. So people seemed to think it was growing more slowly these days, but as the Space Force dudes had explained to her over and over, it was the *diameter* that was growing more slowly. The *area* was growing faster than ever.

All that would be scary enough if it were just out in empty space, but of course Bigballs had put the shade squarely between the Earth and Sun. To help cool the planet, he said. As a gift to the people of Earth, he said. But the fact was, by tipping the shade this way and that way, he could steer it with light pressure from the Sun, and decide which portions of Earth would have their sunlight reduced.

"It's an instrument of climate warfare," the President had said, "in the hands of a known drug user."

So yes, Paramaribo was a busy place, and yes, that mattered.

"We seem to have a visitor," Jeanette said suddenly, looking up at something behind Alice's head. Dona was looking that direction as well, so Alice turned her head just in time to see a buzzing microdrone the size of a hockey puck come whizzing to a stop a few meters from their table.

In a tinny yet creepily natural robotic voice, it said, "Dona Obata. Jeanette Schmidt. Alice Kyeong. Please acknowledge your identity."

"Acknowledged," Jeanette said.

More cautiously, Dona asked, "Are you from Renz Ventures?"

"Yes," the drone replied. "However, I'm not authorized to give any additional information without confirmed identities."

Sighing, Dona said, "All right. Acknowledged."

Annoyed, Alice said, "You know damn well who we are." By now, this little puck could have matched their faces against any number of global biometric databases. That was probably how it knew to approach them in the first place. But it was no more intelligent than a doorbell, and there was no point arguing with it, so she said, "Acknowledged."

The drone chimed. "Thank you. Passengers Dona

Obata, Jeanette Schmidt, and Alice Kyeong are requested to move to their assigned launch site within three hours."

Jeanette *did* try to argue with it, then, by asking, "Right now? Three hours? Why?"

It replied, "Launch schedules have been adjusted, spaceport wide. Passengers Dona Obata, Jeanette Schmidt, and Alice Kyeong are given three hours to collect belongings, perform personal hygiene, and travel to their assigned launch site. Pre-boarding procedures commence at 1:50 P.M. local time and will not be suspended or delayed."

"That's more than a full day early," Jeanette protested.

"Please acknowledge receipt of this message," the drone said.

"Acknowledged," all three of them said, in annoyed near-unison.

The drone chimed again, then retreated into the flow of traffic on the street.

"They could have just called," Jeanette said.

"Someone's checking up on us," Dona said, looking genuinely worried. "Something's not right. They want *us* in orbit early, too, which means the crew ferry's leaving Transit Point Station ahead of schedule."

"Which means what?" Alice asked, not following her reasoning.

"Could be embargo stuff," Dona speculated. "Renz Ventures is afraid of outside forces interfering with Suriname's internal affairs."

If that was true, Alice thought wryly, they were right to be afraid. However, the administration of ITAR sanctions sat largely with the United Nations, and there was no guarantee they didn't have some ham-handed, ground-level operations of their own in the works. Or, hell, even the mammoth U.S. government—five million bureaucrats, and growing!—with its overlapping jurisdictions and spirit of empowerment, might have dozens of operations going on that the President didn't specifically authorize or know about. Banking investigators, tax investigators, the customs service . . . the list was endless.

"That could fuck us hard," Alice said.

"Indeed," Dona agreed.

"Well, let's get going!" Jeanette piped up.

So they took a final sip from their drinks, and slapped way too many paper currency bills down on the table, because who was going to need them after this? Then they rushed out into the street, waving for a taxi.

And now that the launch was only a few hours away, and controlled by these yahoos rather than the U.S. Space Force, and Alice was headed not for a secret training base in low Earth orbit, but for a dangerous mission in the blackness of outer space, far from everything she'd ever known or loved, she did have to acknowledge that yeah, she actually *was* a little bit afraid. Well, damn.

2.1
21 March

✦

ESL1 Shade Station
Earth-Sun Lagrange Point 1
Extracislunar Space

Igbal Eilan Renz—Iggy to his closer associates—
eyeballed the vapor pen in his hands and breathed deeply,
oxygenating his blood for the ordeal ahead.

"You're back to the beta-three mixture," Pamela warned.

"Noted."

"It's going to last about twenty minutes, and you're
going to feel—how did you put it?—'paralytically jammed
in a soft, cold blankness.'"

"I remember, yeah. It was a rough trip. The Beings
barely spoke to me at all."

"Uh-huh. You can stop that deep breathing, you know.
Your pulse ox is ninety-eight."

"I know what I'm doing," he assured her. He was
cramming every oxygen molecule into his bloodstream
that he possibly could, because he knew from experience
that it would hold that suffocating feeling at bay, keeping
him calmer for a longer period of time, allowing him to

retain some control over his faculties. He'd also loaded up with furanocoumarins at breakfast, courtesy of a dense grapefruit paste imported from Earth, and that was going to increase the potency and half-life of the DMT he was about to inhale.

Over the past several years, he'd tried blending straight DMT with 5-MeO-DMT, and everything else from bufotenin to LSD to psilocin and psilocybin, but found over time that all that stuff just got in the way of the Contact he craved. Now he was back to a formula that was almost pure N,N-DMT, solvated in almost pure ethanol, with just a hint of zaleplon to keep his heart rate down and goose up the visualizations a bit. This mix hadn't worked that well for him in the past, but now that he was closing in on *why*, he felt it was important to circle back and retry some of his early experiments.

The two of them were in his office, by a set of enormous windows looking out at the tiny Earth. He sometimes took his drug trips sitting down, strapped into his chair, behind his desk, both bolted firmly to that surface of the room he'd arbitrarily designated as "floor." Today, though, he was floating free, with the air temperature set to a nearly blood-warm twenty-nine degrees, because he figured minimizing bodily sensations was the ticket to better reception.

"Last time I used this was on Earth," he reminded her. "Surrounded by jibber-jabbering radio fields and quantum decoherence. Now even the Sun is quiet. With the Shade-absorbed photons kicking electrons into the conduction band, the entangled states here in the station are minimized, which means less noise."

She rolled her eyes. "Okay, Ig. I'm sure that's correct."

"Oh, don't patronize me. Quantum physics is used to justify all kinds of nonsense, but that doesn't mean *quantum physics* is nonsense." He waved the vape pen at her. "This stuff, this *brain chemical*, activates neuro-quantum computing pathways that can be measured with a goddamn MRI scanner. It's a real brain circuit, that connects you to something outside of the brain. That's *profound*, Pam, and if you're not willing to experience it firsthand, you don't get to judge."

"I most certainly do," she said, fussing with his blood pressure cuff, "and not just because I'm your doctor. *Everybody* gets to. Everybody *is*."

"Not breakin' any laws," he reminded her.

"I could murder you right now and not break any laws. That doesn't make it smart."

"Well then, we'll let history be the judge," he said, in a voice that sounded pompous even to him. Then, backpedaling a bit, he added, "It's not like I'm the world's first innovator to have eccentric hobbies. Isaac Newton was a closet alchemist. All his life, trying to make gold out of thin air. Isaac Newton! Feynman played drums. Howard Hughes? Morphine. I'm not even the only person doing *exactly this*. The Beings are a hot topic on the biohack roundtables."

"Great. That's great. Very respectable."

"I'm just saying. Let people judge me when *they're* generating as much electrical power as the entire United States." Then, sensing that wasn't getting him anywhere, he changed course again and said, "How's the baby doing?"

Pam touched her abdomen. "Not kicking yet, but otherwise good."

"And you're feeling okay?"

"The morning sickness appears to be subsiding, yes."

"All right, well, I know what that means."

"Mmm?"

"The thing you're working on? Your actual job? You're going into stasis soon."

She sighed uncomfortably. "Yeah. I mean . . . Yeah. Are you worried? I mean, it's your baby, too."

He shrugged. "I know it's the whole reason you came to Esley. I'm not going to stand in your way, but yeah, sure, I'm worried. Shouldn't *you* be reassuring *me?*"

"Mmm." Her look was more thoughtful than a glower, less certain than a glare. She looked, for lack of a better word, compromised. "It's possible to want something with all your heart, and also fear it. We really don't know the risks."

"But it'll be okay?" he tried. She knew more about that than he did, so he didn't try to elaborate. But it was true, he also felt uneasy now that the moment was actually upon them. There was a doctor en route to ESL1 who would put Pam in stasis and then take over her job. And there would be no more Pam, not for a long time.

He sighed. In addition to being one of the most beautiful women Igbal had ever seen (with genes from all over the world—red-brown hair, coppery skin and, somehow, blue epicanthic eyes), Pamela Rosenau was a medical doctor, and an expert in hibernation technology. Blowing sunshine up her pant leg was unlikely to work, and might backfire, and she knew damn well he was going to miss her, and worry about her. And the baby. His first and only child!

He grimaced and shrugged instead. "You want to make someone else do it? I've got a whole list of candidates."

She didn't appear to have a ready answer for that.

"Seriously," he said, "You don't have to do this at all. You certainly don't have to be the first."

"If I'm not first then it's never going to happen for me," she answered. "And that's not acceptable, either."

Unsure what to say to that, he simply patted her on the back of the leg and called it good.

Pam and Iggy's relationship was eccentric at the best of times, and uneasy at the worst, and there was no way in hell a guy like him could have put a baby in her if he hadn't been a trillionaire with literally worlds to offer. Even so, it almost hadn't happened, and even now she seemed ambivalent about it. Ambivalent about him, and about the possible futures that might keep them together or apart. So okay, time to change the subject again.

At the left and right edges of the bank of windows, he could see the ESL1 shade sprawling like a blank canvas, almost as big as Germany and with more energy at its disposal than any country on Earth. His most prized possession. He stared at it for a long moment, and then at the round, perfectly lit sphere of Earth. And, far behind it and to the left, the gray-white pinkie nail that was Luna. Some offices had views of mountains or forests or cities or parks; his had a view of everything there ever was.

"I'll support whatever you decide," he said, meaning it, although his heart and mind ached with the possible outcomes. Then, with nothing more to say, he put the vape pen in his mouth and inhaled sharply.

"Bye," she said, now even more clearly annoyed.

Which was dumb, because even as inhaled vapor, DMT didn't take effect *that* quickly. He held the breath for as long as he could, and then exhaled.

"It tastes like mint," he said.

"I don't know why," she answered.

"There's no mint in it?"

"You know exactly what's in it."

"Maybe the zaleplon? Could there be menthyl acetate in it as a filler?"

Pam glared. "I don't know what the fuck any of those things taste like, Ig, and you're the one that programmed the synthesizer. Okay?"

But then, before Igbal could think of a witty rejoinder, the chamber walls were kaleidoscoping around him, slowly lengthening and unpacking and telescoping and folding out into the much bigger (and yet somehow much flatter) space he called the Atrium. It resembled his office in the same way a baroque, stained-glass cathedral resembles a little white church.

"Atrium," he reported, not for Pam's sake, but because he was being recorded.

His voice echoed: *trium . . . um . . . ummm . . .*

"Standard atrial echoes, normal color palette. The space appears at least four times larger than normal in every dimension, and growing."

He felt the words coming out of him, but he couldn't hear them; each syllable rebounded from every surface in an otherworldly cacophony. And what he was saying wasn't precisely correct, either; his office didn't *appear larger*, so much as it appeared to be broken up into facets like folded maps that never stopped unfolding.

"*Not* standard echoes," he reported. "Very strong." *strong...strong...*

Vibrations rang everywhere; even the slightest sounds ringing the office like a church bell. He hit the pen again, drawing deeply from it twice more while he still had the presence of mind, then felt it spinning out of his grasp. The Atrium was collapsing—*fast*, this time—into the dimensionless tube or point or singularity he called the Junction. The Junction had no size, and yet it was made of colored shapes, like a black hole swallowing cartoons onto its infinitesimal holographic surface.

"Junction," he might have said, although the parts of his brain that could speak were lagging farther and farther behind him. He felt himself breathing hard and deeply, drawing more and more and more oxygen into his lungs, because he knew damn well that where he was going— the sacred, sordid, incomprehensible place he called the Tumbles—he would barely be able to breathe at all.

He felt a moment of terror, just like he always did, because THIS WAS A HELL OF A THING HE WAS DOING, RIGHT? RIGHT? RIGHT? Oh godly godly here we godly go.

Imagine a man's voice saying "Murblemiiih! Mih! Mibblemurblemibblemih!" right into both your ears, and conducting right down into your bones and jumbling them into bright soft fragments, except that the man's voice is your own, and you're not there at all, except that the *Beings* are with you, and they are glad, so glad, so very glad you could make it back to see them.

They have some

They have something

They have something really important and wonderful to tell you

because you're

getting

closer

to

the moment of

contact

hello hello hello hello HELLO!

why hello

the message is

yes

the message is a transmission

yes hello

the message is a transmission from a

yes

hello

so glad so glad so GLAD you could make it

here is the message:

here

here

here is the message:

Except you're not there at all, and you're tumbling dimensionlessly in the everything, and you still can't still can't still can't really quite make out what they're saying and

try again

try again

not quite
hello!
not quite integrated
here is the message:

here is
here

hello?
no
damn

"Still too much decoherence noise," a clear voice says,
and that's
Hello?
That's all

Hello?
That's all

The message is a
Hello?
That's all

That's all you get this time.

Ah, damn. Ah, well. DMT hits like a tidal wave and
evaporates like a dream, just a few minutes later. Melting,
forgotten, and yet somehow intensely meaningful.

"You back?" Pam asked, shining a penlight in his eyes.
Still annoyed. Still not into this particular aspect of her
job.

"Ow. Yes. I'm back."

"And?"

"We're getting closer."

"Joy," she said acerbically. She handed him a bulb of orange-flavored electrolyte drink and said, "I realize the ethanol in the vape mix is only there as a solvent, but it's still ethanol, and your blood levels haven't peaked yet. Don't go back to work for at least an hour. And Ig?"

"Yes, Pam?"

"Even if I stay, you need to find someone else to help you with this. I'm not doing it anymore."

1.3
21 March

✧

Paramaribo, Suriname
Earth Surface

The RzVz launch vehicle, *Exultation*, was a good old-fashioned vertical rocket ship with a little shuttle perched on top, with seating for a pilot and copilot who apparently were not actually needed, or at least not going to show up for this particular trip. The empty seats were far more unnerving than if the ship were simply automated and pilotless. Their vacancy contributed to the rushed, half-baked vibe of this whole endeavor.

Separated from the cockpit by a little doorway was the passenger compartment, with two rows of three seats. It looked like maybe two additional rows could be bolted in, but those spaces were vacant as well. The seats had probably been removed to save weight. The seats that remained were pleather in RzVz blue, bright against the cabin bulkhead of gray composite material, much like that of the Space Force's own shuttles. There were video monitors built into nearly every surface, serving as virtual windows looking up at the sky, down at the ground, across at the launch tower and the complex of roads and fuel tanks and support buildings that surrounded it, and out over the sea and the swamp and the rocky beaches and the bricky, tin-roofed sprawl of Paramaribo off in the distance. A ladder led down the left-hand side of the cabin, but it seemed weirdly out of place, because the overall effect in here was like someone had taken a section from the right half of an airliner, and tipped it on its back.

Apparently thinking the same thing, Jeanette said, "Sorry you got the middle seat, Hon. I'll save you the armrest."

That was a joke, because they were all in bulky spacesuits, strapped into their seats, with their heavy arms lying on rather generous blocks of cushioning separated by a good three centimeters from their neighbors. Alice had Jeanette on her left and Bethy Powell on her right, and Dona Obata in front of her, and on either side of Dona were two women she'd met only very briefly, in the gowning area where they'd all been ordered by a chipper young functionary to exchange their street clothes for blue space coveralls covered in patches announcing their status as RENZ VENTURES SPACE COLONIST and MISSION SPECIALIST posted to ESL1 STATION CREW 3.

One of the women was surprisingly muscled, and had short brown curls and a name tag that said R. LEE. The other was tall and thin and vaguely floppy-looking somehow, with shoulder-length aquamarine hair. Her tag said M. AAG.

"Malagrite Aagesen," she'd said with a very slight

European accent, catching Alice's eyes on her name tag as she zipped up her coverall. "But I guess I'm 'Maag' now. That's kind of silk, eh?"

As they dressed and made introductory small talk, Jeanette let it slip that Alice (A. KYEONG) had room left over in her flight bag, and so after some negotiation Alice found herself in possession of the street clothes (and in at least one case, used underwear) of five other women. They'd taken the duffel away from her in the gowning area, and she had no idea what had happened to it after that, or where it was now. She hoped to hell it did not get misplaced in all this amateur-hour shuffling, because she *needed* some of the stuff in there.

Surprisingly, despite all that was in it, the space inside the shuttle did not feel cramped. However, it did seem a bit flimsy; not counting the reentry shield, the whole crew cabin probably weighed less than the women inside it, and although it was mostly carbon fiber and foamed titanium, Alice almost felt she could kick the whole thing to pieces in a few minutes if she needed to.

"Are you ready?" Bethy asked everyone, not over the suit comms (which hadn't yet been switched on), but just calling out loudly through the acrylic of her helmet visor, in a voice like some kind of sports announcer. Then dropped back into her own Kiwi voice and said, "I know I'm not! Ha!"

Two male technicians had led them into the launch vehicle one by one: in through the hatch, down the ladder, across the empty seats and into their own, and then helped them buckle in. "Thanks to carbon bond stripping technology, you've got three hours of breathing from a tank the size of a wine bottle," one of them kept saying, over and over. "That will get you to Transit Point Station, so do not open your helmet visors unless instructed. Thanks to carbon bond stripping technology . . ."

Bethy had gone in first, and then Alice a few minutes after her, and so the two of them had had almost half an hour sitting next to each other, pretending to get acquainted.

Bethy had said things like, "I'm from Middle Earth. You know, where they filmed those Hobbit movies. My pastimes include gardening, bicycling, and beefing exotic billionaires." And, "God loves a fast car. How many kph do you reckon this baby clocks?" And, "Botanist, yeah, but I don't honestly think that's why. I hear they're going to start raising some animals, and I know a little about that." And, "Box of fluffy ducks, we're about to head! Journey of a lifetime and all that."

She was laying it on awfully thick—too cheerful, too Kiwi, too lacking in the kind of nervous tension the occasion actually called for. It looked like an act. It *was* an act. Of course, Bethy always seemed to be acting; Alice wasn't sure she'd ever met her as an actual person. Still, it made her feel exposed, so she responded as noncommittally as possible, with brilliant improvisations like "Uh-huh," and "I moved around a lot as a kid," and "Air Force medic, eight years," and then "Uh-huh" again. Bethy knew all of that already, and while it was a good idea to go through the motions, Alice felt pretty nervous about the whole thing. Bethy wasn't a good liar, and Alice suspected *she* wasn't, either. The less she actually said, the better. But she also realized that wasn't the only thing she was nervous about. In point of fact, she actually felt rather keyed up.

Jeanette, for her part, reached across Alice to touch fingers with Bethy just as soon as the techs buckled her in and climbed back up for their next human parcel. "We're going to be crewmates, so I'm pleased no matter what. Jeanette Schmidt, space resources utilization."

"Bethy Powell, botanist and cattle rancher."

As far as Alice knew, Bethy didn't have any formal credentials in botany—not real ones, anyway—but her family *had* grown vegetables and battled weeds and participated in some kind of Open Source Seed movement, and in her final week at the Marriott Stars the bosses had had her tending a zero-gee hydroponic system made of white plastic tanks and tubes, with help from a consultant they'd flown up under pain-of-death secrecy. So yeah, she probably knew enough to fake her way through.

"Shoulda put some crayfish in there," she'd commented at one point. "They eat anything, and their poop is good fertilizer, because anything's poop is good fertilizer."

Anyway, now they were all strapped in and ready for flight, looking out the "windows" at the scene around them. Their last glimpse of Earth through anything but fire and shock waves.

Alice's attention was directed inside the ship, however; the Air Force sergeant in her felt a flutter of nervousness when she looked at how lopsided the load was here. All the people on one side! The ship was a sort of stubby winged shuttlecraft, with the ladder and cargo holder down one side, and it just didn't look balanced. But that couldn't be right, right? They'd've worked it all out to the third decimal place. It was Alice's keyed-up perceptions that were skewed. Right? When it came to being a Maroon Beret, Alice was very, very good at her job. When it came to most other things, she was a bit of a wreck, and often didn't trust her own judgment. This was one of those times.

Presently, the suit coms switched on, and after a moment of static and feedback she heard one of the technicians saying, "Check, check. Can you ladies hear me? Cargo loading is about to commence, so I'd like to do a roll call and make sure you're all on the network. Elizabeth Powell?"

"Here."

"Alice Kyeong?"

"Uh, here."

"Jeanette Schmidt?"

"Present! God, I'm nervous."

"Just breathe deeply. We can adjust your oxygen mix if necessary. Malagrite Aagesen?"

"Roger."

To which someone said, "I have a brother named Roger."

To which someone else said, "Is he married?"

But the technician was having none of that. "Cut the chatter, please. You're on an open channel with ground control, and we're on the clock here. Dona Obata?"

"Here."

"Rachel Lee?"

"That's *Rock-kale* Lee. Here."

"All right, we're going to start loading the cargo containers."

"Won't that block the aisle in an escape situation?" Jeanette asked.

To which the technician replied, "In an escape situation, this whole structure blows apart and you all come down on parachutes."

"Huh," said someone.

"Yeah, right," said someone else.

"Cut the chatter, please. Pod one is on the rails. Keep hands and feet out of the aisle."

And then a blue barrel came trundling down the ladder on two pairs of motorized gripping wheels.

"Pod two coming."

A second barrel followed, this one covered in cryptic red and white labels.

"Pod three."

This one was white, and square, and looked like an oversized milk crate full of neatly bagged charity donations. Was her duffel in there? Together, the three cargo pods were enough to fill the aisle next to the seats, and Alice's loading questions were answered. *Now* the weight looked balanced. With any luck, these jokers knew the mass of every colonist down to the gram, and had loaded enough ballast, in just the right places in each container, to compensate. With any luck. As much as she distrusted herself, she wasn't too keen on Renz Ventures, either. At least on this particular day, they did not seem to have their shit entirely together.

"Capcom here," a voice said over the network. "Please clear the channel. Thank you. Colonists, I'm going to be talking you through this mission from here on, so please listen closely."

Capcom stood for "Capsule Communications," a job title that dated back to the earliest days of space travel, now almost seventy years ago. The term was one of the first things drilled into RzVz candidates, which Alice found ironic, because as far as Launch Ops was concerned, RzVz colonists were cargo—not much different than the barrels currently sitting to their left. But perhaps RzVz felt it was psychologically important for passengers to feel that sense of connection to someone who knew what was going on. Especially with no pilot on board! A ship full of people who'd never been to space before . . . did they need a strong human voice piped into their helmets? Probably. Probably most of them did, yes.

Of course, Alice was no stranger to pilotless aircraft; these days about half the USAF fleet was on full autopilot all the time. But not the fighter jets. Not the ground support jets or the combat helicopters, not when anything, you know, *hairy* was going on. These days a robot could probably fly combat missions better than most humans, but "most humans" weren't who the Air Force recruited to fly their planes, and when you were risking your neck there *was* something reassuring about a human being (an *officer*, no less) issuing calm instructions and status updates.

Was it different if that voice was on the ground, controlling nothing and sharing nothing of the danger? She supposed it was. But probably still better than nothing. Capcom certainly had a nice, deep voice.

"I'd like you to sound off by seat numbers again," he

said, and then when they'd gone through that, he remarked, almost casually, "All right, the hatches are sealed and if you look out your viewscreens, you'll see the tower beginning to roll away. We're live, and the main engines will ignite in thirty seconds."

"Woooh!" somebody said.

Someone else started breathing really hard and fast into her microphone.

"Cut the sounds and voice chatter, please," Capcom instructed calmly. "Colonist Lee, I'm putting some CO_2 into your air mix to adjust your breathing rate. Breathe nice and deep. That's right."

And then, with remarkably little fanfare, he started counting backward from ten! "Ignition in ten . . . nine . . . eight . . ."

Like a rapid-fire eternity, the numbers came too quickly for Alice to think or to feel or to really grasp what was about to happen, and yet somehow too slowly to release the tension. She was on another rocket ride, just another rocket ride, just another little rocket ride to space, except she was lousy at fighting and she had told the President she would take over Esley Shade Station by force . . .

And then the engines lit up. This ignition was a louder, jerkier business than on a government launch vehicle, and wasn't *that* a strange thing, that private citizens carrying private citizens would be less gentle than the Space Force tossing some hardened Maroon Beret up into the sky.

And through the many video screens she watched the ground fall away and the clouds ease closer. Not quickly at first, but once the launch stack was clear of the tower it felt like a whole 'nother set of engines kicked on, like *kicked* on, and then they were *really moving*.

Somewhere on the voice network, one of the women was whimpering and hyperventilating (Alice thought it was one of the newbies she'd met in the gowning area), and another one was whooping loudly, but only for a second or two, before their voices cut out abruptly, and the soothing voice of Capcom was saying something Alice couldn't quite make out over the rumble and screech of the engines and the air rushing by them faster and faster.

After that, she began to settle in. Her breathing slowed, because riding out noise and vibration was how she'd spent most of her second decade of life. This was her *fourth* trip into space, basically routine at this point, and easily her five hundredth time leaving the ground in some dangerous contraption or other. No big deal at all, no big deal at all.

Interestingly, once the first layer of clouds had shot past them, the view screens all suddenly had a gee-force indicator plastered across them in big white figures. Presently 2.3 g, and climbing. 2.4, 2.5 . . . At 3.0, the numbers turned yellow, which worried Alice vaguely, since it implied that at some point they would turn orange or red, and oh my God the centrifuge drill at RzVz training went all the way to seven gravities. Just for a second or two, but it *hurt*, and Alice had found it nearly impossible to breathe. Was that about to happen here? And if so, why was she just figuring it out *right this second?* Another briefing she'd skipped, or played on her tablet in the background instead of paying full attention?

Jesus.

And then the word STAGING was flashing across the screens in bright red letters, and without warning Alice felt herself thrown forward hard against her seat harness, and then oddly weightless for a fraction of a moment, and then thrown backward or downward really hard against her seat cushions.

"You ready to get heavy?" someone asked. Jeanette Schmidt? Hard to tell; the voice was hoarse and deep and shuddering, barely a woman's voice at all.

Alice, who ate fear for breakfast and had hurled her body out into cloudless stratosphere more times than she could count, found she was maybe not quite ready to get heavy. And yet, the gee counter climbed, faster now. 5.0. 5.25. 5.75! At 6.0, the numbers went red, and at 6.5 they began flashing, and it was too late, already too late to take a breath, and then it was 7.0, and in some weird phase change, Alice's helmet visor suddenly went foggy with condensation for some reason. She remembered to squeeze her lower body, keeping the blood from pooling there like the Air Force had taught her to do, but of course that was for when you were seated upright and the gee force was toward your feet. She was on her back so that wouldn't do any good, and *why wasn't she better at this*?

It occurred to Alice that these people were fucking crazy. There were engineers willing to build rocket ships *this close* to the limits of human endurance. There were owners willing to operate those ships without insurance or really even any government oversight. There were women who, with a few days' training, were prepared to climb aboard those ships and never come back to Earth again as long as they lived.

The gee counter hit 7.4 and then, with a chunking noise somewhere behind and below, began declining sharply. 7. 6. 5. The voice network was briefly dominated by the sound of women gasping for breath, and then Capcom was on again, saying, "We have main engine cutoff. Prepare for zero gravity, just like in your training, and if you vomit inside your helmet remember to press the purge valve on your chin."

There was some whooping after that, which Alice understood completely: The ordeal had only lasted a few minutes (maybe eight? maybe ten?), but it was as terrifying as anything she'd ever done, and she was quite glad it was over. Too, for women like Jeanette, the arrival in outer space was the culmination of a dream, perhaps lifelong, and the start of an exciting new chapter in their lives. Reaching for the stars and all that crazy bullshit.

For Alice it was simply the next leg of a journey that would definitely end in tears. Maybe not for her, but for somebody. And *maybe* for her, yes, or her poor worried mother back in Burning Man.

"Attitude control jets activated," Capcom told them. "We're going to reorient the capsule and then do a slight burn to raise our apogee to the orbit of Transit Point Station."

"Capsule?" Jeanette said cheerfully. "More of a shuttle, really."

"Our?" said Bethy Powell at the same time. "I don't see you up here with us, Capcom. Have you been?"

"Many times, yes," Capcom replied, "now please cut the chatter."

But someone else piped up with, "Something's wrong

with Lee! I think something's wrong with Lee! She's choking or something."

That was Maag speaking—the girl with the aquamarine hair. Alice recognized the voice. And indeed, through the hiss of air valves and the huffing of her own breath, Alice could hear the faint sounds of coughing and retching in the seats above her. Or in front, or whatever.

"We're talking Colonist Lee through a situation," Capcom confirmed.

"It sounds like she's choking," Maag said, fumbling with her harness and finally releasing the buckle. "You can't talk somebody through choking."

Capcom reacted with immediate and stern disapproval. "Colonist Aagesen, I show your seat restraint detached, repeat, detached. Please check your buckles and reattach."

"I'm aware of the problem," Maag replied, floating up out of her seat and catching herself by grabbing one of the seat straps awkwardly with her left hand.

"Whoa," she said, clearly a bit surprised and disoriented by the lack of gravity. Alice felt smug about that for about half a millisecond, and had to remind herself that her own first minutes in freefall hadn't gone so well.

"Colonist Aagesen, you're in a vehicle undergoing orbital maneuvers. You're risking injury to yourself and others, as well as damage to equipment."

"Understood," Maag answered.

Capcom persisted: "When the reaction thrusters activate, the ship is going to rotate around you, and when the main jet fires, you'll experience thirty seconds of about point five gee. Your fall could break someone's neck."

"Then delay the burn," said Dona.

"It doesn't work that way, Colonist Obata. I don't want to be rude, but you folks are cargo."

"Hands and feet inside the ride," Maag said. "I do get it, yes."

Presently, Maag crawled her way across Dona's space-suited form, to where R. LEE sat flailing and coughing. Lee was still cut out of the main voice network, so the sound was muffled and distant, but unmistakable.

And then another noise: a series of rumbling tones, like low blasts of tuba music. RROO! RROO!

"Attitude jets are firing," Capcom warned.

Alice wasn't sure she would have felt anything, if the images of Earth in the view screens hadn't begun a slow spin around them. As it was, she felt a hint of dizziness.

Ignoring Capcom, Maag reached Lee and poked at something under her helmet visor. The suits had a big orange button there marked PURGE, supposedly for situations like this. But a panicked Lee was batting at Maag, trying to push her away. Maag responded by grabbing a fistful of Lee's harness strap and leaning into the button with the plastic armor of her spacesuit elbow.

That did the trick; there was a kind of farting sound, and Lee's helmet barfed out a cloud of, well, barf.

"Orbital burn in fifteen," Capcom warned.

Then Maag was fumbling one-handed with the visor latch on Lee's helmet, saying "Hold still, you fucker, hold still."

And then the latch was open, and the visor was rotating up and away from Lee's face, and Lee was coughing and spitting and screaming into the passenger cabin.

"Fucking fuck! Fucking..." And then she vomited again, launching an arcing stream of it over Maag's shoulder, across her faceplate, and up toward the empty cockpit.

"Son of a..." Maag said.

"Get the fuck off of me," Lee spluttered. "Let me up. Let me up!"

Without gravity to hold Maag down, Lee did manage to throw her off fairly easily. Of course, Maag was holding onto Lee's straps with her left hand, so she just sort of pivoted up into the space above the seats, but that was the moment when Capcom said, "Two, one, initiating orbital burn NOW."

Maag became heavy again, falling toward the back of the passenger cabin. She caught herself with her left hand, pivoted some more, then cried out in pain and fell squarely on top of Alice.

As it happened, Alice was no stranger to situations of this type. When you jumped out of planes for a living, it sometimes happened that somebody's chute didn't open. Twice in her career, Alice had arrested somebody's fall—once by flying down to a dude who had hit his head on the way out of the plane. At three thousand meters she'd tucked in her arms and shot downward face-first, and at two thousand she'd flared and slid a hundred meters laterally, and grabbed the dude and octopused every limb around him and pulled the cord on her primary. BAM! It was too much weight too quickly, and she had nearly dropped him right then, and nearly again several times during the descent, until she'd finally groped her way to one of his dangling carabiners and clipped him to her harness, taking some of the weight out of her arms. And then the fucker had woken up!

His name was Bill Gonzales, and he was *strong*. He wrestled her for a moment, yelping and squawking in alarm, but she had him from behind, and she was saying "Calm down, Gonzales, calm down, I've got you. Calm down. I think you hit your head. Can you look at the horizon for me? Find a spot to orient. I've got you. Can you, yeah, can you grab onto my waist? Brother, you are *heavy*."

The second time this happened, things were nowhere near as calm. A guy called Florida, coming down on a streamer, had landed squarely on her canopy and collapsed it, and before she knew what was happening the two of them were tangled up together in a mess of unbreakable parachute cords.

Almost without thinking she pulled her boot knife and started slicing, with the ground rushing up at two hundred kph. And suddenly everything was in slow motion, and she had *plenty of time* to see where the problems were, and she tied Florida to her left leg and then cut everything else, and while he screamed and thrashed she pounded her reserve chute from the sides, took what felt like a very long breath, and pulled the cord. Then the world went back to normal speed, and the chute opened with a sickening jerk that felt like it had popped every joint in her body, and then the two of them were coming down into a canopy of trees—in cartel country, Panama!—with the hum of bullets in the air all around them.

Alice got a medal and a promotion to Senior Master Sergeant for that one, and she never figured out if it was for saving Florida's life, and her own, or because she broke three bones in her right hand, or because she pulled out her service pistol with that same hand, and started returning fire, and happened to hit somebody who happened to be in view of her jump camera.

(There had been some talk about her meeting the President in the wake of that incident—Yano, not Tompkins—along with a handful of other decorated Spec Ops. But it was election season, and Yano was trying to appease his base by distancing himself from the not-so-secret war against the Cartels, and then he lost the election, so the thing had never quite come together. But apparently Alice had been on some sort of presidential short list after that, which was one of the reasons the new President, Tompkins, had thought to interview her for the RzVz job. So in a way, that incident had been her ticket to outer space.)

Anyway, when Maag landed on her, the situation was familiar enough that she knew exactly what to do, and mild enough that she almost laughed while doing it. But her medic voice kicked in instead.

"I've got you. I've got you. Just hold still."

To Lee, Maag said, "You're welcome, asshole."

But Lee was still mostly just coughing, so Alice said, "Easy now. We don't know what's going on there. We'll give her a proper evaluation in a minute. Just hang tight."

It was a hallmark of the Maroon Berets, that they could speak soothingly to a patient while simultaneously firing a weapon or barking orders at a subordinate. Because patients had to be kept calm, for both medical and tactical reasons. Until this moment, Alice had never really considered how creepy that was, or what it said about her that she'd taken to it without any specific instruction. But of course Maag didn't know any of that. All she heard—all anyone heard—was Alice's soothing voice. They would form their opinions around that—everyone except Dona and Bethy—and think she was a nice person, and it would work out to her advantage. And this thought brought with it the slightest flicker of shame, passing over her and then gone, at least for now. No time for shame right now.

The burn lasted thirty seconds, with Capcom counting up the numbers, now that he could get a word in.

"Twenty-eight, twenty-nine, thirty. Burn complete. Colonist Aagesen, please return to your seat and buckle in. We've got another hour before station rendezvous."

Ignoring him, Alice said, "Hang tight, Lee. We're going to examine you and see what's going on."

"Fuck off," Lee said, gasping, struggling blindly with her seat buckles. Panic attack? Without waiting to be asked, Maag floated up off of Alice and took a position between the cargo canisters and Lee. Alice unbuckled herself and flipped up over the seat, locking eyes with Dona for a moment before gripping Lee's heaviest strap and settling down to clamp her knees against Lee's arms.

Alice said, "Hold still, soldier. I'm a medic, and I'm going to check you out. Can you take a few deep breaths for me?"

But Lee was panicking, not really responding in any meaningful way, and it occurred to Alice that she might, among other things, be feeling claustrophobic.

"We're monitoring Lee's vital signs from here," Capcom warned. "If you don't stay put, you could be liable for any injury you cause."

"Is there a way to shut that guy off?" Alice asked no one in particular. Then, to Maag: "Can you get her helmet off? That's a, yeah, that's a latch. Good. Now rotate and . . . lift, I think? Right. Good."

Maag lifted the barf-stained helmet away, handing it off to Dona. Alice held Lee by the cheeks and looked at her pupils, which were maximally dilated, so that it was impossible to tell what color her eyes were.

"Breathe for me," Alice instructed. "That's right, your job right now is just to breathe. I know you're a doctor, but right now you listen to me. Breathe. That's right. Maag, can you get these gauntlets off her hands?"

At this point, Jeanette piped up, saying, "I think you can relax, Capcom. We've got things well in hand up here."

To which Capcom replied, "Ah, shit. I'm going to get some coffee. Please don't break anything while I'm gone."

3.1
21 March

St. Joseph of Cupertino Monastery
Shoemaker-Faustini Plateau
Lunar South Polar Mineral Territories

My Dearest Father Bertram,

Is it strange, to be the abbot of a place that hangs above you in the sky? You are so sorely missed in this, my chosen exile, as you breathe fresh air not from canisters and walk beneath blue skies. Blue! Already it seems incredible that any sky would dare so bold a color.

It is I, your most humble Brother Michael, writing to you from the third hydroponic module, which we jokingly refer to as the Greenhouse, since it has been modified to grow, beneath its pink and blue diodes and opaque, non-glass ceiling, things that actually sprout from dirt. Our food supply comes, much like that of Nevada's hippy Burners, from plants grown in water troughs and bathed in our own bodily wastes, but our *future* comes from the—well, I almost said "earth," but of course this is regolith. More anon.

May I call you dearest? Although your title is Fa and mine is Bro, I think we both know that my feelings for you—unrequited though God requires them—be neither filial nor fraternal. Although one must observe, "Platonic" is hardly the word for it either, since Plato was assuredly a practicing member of our little club. But if love must dwell separate from physicality, must it also dwell in silence, or shall it, in private letters, dare to speak its name out loud? For dearest you are, and shall remain, as should surprise no one.

Your missive addressed three urgent interrogatives, which I shall endeavor to answer as thoroughly as would a corporate functionary called upon the carpet by his superior to answer for actions deemed unauthorized. I hope to persuade you of both my diligence and my frugality—two qualities thought useful in a man of my position, although I recognize it matters more how such things land than how they're cast. And so we shall see, *nicht wahr*?

As to the question of "why in heaven's name shipments of water have been halted when we've got eight new brothers prepping for launch," you are wise to inquire. It's true that proximity to the ice mines of fair Luna was the primary concern in selecting the site for our moonastery. However, what Shackleton Lunar Industrial Station (or Moonbase Larry, if I prefer) doesn't advertise is that their water (like all such) is eighty-nine percent oxygen, whereas the rocky Moon herself is forty-five percent, and as my gran would say, them economics don't rightly square. Truly not.

As irony would have it, among the many apparatuses and apparati sold to us by Larry Killian's merry band there sits an emergency oxygen generator that, when hit with fabulous amounts of electricity, reduces a shovel full of sand into a pail of oxygen and a fused brick of elemental silicon, plus a little bolus of slag for which no use has yet been found. The process requires methane, but returns it intact, and so costs nothing but electrons, with which we are liberally supplied.

Listen: the bricks, if stacked, will vacuum weld most impressively into an airtight wall of rainbow black, like the feathers of a raven, and it turns out the emergency oxygen can be breathed by God's servants even in the absence of emergency. Or (as Sir Larry no doubt regrets) reacted with still more methane to produce the very water we neglect to purchase, though it be plentiful and close at hand. This may also answer your second question, namely, "why the frig are we having tanks of methane soft-landed from orbit?" I trust that frig is now clarified sufficient, for what I'm doing is simply cheaper, by a factor so considerable that, should your thoughtful attention turn toward it, may be found persuasive. And yes, and yes, Sir Larry Eddie Killie himself fairly protests that his oxygen generator isn't meant for such hard duty. I *do* hear him, and yet a moment's calculation tells me we can buy a new generator every three months and still come out ahead. Whose fault is it that moonwater costs more than expensive machines?

And so one is forced to ask, as we settle into this lifelong, life-shortening task of figuring out how humans can live as happy extraterrestrials: are we in it purely for the good of the future? Shall we shore up the local infrastructure at greater expense to God's church, or shall we go thriftily into tomorrow with a cheat from Orlov Petrochemical? I await, with eagerness, your counsel in such matters.

As for question three, I am having so damn many seeds shipped up (and thus nearly erasing the aforementioned savings) because hydroponics is a losing game. Every gram of food grown in sewage is grown of atoms born on Earth and merely recycled. It admits no participation from Luna herself or, if we buy aqua vitae from Sir Lawrence, no participation save that million-dollar glass of water.

And so it makes sense, to me at least, that most of my personal kilograms hauled moonward were allocated to the seeds of Earthly plants, that I might discover what groweth in the soils of Our Lord's other creation. And a ghastly endeavor it was, for kilogram after kilogram perished badly, ere I found what adornments Luna would permit on her skin.

The soil smells like gunpowder, or the dried-out dust of a mineral hot spring, and this reeky sulfur (being roughly two percent of the local regolith by weight and ninety-nine percent by pungency) doth slay the nitrogen-fixing bacteria I also transported. And so I found I must be satisfied, in the beginning, with plants that fix the nitrogen themselves, for there is no nitrogen, and I mean *none*, in the soils of Lune. This, too, must come from Orlov Petro, as I thought was well explained to His Holy at the very beginning of this venture. Here at my elbow (and also at my knee, for quarters are tight) Brother Giancarlo, being a Vatican astronomer by former profession, attests to such, although in the shuffle of this and that, we can perhaps forgive its forgetting. It is, after all, the least visible and reactible component of the air we breathe. So yes, I am also having tanks of nitrogen dropped from the sky! Mea culpa, Bertram, I thought at least this one portion of the endeavour would not surprise you. Apologies if it were not explained with sufficient oomph to penetrate a human skull.

In any event (or perhaps not in any, but in some), I can now report seed-to-seed growth of four fixers, being (by common name) blue lupin, sweet clover, bird's-foot trefoil, and alfalfa. As it happens, although the lupin is known mainly as an ornamental flower and secondarily as a weed, its seeds are a sort of bean and, though bitter, a delicacy in ancient times, and still today in some parts of the world. Bird's-foot trefoil is an inaquatic relative of the lotus, whose flowers, while non-nutritious themselves, have an antispasmodic effect on the digestive tract and can thus improve the absorption of other nourishments, thereby wringing extra calories from any meal into which they're sprinkled. Alfalfa sprouts are edible, as any Nevada Burner or Vancouver hippie could tell you, and while calorically poor, are a source of vitamins B and C, the latter of which may be quite difficult otherwise to acquire in a land without fruit trees. Sweet clover is inedible, alas, but (as our mass spectrometer insists) pulls more nitrogen from the air and into itself than all others combined, and so earns a place as a servant of Saint Joseph.

Once these proud pioneers have grown and gone to seed, I remove them from the soil, and weigh them, and then bake the moisture out of the soil and weigh what's left, and the difference between that and the starting mass is the Gain—what the plant hath wrestled free of Luna to become, for the first time in eight billion years, living matter. And dearest, if such an alchemical transformation is not called a miracle then I don't know what possibly could be. I am humbled beyond words (yes, I! Wordless!) to be even present for it, much less participant.

And then! Bertram, I then save the seeds from these plants and grind the rest back into the dust, making of it an alien humus that can sustain less hardy crops, that need their nitrogen prepackaged in organic forms. Like a dried-out skeleton, the Moon has plenty of calcium, and like a rusted old sportscar it has plenty of iron and magnesium. No shortage on these fronts! Compared with Earthly earth it's deficient in sodium and potassium, though, and we find here that carbon is but one part in a hundred thousand of the soil. Of all the tested nitrogen fixers, these four plants, then, are the ones that take their carbon most efficiently from the CO_2 we brothers exhale, which comes ultimately from Orlov's methane and Killian's emergency oxygen. And so, even mixed with the corpses of clover and lupin, our soil remains lethally starvaceous to most of what grows back home. Any farmer who found himself parked over such impoverished dirt would surely sell out to developers and see it converted forthwith into suburb! Of course you will ask: Could I not fertilize the soil by pooping in it? Indeed and of course, if I only desired to invalidate the whole experiment. The question is, what grows *here*, not on the atoms of Mother Earth we bring here with us.

It matters to me, and I like to think it matters to Our Father Who Art, that OP's methane and nitrogen come not from Earth but from near-Earth asteroids, and that they also become alive here beneath our humble roof. Might not this greening be an ultimate purpose for which God created Adam afirstplace? I do like to believe we're at the beginning of history, here, as one with the first neolithic goblin-men to scatter seeds deliberate and harvest what they planted, and that the future (though they know us not as individuals) will subsist on the crops we here develop.

(In Ages Middle, toward the end of Ages Dark, monasteries not only trained friars and priests in their childhood letters but, by preserving and endlessly copying the manuscripts of Ages Roman and Greek, whilst nurturing strange crops and livestock the world had forgot, became civilization's sole experts on many aspects of ancient life, including sanitation and medicine, and formed the nuclei of colleges that would blossom into the world's great universities in Ages Renaissant. Is it vanity to dream of future days here in space, where the Church plays such a role again in the secular lives of human beings? Surely this thought drives His Holy and the most generous donors who back this monastery, or why else indeed are we here?)

There are further steps to the growing process, or precursors, rather, for we have to grind the soil to make it safe to bring indoors. Imagine, if you will, that it has lain unweathered in the sunlight for more years than there are humans alive, and each teaspoon is basically a trillion-strong pile of microscopic stone arrowheads that would tear us up inside if we let them. And tear the plants up, too, most likely, unless they have cellular repair mechanisms we ourselves do not. But if we grind the regolith too fine, it becomes airborne too easily in the low gravity, and if too coarse then any water we pour into it slides right through, as through a column of gravel. For posterity, please know that a hundred-micron average particle size does the trick of being soil.

And so, with ground, hydrated, nitrogenated moondust in our greenhouse pots, we have seed-toseeded another subfraction of nature's bounty. What grows, you ask? Spices, for one. We have, for example, field mustard, whose seeds become the yellow stuff you spread on hot dogs, and whose leaves are as edible as kale, with a slightly peppery kick. Also blue stonecrop, which is astringent and makes a good salad dressing, and French marigold, a relative of cloves and cinnamon whose petals resemble saffron in both color and flavor. Also marsh thistle, which gives up a sweet syrup, and given the appetite for sulfur within the genus Allium, I remain hopeful that either onions, shallots, leeks, chives, or garlic can be coaxed to grow as well. So please, yes, send these seeds above all others. As for food crops, there are several that grow but refuse to flower, but we can reliably get seeds back from tomatoes, rye, wild carrot, and garden cress.

Can you see, dearest, the beginning suggestions of a Lunar native cuisine? Already we've served a tangy rye pasta with a sort of red-orange lupini sauce like nothing you've ever tasted, along with a salad of greens and shredded carrots, topped by a citrusy drizzle of pulverized plant matter. Delish! And all of it won, atom-by-atom, from the rocks of an unliving universe, feeding into our bodies matter that has never touched the Earth. And so, bit by bit, morsel by morsel, we become Lunar and asteroidal, leaving Eden behind to the meek, who shall indeed inherit. And if food tastes better when the diner is camping, rest assured it tastes better still when seducing a dead planet to join forces with the living. If there be

a greater calling for any human life, I confess I know
it not and seek it never.

My darling I am, very yours and very truly,
Brother Michael Jablonski de la Lune

✧✧✧

Dear Mike,

Your pomposity, while hilarious, does indeed
teeter dangerously on the brink of vanity. I will
consider your letter a private confession of this sin
and will ask you, in your morning prayers, to add a
daily plea for forgiveness. Please resume ordering
water from Shackleton Lunar Industrial Station. You
can cut the order in half if you like, but the goodwill
of Harvest Moon Industries in general and Sir
Lawrence Edgar Killian in particular is at stake. The
Vatican relies on goodwill more than you seem to
realize, and at the moment the Church appears to be
serving as an important bridge between corporate
and government interests on the Moon. You do not
exist in a vacuum, my friend, and yes, that's a joke.

As for being the abbot of something that hangs
above me in the sky, it may interest you to know I
not only smile warmly at the Man in the Moon when
I see him winking down at me, and think of you guys
standing there on his chin, but I've added an app to
my glasses that shows me the position of the Moon
at all times, including when it's located behind the

ground underneath my feet. So my thoughts are with you and your brothers constantly. Frankly, so are everyone else's; this is one of the highest-profile projects the Church has ever undertaken.

Thanks to generous donations, your seeds are on their way, and should arrive by the end of the week.

With love and kindness,
Fr. Bertram Meagher, MDiv

✢✢✢

My Dearest Father Bertram,

Harvest Moon's public relations gaggle needs to learn how to read a map; Shackleton was the name of their proposed base at Shackleton crater, fully four hundred kilometers from here. Since the U.N. denied their mineral claim for that site, deeming it of greater scientific than commercial interest, the base has instead been constructed along the promontory between craters Shoemaker and Faustini. The new claim is quite a bit larger than the original request, covering both craters lip to lip, with a kilometer-wide strip of land in between, along which they have bulldozed a road. They don't *need* a road, you understand; they simply want to mark the place up so the brochure photos look impressive. For the same reason, I have asked them to bulldoze a driveway to St. Joseph's, which sits a little over a kilometer past the boundary of their claim.

The Chinese, meanwhile, have bribed their way to ownership of nearly the entire North Polar Mineral Territory. One hopes they'll bring a balance of men and women there, for it does seem odd, that here at Saint Joe we have a pile of men, while ESL1 has a floating swarm of women with, somehow still, a man in command of them. Of course, of the billions of women who exist, Renz Ventures selects only those dozens who don't find this too problematic, and yet, strange are the tides that segregate the children of Adam and Eve in this way, and strange is the future ahead, if others should follow suit. Danny Beseman and Sir Lawrence both have a better track record of gender-blending, and one hopes that Mars and Luna, respectively, will benefit therefrom, and yet they still are the fingers of a man's man's world, reaching upward into heaven in a way the Creator does not command nor, presumably, endorse. From the confines of our crater there is little we can do about the patriarchal plight of women, but I can at least write you, Bertie my love, of my concerns on the matter.

In any case, the Mandarins can keep the north pole as far as I'm concerned, for while the overall water content is greater there than here, at the opposite end, the concentrations are lower, whereas each of Sir Larry's craters holds a cubic kilometer of ice so clean that an intrepid astronaut could very nearly strap on skates and a tutu and start tracing out figure eights. I can hear the sprightly dance music already!

You should know, if only for the sake of intellectual rigor and emotional rectitude, that if you blow kisses to us upon the chin of the Man in the Moon, you're more than two thousand kilometers off the mark, for we stand in truth upon his left cheek, like hairs upon a mole.

Oh, and by the bye, could you check on something urgent for me? Since we do not own the mineral rights to the land on which we sit, by my reading of the Reformed Moon Treaty, we're in violation if we invite the boys from Moonbase Larry over to dine on native cuisine, but not if we feed them earthstuff grown from our own shit. Is this accurate? It seems rather rude.

Very yours and very truly,
Brother Michael Jablonski de la Lune

4.1
22 March

✦

Clementine Cislunar Fuel Depot
Earth-Moon Lagrange Point 1
Cislunar Space

"Sir," an anonymous functionary was saying, "we had very little warning you were coming."

His accent was Moldovan. He was blocking the hatchway that led from the pressurized hangar to the station interior, forcing Grigory to hold a grab rail to keep from floating away. The wisdom of including a pressurized hangar in this station was debatable, but Grigory had wanted his men to be able to load, unload, and service gatherbots in a shirtsleeve environment, and that had seemed the easiest way. But the problem with a big open space like this was that if you weren't extremely careful, you could get stranded in midair and have to wait for air currents to drift you toward a surface. Not even microgravity to help you here at L1.

Impatiently, Grigory asked the functionary, "For what do you require warning, crewman? To cover up your failings? This facility should be prepared for all things at all times. May I enter?"

"Of course, sir. Apologies, sir."

The functionary (whose name tag said EPUREANU) was blocking the hatchway, but presently he attempted to bow and fold his hands submissively, and also to step out of the way, but since there was no gravity here both instincts failed him, and he simply flopped and rotated in the air. Grigory felt momentary embarrassment for the man, and also the countervailing urge to simply brush him aside like a curtain and swing into the station—*his* station: the Clementine Cislunar Fuel Depot.

But he reminded himself why this young man was afraid: not of being pushed aside, not of looking a fool. Of losing his job, perhaps, but at the very back of it all he was fearful of being stuffed out an airlock and declared an industrial accident. Such fears were useful, and Grigory knew better than to squander them with petty schoolyard behavior. Instead, he waited silently, which he could see on Epureanu's face was far more effective.

The man got fumblingly out of Grigory's way, and then Grigory did enter. And now that his point was made, he let the sympathy rise to the surface, and he said, "I don't know you. They sent you down here alone, to face whatever mood brought the boss here ahead of schedule, in an otherwise empty shuttle. I spent a hundred million dollars to arrive here early, and this makes them afraid. So they sent you."

"Sir," the functionary agreed, apparently unsure what else to say.

"Rest assured, if I'm indeed angry it is not with you, nor will they succeed in deflecting it onto you by such tactics."

"Sir," the man said again. "Thank you, sir."

"What is your job here?"

"Maintenance supervisor, sir. My crew checks the gatherbots every time they come in."

"Ah. Real work, then."

"I don't hold a wrench," Epureanu admitted, "but I put in longer hours than the men and women who do."

Grigory considered this. For the man to speak so—like a human being talking to another human being—implied some courage back there behind the nervousness. Grigory decided to respond as a fellow human, and so he said, "Men of small imagination expect me to behave like a cartoon gangster, and I find it is easier to oblige them than to explain why I don't need to. Thus, I have brought real vodka with me, and real caviar, and two cigars. Only two, Epureanu, to show who has earned my favor. In two hours' time, you will join me in the mess hall for a public celebration, to show these men they fear the wrong things. What is it with spacemen, ah? So smart, such strong chins, and yet so many of them are fools."

"Yes, sir," Epureanu agreed. Back now to playing recorded phrases from the Obsequious Spaceman Handbook.

Grigory sighed. Perhaps the vodka would loosen this man's tongue, and once the cigars were lit and the caviar and eggs and chopped onion consumed, Grigory would also invite Morozov and Voronin, the station's commander and subcommander, to join the party, lest their offended dignity get the better of them and swing back against Epureanu somehow. And when they'd all had a few drinks, then and only then could they truly speak. He'd often thought this was the real reason for Russian alcoholism; not the grim winters, not the wild gyrations of the economy, but a simple inability to connect, person to person, in any other way, alas. Or perhaps an unwillingness, but it amounted to the same thing; Russian culture admitted few other bonding mechanisms.

In zero gravity, one did not sling one's flight bag over one's shoulder. Rather, one tucked it under one's arm and kicked off with the feet. Grigory brushed past Epureanu and made his way into the station proper.

"Why *are* you here?" Epureanu asked.

"The Coalition has put a naval blockade on Suriname. Surface ships are prevented from entering or leaving the country until further notice."

"Oh. Shit. Really?"

"Yes, really. The bastards fear what they can't beat."

"Well, uh, your quarters have been prepared," Epureanu said, trailing along behind him. "By me, I mean. Personally."

"Good," Grigory said. "I'll take a large shit and then head down to Operations."

"May I ask, sir? Why don't you have any windows in there?"

Because I fear assassins looking in there through telescopes and knowing for sure that's where I am, Grigory was tempted to say. Instead, he answered, "The Sun revolves very slowly around the station, once per month, and when it's on this side I find no window shade ever fully blocks it out. You live here, this should be obvious. But this is not the time for small talk, Epureanu. You're dismissed. No need to hang at my elbow while I shit, ah?

You'll meet me in two hours, and I'll tell you all about it at that time."

"Very good, sir."

Epureanu looked grateful to have the opportunity to retreat.

Grigory sighed. Alone among the Horsemen, he had *not* built his empire from scratch, but inherited the foundations of it from his father, Magnus Orlov, the Great and Terrible. It was hardly Grigory's own fault that he'd inherited a very Russian legacy of violence and corruption, with all the attendant risks. He had standards to uphold, and quite frankly Orlov Petrochemical had always run on fear and jealousy and greed, in that order, and such a legacy was not lightly overturned if one valued one's life. Indeed, it was by paying close attention to this legacy that Grigory had expanded his father's business into nuclear fusion, and then into asteroid mining.

And so, in order to maintain a reputation as the sort of person who could have you killed, Grigory had in fact had people killed. He had, yes, but only twice! And only because there truly hadn't seemed to be any way around it. But twice went a long way, and the people who worked for him sometimes also had people killed, and *all* of that stuck to him, as he supposed it must. The Eastern Bloc energy sector was not for the squeamish or faint of heart. Which of course made it all the more annoying that Morozov and Voronin had sent a junior manager—a *foreign* junior manager—to receive him. After all this time, they should certainly know better than that.

In Operations, Morozov looked up at Grigory's arrival.

"Mr. Orlov," he said, with utmost respect and just a tinge of resignation. "You made it."

"I did."

"Welcome," said Voronin. "I see you dodged the blockade."

There were three other people in here—two men and a woman—but none dared look up from their tasks.

"I did," Grigory said again. In truth, he'd taken what he feared might be the last commercial flight into Paramaribo—a *commercial flight!*—and then ordered a shuttle slapped on top of the next available OP rocket, and he had flown it here himself, not trusting any automated systems because the shuttles were built by Lockheed Martin and not his own people. But he made it here, yes, because he feared what violence might happen to his reputation if the Godfather of Space and scariest of Horsemen should find himself trapped Earthside. Space assets created a small fraction of his total revenue, but close to one hundred percent of his growth potential and perceived importance, and he wasn't about to compromise that.

"What is our status?" he demanded, leaving the question deliberately open-ended just to see what they would say.

It was Morozov who spoke first: "Still operating, for the moment. Enough of our LV fuel production has shifted into Suriname that we'll keep flying for another ten days. But then, if the blockade doesn't open up, we'll be out of launch vehicles. And that's the most optimistic scenario; if the Coalition declares a no-fly zone, we're grounded immediately and for the duration."

"Duration of what?" Voronin asked.

"Of whatever these cocksuckers are doing," Morozov answered.

Men of little imagination, yes. Grigory told them, "Our facility is not the target of this interference. Although we could bomb them from orbit, the governments of the world know we're within reach of their immediate reprisal. What do they fear? Rogue actors."

"Renz Ventures?" Voronin asked.

"Of course," Grigory said. "Who else? But Esley is a long way off. To attack there would be costly, and slow, whereas a naval blockade of Suriname requires only a reallocation of existing military assets."

"Making us collateral damage," Voronin said, getting it.

"Indeed. Along with all space commerce that doesn't go through Coalition governments directly. This is fear, gentlemen. Fear of the unknown, and of the future generally. These governments pine for days gone by, when men like us were under their thumbs, or at their service. And how do we respond to fear?"

He waited a few seconds, for an answer he knew they wouldn't attempt, because they themselves were afraid. Of the unknown, of what he might do to them if the Clementine Cislunar Fuel Depot were idled for even just a few days. Then he answered the question himself: "We *feed* it, while appearing to cooperate. We can still land things on Earth, yes?"

"In Kazakhstan and North Africa," Morozov agreed. "Or on the ocean."

"Fine. That's fine. Order twenty landing bodies from

Renz, one every week until further notice, rush delivery. We'll repay their fuel costs in kind, with fuel. What do we make here, Morozov?"

"Fuel."

Orlov snorted. "You're a small man, you know that?"

Morozov looked offended. "You tell me, then. What do we make?"

"Customers, Andrei. We make customers. Tell Harvest Moon we'll buy their entire output of helium-3 for the next four years."

It was the oldest play from Magnus Orlov's rulebook: find what people need, and position yourself between *them* and *it*, and charge as much as the market would bear, and ignore the weeping of widows and orphans. It had worked for Magnus in oil and gas and the refineries to process them, and for Grigory in deuterium—heavy hydrogen—and the fusion reactors to ignite it, hot as the Sun.

He could see Morozov and Voronin still didn't get it, and right now he didn't have the patience to explain it to them. It was a simple enough plan: monopolize the production of RzVz to deny assets to Harvest Moon, and monopolize the production of Harvest Moon while they lacked their own transportation. If Earth was taking itself out of the picture, then the Horsemen were dependent on one another for resources, and with a little maneuvering that could mean—it *must* mean—that they were all dependent on Clementine, which of course was just a thin mask for Orlov Petrochemical. Named for an American lunar probe (which in turn was named for an imaginary daughter from an old American mining song) Clementine was an independent company, only forty percent owned by Grigory Orlov, and with an international crew, only forty percent ethnic Russians. And yet, most of the startups and nonprofits and hedge funds and high-net-worth individuals who held shares in Clementine were in Grigory's pocket one way or another, and the Clementine entity was self-incorporated according to its own laws. Each man (and three women) aboard had renounced an Earthly citizenship, and held a passport issued by Clementine itself. The station was, for all practical purposes, an independent nation, with Grigory Orlov as its ruler, and any profits that didn't land directly in his pocket came with . . . encumbrances. The arrangement was mostly for the purpose of avoiding taxes, but it had other advantages as well. It let him risk other people's money, for one thing. It let him bring in people eager to take on a large share of his risk, for a relatively small share of his profits, and it gave him a handy pool of scapegoats for when things, inevitably, didn't go according to plan.

As for the business at hand, helium-3 (also known as "tralphium" to nuclear chemists and "threelium" to the tabloids) was simply a lightweight version of the normal helium atom, with only one neutron instead of two. Though fantastically rare on Earth, it was actually rather common throughout the universe, and one of the many volatiles Harvest Moon Industries was pulling out of lunar craters. And the thing about that was, Orlov-brand utility-scale fusion reactors were fully capable of burning a tralphium-deuterium mix instead of their usual deuterium-deuterium. In fact, they *already* produced and combusted tralphium that they produced internally, as part of their normal fusion cycle! Feeding it in as a primary fuel would require some minor plumbing changes and software updates, but simulations suggested the reactors would not only produce *five times* as much net energy, but would last six times longer before neutron-producing side reactions wore out their components.

This was by design, not by coincidence, for Grigory Orlov had always believed in a future when he controlled a supply of ^{3}He. He just hadn't counted on controlling the *only* supply, so quickly. It made sense, though; he already had seventeen reactors operational around the world, whereas Sir Lawrence Edgar Killian, the CEO of Harvest Moon Industries, owned zero, and was presently selling his tralphium output to a diverse and ever-shifting assortment of government labs and quasi-governmental utility companies, plus a trickle to Dan Beseman for his alleged Mars colony. By selling through Orlov exclusively, Killian could probably reduce his own overhead, making it actually a good deal for him, as well as the only deal Grigory left open to him.

It had taken Grigory all of ten seconds to work this out in his head. He could see that Morozov and Voronin needed time to catch up, but they could do that while following his instructions.

"Place the orders," he told them. "Right now, before one of them figures it out and beats us to it."

Of course, Clementine did also produce conventional fuels (hydrogen, oxygen, and methane) and other volatiles (mainly nitrogen and CO_2), so he spent a few minutes thinking about these, and when Morozov and Voronin were ready he told them, "With terrestrial carbon unavailable, extraterrestrial carbon is about to become a lot more valuable. I want you to double the price of CO_2, and triple the price of methane. Triple nitrogen while you're at it. Leave hydrogen and oxygen alone, or we'll simply force Beseman and the Chinese to buy it from Harvest Moon. That must not be permitted. *Drop* those prices if you have to."

"You're cornering the market on three separate materials," Morozov observed.

"We. *We're* cornering the market, and in two cases it's only the extraterrestrial market, so let us not get too excited."

Unlike Renz Ventures, Clementine only sent its gatherbots after carbonaceous, volatile-rich space rocks. Still, they did produce some elemental aluminum and magnesium as a waste product of the processing (for which Beseman was the sole customer), as well as iron and slag, which Grigory practically gave away to the Chinese for radiation shielding. Now, Grigory dropped the price on these, mainly (again) to keep Harvest Moon at bay. Let them control trade on the lunar surface itself— there was little Grigory could do about that!—but he would do what he could to stymie their growth into other sectors.

"Is that all?" Morozov wanted to know.

Grigory thought about that. "It is all I can think of for the moment. Clear a workstation for me here, and I will go through the books. You gentlemen are adequate at following orders, but I'm guessing there are patterns you've missed, and every ruble is going to count in the coming weeks. In fact, order ten kilograms of sulfur and ten of phosphorus from Harvest Moon, right now, before they start raising their own prices. We're going to need it for the food and drug synthesizers."

After that, he drew up orders to convert his fusion energy plants over to deuterium-tralphium—a contingency plan that was already in place for most of them, and easily drawn up for the remainder. And then he simply farted around for a while, looking at numbers and adjusting allocations here and there. For all his bluster, he did tend to hire good people, and they should be more than competent to take matters from here. But he liked to stay closely involved, particularly with his off-world assets, so he dutifully expanded each line of the cash flow statements until he had a clear understanding of what Clementine and its people were doing, and ought to be doing. He could of course have done this work from his quarters, or Earth, or anywhere really; taking up space in Operations was mostly theater and partly social, since even cartoon gangsters need some level of human contact.

Finally, he logged out of the workstation and excused himself to the mess hall, stopping by his quarters along the way for the bottle of vodka and the bento boxes of egg and onion and caviar. And the cigars, of course.

In the mess hall, Epureanu was waiting for him, with a slightly nervous impatience.

"Drinking with gangsters can be unnerving," Grigory told him. "I should know; I've been doing it all my life."

"I don't doubt it," Epureanu said.

There were tables and benches in here, and seat belts, to create the illusion of sitting down to a meal with one's crewmates, who were of course also one's neighbors and coworkers and friends. In early days, the module had simply been a big open space where people could hang about at any angle they pleased. That was certainly a more efficient use of space, but Grigory found it weirdly isolating, so he'd ordered it changed to this admittedly rather silly configuration. There were also festive decorations taped to the walls—paper flowers and paper animals, shipped up from a party supply store in Paramaribo. It was silly, but it worked. It set the tone Grigory wanted for this room: relaxed camaraderie.

Settling down across from Epureanu, Grigory stuck down his bottle and bento boxes on their magnetic bases, and leveled a gaze at the young man.

"I can assure you I'm no gangster, but drinking with the boss can be tricky as well. One worries about saying the wrong thing; will I pump you full of truth serum and then punish you for what you say? This is a legitimate fear. This is exactly the situation I've put you in. But it's also one of the only ways for grown men to make a real connection. This is valuable, particularly for a man in my position, with whom the right sort of people might be loath to connect, while the wrong sort are entirely too eager. I think you're the right sort, Epureanu, and this is why I compel you to drink with me."

"I appreciate the invitation," Epureanu said, with a nervous attempt at warmth.

Grigory smiled at that. "You're very kind to say so, and I believe it demonstrates my point."

He took up one of the cigars, clipped it with a tool snugged into the lid of one of the bento boxes, and let the fingernail-sized cut end drift away as someone else's problem to clean up. He then took up the cigar lighter from the lid of the other box, ignited a butane flame, and puffed the cigar to life. And then, in a naked and admittedly somewhat juvenile show of power, he handed that very cigar to Epureanu.

"It's not Cuban," Grigory said. "For all their vaunted reputation, the Cubans roll a harsh smoke, and this has only grown worse as the global market for tobacco products has declined. No, this is a Don Collins, from the American island of Puerto Rico. The size is 'robusto,' which means it will burn for more than half an hour. Do not inhale the smoke, or it will make you ill."

"Thank you, sir," Epureanu said, taking the cigar from him and puffing from it experimentally.

"Call me Grigory."

"All right."

Grigory then clipped a cigar for himself, and lit it with the little butane torch. An old-fashioned cigarette lighter would never work in zero gee; the lack of gravity convection would turn the flame spherical, and burn the thumb holding down the thumb switch. A *proper* cigar lighter, though, was a pressurized torch that spat its flame a centimeter and more from the butane nozzle. It actually worked better in zero gee than it did on Earth, as the flame shot out straight, rather than curving upward.

Next he saw about the vodka, the drinking of which in zero gravity Russians had been perfecting for decades. Yet another tool clipped into his decadence kit was a stopper syringe, and once he'd uncapped the bottle and tossed the cap over his shoulder, he jammed the stopper part into the neck of the bottle, cold and sweaty with condensation, and pulled back the plunger on the syringe, drawing a perfect shot of liquor into it, which he then withdrew and injected into his mouth, and swallowed gratefully.

He was not above drinking warm vodka, or bad vodka for that matter, but this was *Stolichnaya Elit*, and the bottle had come fresh from the chiller in his quarters, cold enough to freeze liquid water. It would certainly do the trick, and meanwhile taste good on the way down.

He drew the syringe full again and passed it to Epureanu, who sipped from it and mmm'ed his appreciation.

"Don't be a schoolboy," Grigory told him. "You drink the good stuff the same way you drink proletariat swill: a gulp at a time. Come now. There, yes. Let me fill it for you again."

Once you got past the first couple of shots, you had to move the bottle a certain way to get the vodka within reach of the syringe. He did so, and then when he'd filled and handed over the syringe he began prepping crackers and sliced hardboiled eggs with smears of caviar topped with diced raw onion, held in place by surface tension and hope. A few gawkers had stopped by already, to watch Grigory and Epureanu drink and smoke and eat, and that was fine and according to plan. A feast like this was meant to nourish the ego as well as the body, and it did help to have an audience.

He knew he was succeeding when, a few minutes later, Epureanu drew a third shot for himself without waiting for Grigory and without asking permission.

"Yes," Grigory said approvingly, "like a man. Good.

Take what properly belongs to you, without apology. Men like us do not apologize, Epureanu, unless there's something to be gained by it. Or shall I call you Daniel Florinovich? I've read your dossier." Calling a person by first name and patronym was a sign of familiarity in Russia. Not necessarily of *friendship*, though; one could also be "familiar" with underlings, who could not respond in kind. So the question was simultaneously neighborly and domineering.

"If you like," Epureanu answered.

"What did I just tell you, Daniel Florinovich? You must tell me what to call you. Me, your boss's boss's boss."

"Then call me Daniel," Epureanu said. "You are not my mother."

"Fuck your mother," Grigory said, and laughed. The vodka was taking hold, yes. So was the reek of cigar smoke, sure to let the entire station know their leader was on board, for no one else here was authorized to ignite anything but a welding torch.

"Grigory?" A voice from behind him. He turned, and saw Andrei Morozov hovering there.

"The grown-ups are drinking," he said. "What is it?"

"We've received a message on the entangled channel. For you, I presume."

It was a valid presumption; the *ul'trashirokopolosnyy* was for Grigory's own personal use, so any message on it was, by definition, intended only for him.

"Contents of the message?" he asked.

Morozov looked uncomfortable. "A woman's voice, sir. Saying, in English, and I quote, 'The asset is embedded at TPS.' Nothing after that. Do you know what it means?"

"I do, yes."

"TPS is Transit Point Station, I assume. Have you got a *spy* in position there?"

"You're a nosy fucker, aren't you?"

"Just doing my job, sir. Do you want me to reply?"

"No," said Grigory. "The asset has its instructions already. You look thirsty, my friend. You and Voronin should find a squeeze bottle of that drug-printer vodka and join us here."

"All right," Morozov said neutrally. Grigory knew Morozov enjoyed a good party as much as the next man, but he was on edge, and this display wasn't helping his mood. Nor was it intended to, but now that the point had been made, they could all let down their guard. In fact, he required it.

"Your soft, flabby underbelly is showing," Grigory told Morozov. "Get Voronin and have a fucking drink with me and Daniel Florinovich here. Bring everyone, in fact; the world doesn't know it yet, but we made a trillion rubles today. We *took* a trillion rubles from Lawrence Killian, and there's not a thing he can do about it. So now we celebrate."

1.4
22 March

Transit Point Station
Low Earth Orbit
Cislunar Space

"I'm Derek," the pilot said, reaching out to shake her hand.

"Of course you are," Alice said, a bit more snidely than she'd intended. She backpedaled slightly, with, "Sorry. I'm Alice."

She felt embarrassed by her reaction, but not *that* embarrassed, because goddamn it, the male pilots she knew (and she knew a lot) were never "Chris" or "Dana" or "Timmy." Did men with names like that simply never go to flight school, or never get taken seriously there? Or did they all change their names to "Mitch" and "Hank" and "Thor"? Seriously, she knew two guys named Captain Thor! Of course, the female pilots were nearly as bad. She knew a female "Mike" and a female "Brandon," for God's sake.

"Whoa," said Derek, smiling but confused by her tone. "Hostile. What's that about?"

The name tag on his jumpsuit said D. HAKKENS.

"Oh, you pilots and your names," Alice said, unhelpfully.

Derek snorted, then nodded, then tongued his cheek from the inside, seeming unsure what to make of her. "Pilots, huh? Okay. I heard you were pararescue. Is that right? Special Forces medic? I've found . . . excuse me, I need you to sign this." He thrust a tablet computer at her. "I've found Special Forces people sometimes have an issue with pilots. Not tough enough, something like that."

"It's not a toughness issue," she said, glancing at the form on the screen (some kind of safety waiver) and scribbling her finger on the signature block. "I'm sorry, it's not you. Well, maybe it's you; I mean, we haven't met. I've had a lot of soccer dads ferry me around and expect me to swoon for it. *Can I help you with that, sweetheart?*"

Derek laughed out loud at that, cheerfully refusing to take the bait. And why was Alice baiting him, anyway? Was she attracted to him? Was she pushing him away so she didn't accidentally sleep with him? Damn it. That had certainly happened with a soccer dad or two, but she couldn't tell right now if that's what was going on. Was he anything more than just all right? Did she want him to be? Did it matter? Unfortunately, Alice never seemed to be in good contact with her own brain about stuff like this. Like a lot of adrenaline junkies, she was never in touch with much of anything when the world around her was too calm. She *did* have a job to do, so she decided to focus on that.

"My call sign is 'Beaker,' if that helps," he offered. "Probably not the most macho you've heard."

Alice opted not to smile at that. "Muppets fan?"

"My father was."

Was. Past tense. Okay, now *that* was bait Alice wasn't going to take. No, she wasn't going to ask some flyboy about his dear dead father, and listen to all the stories about him sitting in Daddy's lap, landing the goddamn plane at the age of three. Jesus Christ already.

"What did you want to see me about?" she asked curtly. "What's this form I just signed?"

They were floating in a too-busy service hab on this too-empty station, their voices elevated over the surprisingly loud hiss of the station's ventilation system.

Like the spaceport at Paramaribo, Transit Point Station was some kind of joint venture between RzVz and the three other private space companies: Orlov Petrochemical, Harvest Moon Industries, and Enterprise City LLG. And like Paramaribo, TPS had a seat-of-the-pants vibe to it. As the shuttle had approached, Alice and her fellow passengers had seen the structure of it—much larger and spindlier than you saw it online, from angles carefully selected to be photogenic and dramatic. The station orbited at a higher altitude than the Marriott Stars, so the Earth was smaller and rounder below it, and revolving more slowly underneath, than Alice was used to seeing it. TPS had ten cylindrical habitat modules arranged in two rows of five, with connecting modules in between, and the "pier" structure extending upward from that, with berthing slips for, it looked like, ten spaceships at once, although only three were occupied. One was filled by a little shuttle like the one they were in, and one by a deep-space craft Alice actually recognized from one of her briefings, as the L.S.F. *Dandelion*, the "low speed ion ferry" that would carry them out to ESL1. Or a vehicle of the same type, at any rate.

The third ship was so big she'd thought at first that it was part of the space station. It had taken her a minute to recognize it as H.S.F. *Concordia*, the famous ship that was allegedly going to carry one hundred lucky contestants to Mars in a couple of years. "My God, will you look at that," Maag had said. Alice hadn't known what to say. Mars? For real? But there was Dan Beseman's ship, larger than life.

Now, onboard the station, a small Asian man in red coveralls brushed past her and Derek, looking like he was in a hurry, with a larger, ginger-haired man trailing after him. These same two people had swarmed past in the other direction not two minutes ago. TPS had been built to accommodate transient populations of up to a hundred people—literally, a hundred!—but its permanent crew was only ten, and they always seemed to be in motion, on their way from somewhere to somewhere else. Cheerful but harried, clearly overworked in their shitty astronaut jobs and just as clearly loving it.

Transit Point Station was on the same clock schedule as Suriname, an hour ahead of Eastern Standard Time. As Alice and her crewmates discovered shortly after arriving, during the evening and night shifts, these modules unfolded into galleys and bathing areas, exercise rooms and sleeping quarters. It wasn't as nice as the Marriott Stars, but it was a lot nicer than Alice had been expecting. A bit like RV camping, and in the absence of gravity the modules felt pretty roomy inside. With the exception of Rachael Lee, they'd all slept together in the same dormitory module, in sleeping bags like oversized pillowcases hung from the walls. Lee, who had barfed in her helmet, was recovering in sickbay, which was a module unto itself, and capable of serving up to six patients at once. That seemed like overkill to Alice, but it said something about the ambitions of the people who'd built this place. Lots of traffic expected in their future, lots more than today.

But during the "day," most of these same modules packed up into corridors and workstations, plus gowning and de-gowning rooms for people in spacesuits. This particular module—2C—wasn't exactly out of the way, but it didn't seem to be serving any specific function at the moment. It was a good enough place to meet and talk.

Of course, Alice was only here because she was bored and Derek had paged her. She got the sense Derek was here for something more specific than to get a form signed.

"According to your dossier, you're a qualified pilot yourself," he told her.

"Gliders only," Alice answered. "I had some basic single-engine training but not enough to get certified." She paused and looked at him. "Why?"

"They're pushing us out of here ahead of schedule, and my copilot isn't going to make it off Earth in time. I need someone to fill the chair."

Alice couldn't quite help rolling her eyes. "We need two pilots for a slow ferry? Really? I took a big rocket here, and we got all the way through boost phase, orbital rendezvous, and docking with zero pilots."

"True, although that's frowned on. They wanted you out of there, and up here, in a hurry."

She frowned at that. "Yeah, we noticed. Why is that? What's going on?"

Derek demonstrated the art of the zero-gravity shrug. "Not sure. Something about government interference. You heard about the blockade of Suriname?"

"People have been talking about it, yes."

"Well, that's part of it, but there seems to be something more going on. Igbal's worried about, quote, 'more invasive government assistance,' close quote."

"Even up here?"

Derek shrugged again, and for the first time, it occurred to Alice that it might be *her own operation* that RzVz had caught wind of. The thought gave her instant goose bumps, though whether of fear or excitement she couldn't tell. Like most Maroon Berets, she had those two emotions pretty well twisted together when she had them at all.

Changing the subject, she said, "How does it help you, to have a glider pilot on a spaceship?"

"In terms of flying, it doesn't. You'd be redundant and actually kind of in the way. In terms of *my pay*, it's the difference between tending a semi-robotic flight and *commanding* a fully manual training mission. That's six thousand dollars in my pocket."

"Ah." Six thousand dollars didn't buy as much as it used to before the currency collapse, but for most people it was still a month's rent or two years of decent haircuts— nothing to sneeze at. That made enough sense to calm Alice down a bit. As a motivator, simple human greed was easy to relate to. RzVz wasn't a drug cartel; they weren't going to put a bullet in the back of anyone's head or anything like that. But they did want their precious profits, same as Derek, same as everyone else in the world.

They also wanted power, she supposed. Not just the power to buy and sell what they wanted, and place their space assets wherever they wanted, but to sidestep government influence in every big and small way they could. To operate out of third-world countries that did their bidding. But even *that* wasn't so sinister, because what was the point of power, if not to satisfy greed? Cartels were *not* motivated purely by money. They were quick to anger, quick to take offense, quick to solve problems with insane levels of highly targeted violence. Corporations—even shady ones like Orlov Petrochemical—were calmer and more predictable. Still, if it were up to her, she would have liked to see them under better control. Bridle the Horsemen, so to speak.

Alice realized, suddenly and with some surprise, that she was a bit of a socialist. Huh. If she really thought about it, most Air Force people were! Praise Jesus, all their *actual needs* were met by shared facilities and a government salary, and few of them traded it for the private sector until their pensions kicked in and it was safe. Funny, that people like her would rather parachute into a hot landing zone than risk their pride and treasure in the job market.

And it did sound kind of silk, learning to fly a spaceship. Also, and more darkly, she might learn something that would help her escape from Esley Shade Station if her betrayals somehow failed to deliver the station into government hands.

Playing along, she asked, "What do I get out of it?"

Derek seemed to ponder that for a while, before answering, "I guess I could sleep with you."

It was such a flyboy thing to say, it almost didn't surprise her, but she pushed him for it, lightly on the chest, with her other arm braced, so he tumbled away from her.

"Try again."

Snorting as he caught himself, Derek said, "You'd be surprised how often that works. But okay, you're a cut above the schoolgirls. Duly noted. You want a third of the bonus money?"

"Half," she said, not meaning it, just wondering what he'd say.

He looked at her sideways. "Fuck are you going to spend it on, Colonist?"

"Don't care. Oxygen, maybe."

He snorted again, but with a bit less amusement.

"One third. Final offer. And you get a flight approval on your personnel file, and a pile of hours toward your certification, so I don't want any shit from you."

"Deal," she said, after pretending to think it over. Then, just to be an asshole, she added, "I'd've done it for free."

He nodded. "Yeah, me too. Fucking spaceship, am I wrong?"

And then the two of them were laughing, and that was that.

Changing subjects, she asked him, "If we're shipping out later today, what's going to happen to Rachael Lee?"

"Colonist Lee is staying here. I'm told she's on some kind of probation, might get shipped back home."

"For barfing in zero gee?"

"For losing her shit about it, yes."

"Mmm." That seemed fair. RzVz was no military operation, but it did seem to have a bit of the same flavor, including a low tolerance for bullshit. For a moment, Alice caught herself thinking that was good and would make her happy in her new life.

Derek handed her a little Velcro-backed rectangular patch that said PILOT TRAINEE in gold letters. It was fresh off the fabric printer, still warm.

"Once you put this on," he told her, "you outrank the other colonists, at least until we reach Esley. So I need you to go round them up, get 'em ready for the flight."

He looked her over for a moment, and then added, "I was an Air Force captain, you know. Fighter pilot. I flew top cover on fifteen Coffee Patch missions, making sure you people had clear skies above."

Alice considered that. "Am I supposed to be impressed?"

"Just saying, you're not the only one who's been shot at." Then, to her unspoken question, he answered, "The June Massacre? Yes, I was there."

Hmm.

Once the bankrupt U.S. government had finally given up its drug war and Big Pharma had taken over the job of getting people high, the Cartels had not taken it well. They'd started straight-up taxing the people and businesses in their territory, like legitimate governments high on blood and cocaine. And the actual legitimate governments had taken *that* badly, and soon everybody was shooting everybody. And yeah, the second time an American judge was murdered right there on the bench of his own courtroom, the U.S. was officially back at war with the Cartels again, and it was *personal*.

Things had gone well for Uncle Sam, and then *really* well, because it was finally just a matter of identifying what needed to be blown up, and then blowing it up. Hard times or no, these things were still very much in the American wheelhouse, and the Air Force started racking up impressive numbers, until it was time for the Marines and Army to start actually capturing back territory. Boots on the ground, as they liked to say. Even that had gone well for a while, until the Medellín Cartel had somehow gotten their hands on a shipment of Chinese jet drones, packing enough EMP wattage to microwave a human brain from two kilometers away.

That day—known to the media as the June Massacre and to the Maroon Berets as Zero Extract—was the war's highest Coalition body count by a factor of ten, and it had been largely responsible for pushing the U.S. back into covert ops, where it was easier to literally hit the Cartels where they lived, with deniability for any atrocities that might occur. Not deliberate atrocities, of course, but there were plenty of fuckups in the heat and confusion of battles taking place on remote, mansion-covered hills poking up out of dense jungle. The Medellín and Chocadores used their own children as human shields, and other people's children as torture porn to bait ambushes.

"I'm sorry for your loss," Alice said to Derek. What else could she say?

He nodded. "Yeah. Thanks. We undock in three hours."

He turned to go, on some inscrutable pilot business of

his own, before turning and adding, "That trainee patch puts you in my chain of command, by the way."

"Well, duh," she answered. But his meaning was clear: Until they got to ESL1 and she reported to whomever, he in fact couldn't sleep with her, even if he wanted to. Sleeping with direct subordinates was universally forbidden, both in and out of the military.

"Understood," she added, just to make sure he knew she knew what he was getting at. But it did cross her mind that military and corporate ethics rules probably didn't apply out here. Maybe not even maritime law, because who was going to enforce it?

When Alice got back to the sleeping quarters, she found Dona Obata engaged in a fierce argument with two men wearing the red jumpsuits of Transit Point Station crew.

"I'm sorry," one of them was saying, "but your file is red-flagged. Some of the answers on your application don't line up with your background check, and the AI kicked it back."

"My background check was finished months ago," she snapped at him, "and I passed."

"Data sniffers," the guy said, shrugging. "They never sleep, they just keep searching."

"Fucking AI," Dona spat. "You let me talk to a *person* about this."

"I'm a person," he said. He was black, though not as black as Dona herself. The name tag on his coverall said CMDR. C. OLIVER. "I reviewed the discrepancies myself."

"What's going on?" Alice demanded.

"Big Brother, here," Jeanette mumbled.

Moderating her tone, Alice tried, "Commander, I've known this woman for"—for what, a few days?—"a few days, now. I've seen nothing suspicious."

"Reeeally," Commander C. Oliver said, glaring sideways at her. Not impressed.

It did sound kind of thin. Why had she said that?

"What exactly is the problem?" she tried. Oliver looked at her name tag, saw the trainee patch. Looked back up into her eyes.

"Anomalies," he repeated. "I mean, people lie on their résumés, it happens, but not everyone has *École Polytechnique* lying on their résumés for them."

Improvising, Alice asked, "Meaning what, she hacked her records?"

"I don't know," Oliver replied. "I don't know what it means, but it's not my job to know. Our instructions are to put her back on the shuttle that brought her here. And so far she's noncompliant. Are you military?"

"Formerly, yes."

"You want to give us a hand with her?"

Physically, he meant. Because even out here in low Earth orbit, he didn't want to assault a woman, or be accused of touching one inappropriately.

Alice looked him over. It was hard to say what separated civilian types from military and first responder types, because civilians could be tough and disciplined people. Football players and street brawlers, CEOs and Cartel jackboys all had their strengths. And yet, she could spot at a glance who was and wasn't currently in the military. Former military took only a moment longer to sniff out. There *was* something disciplined and tough about Commander C. Oliver, but he was definitely a civilian. This amused Alice, who had spent her adult life around Spec Ops men who'd think nothing of grabbing Dona by the tits and slamming her head against the ceiling, if the tactical situation appeared to call for it.

However, Alice's special relationship in this situation offered a whole 'nother approach: throwing Dona under the bus. Dona was *burned*, as the intel people liked to say, and if Alice tried to defend her, she could end up burned as well. No, thank you.

"What's your strategy here, Dona?" she asked in a loud voice. "Whatever you were trying to get away with, it didn't work, and now these gentlemen want you gone. Your new employer wants to stop employing you. And you're *arguing* with them? Do you think that's going to work?"

"What are you doing?" Dona demanded, glaring icily. She was far off script now, and Alice could see that made her dangerous. She would turn to violence if she thought there was an advantage in it. But there wasn't. What could she do, beat up everyone in this room, and then just board the ferry to ESL1 like nothing had happened?

"Helping, Dona. Are you listening? I'm *helping*. I don't know what's going on here, but if you're some kind of a spy, I'd say your cover is blown. If you're not a spy, if you're some plain old liar, your cover is still blown. Apparently Igbal doesn't want liars on his station, and I can't say I blame him. Would you? You're *fired*, girl. They're not letting you on that ferry. So what are you trying to do?"

"Steady now," Bethy said from across the room. "Nobody wants trouble."

Dona turned her glare of cold fury in Bethy's direction, and right there, from the look in Dona's eyes, Alice could see she'd made the right move. If Alice and Dona and Bethy were all in this together, Dona would know that her own exposure could, ironically and indirectly, make Alice and Bethy more secure. Problem solved, everyone! Government interference found and neutralized! But no, Dona didn't appear to see it that way. Dona was *not* in this together with Alice and Bethy, but had some other sort of plan in mind. To cut Alice and Bethy out? To seize the station and all its assets for France, or for the Congo, or for the highest bidder, or whatever? Maybe even for the fucking Cartels. Oh, Dona.

"Maybe *you're* a spy," Dona said to Bethy, then turned to Alice to include her in the statement as well. It was a naked threat—*I can expose you right here and now*—but Dona's heart did not appear to be in it. She was compromised, all right, but she and her backers still had a good deal of deniability. If she went and compromised the *whole operation*, there'd be nothing but ass fuckings all around, and the ESL1 Shade still in the hands of a nutjob.

Dona sighed, and then the tension went out of her, and she did a remarkable job of starting to actually cry. "I just wanted to be here. The future, outer space. Didn't you? Oh, damn, I knew it was too good to last. I went to college, okay? Free online college is still college. I know what I know! Give me an aptitude test!"

Commander Oliver now looked embarrassed. "That's

not my department, Ms. Obata; I don't even work for Renz Ventures. When you get to Earth, I'm sure you can petition your case with the admissions board. Right now, I'm afraid Pilot Trainee Kyeong is correct: you've been fired. If you don't get on that earthbound shuttle ASAP, you can be charged with trespassing, and billed for the air you're breathing. Which isn't cheap. That *is* my department, so I'd encourage you not to test my patience."

"So what am I supposed to do?"

"Put your spacesuit on. Now. I'll have someone stow your belongings on the shuttle for you. I don't have any pilots to spare, but the shuttle can take you back to Suriname on its own. It'll be a few hours before the orbits line up, but you can spend that in the shuttle, floating free. Not here."

"Damn it. Damn it. Really? Are you serious right now?"

Oliver's silence said it all.

Bethy, wisely, looked away rather than involving herself any further in the dispute. And so it was Maag and Alice who wound up escorting Dona to the gowning module, and watching while she stripped to her 3D-printed "space underwear" and sullenly donned her spacesuit. Distinctly unfashionable, the space underwear consisted of a dark gray, stretchy, remarkably slippery T-shirt with a kind of shelf bra built in, and a pair of tight-fitting shorts in the same color that reached almost to the knee, like bicycle shorts. They were basically just to keep spacesuits and coveralls from chafing or sticking or stinking in the wrong places. Loaded with antimicrobials and "odor-neutralizing and odor-sequestering molecules," they were designed to go a whole week between washings, and to permit the aforementioned spacesuits and coveralls to be used for *months*, because apparently laundry was hard to do in outer space. It used up a lot of water or something. This had been invisible to her at the Marriott Stars, but people made a big deal about it here.

"You're going to be going through atmospheric reentry by yourself," Maag told Dona. "I don't care *who* you are, that's going to be scary."

"I'll be fine," Dona snapped, because of course she'd been through several reentries already.

But it just looked like bravado to Maag, who offered Dona an awkward hug. Dona accepted it, but shot Alice a look that said, *I might very well murder you for this.*

Once they had her in the spacesuit, they escorted her onto the shuttle and helped her buckle in like it was their job. Perhaps it was? They chose an aisle seat for her, closest to the vehicle's center of mass, presuming that was better somehow. Then one of the red-jumpsuited station technicians came around with a box containing Dona's flight bag, and secured it to the rail across from her seat.

Maag offered her another awkward hug, and said good luck.

"And to you," Dona said sourly, and with a bit of acerbic irony. Like, *Good luck, blue hair, when Pilot Trainee Alice Kyeong turns on you, too*. Her voice was muffled by the bubble of her spacesuit helmet, but that tone came through loud and clear. Well, good. At least she was playing the part—hurt and confused, a little panicked at how fast this was happening and how little control she had over it. The nastier truth was something Alice wasn't sure she wanted to know, but meanwhile she had her own part to play: ashamed. If she simply pretended in her mind that Dona *wasn't* a dangerous government operative, then this was a shitty thing they were doing to her. Shitty and scary.

"I'm sorry," Alice told her, not meaning it in the slightest.

There wasn't much else to say, so the three of them—Alice and Maag and the red-suited technician—retreated back into the station under a cloud of shame.

"Not exactly teamwork," the technician said, putting voice to it as he dogged the double hatches closed. "Not exactly professional."

"Right?" Maag said. "We're just kicking her out in a lifeboat. For what, exactly?"

"For being a security threat," Alice said. And this time she did mean it.

The technician leaned on an intercom button and said, "She's ready to fly, Cap'n." His name was D. Nguyen, and he looked about as far from a classic astronaut as you could get. Lacking the chiseled flyboy jaw or the smug PhD certitude, he had that harried Transit Point Station thing going on, and he looked, if anything, like the janitor from Alice's high school. Was it possible to "stoop" in zero gravity? If so, this man was doing it.

And yet, he must have passed through some kind of selection process to be here. With nothing to explore or build, and no research to perform, the TPS joint venture had more in common with the Marriott Stars than it did with anything out at ESL1, or on the surface of the Moon, or whatever. But the staff of the Marriott Stars were fit and friendly and extremely good at their hospitality jobs. Alice had imagined them being recruited from resorts all over the world—every one of them a multilingual kite-surfing instructor and tennis pro and five-star chef with somehow no ego about it. She'd been discouraged from fraternizing with them, and with one sweaty exception she had in fact kept her distance, though she'd liked them well enough. But D. Nguyen was not like those people, either.

"What's your story?" Alice asked him. She liked to think of herself as the sort of person who could get away with questions like that.

He was actually upside down from her at the moment, so his expression was difficult to read, but he'd understood the question, and his answer was clear enough: "I worked twenty years on deep-sea natural gas rigs. Maintenance division." He made a swimming motion with his hands. "Spent years of my life underwater, and years more in decompression chambers, gassing out the nitrogen bubbles. But I had a window that looked up at the stars. Every night, they kept me sane! Dreaming of the sky. Dreaming to live in the sky."

"Ah."

"Nobody more qualified than me," he said with a little laugh.

Intrigued, she asked, "You work outside much? In a spacesuit?"

"EVA? Yeah, we go out in teams of two to swap out components and such. I'm usually one of the two. But I also keep the 3D printers running, and the toilets, and every other thing. These boys would die in half an hour if not for me."

Turning right side up, he gave Alice and Maag a sidelong look and observed, "Mostly women where you're going. Trust me, I seen them all when they come through here. The only men out there are pilots. You tried zero-gee sex yet?"

Maag looked annoyed at that, but Alice just laughed. It was the sort of pass an Army Ranger might make—direct and to the point, and without much riding on it.

"You're at the top of my list," she assured him.

"Got more experience at that, too," he assured her right back.

Then, suddenly, there was a banging noise from the double hatch, and through the little round window Alice could see the shuttle falling away. She couldn't help crowding forward to look out the porthole, and apparently neither could Maag. The two of them crowded in together, as much as the lack of gravity allowed, and watched as the shuttle—*their* shuttle—drifted away into empty space.

"Damn," Maag said.

She smelled of Paramaribo and wet wipes and some sort of fruit-scented shampoo, and the new-car aroma of 3D-printed clothing.

"Yeah," Alice agreed. If she thought about it, she actually did have some complex feelings about what had just happened; she and Dona had spent a lot of time together at the Marriott Stars, in training and conversations and the curiously intimate business of wrestling each other into submission. Well, Dona wrestling Alice into submission. They weren't *friends*, exactly, but they had headed off into danger (and probable combat) together, which made them a lot closer than office colleagues.

On the other hand, it really did seem like Dona had been planning all along to betray Alice and Bethy, and their respective countries, which was awful, of course, and made Alice very glad to see her leaving in disgrace. But it somehow didn't erase the other stuff, not completely. And then, yes, there was also the slipshod way the thing was being handled. Kicking someone—anyone—out into outer space by herself was a cold move. She wasn't sure what anyone could have done differently, with no security personnel on the station, and presumably no weapons, and no spare pilots, and everyone in a huge hurry to pry these colonist women away from the grasping hands of Earth.

But it did leave a bad taste. Unprofessional, yes, on multiple levels, because *everyone* was off script. How could there be a script for something like this?

The shuttle simply drifted for a minute, and then little plumes of gas started jetting out of little recesses in its hull, and it began to rotate, and then more jets fired, and the rotation stopped. Then, with eerie silence, the main thruster fired; a blue-white umbrella of flame and gas, blasting from a cone-shaped nozzle mostly hidden from view.

For a moment, the ship barely moved, and for another moment it moved sluggishly, like a motorboat churning at the dock. But then, with alarming swiftness, it pulled out of view. Both Alice and Maag craned at the window, trying to angle for a better view, but the shuttle was gone. Reluctantly, they turned away.

"She'll be okay," Nguyen assured them, although it was hard to say what, if anything, he was basing that on. "That shuttle was supposed to leave empty tomorrow. It knows its way back home."

"I feel unclean," Maag said, half jokingly and half . . . what, despairingly?

"Space is grungy," Nguyen said to her, nodding vaguely. "You have to do everything. Fix the climate controls or you broil and freeze. Clean the toilets or you shit yourself. You have to deal with problem people, and with good people on problem days, and I'm saying *really deal* with them. Or what happens? It's not pretty. That's the thing, eh? Not pretty. Guys like me, we know that."

Unhappily, Alice said, "She *was* a problem person. Bad enough her story didn't line up, but her reactions didn't, either. Did you buy any of that?"

Maag shrugged.

Alice thought: *Do you buy any of* this? *From* me? *Shit.*

"Do you have access to any medicinal comforts?" Maag asked Nguyen.

Somehow, his answering smirk was simultaneously filthy and guileless. "Alcohol? Could be. If I take you on a date, show you the sights . . ."

Maag appeared to be considering that for a moment— like a woman contemplating a tray of greasy gas station hot dogs before a long desert drive, and wondering if she dares to eat one, so to speak.

But it was Nguyen himself who saved her the trouble. "The drug printer's idle time program is a never-ending experiment to create drinkable booze. Some of it's pretty good stuff, and if you throw some orange drink in it, it makes a decent cocktail. You want some, I can set you up, no strings attached. This was an ugly business; I can see you're upset."

And it was Alice who stepped in humorlessly with, "We have to *go*, Maag. Our ship leaves in about two and a half hours. We've all got to pack up our shit and get our spacesuits back on."

"Why?" Maag wanted to know.

"Still running from government interference, it sounds like."

"I mean, why the spacesuits?"

"Any launch, docking, and undocking maneuvers," Alice said, for once remembering a line from the RzVz training. "In case we rupture a seal."

"We're not wearing them now," Maag said, sniffing and flourishing a hand at the now-vacant airlock. *Wasn't that an undocking procedure?*

"We're not civilians here," Nguyen told her. "All veteran astronauts here. Also, we got a lot bigger volume than a spaceship. We spring an air leak, we might not even notice right away. And even then, we just close a door, seal the module until we find the hole. It's happened more than once—no big deal. And heck, if we suited up for every docking and undocking here, we'd never do anything else."

"Hmm."

"She'll be okay, we'll be okay," Nguyen said. "Everybody be okay. Come on, I'll send you away with a little something."

Maag shook her head. "Nah. Thank you, no, I changed my mind."

Maag was clearly not going to be made happy about any of this. Well, fine. Cheering her up wasn't in Nguyen's job description anyway, or Alice's. But getting her on the ship *was* Alice's job, so she beckoned, and Maag followed.

They made their way back to the gowning area, where the women had already received word of their impending departure, and were already shrugging and twisting their way into spacesuits. This was a tricky business, like fitting yourself into a very heavy, very stiff, pullover winter coat and snow pants. And once you had them on, you had to rotate the seals and lock them together, and then you had to pull your helmet down over your head and lock it into place, and turn on your air, and then put the gloves on and lock their seals as well. Then check for leaks. It was serious business, but also harried and rushed. They were, once again, being moved along like UPS packages. Ah, life in space.

There were originally supposed to be nine colonists in this shipment, but with Lee and Dona out of the picture, they were down to just a lucky seven. There was Alice, of course, and Bethy Powell, and Malagrite Aagesen, and Jeanette Schmidt, and the three new faces who'd been waiting here at Transit Point Station for a couple of days.

The women had dined and washed and spent the night all in a single hab module, hung in thin sleeping bags from every available surface. When the "night" shift started, the windows slowly frosted themselves white with some sort of liquid crystal thing, and the blue light reflected up from the Earth on one side of the module came through as a sort of midnight purple, while the sunlight on the other side came through as a smoldering campfire orange—first through one set of portholes, and then another, and then dark for a while as the sun slipped behind the Earth, and then rising again, never brighter than a DON'T WALK sign. The hatches at either end of the module remained open, and a constant breeze flowed through from one end to the other, making the place feel almost outdoors, like a mountain cabin with all the windows open.

The seven of them *had* slept (maybe five or six hours?), and these were mostly quite serious women, no less than Alice herself, though in different ways. And yet, the night shift had passed with the dreamy excitement of a grade-school slumber party, or the first night of summer camp, full of whispered biographies and bursts of giggling. And Alice, who'd shared a room with her hissing goose of a mother for a while, and who'd spent much of the last eight years sleeping in ditches full of rough-talking men, was unable to resist being drawn in to this girl talk. She'd told the new women more about herself than was probably wise, and had listened raptly to their own stories.

There was Nonna Rostov, a materials scientist from the Russian Far East, with Asian-looking features and wavy chocolate hair, who carried herself with a nervous determination that reminded Alice of kids about to go through Navy Dive School. (That was one of the harder, scarier courses the military offered, where drowning was a very real possibility, and the reward for passing was even more chances to drown.) Every time Nonna drifted away from a secure hand- or foothold, she seemed to panic a little, flailing wide-eyed for a few moments until she remembered she wasn't falling, wasn't in any sort of immediate danger. After three days in zero gee it seemed she should be wearing it better, but Alice had seen people acclimate at different rates, so okay. It was poor but not terrible. Nonna had brought a little guitar with her to outer space, sized like a ukulele but shaped like a battle axe, with a surprisingly deep tone, and she'd spent a few minutes strumming it as the lights were turned down. She wasn't bad.

And there was Saira Batra, a walnut-skinned little thing with a halo of zero-gee frizz bursting out of her head. Her blue RzVz coveralls looked official enough, but stripped down to her gray space underwear she'd looked vaguely like one of those dolls you could win at carnivals by knocking things over with a baseball. She had a PhD in something Alice couldn't quite grasp. Topo-histo-smorbologicalism? Something like that. As near as she could figure it meant finding practical applications for geometry involving more than four dimensions, and why *that* was needed at ESL1 was anyone's guess. Saira herself seemed a bit confused by her selection, though in an upbeat sort of way.

"Of *course* I'll get pregnant for this," she said at one point. "I was planning on getting pregnant in the next few years anyway, and now my child will be part of something really big. Esley is supposed to get a spin-gee extension at some point, and that should be fine for physical development of a growing body. All the animal experiments have turned out fine. There've even been some healthy animals that were born and raised entirely in zero gee. With the right drugs and exercise, the body can be fooled into not knowing the difference."

Dona Obata, obliged to share a biography when her own turn came, had seemed cagey about relying too much on her cover story, so she hadn't said much. But she did tell a story—probably true—about fishing in some African river when she was a little girl. Bethy Powell, similarly, had told a couple of funny stories about growing up on a New Zealand cattle ranch.

And finally there was Pelu Figueroa, the oldest of the group at the age of exactly forty years, which Alice for some reason guessed correctly on the first try. Pelu had PhDs in both mechanical engineering and astronomy, and she'd run four ultramarathons and could swim a mile in just under twenty minutes. That wasn't going to win any records, but it was really, really good. Pelu was also a certified yoga instructor and weightlifting coach, and Alice pretty much hated her on sight. Not a strong hatred, not any sort of *loathing*, but that super-duper can-do attitude really rubbed her the wrong way for some reason. Pelu did seem to feel she was locked in competition, and was winning fiercely, and deserved a nod of recognition for it. *Well done, madam. Well done indeed*. Pelu also seemed to think she was tough, although Alice could definitely kick her ass. Hell, Alice could probably kick the asses of everyone here, all at the same time, if only Bethy would sit out. So whatever.

Last night these were just idle thoughts, but here and now, they took on a more sinister edge. Alice had *just* kicked Dona out into space, and it occurred to her that in completing her mission, she might very well have to hurt some of these women at some point, and by the light of day it just wasn't all that cute.

"Let's pick up the pace," Alice told them all. "I want everyone suited and cross-checked in thirty minutes."

"Who put you in charge?" Jeanette asked, not sharply but, like, actually asking.

"Our pilot."

"We have a pilot?" Jeanette said, with exaggerated glee. "Ooh, swanky. We're moving up in the world. Now if only we were leaving on a normal schedule, I might feel almost like a respected human being."

Maag said, "Good luck with that. Bunch of men running things up here. *Cave* men. Bloody competitive assholes. I'm the *first*! Yeah? Well I'm the *best*! Yeah, well I've got the *biggest dink*! Yaaaargh!"

Alice paused, looking at Maag. This was interesting, because last night Maag had been gung ho about her upcoming job, as a chemical engineer and manufacturing process specialist, and excited about the chance to "be part of something so much bigger, so much bigger than any of us have ever dreamed." If she had a problem with Igbal Renz, she certainly hadn't mentioned it then. But Alice had a professional interest in people who had a problem with Igbal Renz.

Jeanette, however, did not. She said, "Jesus, girl, what crawled up your ass? It's a bit late for that kind of talk, don't you think?"

"No," Maag said. "I don't. Obviously, I wanted to be here. I *want* to be here. But why is it, if you want to get to space, you have to pick a Horseman? You have to be exactly what some rich man is looking for. It's a rich man's sky, isn't it? And why is that? So all right, I've picked my Horseman, all right. Igbal is my guy. But I don't have to love doing that. Do I? I don't have to love every aspect of everything. My God, we just pushed a fellow traveler out into space, alone, because she lied on her résumé. Because she's not exactly what the rich man wants."

"That's crap," said Nonna Rostov, in a heavily accented voice. "She seemed nice enough person."

"She shared a candy bar with me," said Saira Batra.

"She was up to no good," Alice said, in a tone she hoped would end it. "Can't you *smell* it? She wasn't just lying on her résumé, and she wasn't alone. Wasn't *acting* alone, I mean. There's a lot going on up here. Probably more than we know."

"Definitely something wrong with her," Bethy Powell agreed. "Good riddance, I say. Now let's get to Esley Shade Station and let that pervert knock us up!"

2.2
23 March 2051

ESL1 Shade Station
Earth-Sun Lagrange Point 1
Extracislunar Space

Igbal flung himself into the computer lab, saying, "What the hell, Sandy?"

Sandy Lincoln, buried in VR gear, looked around blindly for the source of the voice, then switched her view to translucent and swiveled the bug eyes of her headset toward Igbal in a way he still found creepy, though it had been normal human behavior for decades.

"Huh?"

"We're doing the Mach drive test. Right now."

"Oh. Okay."

"Your numbers are way off."

"Okay. You checked the model yourself."

"Well, it's crap."

Dead-eyed as a lobster, Sandy replied, "I'd blame the MechanoLab software before I blamed the actual model, Ig. It's really not designed to simulate these kinds of exotic theories. It's for gears and stuff."

"We bought the quantum gravity package for it. For twenty-eight thousand dollars!"

"Still."

Igbal sighed. The Mach-Fearn effect was a kind of quantum gravity assist, not unlike a slingshot orbit around Jupiter. You could launch yourself right out of the solar system by stealing an infinitesimal amount of momentum from a planet during a close flyby, slowing it down ever so slightly in its orbit. Boom. Hyperbolic trajectory for your spacecraft, right out to infinity. Unmanned probes had been doing it since the 1960s, and human-crewed missions in cislunar space regularly slingshotted around the Moon to get higher and farther away from the Earth. The Mach-Fearn effect was a similar thing, except you were stealing energy from the expansion of the universe itself, pulling it back in toward you by literally the smallest possible quantum of movement. By firing a bunch of steam-powered pistons!

Actually, the pistons could be powered by anything—nuclear fission, nuclear fusion, or what have you—but Igbal had personally built a sealed, hubcap-sized prototype that ran on vapor expansion because he had the parts lying around, and it *worked*. He had stolen a small amount of velocity out of nowhere, or out of everywhere, without expelling any sort of exhaust or propellant. It was amazing, and for many people it could have been the signature achievement of a lifetime. For Igbal it just meant there was more work to do, so then a team of four engineers (and yes, one of them was male, goddamn it) had scaled his design way up, to a version slightly larger than a traffic roundabout, and it was outside right now, thrumming away.

"Come with me," Igbal said.

"What?"

"Come with me, dammit. No, get that stuff off your face and leave it here. Right. Right, yes. Now come on. I need your eyes on this."

Sandy was one of those appallingly stupid smart people. With a genetically fit body (of course), she boasted a PhD in theoretical physics from M-I-betyourass-T, and a master's in mechanical engineering from Purdue for some reason, and she was creative and whip-smart and generally perfect for this place, except that she was a goddamn idiot. Her medical records indicated she was "cured of autism" at a young age, which was fine; a lot of smart people were on the spectrum. Hell, Igbal himself was on the spectrum. But Sandy took it to a whole new level. She was in constant danger of walking out an airlock or cutting an artery on her goddamn zipper, and Igbal should probably have sent her home twelve months ago and let her work remotely from Liberia or Suriname. Would he have, if she weren't so goddamn gorgeous, and occasionally sleeping with him when the mood randomly struck her?

"I really like sex," she'd told him once. "It just doesn't occur to me." Uh-huh. She was good at it, too.

"Sandy," he said, as gently as his impatience and general asshole-ness would allow, "you're hooked on some wires. Jesus. Jesus Christ. Jesus Christ, are you ready? Come with me. I need you to see this and tell me what's going on."

"Okay, Ig," she said, as though he were the weird one. As quickly as he could safely move, he swung from handrails and kicked off from corners and hatches, ricocheting from computer lab to nanofabrication lab, past the main kitchen and through the secondary hab corridor, to his office, with its gigantic windows—the best view available from inside the station. And why not? He owned this whole place, and the Shade, too, or anyway sixty-five percent of the corporate entity that controlled them. So yes, he had bigger quarters and his own luxe workspace, right?

Pam was still there in the office, looking mournfully out at Mach-Fearn Test Probe Mark II, or MFTP2. There were two astronauts floating outside, at a presumed-safe distance, but the disc-shaped probe was decidedly *not* gathering momentum from the expansion of the universe. Not pulling the universe in around it like a warm blanket, or not much, anyway, and certainly not symmetrically. The probe was crawling away from the Shade, toward the blue-white billiard ball of Earth (a ten-ball, he supposed), at pretty much the exact same speed as MFTP1 had done, and it was not accelerating. Unless you counted rotation! The thing was slowly swinging its face around and around, like a quarter spun on a tabletop, about one revolution per minute. And that didn't seem to be changing now, either.

"One of the pistons is stuck," Sandy diagnosed immediately.

"No," Pam said, glancing at the columns of glowing numbers marching across the windows. "Telemetry is normal on all twelve hundred of them, and we're not picking up any vibration anomalies. Anyway, the thing's not accelerating."

"It's not accelerating," Igbal repeated. "Talk to me, Sandra."

Sandy frowned, moved closer to one of the windows, peered out for a few minutes, and then shrugged.

"The Mach-Fearn effect is theoretical."

"Theoretical."

"Yeah."

"Then why did MFTP1 work?"

"It didn't work very well."

"I know that. That's why we built MFTP2, with fifty times as many pistons. Fifty times!"

"I don't know," Sandy said, a bit defensively. "Maybe the effect doesn't scale. Maybe there's a maximum impulse you can attain, and that's all you can get before the universe starts pulling it back. Remember, the equations say the *mass* of the pistons is irrelevant. That's why I was advocating for MEMS."

Igbal huffed and grumbled and ran his fingers through his beard. MEMS stood for microelectromechanical systems, and in practice it meant little gears and motors machined out of silicon, using semiconductor photo-lithography techniques that had barely changed since the turn of the millennium. It would have taken a lot longer—weeks longer!—to get something fabricated, and even then there would be a lot more variables to consider. The vapor expansion design was simple to build and easy to diagnose, which is why Pam—who wasn't even an engineer!—could tell from here that it was working flawlessly. It was the *universe* that was malfunctioning.

"Why is it spinning?" he asked, trying hard not to make it sound like an angry demand. "Why would the force on one side be different than the force on the other?"

"I dunno." Sandy now sounded interested. "Some kind

of asymmetry in the expansion of the universe? Hell, Ig, we might just have invented a new kind of telescope. Or discovered some new physics."

Igbal groaned. To a physicist, "new physics" was like getting the universe to suck your dick. It was the ultimate prize. To an engineer, it simply meant your machine didn't work, and nobody could tell you why. Maybe for years.

"Something's wrong," Pam said, looking up sharply from the tablet in her hands.

Igbal followed her gaze, and saw she was right; one of the astronauts had drifted too close to the spinning probe and intersected one of its edges. The probe, with considerable momentum behind its spin, had caught and *heaved* her toward the distant Earth. Now she was tumbling away—not fast, but at a decent walking speed.

"Ah, damn it," he said. "Is she hurt?"

"Heart rate is one-fifty," Pam reported. She did something on her tablet, and suddenly the room was full of the sound of screaming.

One of the astronauts was saying, "Hold on! Hold on! I'm going to come and get you! Yuehai, I'm coming to get you!"

The other astronaut was simply screaming, and even though the radio channel was full duplex entangled, her voice was stepping all over it, making it difficult for any questions or instructions to get through.

Igbal found a comm panel and pressed a button. "Shut up! Shut up! Shut up! Both of you shut the hell up! Yuehai, are you injured?"

"Aaaah! Aaaah! I'm loose! I'm falling!"

"You're not falling," Igbal said, as calmly as he could

manage. "You're drifting away from the station, which is good, because the nearest thing for you to collide with— will you shut up? The nearest thing for you to collide with—Yuehai, you've got to quiet down. The Earth is a *million miles away*. Almost two million kilometers, all right? Now I need to know if you're injured."

"My arm! My arm is . . . broken, I think!"

"I'm coming!" screamed the other astronaut, Sienna Delao. Sometimes, but not always, known as Dee.

"Will the two of you shut up?" Igbal said again. To Pam he said, "Is her suit breached?"

Pam studied the tablet in her hands and said, "Pressure normal. Tank flowrates normal. Strain gauges say her arm's not bent at the wrong angle, either. If there's a fracture, it's a hairline fracture."

"Jesus. Sienna, do your job, all right? Don't—will you be quiet, please? Don't hit the probe. Take a straight line out to the side of it, and then a straight line to where Yuehai is going to be. Not where she is, where she's *going* to be."

"Are you sending help?!" Sienna shouted into the channel.

"No, I'm—No—look, Jesus. Pam, can we send Derek or Hobie out there with an inspection pod or something?"

"Hobie's in stasis," she reminded him, "and Derek's in transit."

"Oh. Right." He leaned on the button again. "Sienna, do you need someone to suit up and come out there and rescue you? Do you expect *me* to do it? Those suit jets have about as much thrust as a can of hair spray, and unless you really fuck with the controls they're going to push you in a *straight line*."

"I'm not trained for this," Sienna complained.

"You *are*, Dee. As much as any of us. Just stay calm for me, all right? If I come out there with a relief team, it's going to take us ten minutes to suit up, and then another fifteen to decompress in the airlock. If we really push it, we could be out there in twenty minutes, maybe, but how far away do you think Yuehai is going to be by then? She's, like, half a football field away from you. Just go get her."

Sheee-it.

All of the station's second-wave inhabitants—the women housed in Beta Corridor—had been selected mainly for their brains, and it showed. Hopefully the new ones currently en route from Earth—the Gamma Girls, as he privately thought of them—would show these Betas a thing or two. If not, he was going to have to get *really serious* about recruitment. Assuming Earth would even let him get another batch of colonists up here, which was looking doubtful.

It took about half an hour for the whole spacesuit escapade to sort out, for Sienna to catch Yuehai and arrest their gentle rotation, and gently nudge the two of them back to the station and into an airlock, where it would take another fifteen minutes for them to recompress to full station atmosphere.

"Is there a medical team standing by?" Sienna demanded, as she struggled out of her suit.

Sighing, Igbal cut the voice channel, though he left a video feed up on one of the windows, so he could keep an eye on them.

"Ass clowns," he complained. "This is the best we can recruit? Really?"

"We've got some promising candidates in the next batch," Pam said.

"We'd better. Jesus Christ."

Meanwhile, outside, the probe continued its lazy retreat from ESL1 Shade Station—already a kilometer away, and shrinking. "Sandy, is it going to hit anything if we just let it go?"

"It might hit *us* in about ten months, if it doesn't start accelerating again."

He sighed. "Wonderful. Can we blow it up?"

"Then the fragments will hit us." For once quick on the uptake, Sandy said, "We're going to have to send a ship after it, yes. Unless . . . if I can figure out what went wrong, I might be able to upload a command sequence that will move it into a harmless orbit. We really should have put those ACS thrusters on it."

"And cost ourselves three weeks, yes."

The Mach-Fearn effect was admittedly a crazy idea: that dissimilar masses approaching and retreating from one another in a particular pattern could suck energy out of nowhere. But not *that* crazy, because the probe was clearly doing *something*. It had been worth trying, and it *would* be worth following up to see what was going on. But in terms of building a starship drive here and now, this year, it was a total bust.

"Damn it," he said. "I thought this one might just be the one."

Sandy put a hand on the small of his back. "Sorry. I'll try to piece together what's happening. No matter what, we should get some great journal publications out of it."

"Journal publications."

"Uh-huh."

"Jesus. Pam, what's next on the strike list? Is it the gamma ray mirror thing?"

"Yup."

"And remind me: how long do we need, to build a testable prototype?"

"We haven't even got the mesh simulations running yet."

"Best guess?"

"I'm an obstetrician," she reminded him.

"You're a goddamn space colonist. You're whatever needs doing, and you've been managing these projects, so what's your best guess?"

"Eight months. And that's if we can get the terahertz confinement pulsers shipped from Earth, which, I mean, your guess is as good as mine. They're made in Switzerland."

"Ah."

Switzerland wasn't a Coalition country, but they *were* an ITAR signatory, so even if the blockade and embargo were magically lifted, they might balk at shipping anything to Suriname that wasn't made of chocolate. Day by day, the bureaucratic noose was tightening, and it was honestly starting to freak him out. Why did the governments of Earth care so much what he was up to?

"How long if we make the pulsers ourselves?"

"Oh, crap, Ig. Can we even do that?"

"We might not need to," Sandy opined. "I've been

thinking about that fractal surface for the plasma injectors. If we can induce a controlled flutter at the ignition point, we could get the same kind of ripples running through the confinement vessel, without any kind of timing mechanism."

"The same?" Igbal asked skeptically. There was no solid material capable of reflecting gamma rays, but it appeared that relativistically moving plasma shock waves could do the trick. Which meant, in theory, that an ordinary proton fusion reactor could be turned into a rocket engine. Possibly even the best rocket engine the world had ever seen. It also provided a pathway to a working antimatter photon drive—one of the holy grails of interstellar propulsion research. That would still be a distant second to the reactionless, propellantless miracle of a working Mach-Fearn drive, but of course you had to go with what actually worked.

"I can get started on the simulations today," Sandy told him. "MechanoLab should do a lot better with that one."

He felt his face pulling down into a frown. "So which is it? Are you going to simulate fusion drives, or are you going to write papers about the Mach-Fearn effect?"

"Both."

"Both?"

"I don't sleep much, Ig, and these are exciting projects."

He thought about that. Local custom said he could only expect ten-hour workdays from his people here. Meals and cleaning and laundry services were all provided, so hopefully people didn't have much in the way of personal chores taking up their extreeeemely valuable time, but he also could not afford to burn anyone out. Not here, not now. Also, he was dubious about anyone's ability to focus on two such demanding and largely unrelated activities.

Truthfully, the work Sandy had gravitated to here on the station could technically be downsourced to any of ten RzVz facilities back on Earth. But the security risks were substantial, and he would have a much harder time directly supervising what was happening. As someone who'd enjoyed phenomenal success with personally supervised projects, he was not real interested in doing it any other way.

Sighing, he said, "Mach effect on your own time, and I'll need you to check in with me every few days to follow your progress. I'll have Lurch set up the calendar invitations. I also want you to meet with Pam every week to make sure you're taking proper care of yourself. We spent a lot of money bringing you up here."

Sandy shrugged. "Okay, that's fine."

Lurch was the station's administrative assistant program—one of those autonomous agents that was always listening and learning. Igbal didn't need to "have it do" anything (this conversation alone was enough to get it going), but old habits died hard. Employees were prohibited from having their own *personal* digital assistants on RzVz off-world properties, and although Lurch was technically Igbal's assistant, it was more than capable of doing the job for all twenty-three of the people currently on ESL1 Shade Station.

He still found it creepy that Lurch rarely spoke, but okay, that was how people liked it these days, and it did keep down the chatter.

Sandy put her hand on the small of Igbal's back again

and said, "Don't worry. The gamma mirror is a good idea, and even if it doesn't work as a fusion drive, there's always the antimatter. If that works even a little bit, it could be enough to get us to Centauri."

"Yeah. The antimatter." He clicked his cheek a few times. "Okay, well, Pam, will you please meet Tweedledee and Tweedledipshit at the airlock, so we don't get some sort of remote workplace safety lawsuit?"

Pam scowled at that—not at what Igbal was saying, but at the way Sandy was touching him—and Igbal knew he was in trouble there, too. Pam wasn't officially a jealous or possessive person, but unofficially he was seeing more and more of that from her, now that her time among the living was growing short.

"I'll see if Yuehai's arm is broken," Pam said, "or just her dignity. You two have fun while I'm gone."

"Thank you," Igbal said, and watched her leave.

Jesus. It seemed stupid now, but in all honesty, during all the planning it had never actually crossed his mind that a space station full of women was going to be this much trouble.

5.1
23 March

✧

H.S.F. *Concordia*
Moored to Transit Point Station
Low Earth Orbit

"Well, that sucks," said Dan Beseman. "Did you try begging?"

"I actually tried prostitution," said his assistant, Miyuki Ishibashi. It was a joke, of course, but it hinted at her frustration. She was a problem solver by nature, but some problems were harder than others, and she'd tried her best at this one before bringing it to Beseman's attention. "No takers. Orlov had them over a barrel, and forced them to sign a four-year contract for their entire output. We won't get *one atom* of tralphium from Harvest Moon until after this beast"—she pounded the bulkhead with her fist—"is on its merry way."

"Well, shit."

Beseman was a fit, handsome man—the youngest of the Horsemen, and arguably the most charismatic. But he was her boss, and like a lot of powerful people he sometimes lost his temper in the face of bad news. Which meant, as often as not, that Miyuki was the one who bore the brunt of it. Such was the life of a personal assistant! A thick skin was the first and most important qualification for the job. So far, Beseman seemed to be taking this news pretty well, but she had her guard up just the same.

The two of them were on the bridge of the H.S.F. *Concordia*—or rather its "operations coordination center" as the engineers insisted on calling it. (Why did engineers always insist on creating their own dense jargon to identify things that already had perfectly good names? Beseman had sent out companywide memos on the subject, even threatened to fire people over it, but the problem stubbornly persisted.) They were looking out and downward through the windshield (or "forward transparent hull panel") at the spindly mass of Transit Point Station, reaching down and away toward the rolling landscape of Australia, far below. The view was nothing short of breathtaking, and the first few times Miyuki had seen it, it had made her feet and stomach tingle with vertigo, but after seeing it every day for months, she was adapting. Breathtaking was now the norm, which was probably good, because the endless unspoiled wilderness of Mars seemed capable of breaking her brain. Even glimpsing it through the eyes of a robot—one that wasn't under her command, and was in fact separated by a speed-of-light round trip lag of fifteen minutes— sometimes brought tears to her eyes. *That* was the prize. Everything she did, everything she sacrificed, was in pursuit of that one simple goal. If she had to put her life on hold—for *years*—in loyal service to someone else (some trillionaire, specifically), she counted herself

fortunate to be handcuffed to the one—the *only* one—
who could take her to Mars. Or rather, who could greatly
improve her chances of winning the competition for a
berth on his ship.

The bridge was basically Beseman's office right now;
he came here for hours every day to work or to think.
From here he could monitor all of the ship's systems as
they slowly came together. He could call or email or vmail
anyone in the world, and he could watch the fuel tanks
slowly filling up with hydrogen and oxygen, shipped
monthly from Clementine Cislunar Fuel Depot. Being
here seemed to comfort him, by providing a direct
connection to that future on Mars, which he wanted every
bit as much as she did. It was the biggest common
denominator between them; they might come from
different strata of different worlds, but they shared that
goal. Of course, so did hundreds of other men and women
who'd applied for the job of Beseman's assistant. She'd
gotten appallingly lucky, and she tried hard to never lose
sight of that fact, when he was texting her at 3:00 A.M. or
venting his frustrations, or whatever.

Ready for the cameras at all times, she wore the beige,
close-fitting, two-piece uniform of Antilympus colony
hopefuls, with her hair pulled back in a plastic claw. This
was necessary, because of course she *wasn't* guaranteed a
berth. She was in the lead right now; of the thousands of
semifinalists, she was currently ranked fifty-ninth. Since
there were one hundred berths on the ship, that nominally
implied she was making the cut, and would be making the
trip, but the rankings were *volatile*, and her public image
was critical to her success. Since cameras were literally

everywhere, and since *Concordia* was the subject of great public interest and the particular, constant scrutiny of its sponsors, she left nothing to chance. But this also highlighted the status gap between her and Dan Beseman, because right now he was wearing a green velvet track suit, a pair of running sandals, a four-day growth of beard, and a look that said he did not give one shit what anyone thought about his appearance. Why should he?

"What are we supposed to do for power?" he asked her, mostly rhetorically.

"Solar?" she tried. It was a running joke between them, and not a very funny one. Mars got less than half the sunlight the Earth enjoyed, and it would take eight thousand square meters of high-end photovoltaics, coupled to high-end batteries and ultracapacitors, to supply even the initial power requirements of Antilympus Township. Right now what the empty, robot-haunted Mars colony had in place, at great cost, was about a tenth that much. Which was a problem, because if they stuck to plan, they were going to be *smelting iron* out of the Martian soil (or "regolith") within three months of landing, and that kind of thing did not come energy-cheap. Of course, a Compact Rare Earth Fusion Tokamak, inefficient as it was, only needed a few grams of ^{3}He and a few of deuterium to see them through that first Martian winter, so for years it had been Plan A for the colony. Basically, from the moment Beseman was sure that Lawrence Killian and Harvest Moon really were going to be selling ^{3}He (or "tralphium") on the open market. But apparently that wasn't going to happen, because apparently Grigory Orlov had somehow bought all of it. *All* of it.

That didn't leave a lot of options. *Concordia* presently had about half a gram in stock, which wasn't enough to help. It wasn't enough to justify dragging the mass of a tokamak reactor all the way to Mars.

"I'm serious, Miyuki. Did you ask NASA about a fission reactor permit?"

"I did, and they just laughed. They said even *they* can't get a license to launch more than an RTG. These days, U.N. safety guidelines rule the roost."

"Ugh."

RTG stood for radioisotope thermoelectric generator—basically a five-kilogram block of plutonium generating heat, that could be turned into electricity by thermoelectric panels. The plutonium core was encased in heavy, catastrophe-proof ceramic, and could not only survive the explosion of a launch vehicle, but could be recovered intact from the ocean floor and re-flown on another mission. RTGs were great for powering spy satellites and space probes to the outer planets, but they were useless if you needed more than a few hundred watts of electricity. *Real* nuclear reactors were a lot bigger; even a little two-hundred-kilowatt sealed fission reactor was the mass of a shipping container full of cinder blocks, and at least twenty kilograms of that was tightly controlled fissile material. To launch something like that into space involved a lot of risk, because if a rocket blew up or crashed, it could scatter those fissiles across a wide swath of land and sea or, even worse, land the reactor intact but supercritical, and melt a radioactive hole straight down to

Hell. And two hundred kilowatts was barely enough to run the lights and toilets at Antilympus.

Despite appearances, Miyuki was no secretary; she had a physics degree and had worked in energy startups for twelve years before coming here. Her work with Beseman—now six years and counting—had forced her to learn five college degrees' worth of engineering, finance, logistics, government regulation, and conflict management. At this point, if she wanted to, she could step into a CEO job almost anywhere. But instead she kept Beseman's schedule, and sent out email and made phone calls for him, basically letting him be in two places at once. Which meant she needed to be his equal, or nearly so, and *also* be a good secretary. She sometimes wondered if he knew what a demanding role it was, and how much it took out of her, but she wasn't about to utter anything that smacked of complaint. No sir!

All things considered, Miyuki would rather be working for somebody like NASA or ESA or the short-lived U.N. Space Agency. She'd've had to eat shit there, too, but in a more egalitarian way. But alas, with the exception of the Chinese and, to a much lesser extent, the Russians, there were no public space programs anymore. Through some combination of deficit spending, warped priorities, and desperately short-term thinking, the governments of the world had starved themselves right out of the civilian space business. The last gasp of American adventurism— NASA's Mars program—had just been handed over to Beseman's control, because yes, the Horsemen had expanded into that power vacuum very nicely. And then they kept right on expanding, because people needed things the Earth could no longer provide—not just frontiers like Mars, but simple things like rare earth metals and tralphium.

She supposed she might also have preferred to work for a Horse*woman*, if such a thing existed, but there were no female trillionaires and, quite frankly, not even really any female billionaires who'd made their fortunes from scratch. Why? Miyuki didn't know. But she didn't suppose it would change the dynamic very much if there were; if you wanted to gather resources on that kind of scale, you couldn't also be a kindly and generous person. Even Sir Lawrence (or "Saint Lawrence," as Beseman sometimes mockingly called him) had built Harvest Moon Industries on the backs of eighty thousand underpaid, overworked creatives. And with his blimps and parachute jumps and motorcycle races (right into his eightieth birthday and beyond!), he wasn't exactly the most grounded business leader. Other nicknames Beseman had for him included "dare geezer" and "floaty the butterfly."

Miyuki could do a lot worse, and she knew it. Beseman was the second-kindest Horseman, who'd made his money selling appliances and consumer electronics that were designed and built by other companies. It was the oldest business model in the world, but to do it—to crush all competitors at it—he'd developed quantum-AI logistical systems unlike anything the world had ever seen before. At the age of twenty-three he was running warehouses full of entangled data servers, and the small army of people required to maintain them, and the gambit was so successful he'd pretty much single-handedly revived the bricks-and-mortar retail sector by the time he was thirty. By forty, he'd already purchased three of the multinationals whose wares he peddled. Enterprise City was *where you went to buy stuff*. Period. And thanks to "creepy" predictive traffic analysis they nearly always had what you were looking for, and ten other things you didn't know you needed. Who didn't spend money at Enterprise City?

So yeah, Beseman wasn't a bad guy by any means. But he was very focused, and tended to divide the world into (a) what helped him, (b) what thwarted him and needed to be battled or smothered, and (c) what didn't matter and deserved no attention. Most things, on or off the Earth, were "c," but now Miyuki could see that both Harvest Moon and Orlov Petrochemical had moved themselves to column "b," and were going to be high on her radar for the foreseeable future. Well, fine.

"Shit," Beseman said to her now. "They can't get a license for their own use? Is that literally what they said to you?"

"It's literally what they said," she confirmed. "Do you know Ewin Stoycos? The nuclear guy from Johnson Space Center? I talked to him for about half an hour, and that's literally what he told me."

"Did you . . . did he, you know, have any suggestions for what we *can* do?"

She nodded. "Actually, yes. He did."

"And?"

"He's really into thorium these days. He said we should look at something called a LIFTR, which stands for liquid fluoride thorium reactor. He says we can get a megawatt of throttleable power for about two hundred million dollars. It burns unrefined thorium metal, straight out of the ground, which isn't even radioactive until you hit it with neutrons. But that's also the bad news, because we'd still need an RTG as a neutron source, which invokes ITAR *and* the nonproliferation treaty."

"So we'd have to launch out of the United States?"

She shrugged. "Unless we want them to throw us in jail, yes. But it's worse than that. Even though thorium's not radioactive, it's still categorized for some reason as a fissile material. We need three hundred kilograms of it, and we might need to spread that over as many as twenty launches."

"Seriously? From the United States? That would take years. Oh, my God. That would take *years*. We can't get an exemption?"

This wasn't good. He was getting really angry now, and that could go badly for her if she didn't tread carefully. In measured tones she said, "Stoycos asserts that it's possible to get one. There's a mechanism for requesting it, but we'd have to go through Congress *and* the United Nations Security Council. Given the high profile and popularity of our project, he says we'd probably prevail, but . . ."

"But that would also take years."

"Exactly."

He sighed. "Damn it. Damn it. If we miss this launch window, Miyuki, it'll be two years before the next one. Given our burn rate, we'd need a hundred billion dollars to bridge the gap."

Miyuki had already done the math on this, and he was right, so all she could say was, "Yup."

"Do we even have that much cash?"

"Cash? No. You'd have to liquidate some substantial holdings. So, I mean, yes, in principle we can afford it, but it would be painful."

"Jesus. This *can't* be the reason we miss our launch window. That's just too stupid. Orlov seriously won't sell us *five grams* of tralphium? At name-your-fucking-price?"

"Nope. I asked every possible way. I offered every possible thing including, seriously, going on a date with him. His people just laughed."

"Wow," he said. "Huh."

She really had done that. It was *way* above and beyond the call of any reasonable duty, but Beseman's lack of praise or even acknowledgment of it didn't surprise her. She knew better than to expect that from him, and if Beseman knew her at all, he'd know she'd done it as much for herself as for him or anyone else. She wanted her shot at Mars that badly, yes!

"Wow," Beseman said again. "Is Orlov *trying* to make us fail? Is that why he bought up every single atom?"

She shrugged. "Maybe? If you see life as a zero-sum game, it means somebody's got to lose. Somebody *else*, specifically. Dan, I don't honestly know why a pig like Orlov is in space at all. What's his vision? Colonizing the bank? Exploring the balance sheet? It's just numbers to him. I think, honestly, *we're* all just numbers to him."

She shuddered to think what would have happened if she had actually gone on a date with Orlov. Even being in the same room with him sounded nauseating; the thought of actually making dinner conversation, while he pretended not to leer at her body, was almost more than she could bear. Almost.

"Oh, he's not that stupid," Beseman snarled, making a tight, angry gesture in the air. "It's not zero sum. Any idiot can see the growth up here. It's highly, *highly* positive. It's an exponential sum! Even if he slows everything down, even if he stands between us and Mars, how is that a win for him? It's not a race; he's not competing with us. I think that bastard just likes watching people lose. We're not numbers, we're *enemies*. You want an explanation that fits the data? It's malice, pure and simple."

But as satisfying as it was to hear Beseman say that, Miyuki knew it was wrong. It was like that old *New Yorker* cartoon, where Olrov was saying "PAY ME TO EXIST." Yes, there was enough truth there to make it funny, but people weren't caricatures, and their hopes and dreams weren't cardboard signs. Even very stupid people were complex creatures, and lord knew Grigory Orlov was not stupid. Not even a little tiny bit. It had been foolish to think, even for a moment, that he'd be influenced by anything as ordinary and commodified as a female body. But okay, if pure greed and pure malice were insufficient explanations for what made Orlov tick, they were still definitely useful models. Any physicist could tell you that a simple model, even if technically incorrect, often got you close enough to the right answer that the wrongness didn't matter. So if it worked— modeling Orlov as an engine of pure greed or pure malice—then did the deeper truth really matter?

Miyuki just shrugged. "Okay, yes. He's a bastard. That's not exactly new information. What do you want me to do about it?"

"I don't know. I don't know." Dan ran his fingers

through his weightless, not-washed-in-a-few-days hair, and sighed. "What happens if we cut Earth out of the picture? Can we find a derelict Cold War satellite with a working RTG? Maybe Harvest Moon can dig up some thorium for us. Are there supplies of it anywhere on the Moon? Find out for me, please. Meanwhile, what's the status on the fusion tokamak? We launched that one already, right?"

She nodded, and pointed a finger toward the ship's aft. "It's in the lander's cargo hold right now. The hold was specifically designed to accommodate it, Dan. If we put something else in, we might need to rip out bulkheads or pound a big dent in the wall. Something. It's late in the day for this kind of disruption."

"And yet, here we are," he said. "Great. That's just lovely. Still, there's no point crying about it. Let's figure out a replacement power supply, and get it the hell in here."

Miyuki, who needed Mars more than she'd ever needed anything else, looked him in the eye and said, "Will do, boss."

4.2
23 March

✧

Clementine Cislunar Fuel Depot
Earth-Moon Lagrange Point 1
Cislunar Space

"Why didn't you wake me?" Grigory demanded.

Nervously, Andrei Morozov answered, "You said the asset at TPS had its instructions already. The same woman, on the same channel, contacted me a few hours later, saying she was in control of a shuttle departing Transit Point Station. She demanded I upload rendezvous instructions to get her to Clementine, and I did so. I assumed she was working for us."

"She was," Grigory said, "but not *here*. She's not supposed to be *here*, Morozov."

The two of them were in the pressurized hangar, holding onto grab rails with their feet. They were contemplating an entire space shuttle that didn't belong in here. Parked in the arms of an insectile handlerbot, beside a similar structure holding Grigory's own shuttle, the new arrival seemed to glare accusingly. It might as well have STOLEN PROPERTY spray-painted on it in big Cyrillic letters.

155

"This is a major fuckup," Grigory said heavily, though Morozov's explanation did make sense. "You have fucked us all right in the ass."

"I take it that's not our shuttle," Morozov said. Quite unnecessarily, because although the two side-by-side spacecraft were identical Lockheed Martin LMS-50s, the new one had the RzVz logo painted prominently on the tail.

"Funny," Grigory said, then sighed. "How many people know she's here?"

Morozov rubbed his hands together uneasily. "You mean, besides the radar satellites of every space-faring government? Six. At least six. Maybe more; she's sitting in the mess hall right now."

"Wonderful. Really exceptional work."

This was exactly the sort of problem best handled with a quiet disappearance of the person involved. Poof, gone. Unfortunately, six people were too many to trust with a secret like that, even here. So, since true quiet didn't appear to be an option, Grigory must roll hard to the opposite rail.

"What else did she tell you?"

Morozov shrugged. "Nothing, until a few minutes ago, and even then she didn't say much. She said she was 'burnt,' and they put her on a shuttle home."

"This is not her home."

Morozov paused a moment and then said, "Understood. She did at least hack the running lights on that shuttle. And the location transponders. She came in dark, so it's *only* the superpowers who could've tracked her course changes."

"Only our greatest adversaries, you mean. Only the people capable of doing us real harm."

That didn't please Grigory, but it did give him an idea.

"If the crew of Transit Point put her in there alone, that technically makes her the captain of the ship, as well as an obviously persecuted individual. If she was seeking asylum here on Clementine, *of course* she commandeered the ship. How else could she get herself to safety?"

"So we return it, then? The shuttle?"

"No," Grigory answered. "Not unless they sue for it, in which case we'll demand proof they know it's here. But for now we keep the whole matter as quiet as possible. Make sure everyone who has seen her knows this. Quiet."

It wasn't easy to keep things quiet in this chattering age, but Orlov Petrochemical and its associates did have a better field record than most, and Clementine was a small and frankly elite community within it. His people knew what was good for them and, more importantly, what wasn't. And when they failed and word got out, which it certainly must at some point, then it would be Grigory's own version of the story that circulated. It was hardly the best solution, but it was all he could come up with on short notice, and so it would have to do.

"And what do we do with her?" Morozov wanted to know.

"An excellent question. I'll go and speak with her, but unless she steps outside for a breath of fresh air, she's going to have to stay here for the foreseeable future. And it occurs to me, I'll need you to strip all the identifying information off that shuttle. Not enough to fool a crime lab, you understand, but enough to thwart a casual inspection. You, personally, must do this, and keep everyone out of here until it's done. The transponders were deactivated? Yes? Replace them with our own— something from the gatherbots; I don't really care. Suspicion is fine; people are suspicious of us all the time. But let's have no smoking guns in plain view, ah?"

Morozov, who'd worked for Grigory a long time now, simply nodded.

"Understood, sir. I'll order some clothing for the woman; right now she's dressed in RizzVizz blue. Not exactly blending in."

"Mmm. Damn. All right, I'll go talk to her."

Morozov nodded, happy to have the problem out of his problem basket. "Right. Do we know her name?"

"Not officially," Grigory said, and kicked off toward the hatchway to the station proper.

"Ms. Donna," he said to her.

She was a slight woman, but wiry with muscle. Her skin was very black against the blue of a Renz Ventures space coverall, and she smelled of sweat and perfume. A forlorn little flight bag hovered beside her on a strap.

"Ms. Obata," she corrected. "Dona Obata."

Indeed, it said so on her name tag.

"You're African," he said, surprised by her accent. "They told me you were French."

"I can not both?"

Ugh, her Russian was atrocious, and Grigory had no French at all. Annoyed now, he asked her in English, "Why did you come here?"

Grigory rarely spoke English, but only a fool didn't

know it well, and he was no fool. He'd been told, in fact, that his English was quite good. When foreigners made the mistake of speaking "privately" in English within his earshot, they usually found cause to regret it later.

She replied in the same language, "It was that or go back to Earth, where I'd be no use to anyone."

"Mmm. And what makes you think you are of use to anyone here?"

She had no reply to that, but neither did she look embarrassed or nervous, or anything really.

He told her, "Your persecution was political and perhaps racial in nature. From the way you'd been treated, you feared for your safety should you return to Paramaribo. You were sent off alone in that shuttle, and by your understanding of maritime law, this entitled you to commandeer the controls and set a destination of your own choosing. You are thus a refugee, and you saw Clementine as a possible refuge. You have asked me for political asylum. You are to volunteer no information, about this or anything else, to anyone save myself, and if anyone questions you, you are to answer in small words. But this is the story people will glean from what little you tell them."

Again, she said nothing. Her face impassive, unafraid, simply waiting.

"You will, furthermore, renounce whatever Earth citizenships you hold, and be issued a Clementine passport."

That she *did* reply to, saying, "That sounds difficult to undo."

"Is it? Hmm. Not my problem. You have created a

number of issues by coming here, where you are neither trusted nor known. These are issues that I and my people must now deal with, while you stay hidden from public sight."

Carefully, she asked, "What if I don't want to renounce citizenship?"

He snorted. "Are you really asking? I could, for example, put you right back on that shuttle. Or out an airlock."

"You could try," she said, an edge of warning now in her voice. He reminded himself that this was a dangerous person, trained by the French and U.S. militaries to kill with her bare hands, in zero gravity. And she'd had no compunctions about betraying France and the U.S. on Grigory's behalf, for the promise of money. That made her even more dangerous. But Grigory was dangerous, too, and laughed.

"You have what the Americans call a 'bias toward action.' I approve of that. Truly. But you are being more rude than smart, and I haven't got time to explain to you just how fucked you are. This is no soft target, Ms. Obata. My people are not soft people. Nothing is owed to you, and the thing *you* owe *me* is nowhere in evidence. You've failed in your mission, and you've come straight to me with your failure, which is in itself another failure, because now you and I are linked. For nothing. For no reason and no gain. Do you see?"

After an uncomfortable pause, she nodded. "Yes. Sir."

"Good. Then we understand each other. We will create some paperwork for you to sign, as a refugee seeking political asylum. It has never happened in space before, so the precedents are ours to set. Look on the bright side: you will owe no taxes to any nation."

Carefully, she asked, "What else?"

He laughed sourly. "Ms. Obata, what I wanted from you, what I wanted you to secure for me, is now beyond your grasp. For the moment, you are pure liability. Every time you open your mouth to speak, I would like you to consider this. We also have no empty quarters in which to stash you. The station is quite full, and in need of expansion. But this gives me another idea: you will sleep in my own quarters."

She raised an eyebrow, and the corners of her mouth turned down a bit.

"Relax," he told her. "This isn't Renz Ventures. We will sleep separately, in shifts, and you will not be touched. You think I have nowhere better to ink my quill? But placing you thusly will further tangle any rumors that might attach to you. People will see you coming and going from there, and it will make them think still another thing about why you are here with us. And they will *not* ask questions about *that*. Do you see? The more different stories there are about you, the less anyone really knows. And you want them to know nothing, because if the real truth came out about what you were *supposed* to be up to, you would be *real* liability. No, if we play this right, your stupidity can still be useful, in confusing and wrong-footing our opponents."

The woman thought about that, and said, "I'll take it as a positive omen, that you said 'our.'"

"Inefficiency of the language," he said dismissively. "The Russian word, *nash*, is more precise. I did not mean to include you, verbally, as part of the team here. But your words are also interesting, as the interpretation of omens says more about the . . . interpreter than it does about the ominous facts themselves. Your point is visible: having accepted an offer to corrupt yourself and betray your government and your strike team for me, even having *failed* at it, you imagine yourself now in my employ."

She shrugged. "That's accurate, although it sounded a lot less stupid in my head. I will tell you, it wasn't the money you were offering that attracted me. It was the offer itself—the fact of what you intended. ESL1 *is* a soft target, and the future belongs to the bold."

"And the competent," he said, snorting. "There are two other operatives on their way there, yes? The American and the Kiwi, who will seize Esley Shade Station without your help. Benefiting no one—not even the governments ordering the seizure. It is shortsighted foolishness, and an excellent example of why I have cut ties with the governments of Earth."

A middle-aged workman in the stretchy gray uniform of Clementine stuck his head through the doorway.

"Good morning, sir," he said in thickly accented Russian. Bulgarian? Polish? His name tag said SZCZEPANSKI. A Polish mechanic or tank handler? Something like that. "Is breakfast still serving?"

It was a foolish question; the serving windows were closed, and the drink dispensers and food printers covered. Grigory didn't know this man; Clementine had staffed up quickly to get ahead of the growing need, and Grigory hadn't spent enough time here in the past several months to know even half of the senior staff. The junior staff he wouldn't normally bother with, except to tweak the noses of the people above them, and Grigory frankly didn't know which category this man belonged in.

"No breakfast," Grigory told him, regretting not having closed the hatch on his way in. "And we're having a meeting here."

"Ah," said the man. "Who's the new meat?"

"Her name is get the fuck out of here and close the hatch behind you."

"What? Oh. Sorry."

"Indeed."

The man retreated into the connecting module, closing and latching the bright yellow hatch behind him.

"The famous Orlov charm," said Dona Obata, with something like approval in her voice. Clearly, she'd understood at least something of that exchange. He couldn't tell to what extent she was joking or serious, and he didn't really care. But all right, part of him was beginning to warm to this strange woman.

Sighing, he asked, "You wish to remain here as part of the staff? Is that your goal?"

"Basically, yes," she agreed.

"Hmm. Hmm."

Under the circumstances, it was a bold request indeed. He tried to imagine what sort of job she'd even be qualified for. Throwing people out of airlocks? He already had people for that, or people who he believed were at least capable of it. Clementine was fully staffed with, despite his grousing, mostly quite competent, no-nonsense-type people. But he considered personal initiative one of the greatest qualities an employee could possess, and he had to admit, stealing a spaceship and coming here uninvited—to demand a job!—showed rather a lot of balls.

"My better judgment bends two directions on this," he admitted, "but you have . . ." he struggled for the right English words ". . . roused my curiosity. So very well, I will set you a task, to spend a quiet week figuring out what you can do for me. Without drawing attention to yourself or causing any additional problems. Impress me, Ms. Obata, and you may find . . ." he paused a moment for dramatic effect ". . . that the future still has you in it."

3.2
23 March

St. Joseph of Cupertino Monastery
Shoemaker-Faustini Plateau
Lunar South Polar Mineral Territories

My Dearest Father Bertram,

This letter hopefully answers your queries about a day in the life of a Lunar monk, of which there may be only three at this moment, but still. As we prepare our souls and ourselves for the imminent touchdown of Brers Fox, Bear, Huey, Dewey, Dopey, Grumpy, Ham, and Eggs, we are indeed well advised to advise them well. And you, their sternest taskmaster!

Each day is different, and being that they are 709 hours long and varied, I shall presume you mean an Earth Day, which we Lunatic Monastic refer to as a Vatican Day, relic as it be of a past we've shed like skin cells.

The valley in which St. Joseph sits is a kilometer off the Harvest Moon mining road, and bears some description since I get the impression you don't quite understand how it's situated. Craters Shoemaker and Faustini sit within a few latitudinal degrees of Luna's southern rotational pole, which puts the noonday sun here just a few degrees above the horizon, and the midnight one just a few degrees below. This casts the broad, flat floors of both craters in full shadow all the time, which over geologic ages has permitted water ice to accumulate there, though it elsewhere sublimates and escapes as cosmic vapour upon the solar wind. This much I think you understand.

What may be less clear is that the taint of land betwixt these holes is in permanent sunlight, albeit slanty and long-shadowed. For this reason also, the Earth we send you in pictures always appears to be newly risen or else about to set, when in fact neither thing has occurred or is about to, or ever shall. This is also the reason our solar panels sit upright, like the playing-card soldiers of Wonderland's Red Queen, guarding the rim of Saint Joe's little valley and turning slowly about on their heels, completing a revolution once per month.

I mention this because said valley splits the difference, with low hills and dips that first block and then admit and then block again the nourishing rays of Ra, so that rather than enduring a fortnight of harsh day followed by a fortnight of harsher night, we get four "nights" per month of durations 26, 22, 49, and 17 hours respectively, where the sunlight doesn't reach us direct, but only reflected from the crests of the opposite hills. Call it twilight if you must, although black sky and bright gray hills are not particularly "twi" in the sense you might mean it.

At "night" we can see the brighter stars, and in the intervening "days" we cannot, although the planets Venus, Mars, and Jupiter remain visible as the zodiac permits. The Milky Way, alas, eludes us always, which is a fine strange loss for those who've relocated permanent to spaces outer. We can, however, see it beautifully from the ice mines themselves.

So understand, Bertie my love, that "morning" comes when it pleases, and any circadian rhythm that attempts to track it is doomed to disappointment. Melatonin is the main product of our drug synthesizer, and also guaifenesin booger liquefaction syrup, about which more anon.

One awakens with the shift clock, which is set to Vatican time, in case His Holy deems it prudent to raise us on the horn and shoot breezes. This hasn't yet transpired, but you never can be too careful with God's own right-hand fellow, I'm thinking.

One sits upright, and like as not bangs one's head on the ceiling, for the bunks (with their desks and storage spaces beneath) are too high, and the gravity too light, and the muscle of a human buttocks too strong, for this event to be in the slightest unlikely. This is why the new modules are a full meter taller than the old, and it's better the skull of a monk get bashed than that Sir Lawrence Edgar Killian's actual customers find the flaw in his first design, for we are beta testers to what he dreams will soon be great Lunar cities of loyal subscribers.

One grabs a roller of tacky rubber, and patiently rolls the dust off one's bedding and bedclothes, for it gathers there all day shift and all night shift. You asked why the modules are so much bare metal inside, and the reason is static electricity, of which conducting surfaces carry none. Even the painted parts are high-metal-content powder coat, baked into place in Sir Larry's robotic manufactories. And each module has at its floor an electrostatic precipitator, to pull dust from the air, and a humidifier, so that a monolayer of water molecules adsorbs to the surface of every mote and speck, rendering them more prone and liable to precipitate out and stick to surfaces. And yet, there's always more dust—a whole planet's worth— waiting to be a problem for God's servants.

The bane of us is cloth, which, no matter how treated, catches moondust as a six-pack holder catches wildlife, which is to say, decisively. And so we tacky-roll the dust away, and rinse it into the sink, of which each module has at least one, and we spray all the bedding down with antistatic fabric softener, which is a conductive diester of phosphoric acid and stearyl alcohol, solvated in ninety percent water and ten percent ethanol. Drinkable, you ask? Well, what doesn't kill you tastes like it ought to.

A word about this, for the chemical synthesizer that produces our soap and softeners and whatlike is not the same machine as the atom-precise drug printer. It tolerates parts per thousand of impurity, and so the antistatic, which we spray liberally on everything but foodstuffs, whiffs faintly of formaldehyde. Should this be corrected it would invert some frowns round here, though it cost His Holy a dainty dollar.

(Also not the same machine is the CHON chow printer, which consumes only water and nitrogen and methane, and is capable of manufacturing the very basics of sustenance: starch, glucose, oil, and a protein with the broke-tongue moniker HILLPTTAGGPT, which incorporates eight of nine essential and five of six conditionally essential amino acids. The contraption's patties and noodles and pastes are edible in the strictest sense, but diresome bland without copious amounts of salt and pepper— two exceedingly costly commodities, as well you know. Too, anyone subsisting entirely on CHON chow will die a slow, fat, degenerative death of sulfur deficiency, so we treat it as a backup to a backup and try to limit reliance thereupon to half our total caloric intake. And yet, it has crossed my mind more than once that if a CHON printer didn't cost as much as a house, these machines could eradicate poverty worldwide, or at least change the face of it extremely. In this way, as in others, life in space points the way toward better lives on Earth. But I digress.)

One then brushes teeth and hair, and bathes with a washcloth that is then immediately placed in the laundry. We do a lot of laundry, Bert! One drinks one's snot loosener with a big glass of water, for we've all got the dust sneezes something awful, and it turns quickly to a cough if not attended.

(This, I'm assured, will be the death of us in the long run, as chronic lung inflammation tick-tocks away the moments of our lives, but if not that then something else to bring us whole with our maker, so it's quite literally all the same in the end, except whether a new world has been won.)

One dresses in the traditional habit if attending indoors, and in space underwear if venturing EVA, which is astronaut for "extravehicular activity" or simply "going outside." The abbreviation applies even if the portal of egress is from a fixed location, nonvehicular, which goes to show the power of acronym to shape our thoughts. Imagine, were they all spelled out for one whole day, how wide the mark we'd find 'em!

Now together with one's brothers, we break our night's fast, perhaps with CHON egg-white-and-toast recipe and some hydroponic carrots, or instead perhaps starch puffs and printmeat patties fried in oil, on a tall bed of cabbage or spinach leaves. And in either case, yes, a mug of glucose-sweetened, caffeine-doped chicory brew, which, though irresemblant of coffee or tea, is at least a renewable resource.

From there the days are marvelously different, for there is much to do in preparing a world for peopling, and unlike Our Father Who Art, we've thankfully more than six days to accomplish it.

(And doesn't that, if you think about it, make Pope Dave a kind of Fifth Horseman? Danny

Beseman the game show host, Iggy the Rake, Sir Lawrence the Adventurer, and Baron Grigory the Black . . . Do we add to the list Davey the Piocrat? No capitalist ambitions there, but he is the most absolute monarch the Old World has left, and he does hope to bring all the New Worlds under his sway. These are the humans who, at present, steer humanity, and a strange and potbellied assortment it be. Mayhap we'd do well to have more *women* in that mix, but since Sir Larry be a widower, that leaveth Carol Beseman as the only Horsewoman, although one could sadly argue she is more of a Horsewife than an entity unto herself. There are, too, some horse girlfriends kicking around, but how much power is that really, to shape the future of the future? God cannot want so narrow a sample determining so wide an outcome, but He seems also not inclined to intervene, so I shall just live out my own little role and shape what I can, and let the angels weep.)

Anyhoo, to pick an example day at random, yesterday after breakfast this guy spent an hour in the greenhouse tending to his own little corner of the future of worlds, and then joined Brers Geo and Puke in the gowning area, for today was a day for EVA, and we were all in finest Underoo.

Donning a spacesuit resembles in some wise making love to a bin full of rubber bands and plumbing conduits, and easier done with help than without, for Lunar gravity is enough to thwart weightless grace and weighted certainty both. The suits themselves I think you've seen; there's nothing monastic about them, aside from the necessary ascetic virtue of carrying one's own atmosphere on one's back.

Once fully clad for vacuum, we passed through the shower, which gave a momentary spritz of fabric softener, which subdues static electricity a bit even in the absence of air.

Thence to the airlock, which provided as always a righteous fifteen minutes for meditation and prayer, and thence to the front yard.

Making fresh footfall in Lunar powder is an awe-dropping experience the first few times you do it, for it has lain there unmolested for half the age of the universe and more. But the thrill wears off, and there's something to be said for stepping again and again in the same spots, for this does bit by bit grind the sharp edges off the dust. I wonder, Bertie, whether Harvest Moon will lend us a steamroller for a Lunar day, that we might grind down the grit of this entire valley, and save ourselves a bit of sneezery. About which, by the way, stands the least glamorous aspect of astronautics, for one cannot blow in a hankie whilst space-suited up, and we sniffled and snuffled our way down the wheel ruts left by Larry's delivery van, passing my forlorn heap of silicon bricks on the way.

These turn out to be harder to use than I'd daydreamed, as the vacuum welding of silly to silly is a chancy business. One atom seated next to another of its kind has no way of knowing they're in

two separate objects, and so they join hands easily
enough. Aye, but one fleck of dust will keep them
acres apart, and the static-electric fountains kicked
up by the Sun from Luna's dusty surface (and all the
more insidious for being invisible!) come and go like
will-o'-the-wisps prowling for an unwary traveler,
spraying at least a few such motes all over everything
nonconductive. And will a monolayer of fabric
softener help us out? God laughs, for that also keeps
silicon from silicon and thwarts the weld. There's
more to be learned here, but scarce the time, and
so the bricks pile up to mock me.

The sun was behind us, fierce and unblinking,
and long crisp shadows bounded out ahead as we
walked, making good time with the absurd, but
absurdly efficient, bunny-hop stride. This takes
some getting used to in a General Spacesuit Heavy
Rebreather; the first few steps are just a flick of the
ankles and a forty-five-degree parabolic bounce, all
well and good, but to keep it up for any amount of
time requires strong, patient calf muscles and a
willingness to lean forward as though running
through a chest-deep swimming pool. One feels
more a cartoon character than a servant of the
Creator, so it's a strange sort of workout, but also a
break from being indoors. No ceiling to bang one's
head out here!

Craters Shoemaker and Faustini are 176
kilometers apart, lip to lip, and the Ernest
Shackleton Center for Misnamed Moonbases sits
midway on the road between them, about ten klicks

closer to Faustini. Saint Jay is three klicks away as the crow can't fly, and a klick off the main road, but actually closer to four kilometers from Moonbase Larry as an actual walk. Some exercise, then!

Among ourselves we tend to hop in silence, reserving vocalizations for necessary warnings, instructions, or calls to attend some detail of particular use or interest. Monastic and also conservative of oxygen! However, upon reaching the road we swapped our radios into the Harvest Moon Industries voice network, and were met at once with exuberant chatter, for only the most effusive of extroverts can stand long in Sir Larry's corporate culture without melting into puddles of sad, colorless wax.

I call them Larry's Boys, for though the station commander is a woman, and a good one from what I can glean from the chatter, I have never met her, for she does not often venture outdoors, and certainly not for such activities as would draw a monk from cloister. Other women are hard to hire, I hear, as the ones with appropriate skills and psych profiles tend to find their way instead to the Convent of Igbal Renz, where the pay is better and the future more mysterious and grand. What do you suppose they are scheming up there in their sun-blotting fortress? Surely not the mere fabrication and sale of gear and tack that others might use to colonize the void! No, there's more to Iggy the Rake than the eye readily meets. Of Killian I'm not sure the same can be said, for he wears his plans right out on his sleeve, and approaches them timid and slow. Of all the Horsemen, isn't it odd that

Sir Larry is the one who lives not in space? Should he take a break from ballooning across Hyperaustralis in his personal air yacht, well, he'll spend that break in dreams of simple commercial plenitude. No conqueror he? Or perhaps I misjudge, and he simply loves the Earth too well to part ties with it, or is finally too old to survive intact the rigors of launch, or both, and this is why he ain't up here with the spacemen.

This day we were to receive our newest crew hab module (which my Trailer Trash origins cannot help labeling a single-wide, but which Harvest Moon calls a Rack Vault), and it was beneath God's dignity to let Larry's Boys deliver and install it unassisted. Indeed, one imagines a future when there are monks enough and equipment enough to take delivery straight from the high-roofed, airless dome of the factory itself, and trouble Harvest Moon for naught but the hardware alone. But that day is not yet upon us, nor shall it be afore you yourself are here among us to order it so. And thus, we arrived to help foreman Huntley Millar and his crew of four to load our module onto the bed of a truck with cranes at either end.

Lunar gravity or no, these modules are *heavy*. Designed to sit aboveground and provide adequate protection against cosmic radiation and mild solar flares, the arched hemicylindrical ceilings are hollow vaults of thick iron plate, and the windows are ten centimeters of solid monocrystalline quartz. For shielding against major flares, or for namby-pamby cumulative dose limits that equal the surface of

Terra, one must of course burrow, and that is why the oldest originalest outpost of St. Joe, where yours sincerely first put his feet up and slept a Vatican night shift, is a dug-in bunker, and still where we cower when Apollo is angry and spits his wrath upon fair Luna. We sworn Conquistadores, being neither namby nor pamby, suffice a dose of three millirads on an average day, and trust the drug printer to hold our cancers at bay when time arises, as it shall.

But Larry finds such burial-alive unphotogenic, and gives a hefty discount for surface modules whose photos he can paste in his brochures. And yes, even proud vainglorious spacemen need some shielding o'er our heads, about which you also seem confused. May I explain? The solar wind contains helium nuclei, hydrogen nuclei, and the electrons stripped therefrom, otherwise known as alpha, proton, and beta radiation, respectively. These can to large extent be deflected by the electromagnets topping the aforementioned solar panels ringing the Valley of Saint Jaycoop, even up to the strength of a minor flare. Cosmic gamma rays are more problematic and can really only be shielded against by lots of mass, and so are solar neutrons, which are a gift that keeps on giving, for like Satan they can corrupt the innocent, turning the atoms of our bodies radioactive. Ironically, these are only effectively blocked by *low*-mass shielding, preferably rich in hydrogen, which is an atom that can absorb Satan's touch once (though not twice) without turning vile.

Cumulatively speaking, the realest danger is

cosmic radiation, for the death screams of collided neutron stars, flung into the void at fantastic speed, consist of nuclei from all over the periodic table, stripped of electrons and fiercely charged. The lightest and slowest of these are turned aside by the superconducting tower coil that looms above the monastery, but the heaviest and fastest are bare iron and gold and even uranium nuclei, traveling at ninety percent of light speed and with a million light-years of running start. These angstrom-scale machine gun bullets will tear straight through a human body without pausing, which is bad enough, for it leaves a line of broken and ionized biologicals where'er it hath traveled (whether through the brain or liver or gonads or what have), and there is only so much that antioxidants and DNA repair enzymes can do about that. But what really gets you is not so much the bullets as the shrapnel, for when God's ancient wrath strikes the skin of a space habitat, it's like to strike a stationary iron or aluminium or titanium nucleus and smash it to subatomic flinders, which explode relativistically in all directions but mostly forward, and may strike still other nuclei, kicking forth a heterogeneous mix of every noxious particle and wave in God's menagerie.

As for the electrons these atoms have lost, these also travel through space, and what gets through our magnets strikes the armor of the Rack Vault and slows the Hell down, creating fierce transient electromagnetics that kick loose a shower of what Germans and physicists call Bremsstrahlung radiation—mostly X-rays, which also need mass to halt them.

And so, the shielding is, from outside in, plastic upon aluminium upon iron, and then a gap that is eventually filled with liquid water (though not this day, or the next), and then graphite, and then more iron, weighing in total some two hundred kilograms per square meter, about half of which is the aforementioned water and not lifted by us this day, and the other half that isn't, and was.

Now, even with prompt and vigorous treatment, a dose of a thousand rads is universally lethal, whereas two hundred rads is a therapeutic for tumor eradication, and can be repeated daily for a week, so long as it's focused mainly on the tumor site itself. A mere twenty-five rads in a single shot will agitate your blood cells, and is the threshold where serious increases begin to the risk of eventual cancer. Were the Moon not here to block out half the sky, and the hills and Earth shadow another percent or two, this location would receive about a hundred rads in a good year, or a thousand in a particularly bad day. And yet, with all countermeasures in place these values are knocked back to a mere ten and one hundred, respectively, even if we ne'er sleep in the bunker, which when a bad coronal mass ejection passes through, we certain do. Dosewise it's no worse than living on airplanes, which some Earthmen do. So the only really real problem is venturing away from all that, to walk unprotected upon the surface of Lune. This (and thermal management) is why the General Spacesuit Heavy Rebreather has water tubes all through it, and weighs near as much as the man who wears it. And even so, one's eye doth occasionally see a flash of light that means another retinal cone or rod cell has just bitten the radioactive dust. Alas!

But yes, the Rack Vault is exceeding heavy, and must needs be craned onto the truck bed one end at a time, slowly and carefully and with many a monk and friend of Killian monitoring stresses and pressures and tensions and tilts. It took two hours and change, after which the truck was driven also very slowly back to Saint Joe, with God's loyal clinging to the sides, and mooching complimentary oxygen through a device artfully known as a rape hose, which one unrolls and jams into an umbilical port at the approximate height of one's navel.

With equal slowness the trailer was then unloaded, and the module connected as you see in the attached photo. There being no time left in the day shift to hook up consumables, we left it like that, vacuum-empty with hatches closed, and bid our goodbyes to Larry's Boys, who rolled their empty truck considerably faster in the direction they had come.

Returning to the monastery's interior, Giancarlo and Purcell and I stepped one by one through the airlock hatch, which I closed behind me and seated myself down on the bench beside them for fifteen of silent meditation, broken only by a statement by Purcell, to the effect that future module deliveries (of which there will ultimately be three, and probably no more after that) will have a wider variety of Brothers to oversee them, and this could well be the last time the three of us were in the lock together simultaneous. We'll see how Brothers Ferris, Bryant, Hughart, Durm, Duppler, Groppel, Hamblin, and Ovid feel about that; Eggs at least is no outdoorsman, no athlete and no heavy laborer, and likely to stay in with his telescope monitors most of the time, and perhaps Geo with him, for it truly is a lot of work just getting in and out the door!

Once the pressure has equalized, one opens the inner hatch and steps through into the shower, where first jets of ionized air and then jets of water and surfactant seek to clean off the dust that clings to us despite best efforts and antistatic spray. And then jets of air again to dry the suits, and then finally we may doff them with difficulty even greater than that with which we donned. The suits are finally crucified on their hanging racks, and we strip off the space underwear that has come in contact with them, for it too is contaminated with dust and must needs be fed through the laundry lock before permitted in the dormitory.

Nude as newborns, we then slip back into the shower to clean off the dust of Lune and the sweat of long exertion, paying careful attention to the head hair and body hair, for grit does love to accumulate there. Finally, still nude, we slip indoors, to find ourselves some fresh clothing—inevitably now the traditional monk's habit. And then finally, with much gratitude, we blow our damned noses.

On this day at shift's end we were starving, and no one had thought to pre-program the CHON printer or wanted to wait for it to churn out three meals' worth of slop, so we raided the hydroponics and gorged on sewer-grown carrots and tomatoes and cabbage (all carefully washed and irradiated, of course), then cleaned and stacked the dishes. Then came vespers, for praying in the evening helps one make sense of the day, followed by an hour of personal time which I spent reading academic papers on the art and science of growing edibles in nutrient-poor soil. "Add fertilizer" seems to be the consensus, by the way, which defeats my purpose, and thus it's between the written lines that I must read, to glean the information I require.

Afterward, more tooth brushing and hair combing, and thence to bed. And there you have it: a day in the life.

I hasten to remind my beloved that this is but one of the eighty-two Vatican days I've dwelt here upon the South Arse of Lune, and that the days and times are as varied as those of any nomadic hunter-gatherer or colonist farmer who ever trod the hills of Earth. I shall, for the moment, leave it to your imagination to describe the other eighty-one behind me, and the hopefully much larger number stretching out ahead. I remain:

Very yours and very truly,
Brother Michael Jablonski de la Lune

4.3
23 March

✦

Clementine Cislunar Fuel Depot
Earth-Moon Lagrange Point 1
Cislunar Space

A staffer came into the mess hall to issue Dona Obata, a freshly printed uniform (with, unusually, no name tag on it), and to show her to the trillionaire's quarters, which seemed to have been designed by the same people who did the guest rooms at the Marriott Stars. There, alone, she spent little time contemplating her fate. Things had gone wrong, indeed, and she was not in control of this situation at all, but she had spent much of her life in survival mode, and some in outright fight-or-flight, and she knew very well how to stay loose in a crisis. Instead of fretting, she took a shower, and then slid herself into the soft envelope of a queen-sized zero-gee bed. Sleep found her quickly; she'd been running on coffee and adrenaline for almost three days. She slept hard for a couple of hours, her body actually quite enjoying the reduction in stress that came from no longer being undercover.

Then she awoke, poked around in the trillionaire's

dresser drawers and medicine cabinet, and found a stout metal safe hidden behind one of the padded vinyl wall panels. It was an older type, purely mechanical, and by the looks of it, it had no way of tracking or logging attempts to open it. That was good, because she meant to find out, sooner or later, what was in there. However, it could potentially take her hundreds of hours to crack it, spread out over a couple of weeks, and she needed to know her efforts would remain undetected. In any event, today was not the day to begin; she doubted there were surveillance sensors of any kind in the trillionaire's private quarters (except, perhaps, aimed at the bed to collect a record of his sexual conquests) but the chance of his coming in randomly to check up on her was significant, and until she knew his habits better, she would not trust to luck.

She would, of course, have to seduce him. Her very survival could depend on it, and she was quite good at looking after her survival. In her six years of professional spycraft, she had certainly seduced her share of men. It was easier and tidier than killing them, which she also sometimes did. There were three that she had definitely killed and confirmed, and another three that were . . . probable. So there you had it. But the task in front of her now was to secure a position for herself here at Clementine and, as the trillionaire had said, ensure that the future still included her. To do this, she had to get him not only into bed with her, but actually *on her side*. And she knew how to do that.

Of course, expecting to win his *trust* would be stupid. At his behest she'd already betrayed her former employer, which was also her country, and she'd been fully prepared to shoot her colleagues, Bethy and Alice, in the backs of their heads and turn control of ESL1 over to Grigory Orlov in perhaps the boldest act of piracy the modern world had ever seen. Naturally, the trillionaire was plenty smart enough to know that if she'd do it *for* him, she'd just as readily do it *to* him if a better offer came along. And she would, yes, obviously. But what he also needed to see, and probably didn't, was that nobody was ever going to have a better offer than he did. Nobody else, in all the universe, could offer her *the universe*. Occupying ESL1 Shade Station would never have been anything more than a temporary assignment for her, and then back to Earth for more skullduggery in all the places France liked to meddle. Ironically, she'd've made a better future for herself by simply signing up for ESL1 as an actual colonist! But that RzVz contract, that *mandatory pregnancy clause*, was a nonstarter, and anyway by the time she'd realized going there was even a possibility, she already knew that place was in the Coalition's crosshairs, and its days of normal operation were sharply numbered.

So, what did that leave her? Find a way onto *Concordia*, Dan Beseman's Mars ship? That would take tens of millions of euros, maybe even *hundreds* of millions, to bid successfully for one of the hundred slots, assuming she could even persuade the backers that her skill set matched the basic admission profile. Or somehow get herself hired by Harvest Moon, and somehow persuade them she was one of the very few who actually got to live at Shackleton Lunar Industrial Station? Or maybe she should just suck it, give up on the universe, and move her ass to Burning Man in the U.S., or Ciudad de Esperanza in Antarctica, or even Mustaemara in southern Libya, in the crook of the Sahara's Ramlat Rebiana dune sea. Somewhere essentially uninhabitable, without the aid of space colonization technology. Someplace she could *start something* and *build something* and *be someone*, in a way she never could in France or even the Congo. People like her—females of modest means and great determination—were in the First World seen fit to be excellent whores and hotel maids, and in the Third World as wives for gangsters and warlords, petty politicians and businessmen. Government service within the E.U. had offered her a slightly better alternative, but Orlov had opened up the possibility of something more. Something *real*.

In France's *opérations secrètes* community, RzVz's ESL1 Shade was seen as both a major geopolitical threat and an easy target for wet-ops intervention. Hence her mission there. But Clementine Cislunar Fuel Depot scared them in a totally different way; it was often discussed by Dona's superiors that Grigory Orlov—a "known bad actor"—could "drop a rock" any time he wanted to, and level any square kilometer on Earth with perhaps twelve hours' notice at the very most, and perhaps a lot less if the rock were first painted black and swaddled in radar-absorbing material, so that only quantum radar could pick it up as it passed through low Earth orbit. But in this case, it seemed the best defense was not a strong offense, but simply the constellation of American orbital lasers. Those were nominally to protect against Earthly missile launches, but there was also talk about using them to enforce the no-fly zones in Central and South America, and apparently they had been secretly used to shoot down natural meteorites. And so, Dona had heard those lasers referred to more than once as "rock block" weapons, that could divert the course of an incoming asteroid small enough to be flung by Clementine's gatherbots, breaking it into smaller pieces that would burn up better on reentry, or at least steering it toward unpopulated areas. Because yes, even if Orlov Petrochemical were somehow taken out of the picture, there were enough people in space these days, with little enough supervision, that in paranoid government circles it was understood that a dropped rock from somewhere, against someone, was only a matter of time.

But that left no need for the Coalition to take Clementine Cislunar Fuel Depot away from Orlov, and he seemed somehow to know it. Perhaps he knew more about it than she did. So yes, Clementine was the one place she could think of that made a real future possible for her. And to access that future, she needed to get Orlov's hormones working on her behalf. And really, she felt the work of seduction was half-done already; by asking her to stay in his own quarters, she sensed he was in effect *reserving* her, basically sequestering her away from the eyes and deeds of other males who might catch her eye. She supposed it was a piggish move. She supposed many women in her position would be offended or afraid, but truthfully she felt neither thing. If parking her in his own quarters was crude in method, well, it was also quite precise in effect, and exactly the sort of thing she would have expected from a man with his very particular kind of power. She'd be in trouble if he *weren't* interested. *That* would be worth fretting about.

It was not like this seduction would be a particularly odious chore, either; she was attracted to powerful men in general, and she tended to fall for dangerous, unrepentant men in particular. Call it a weakness. Of course, some such men were also fat or sweaty or pointlessly cruel, or precocious in youth, or else they were old men pining for the precocity of youth, and these were *not* attractive qualities. The trillionaire, though, seemed in fine control of both his body and mind, and his chiseled tough-guy frame suggested he could possibly beat her in a physical fight as well. Call it another weakness, but this engaged her own hormones like nothing else. So yes, as far as she could tell, Orlov was very much her type, and this was her kind of place, and she had done the right thing by coming here.

Next, she did a quick inventory of what she'd managed to bring with her in her flight bag: an extra set of dark gray space underwear, some colorful scarves, a pair of bright red, wedge-heeled, magnetic-soled shoes, a maximally equipped Swiss Army knife, a tube of red lipstick, and a pair of inert, flip-lens magnifying eyeglasses that had no electronic features, save a pair of small, forward-facing lamps on the sides of the lenses. And finally, the now-useless radio: an entangled ultrawideband disguised as an old smartphone handset (the kind people still watched movies on when they were too fashion-conscious for augmented reality glasses). It had one more trick hidden up its electronic sleeve, but today wasn't the day for that, either.

Dressing in her Clementine uniform of dark gray spandex, she tried on the high heels and found they looked pretty good with it. She then tried each of the scarves, first loosely around her neck and then tightly along her hairline, until she found a look that hit the right combination of "accidental" sex appeal. She even tried the glasses with it and found, to her surprise, that they somehow made her look more like she belonged in a mining outpost, like some saucy records clerk accustomed to "hanging with the boys." She decided the lipstick would push that too far, though, so she put it away for now.

Then she stripped back down to space underwear and slipped back into bed for a few more hours of sleep. Her mind—itself a disciplined instrument, and a relieved one—did not prevent her from performing the two-minute progressive relaxation ritual that put her body at rest and sank her into what she called, without irony, *le sommeil du juste*—"the sleep of the just."

1.5
22 March

L.S.F. *Dandelion*
En Route to Earth-Sun
Lagrange Point 1
Cislunar Space

"You monitor the thrust and engine temperatures over here," Derek was saying, pointing to indicators on the Flight Management screen of the ship's virtual control panel. "That's acceleration there, and calculated mass over here. That always fluctuates a bit in the third decimal place, but if it changes more than that, or you see a consistent downward trend, it means we've got trouble. You can set a trigger alarm if you want to, but it's boring enough up here without automating yourself out of existence."

"Plus we need the benefit of human judgment?" Alice asked.

"Only when something unexpected occurs, but then yeah, definitely. And it happens more often than you might think. Machines are fine at anomaly detection and fair to middlin' at diagnosing a root cause, but they know fuck all about how to improvise. That's why human pilots still exist, maybe for a good long while. Okay, propellant mass has its own separate calculation, right here, based on acoustic and optical readings inside the tank. And no, the fuel tank is not going to blow up, so get that look off your face."

"What look?"

"It's xenon. It's an inert gas."

"I didn't say anything."

"Okay, fine. But you do have to watch it closely. An anomaly in fuel mass is not as bad as a leak in the air or water supply, but it's still very bad, so it's something you want to keep an eye on."

They were orbiting the Earth and thrusting lightly along the direction of their orbit, slowly spiraling outward on a trajectory that would take them out past geosynchronous orbit, past lunar orbit, and eventually all the way out to Earth-Sun Lagrange Point 1. This meant that for the majority of the trip, the Earth would be invisible through both the windshield and the rearview mirrors. The Sun and Moon would occasionally pass into view as the weeks unfolded, but right now the Sun was at their side, casting glints off the edges of the rear-view mirror frames and mostly drowning out the starry night in front of them.

Derek selected a different tab at the top of the screen, and brought up the Engine Management screen. He pointed: "Temperature. Efficiency. Specific impulse. Flowrate. Voltage. Wattage input. Wattage output. Problems here are even less urgent, but still, you know, extremely urgent. We'll be two months on this tub if everything goes perfectly, and forever if it doesn't."

"Yep. Got it."

Alice tried to keep the sarcasm out of her tone, but this was the third time he'd gone over the exact same material, after making her memorize the positions and functions of every physical control in the cockpit. In the unlikely occurrence that Derek died and the computer shut down and someone needed to guide the ship manually into a docking port, Alice had a one hundred percent theoretical knowledge of what to do. Emphasis on the theoretical.

Derek continued: "Point is, if you find *any* kind of problem, anything, no matter how small, you wake me up. If *I* find a problem, I'll wake you up on the theory you can help me deal with it, or at least learn from watching me."

"And how long does it take to wake someone up?"

Alice looked back. Behind them, the cockpit door (a two-piece sliding hatch about twice the thickness of a highway sign) sat open, looking back on six women in their space underwear, hanging from the walls like sides of beef. Goggles over their eyes, headphones over their ears, IV catheters in their arms, and various wireless monitoring patches stuck to their necks and hands and feet, and hidden beneath their T-shirts.

It was cold as fuck back there, only eight degrees above freezing, and with the door open that meant it was cold here in the cockpit, too, because the climate controller was too smart to waste very much energy trying to heat one space while it was open to one that was being cooled.

Passengers on these low-speed ferries spent the whole trip in what was called "squirrel hibernation," which was a much colder, much deeper sleep than "bear hibernation," which is what Derek was preparing to go into. Derek looked back. "For them, about two hours. It's no joke; you'll kill them if you try to rush it. Bear hibernation is a lot more flexible, so you can wake me up in about fifteen minutes under normal circumstances, or five minutes in a real emergency. But try not to have one of those, okay? It wouldn't be fatal to wake up that fast, but I'd be sick for days." He paused, then said, "Seriously, are you going to be okay? This is your first space mission. If it's too much, I can just put you under and take the whole flight myself."

"I'm fine," she assured him, although there was something unnerving about the whole situation, even to Alice, who'd dealt with quite a lot of scary things in her life.

But the two of them had been awake together for almost twenty-four hours, which was enough of a strain on the ship's resources that they pretty much had to put a stop to it now. One of them had to go back in the hibernation bay for a few days, and if Derek did it, then Alice would build up flight hours toward a certification. It wasn't hard to pretend to care about that, as part of her imaginary future in space, but it did mean spending a lot of long hours alone with her thoughts, and with seven cold coma patients on the very very brink of death.

By now she'd figured out the other reason Derek wanted her for a copilot: because she had field experience with hibernation drugs. Maroon Berets used a mix called "The Pillows" on wounded soldiers, mainly just to drop the blood pressure and slow hemorrhaging, but with rapid unconsciousness as a convenient side effect. And yes, the core temperature of those patients did drop, along with heart rate and respiration, until the drug wore off, usually in about four hours. But "bear hibernation" was a whole level beyond that, and "squirrel hibernation" was even more extreme.

"It's a lot of responsibility," he said.

"Yeah, I get it."

"You know, this is the first deep-space vessel built entirely in outer space, from something like ninety percent lunar- and asteroid-mined materials. Most efficient human transport ever built, with a *way* better mass fraction than a chemical rocket. I named it myself."

"That's nice."

"You know when you blow on a dandelion, and scatter the seeds all to hell, contaminating an entire neighborhood? That's us. Colonizing space."

"Charming."

He frowned, then let it go. "You're a sweet one, aren't you? All right, then, I'll stop trying to converse with you. Let's do this high-bo thing." High-bo was apparently slang for hibernation. He started unzipping his coverall, revealing space underwear that for some reason was bright orange.

"Hey, why do you get nicer underwear than the women?" she complained.

"Quit looking at my dick," he told her, in a tone that might or might not be joking.

"Our underwear is gray," she said.

"Yeah, I know," he answered, because derp, there were six examples of it just a couple of meters away. "Printer pigment costs money, and y'all haven't earned any."

"Wow. Seriously, you spend yours on underwear?"

"Some of it. Seriously, fuck off with that and get me some biotrackers."

"Okay, okay." Leaving him, she swam back to the equipment lockers and, after a brief search, pulled out a pack of radio patches and handed them to him to stick on various parts of his body.

Soon Derek was packing his things in a locker, and getting strapped to the wall, and developing a half erection that the space underwear couldn't hide. Alice did her best to ignore it as the hibernation cuff slid up and around his arm and then tightened at the elbow.

"Ouch," he said as the pressurized IV needle penetrated his skin and wormed its way into a blood vessel.

"Good vein," she reported.

"Quit looking at my dick!" he said again.

"I'm really not," she assured him.

"It's these cuffs."

Alice was attaching Velcro straps to hold his wrists down at his sides, to hold his ankles together against the wall of the hibernation berth. For a moment, the operation put her face uncomfortably close to his groin.

"Woman cuffing me to the bed, oh Jesus. I can't help it. It'd be bigger if it weren't so fucking cold in here."

She secured the head strap around his forehead and said, "I have patients machine-gunned in a jungle who whine less than you."

"It's normal sized. At least normal." He was starting to slur his words now. His skin was turning pale and sweaty.

"Dude, I'm a medic. I don't care how big your dick is."

"You will," he murmured, and just like that he was gone. His body tried to curl up into a fetal position, but was stopped by the straps and cuffs, so he just hung there, barely breathing. Alice had watched this process six times now, and it still creeped her out. She'd doped her share of patients up with Pillows, but she hadn't left them like that for sixty-six days, and anyway those patients were going to die without the drug. These were *healthy* people, put to sleep for mere convenience, and that was different.

"Night night," she said to Derek, knowing he couldn't hear her. He wasn't as pale as the women around him. He didn't need anything over his eyes and ears. He was more than asleep, but bear hibernation was a long way from death, and so actually not as creepy. She could wake him up if he needed to, and it would only take a few minutes. Not unlike Pillows, which could be counteracted with a different shot called Risers.

And then, with a sigh, she looked around her at the cold ship interior, already feeling the days and weeks stretching out ahead of her. Already realizing yet another reason she'd been chosen as a copilot: because Captain Hakkens of the Normal-Sized Dick preferred to sleep through as much of the boredom as he could, not dreaming, barely ageing, while still earning a full paycheck. Damn it.

For lack of anything better to do, she checked the vital signs on all the sleeping beauties, and then checked their exposed skin for signs of abrasion or infection or anything else out of the ordinary. Checked over the three empty beds—one for her, one for Dona Obata, and one for Rachael Lee, to make sure the equipment was in good shape. And then checked her watch, and saw that six whole minutes had gone by.

Sighing again, she started, very unprofessionally,

checking out the bodies of her fellow space colonists. She was under recorded video surveillance, so she couldn't be too obvious about it, but of course it didn't really look like much, to be looking.

And yes, she had to admit they were a fine collection, good enough for any trillionaire's harem. If you overlooked the sickly gray-blue skin tones, and the goggles and headphones hiding their faces, these were symmetrical, smooth-skinned, well-proportioned humans of many different sizes and shapes. Jeanette was voluptuous and soft. Malagrite—Maag—was tall and slim. Nonna Rostov was even thinner—almost bony, really—but proportioned like a 2030s swimsuit model. Saira Batra was petite in almost every dimension, and Pelu Figueroa was also voluptuous, but in that almost-middle-aged way that said she had put on two pounds a year for twenty years, and her athletic body had found artful ways to distribute it. Bethy was short and compact and rather muscular, with unaccountably large breasts. Dona, though absent, was tall and thin and muscular. And all of them, now that she thought about it, had wider than average hips and narrower than average waists for their respective body types.

Alice herself . . . Alice had never thought of herself as particularly good looking, except in that generic chubby-Asian way she'd inherited from her mother. But she'd always known her hips were her best feature. "Good birthing hips," Soon-ja Kyeong had called them, in a rare moment of quasi-praise. Airmen and soldiers and civilian boyfriends had made less polite comments of their own, but for basically the same reason.

It certainly appeared that the prospective colonists had been selected not only for useful skills and "genetic fitness" (which of course was code for physical beauty), but also for genetic diversity and yes, good birthing hips. Because there was genetically diverse birthing to be done, out here in the Great Beyond. Yes indeedy.

And then, ashamed at how long her gaze had lingered, she turned away and launched herself back into the cockpit, closing the hatch behind her so the place could warm the hell up.

4.4
29 March

✦

Clementine Cislunar Fuel Depot
Earth-Moon Lagrange Point 1
Cislunar Space

Over the next several days, Dona did her best to stay out of the trillionaire's sight, and to poke around the Clementine station, learning its places and rhythms. It resembled both the Marriott Stars and Transit Point Station in certain particulars—the general sizes of modules, the spacing of grab bars, etc.—but a lot of things here seemed to be made of plastic. Also, where the Marriott Stars was basically round in its overall design, its modules huddled around the gymnasium bubble that was its main attraction, and where Transit Point Station was long and spindly to accommodate docking spaceships, Clementine was arranged in a large, rectangular block of trusses and modules, huddled (she supposed) around the pressurized hangar and the outgassing oven that were *its* central features. The layout seemed, in a way, to have been inspired by offshore oil drilling platforms, and for all she knew that might also be the basis for the station's schedules and routines, which did include a false "night" of reduced lighting, but not really much of a pause in activity at that time. But finding her way around, while the crew ebbed and flowed around her, helped her develop a routine of her own, which in turn helped her stay mostly quiet and mostly invisible.

Of course, she was still a new face in a crew of only fifty people, and also the only black person on board, and only the fourth woman, so a certain amount of notice was inevitable. When people introduced themselves to her, she told them her name was Dona and she'd come here from Transit Point Station. If they pressed for details, she turned it around by asking them questions. If they asked, for example, what her job here was, she'd reply, "Oh, are you with payroll?" If they asked about her nationality, she'd say, "I'm guessing you're good with accents." If they asked whether (as a person freshly arrived from Earth) she had any information about the embargo or the blockade, she'd ask if they followed politics closely, and whether they thought the Cartels were going to survive through the end of the year. She was at once friendly and distant, eager and yet curt, sexy but unavailable, and so she became a familiar enough face and voice to stop drawing much attention, without anyone actually learning anything about her.

She learned the station's systems, too; not only how to eat and shower and find the bathrooms, how to use the gym to keep her body strong, but also the way the gatherbot crews would swarm into the pressurized hangar every time one of their charges came back with a rock. Through portholes in the station's hull she might see a bot, dwarfed by its shrink-wrapped cargo like an ant carrying a chocolate kiss, inching its way toward the Hopper, where the rock would be snatched from it and closed within the gigantic outgassing oven, its volatiles blasted away with beams of focused sunlight, blinding even through the polarized coatings of the observation porthole. And once the easy volatiles were cooked off, the beams got even hotter, vaporizing the rock itself, square millimeter by square millimeter, so that chemical extractor wands could take it apart into component atoms, like a drug printer operating in reverse. Then the bot itself went into the pressurized hangar, and was swarmed by a pit crew of human beings doing stuff she wasn't yet sure about, but involved checking the status of the bot and getting it ready for its next outing. From what she knew of life out at ESL1, their systems were substantially more autonomous than this, so it surprised her to see so many people working, it seemed, for robot masters.

She also watched a crab-shaped robotic lander arrive from the surface of the Moon, and a robotic landing body, like a miniature space shuttle, arrive from ESL1. She watched that same crew take a little pressure bottle out of the lander and put it inside the landing body, which they then launched on a trajectory toward Earth. The landing body was the size of a delivery van and mostly hollow inside, and it looked to her like there was a *lot* of room left over in its cargo hold, which told her that bottle must be very valuable indeed.

On the fourth day, the outlines of a plan began to take shape, and that "night" she dared to climb into bed with Grigory Orlov while he slept. She did nothing more than put an arm around him, not trying for anything more physical than that. He stirred and mumbled a bit, but didn't resist or wake up. She liked the warmth of his body, and let it lull her to sleep. In the morning, when he began to stir, she awoke immediately into alertness, but pretended to be asleep as he roused and dressed, not lingering very long between sleep and wakefulness. She was still "asleep" when he left on his morning's business, whatever that was.

The next night she did it again, and then the morning after that it was time, finally, for her to show her worth around here.

"I've been working on a project," she said to him, after he was awake but before he'd gotten out of bed.

"Hmm?"

"I can show it to you in about two hours, if you like."

"If I *like*?" he answered gruffly. "I insist on it. I was not joking about your need to be useful here."

"I know. I'd expect nothing less. The fact is, I can be very useful in station security, and I think you know that. But if that's all I was good for, I wouldn't expect a lot of patience from you."

"Mmm. That is wise. Meet me in two hours, then. In the mess hall."

"Let's make it the infirmary," she said.

That seemed to surprise and intrigue him a bit, though he hid it well. "Hmm? Yes, very well. But do not expect to take much of my time. I have several large enterprises to run."

"I appreciate that," she said, then shut up and watched him dress. She could see he spent time in the gym, and of course took weightlessness drugs to retain bone and muscle mass, and it showed. His body did have some fat on it, but not as much as she'd've expected for a man in his mid-fifties. He was in better shape than most manual laborers his age, and *much* better than most desk drivers.

"You're handsome," she dared to tell him.

"You're a flatterer," he said, unimpressed, then combed his hair and left.

Two hours later, she was in the infirmary with Sergei Golubev, the station's doctor.

"You ready?" she asked him in bad Russian.

"For what?" he answered in bad French. "I am bystander here."

"No. I could not done without you."

He shook his head emphatically. "No. Is no blame here. You blame. I help because of nice, because of bored, because of beautiful. Only. Understand? I no blame."

"No credit, then," she said in English, since she didn't know the Russian word for that. It didn't get a lot of use around here.

"Fine," he said, also in English. "No credit. I am physician. What do I need with credit?"

"Credit for what?" asked the trillionaire, also in English. He'd materialized in the hatchway, looking stern and impatient.

"Your new product line," Dona told him. She held up a plastic squeeze bottle, one of several popular types used for drinking liquids in zero gee.

"Raketnoye Goryuchiye," he said, reading the freshly printed, red and yellow and black Cyrillic label, which depicted a winged wine-bottle shape with a tongue of flame extending from its neck. "'Rocket Fuel'? What is this?"

"Vodka," she answered. "Here, try some."

She attempted to hand him the bottle, but he wouldn't take it. He looked cross and . . . disappointed?

"Drug-printed vodka? My dear, a liter of this ties up the printer for over an hour."

"Try three minutes," she told him. "This came out of the chemical synthesizer. Like soap."

"Then it isn't fit to drink. It's polluted with toxins from side reactions. It probably *has* soap in it. Listen, if this is what you have for me—"

"One million euros," she said quickly, before he could look away.

He raised an eyebrow. "What?"

"One million euros. That's how much money this will make you next week, when the next landing body goes out."

He looked at her for a long moment, and then said, "Firstly, a million euros isn't that much money. We'll make a *billion* on the tralphium in that shipment."

One can't really lean forward in zero gee (not without rotating and translating one's whole body in the process) but Dona made other gestures of engagement. "I understand, sir. But if it isn't much, can I keep it for myself?"

He snorted. "You're a bold one, aren't you?"

"It's the reason I'm here," she confirmed.

He glared at her for another long moment, and then said, "You'll make salary if you're lucky. And by lucky, I mean you'll impress me with what you say next. Explain this million euros to me. Explain it *zhato*, please. Succinctly."

She nodded. "Yes, well, the activated carbon wafers produced by the drug synthesizer for accidental poisonings"—she pointed at the aforementioned equipment—"are basically identical to the carbon ultracapacitors they print down in the machine shop, and structurally similar to the six-micron pump filters we use on liquefied volatiles."

Orlov cocked his eyebrow again. "'We'?"

"You, then. The six-micron filters *you* use on liquefied volatiles."

All this she had learned in the last forty-eight hours, and she stated it with confidence. She was wearing her red heels and her blue-and-yellow scarf and her glasses and her lipstick, looking just as intelligent and productive and sexy and eager to please as she could manage under the circumstances.

He checked his watch, looking bored. "I said succinctly, woman. What do you have for me?"

"You're correct, the liquor that comes out of the chemical synthesizer is *poylo*. Rotgut. *Dechets*, as we say in France. Possibly even lethal. But we force it through an activated carbon wafer, and it becomes premium liquor, or passable at any rate. This man"—she pointed at Doctor Sergei—"confirms it's safe to drink, and you yourself can confirm the taste. We throw the wafer away when it's filtered ten bottles; it simply joins the sewage stream, and helps feed our, or rather *your*, hydroponics."

"How is this one million euros?" he demanded. His face remained impatient and skeptical, seemingly unimpressed by anything she'd said so far. But he hadn't actually left yet. He was actually listening for her explanation.

She gave it to him: "I found a luxury liquor distributor in Spain who'll buy these bottles—these 3D-printed, extraterrestrial plastic bottles full of exotic extraterrestrial liquor—for ten thousand euros apiece. I can fit a hundred into the landing body, packed around your little pony bottle of helium."

Orlov looked thoughtful for a moment, then frowned and shook his head. "This can be counterfeited. It *will* be counterfeited; if it's that simple to make, even the bottle can be faked, and the profit will go all to Spanish gangsters. Assuming the man you're speaking with isn't gangster himself."

"No," Sergei piped in, in Russian. "It will not be easy to fake. The isotopes don't match. Asteroidal hydrogen has actually about the same percentage of deuterium as Earth's hydrogen, but our oxygen and carbon are a little bit lighter, and our nitrogen is a little bit heavier. Earth-printed fakes could be caught by any chemistry lab with a mass spectrometer. We are in negotiations with several right now that are local to this distributor."

To that, Dona added: "And we've *warned* him, we'll cut him off at the first sign of tampering, anywhere in our value chain. It actually *is* possible to counterfeit every part of this, including the isotopes, but doing that would cost a lot more than what we're charging. Now will you please have a taste of this?"

The trillionaire glared at the doctor and asked, in Russian, "You're certain this is drinkable?"

"I've drunk it myself, sir, with no puking and no hangover. I print a lot of booze for people as it is, so I'm in a position to say, it's at least as good as the drug-printer recipe."

Dona was now impatient herself, so she tossed the bottle toward Orlov, who caught it with a slight fumble. *His reflexes still haven't adapted to weightlessness*, she noted, filing the information away in case it might be useful. *He hasn't personally spent very much time in space.*

Orlov pointed the spout of the bottle into his mouth and squeezed. Nothing happened.

"Oh, you have to take off the safety seal," she told him. "We thought of that, yeah, so they don't get tampered with, and so they don't leak during reentry."

Grumbling in annoyance, the trillionaire unscrewed the cap, peeled off the plastic seal, tossed it behind him into the corridor, and then screwed the cap back on. He'd spilled a few large drops in the process, and these he scooped with his hand, casting them, clear and shimmery, into his mouth.

"It's warm," he said, wrinkling his nose.

"Apologies," said Sergei. "This is freshly printed and filtered; there was no time to chill it."

Orlov took another taste, this time from the spout as intended. He swished and swallowed. Took a third taste. Then he tossed the bottle at Dona, and said, "Very well. Double the price every week until this distributor stops ordering. Then find another distributor who'll buy at that price. The first man tells us what the market will bear, you see? And the second man actually bears it. Apparently, ethanol is one of the hydrocarbons we now produce, but the game remains the same as any other product."

"I did well?" she asked, perhaps too eagerly.

He seemed to think about that for a moment before answering, "Better than expected. Imaginations tend to be limited here. This is not impressive, but I am glad to see you are at least capable of original thought."

And that was how Dona Obata joined Orlov Petrochemical.

That night, she did more than just put her arm around him. A proper seduction was slow, not quick, and so it was a small beginning—a hand job in the dark, like a good, chaste girl might do. Not that she was fooling anyone— he knew perfectly well who and what she was—but the body wants what it wants, and even a bastard like Orlov wanted to feel like somebody liked him the proper way. And she did *want* to like him, first of all because that was easier than pretending, even for a practiced liar like her. And second of all because here in space, making a trillionaire her lover was clearly the best of the available options—all the more so if both of them were actually feeling it. Obvious, right? And third—there was a third!— because she was *also* a bastard, and she thought perhaps around Orlov she wouldn't have to pretend otherwise. It might just be that for the first time in her life, she could think of showing a man her true face, and be accepted for it. It was a surprisingly nice thought.

1.6
12 April

✧

L.S.F. *Dandelion*
En Route to Earth-Sun
Lagrange Point 1
Cislunar Space

They traded off hibernation cycles, with Derek asleep for a week and then Alice asleep for a few days, and then Derek asleep for *a week and a half*, and it confirmed for her that he really did want to spend as much time as possible in hibernation, drawing a salary but barely breathing, barely aging, totally unaware of the boring boring BORING passage of time.

Alice skimmed every operator's and maintenance manual for the *Dandelion* that she could find in the onboard systems. Other than a few introductory pages and the odd wiki article copied from public sources, most of it seemed machine-written from CAD drawings and circuit diagrams, and maybe even from AI observations of the actual ship in action. It made for tough reading, but having nothing better to do, Alice skimmed every page and then, with still more time on her hands, carefully read every word.

She lacked the physics and chemistry background for some of it, but on her third full pass through the documents, with numerous dictionary and encyclopedia lookups along the way, things started to come together. The ship operated by accelerating ionized xenon gas out the back, which was efficient but also provided extremely low thrust, which is why it took sixty-six days to get from low Earth orbit to ESL1, whereas a typical flight to the Moon—about a quarter the distance—took only three days with chemical rockets. But that required fuel tanks the size of grain silos, as heavy as a whole fleet of buses, whereas *Dandelion*'s fuel tank held just two hundred fifty kilograms of liquefied xenon gas. Basically, the mass of a very fat human being. That was a *big* difference, but it was also why the passengers needed to sleep through the journey—because even with excellent air and water recycling, the ship would need to be much larger and heavier to support a full complement of non-hibernating passengers and crew for that long. It would eat up all the savings.

Through these awful documents, Alice learned all about the plumbing and electrical and propulsion and data systems of the ship, and about what was behind the walls and panels of the bridge and hibernation stations. Emergency procedures were worryingly sketchy, but she learned what she could, and tried to fit it in a framework of everything she knew about aircraft and ground vehicles, emergency medicine, and basic human health. She would have liked to have known a lot more, but when she downloaded some textbooks over the ship's reeeally slow data connection, they were basically impenetrable to her.

She was, after all, a glorified paramedic, and had reached the limits of what her brain could process. Ah, well.

When learning slowed and stopped and even threatened to reverse itself a bit, she turned to exercise to pass the time. The ship had a little treadmill in back, to which you could strap yourself with gravity-simulating bungee cords. Boring as hell, but at least she could listen to music. And yet, there were only so many hours a day you could slog pointlessly. Eventually she took the bungees off and just danced in midair, until even the music was tiresome. And then, with *still* nothing to do, she went back and actually read every crew briefing RzVz had ever sent her, and some publicly available stuff about the ESL1 shade, and the company (and the man) that had built it. For a spy, she'd done a pretty lousy job of knowing what was going on, but finally she began to feel at least vaguely ready to pass herself off as a genuine space colonist. And then, yes, to perform her mission, whatever that might turn out to be.

5.2
15 April

✧

Mars Today
Premium Downloadable Content
#Marsnow #takeme #iwanttogo

(ERROR: ActivAI sound mapping features not enabled
    for 3D viewer)

GLASS: We're here today with Dan Beseman, founder
    and CEO of both Enterprise City and The Tunneling
    Corporation, and the single greatest force behind
    space colonization in our time.

BESEMAN: Whoa! I don't know about that.

GLASS: False modesty is uncalled for, Dan. Our audience
    knows exactly who you are and what you've been up
    to.

BESEMAN: They also know we're not the only game in
    town, Howard. Let's not dumb this down. Now, you
    put the word "Mars" in there and absolutely, we're the
    clear leader.

GLASS: Who else is even in the game? Mars, I mean.

BESEMAN: Well, the Russian and Chinese governments,

obviously, although they're five to seven years behind us, at best. The U.S. government is no longer on that list, though. You may have heard: as of last month, NASA has officially subsumed its Mars colonization efforts into ours. This vastly decreases their budget, which was a primary motivation for them, but it also vastly *increases* ours, with the only stipulation being that the U.S. government gets to select two of the male colonists, and two of the females, with no input from Enterprise City, Incorporated.

GLASS: Which you've agreed to.

BESEMAN: Which we've agreed to, yes. On a per-person basis, these four people would be the highest-sponsored candidates in the whole expedition, by at least a factor of five, and we also expect them to be among the most qualified. Since literally anyone can buy a berth in the colony, it's mainly a matter of definitions; the U.S. government has bought four seats that simply won't be outbid. Any government could do the same, and in fact at least six of our candidates include national governments among their key sponsors. So the U.S. offer makes sense for us on basically every level. We'd have to be crazy to turn it down, and as NASA itself has reaffirmed, we're not crazy. We're very serious about putting a hundred colonists on Mars within the next five years, and we're going about it very systematically, trying to head off literally every problem the human mind can anticipate.

GLASS: Such as?

BESEMAN: Well, for example, we've got provisions for up to half of the colonists to chicken out after six months on planet. We hope nowhere near that number take us up on it, but I can virtually guarantee that return flight will not go back empty, either. So it could be anywhere from, say, five people to fifty. The fact is, we simply don't know. We don't have any *way* to know, because nobody's ever done this before.

GLASS: And what if more than half the people want to go back, and your return ship can't hold them all?

BESEMAN: In that unpleasant scenario, we can put those excess people into hibernation on the ground for six months, until the next resupply mission brings another lander. They won't experience the passage of time, and their resource utilization will be less than a fifth what it would be if they were awake. Like the first fifty returnees, they'll simply wake up back on Earth. Now, that kind of very long hibernation is an extreme solution, and a health risk, though presumably less of a risk than letting a very unhappy person walk around in a deadly environment like Mars. I don't think we're going to need that, but honestly, even knowing the possibility is there may serve as a kind of psychological safety valve. Nobody's going to feel trapped.

GLASS: You'd still need some people awake to care for those hibernators, though.

BESEMAN: Probably ten people, yes. So we can afford a ninety percent washout rate and still move forward to a second wave of colonists. Who will *still* arrive years ahead of the Chinese and the Russians, assuming they're coming at all.

GLASS: And despite what you said earlier, you don't take just anyone for this mission, right? There are fairly strict qualifications each candidate needs to meet.

BESEMAN: I'm not sure what you mean by "strict." Most
able-bodied humans can meet the base requirements,
which amount to little more than a doctor's note
stating basic physical and mental fitness for space
travel. We don't begin any sort of weeding-out process
until an applicant has raised a minimum bid of one
million dollars, a hundred thousand of which is
nonrefundable, to defray the expenses associated with
each application. So in that sense, we're selecting for
people who can find a million dollars somewhere,
from someone. Is that "strict"? Not really. Again, the
way the sourcing program is set up, that's not a high
bar. Micro-sponsorships alone account for nearly
twenty billion dollars of our total donation pool. That's
just ordinary people who want to help, or who dream
of going to Mars themselves one day, but don't want
to be first.

The primary requirement after that is to submit to,
basically, eight weeks of house arrest with a bunch of
sensors strapped to your head and chest. We *do* want
to eliminate people with heart conditions, or who take
poorly to captivity, and we want to encourage people
who stay fit and active during that confinement. Also,
every applicant has to specify which of twenty-five
different job descriptions they're applying for, so in
that sense, yes, people do need to convince their
sponsors they can do that particular job. But to the
extent there's any enforcement there, it's the sponsors
themselves who are doing it. I mean, we have exactly
four pilot slots, exactly two of which have to be filled

by women, so if you're going for one of those slots, you'll need to stand out in the crowd. Actually, pilot is a bad example, because that's our single smallest applicant pool, and two of the slots have been very decisively claimed by NASA. A better example is janitorial, which can be done by literally anyone. You don't need to be anything special to fill that job, and so, ironically, it winds up being our most competitive category. The male janitorial slot is currently bidding at four billion U.S. dollars, and looks to go higher if Oliver Wang sells his company to regain front position.

GLASS: Strange to think a billionaire would give it all up to push a broom.

BESEMAN: On Mars. Again, if you add that word in there, it makes a lot more sense. Oliver's a very driven person, and on Mars he can leave a mark on history that he never could on Earth. He may start out pushing a broom, but who knows what that's going to look like five or ten or twenty years from now? Who knows how that society, and the people in it, are going to evolve?

GLASS: Are you rooting for him, then?

BESEMAN: I can't play favorites, Howard. You know that.

GLASS: All right, well, I hope your friendship can survive whatever happens. Now, let's talk about some rumors that have been swirling around you lately.

BESEMAN: [Laughs] It's not true that I'm planning to crown myself King of Mars. In fact, the only government on planet will consist of a five-person steering committee, elected annually, and while I do plan on running for that, and so does Carol, it's up to the colony whether they want either one of us, much less both at once.

GLASS: You've sunk more than a trillion dollars of your own money into making this dream come true, and it's hard to imagine anyone with a firmer grip on the issues your colony will face. Surely the voters will appreciate that they wouldn't be there at all without you.

BESEMAN: [Laughs] Thanks. We'll see.

GLASS: Of course, you'll still be CEO of Enterprise City, the company in sole control of supply lines from Earth, and crew transit back and forth between Mars and cislunar space. So whether the colonists elect you or not, you'll still be in a very powerful position.

BESEMAN: Is that a question? It's true, I'm going to continue to run the day-to-day operations of Enterprise City as my primary job. If anything, that makes me *less* involved in the day-to-day operation of the colony. But I'll have the ultimate skin in the game, which is to say, my own skin, and that of my wife. We have the same vested interest as everyone else, in those supply lines running smoothly. But people in the township will also be counting on life support to function, every minute of every day. And food production, and even janitorial services. In a space colony, every person is critical to every other person. That's why the real magic is in the interpersonal relationships we're forming right now, even before we get there.

GLASS: Okay, but isn't that at odds with selling berths to the highest bidder?

BESEMAN: Not at all. Our process has the happy side effect of selecting for only the most determined and qualified people. There aren't going to be any free riders at Antilympus Township, I can promise you that. We all know that about each other, and it's an excellent starting point for any type of personal relationship. So no, not at odds.

GLASS: Talk to me about that name, Antilympus. You came up with that yourself, right? That's not any sort of astronomical designation.

BESEMAN: That's correct, yes, although it was actually Carol who came up with it. There's a thing called "areoid," which is the equipotential surface in the Goddard Mars Gravity Model. Areoid is the Martian equivalent of sea level; it's how we measure altitude. So, Hellas Basin, also known as Hellas Impact Crater, is the lowest-lying ground on Mars, an average of seven kilometers below areoid. So, a fairly deep depression in the surface, right? And by *miraculous* coincidence, it's roughly antipodal to the Tharsis Bulge, which is the region that's highest on Mars, at about six kilometers *above* the areoid. That is, they're on opposite sides of the sphere. The thinking is that the asteroid impact that formed Hellas also formed Tharsis, by literally directly pushing a cylindrical plug of matter several kilometers along its long axis. We're talking about a plug of matter extending all the way through the planet, just pushed, like that. Now, the highest point on Mars is the summit of Olympus Mons, and our little crater, Antilympus, isn't *literally* antipodal to that. It's actually about eighteen degrees off, but we figure, hey, eighteen out of three hundred and sixty, that's close enough. We're at the very lowest point on Mars, *nearly* opposite to the very highest.

GLASS: And when you say *we* . . .

BESEMAN: The robots building the township, yes. We like to see through their eyes, and we often talk about it as though we're actually there with them. It's their township now, but not for very much longer. We like that word, township, by the way. Like a spaceship, fully enclosed and self-sufficient, except it's on the ground and it's a permanent home to hundreds of people. Eventually hundreds. So it's a town, ship.

GLASS: And how are the robots doing? How is that very important part of the project coming along?

BESEMAN: [Laughs] Well, let's just say it's not the limiting factor in our timeline. Landing hab modules and cargo pods is a lot easier than transporting a hundred living people. The H.S.F. *Concordia* is a spaceship like no one has ever built, with crew space and stores sufficient to support ten people for twelve months, plus ninety sleepers in live cargo, plus a hundred kilograms of personal effects for each person, and certain other supplies to help the township through its first Martian year. There's already food and seed and a certain amount of water in place at Antilympus; that's easy. *Concordia* is transporting more difficult cargo like live plant cuttings, emergency medicines, emergency oxygen, stuff like that. So it's a lot of delicate machinery, packed on top of the world's first self-refueling planetary lander and return vehicle. And all of that is packed on top of a giant, reusable chemical rocket the size of a skyscraper. The H.S.F. stands for high-speed ferry, but it's basically a hospital ship strapped to a fuel tanker strapped to a heavy-lift booster. People think building a base is the hard part, but nothing could be further from the truth. Building the ship to get us there is much harder.

GLASS: Good to know. We'll follow up on that in a future show. However, right now most of our viewer questions center around what happens when you all get there. Tell me about this crater you're going to spend the rest of your lives in.

BESEMAN: Whoa, probably not our whole lives in one crater, Howard. If we're successful, there will be other settlements, and regular commerce between them. But okay, imagine a valley twenty-eight kilometers across, ringed by mountains averaging about nine hundred meters in height above the valley floor. Looks a lot like the area around Phoenix or Mexico City, except it's an impact crater, not a caldera or a dry lake bed, which means the center of it is raised a bit, in a ring-shaped mesa that erosion forces have flattened over time. It's on that mesa that the township rests. If you're interested, you can download the view into your glasses and see for yourself. There's a static-view camera slowly rotating on the east side of the township, and for a small subscription fee you can also see directly through the eyes of most of the robots on site. Those feeds are very popular; we've got about a hundred thousand subscribers, more than half of whom view for an hour or more every day.

GLASS: It sounds breathtaking, if you'll forgive the pun,

but of course Mars is a big planet. Why that spot in particular?

BESEMAN: Well, it simply has the most Earthlike conditions. With an atmospheric pressure of thirteen millibars, it's still the equivalent of Earth's stratosphere, about twice the height of Mount Everest, but that's quite substantial by Martian standards. It means we get wind and clouds and frost and even occasional snowfall, from a sky that's sometimes actually blue, especially around sunrise and sunset. It's also warmer than Earth's stratosphere— enough so that on the hottest summer afternoons, we actually expect the valley floor to be muddy. Muddy! We're thirty-five degrees south of the equator, about the same latitude as Cape Town or Sydney, which means good sunlight and nice, long days. That's why we're there. And of course unlike the Moon, we can pull breathing gases and even water vapor directly from the atmosphere. Thin as it is, it's still enough to support human needs.

GLASS: From the safety of a pressurized dome.

BESEMAN: [Laughs] That dome gets a lot of attention! As you know, most of the township doesn't look like that; it's either buried or opaque, with the kind of small, rounded windows you typically find in spacecraft. We've all seen them: specially adapted modules from Harvest Moon and Renz Ventures, with bits and pieces from Lockheed Martin and General Spacesuit. But there are a few spacious, highly transparent common areas, like that dome, that were scratch-built by Enterprise City, on Earth, and shipped in flat-pack kits using some of the same techniques we used to construct the Marriott Stars. We feel these features are very important psychologically, but they do force some design compromises. To minimize the risk of explosive decompression in these areas, we'll be running the interior of the entire township at an atmospheric pressure of just three hundred millibars. That's fifty percent oxygen and fifty percent nitro-argon-CO_2 mix, which is a proven recipe for good lung tissue hydration at these low pressures. Now, that's some pretty thin air! It's breathable, but it takes acclimation, which we'll get during the four-month transit from Earth. But it lets us have our big, clear, geodesic dome.

GLASS: This has been fascinating, Dan, but we're almost out of time. Until we have you back, is there anything else you'd like to say to our viewers?

BESEMAN: Just that we still need your pledges. Please, seriously, log on and review the candidate bios. Find someone you really like, and sponsor them. Columbus crossed the Atlantic on Queen Isabella's hocked jewelry, and it changed the world forever. Now an even bigger change is coming, and you, personally, can play the part of Her Majesty, and shape the future you personally want to see. So I urge you not to miss out on the opportunity.

GLASS: Right! Okay, thanks for joining us again here on *Mars Today*.

BESEMAN: It really is my pleasure, Howard. Thanks for having me.

1.7
19 April

✦

L.S.F. *Dandelion*
En Route to Earth-Sun
Lagrange Point 1
Cislunar Space

The times when Alice and Derek were both awake were necessarily brief, but she *craved* them more and more as the journey wore on. "Tell me about your childhood," she would say. "Did you go to college? Have you ever been married?"

His answers: Normal, yes, and no. When he was trying to wake up or trying to wake her up, he had a set schedule of things to get through, and was not much in the mood for chitchat. It was only during the times when *he* was putting *her* into hibernation, that he seemed to want to talk at all, and of course at those times she was self-conscious about her state of undress, and his hands close to her body, strapping her to the wall. And of course the procedure itself made her nervous, because what if she never woke up? But always, before she knew it, she was drugged and slurring and gone. So meaningful conversation never really quite came together for them until three days before the end of the trip, when he woke her ahead of schedule.

"Get up," he said, holding one of her eyelids open.

"Nnngh!" she protested, trying to twist away from him and feeling her wrists and ankles come up against their Velcro restraints. She was cold, and groggy, and absolutely hated this part.

"Come on, get up, you're going to miss it."

"Nnngh," she replied.

He did something to one of her hibernation controls, and she began to feel warmer, and more awake.

"Are you up?"

"Ugh. Yeah, I guess." She took slow stock of herself and then said, "I have to use the, you know. I have to do stuff."

"Okay, yeah. Meet me in the cockpit. You've got about fifteen minutes."

When she finally got dressed and opened up the cockpit hatches with nearly numb fingers, she sipped from a squeeze bulb of coffee and settled into her copilot's chair.

"What?" she demanded.

"Look."

He was pointing out the right-side cockpit window, at one of the enormous rearview mirrors that projected out from the sides of *Dandelion*'s hull. He was pointing at the reflection of the Sun.

"What?" she demanded again.

"Watch."

She squinted against the glare. The cockpit windows

were dialed so dark she could barely see the nose of the ship or the outlines of the mirrors, and yet the Sun was still too bright to stare at.

But.

"What's happening?" she asked. The Sun was getting brighter along one edge somehow. Or dimmer in the center?

"It's the Shade," he told her. "It's big enough to cover the Sun, now, and we're moving into eclipse position."

Ah! She could see it now: the Shade barely bigger than the Sun itself. The Sun a crescent peeking out from behind it. And yet, it wasn't like watching a solar eclipse from Earth. Alice had seen two of these in her life, and they looked different, because the Moon was *opaque*, whereas the ESL1 Shade wasn't. Not completely; the light coming through it was not nearly as bright as the light leaking around it, but still it was much brighter than empty space. It was very clear that she was looking at something artificial.

"I thought you'd want to see this," Derek said.

"Yeah," she agreed, taking her eyes away from the glare for a moment. She looked at him, watching the Sun through his outstretched hand, a look of wonder on his face. She realized all at once that this tough guy really loved his job, that the grungy boring realities of it had not soured him on the wonder. Huh. When she looked back at the Sun again, she thought perhaps the Shade had moved a little, or grown a little, or both.

"We're about five minutes from totality."

"Okay."

She glanced at the instrument panel, and felt a shudder

of something like superstitious dread, because they were still *three days out*. The Shade was 24,745 kilometers away! The whole of planet Earth could easily fit between *Dandelion* and the Shade, with plenty of room to spare. *Two* Earths could almost fit in between! It was a large distance, and yet, the Shade was already more than big enough to cover the Sun.

"It's the size of Colorado," she said, quoting something she'd read in one of the briefings, or something President Tompkins had told her, or maybe one of the space marines at the Marriott Stars. "It could cover half the island of Britain."

"Five years ago, it was the size of Connecticut."

"Jesus. How did it get that big, that fast? Seriously! How is that even possible?"

Still looking out through his hand, he said, "You have to remember, it's thinner than a sheet of paper. The whole thing weighs less than an aircraft carrier."

"Still," she said.

Slowly, slowly, the ESL1 Shade covered the light and warmth. Alice could actually feel the cockpit growing colder. Because yes, even though the Shade as seen from Earth was just a black speck in the middle of the Sun, it was still capable of measurably affecting the planet's climate. From *here*, it was capable of a lot more than that. She tried to picture *Dandelion* moving into a cone of shadow.

"Seriously," she said, "how did they get it that big?"

He considered the question for a moment, not saying anything.

"Hello?" she tried.

"If you want, I can show you. I've got an inspection pod trip scheduled a few days from now, out to the rim and back to look at some damage sites."

"You and me alone, eh?" She tried to sound jocular, but it came out bitchy instead.

"We're alone right now," he reminded her.

Finally, the Sun was down to just a fingernail, and then nothing at all.

And then something odd happened; her eyes adjusted. Although the light of the Sun was now only one percent as bright—like a really dark pair of sunglasses, further filtered through the tinting of the cockpit windows—it was still too bright to look at without squinting.

"Whoa," she said.

"Just watch."

"For what?"

"Look past the edges of the Shade."

The edge of the Shade was barely visible now, a circle slightly bigger than the Sun, a little off-center from it, the edges ever so slightly brighter than the black of space behind them. No stars were visible, of course. Not with all that light and all that tint.

But.

Outside the edges of the Shade, the Sun's corona was faintly visible, like a blue-white crown of thorns. Like a too-dim photograph of a gas stove's burner, if the flames shooting out of it were ropy tendrils of special effects magic. It looked nothing like an Earthly eclipse. It was bigger, fainter, more complicated.

"Whoa," she said again.

And then the Sun flickered! It brightened in some

places, dimmed in others—a ripple of light and darkness passing across its face.

"What was that?" she asked, startled.

"Shade steering," he answered. "The middle third of the Shade—the older part—is just a translucent semiconductor weave, but the outer two thirds are variable transparency, like these windows. Changes in the distribution of light pressure affects the Shade's orientation and position. If you look at a trace of the orbit over time, it wanders all around the Lagrange point, sometimes by thousands of kilometers."

That *almost* made sense to Alice. She knew the Shade "hovered" above the Sun, held up somehow by the pressure of photons striking it. And she knew that it could *controllably* affect the Earth's climate, giving more sunlight to some areas and less to others. That was why the President of the United States had sent her up here.

She knew that, and yet. With the Sun's corona flaring around it, the rippling Shade was like something out of a dream.

"It's beautiful," said Alice, the coldhearted spy.

"Indeed. Where else are you going to see that? You're one of, like, six people who've ever seen this."

When she didn't say anything, he added, "You're welcome."

And suddenly she was angry with him: "Oh, wow, did I forget to show proper gratitude to the gallant flyboy? Give me a break."

He didn't immediately reply to that, so she pressed onward: "You want to take little old me out in an *inspection pod*? Show me the sights? Get me all worked up? Jesus fucking Christ."

And just what the hell was she doing, there? Derek was trying to be nice to her, and doing a pretty good job of it. He hadn't done anything or said anything even remotely out of line, except talk about his dick when the drugs were kicking in. And he was a pretty good-looking dude, all things considered, and Alice had not enjoyed human intimacy for, like, nine months at least. Unless you counted that shy Marriott Stars porter with the pencil mustache, but that had only been hand stuff, and only one time, so yeah, Alice was about due for some male attention.

And doing a really fine job of it.

Derek made a scoffing noise. "Okay, Colonist. Have it your way."

Alice didn't say anything at first, but finally screwed up her courage and her charm and said, "Sorry. I'm out of practice."

"At what? Being super entitled and difficult?"

"Dating."

He looked at her, almost glaring. "Who said anything about dating?"

She thought about that for a moment, and answered, "You won't be my superior officer. After we dock, I don't report to you."

"Yeah, so? That means we're dating?"

She sighed, tucking loose hairs back behind her ear. They drifted immediately back in front of her face again.

"Look, it's not you. You're a good guy. I'm just really bad at this."

"At what?"

She sighed again. Sighed a third time. Tucked her hair behind her ear again. "You know, stuff. Relationship stuff."

He scoffed again. "Oh, so now we're in a relationship?"

His voice and expression were so stern, so humorless, so thoroughly out of character that she suddenly realized he was fucking with her. He was typical flyboy after all; he just *knew* he was catnip to women, just knew she wanted to be with him (because why wouldn't she?), just knew that all he had to do was sit back and wait for her to pounce. And in the meantime, poke fun at her. And he was right, goddammit.

"Oh," she said. "You're *such* an asshole."

And then they were both laughing.

And then somehow they were kissing, and fussing with each other's coverall zippers in the weird light of the Esley Shade.

And then they were naked, in a drifting cloud of socks and shoes and coveralls and space underwear, ever so slowly falling aftward in the ten-thousandth-of-a-gee acceleration of this low-speed ferry, and fuck the regulations anyway, if there even *were* regulations, because who exactly was going to find out?

Afterward, Alice felt a little embarrassed, as she generally tended to in situations like this. So many situations like this! It was just like her, to sleep with a coworker she then had to work with.

Derek seemed a bit edgy as well, though also amused and refreshed and a tad smug, for having bagged a tough customer like Alice. Well fine. He was better with his hands than a lot of smug flyboys, that was for sure.

As they smoothed their clothes and hair back into place, Derek said, "I'm glad you got to see the eclipse."

"That's not all I got to see."

"Right. Yeah, well, for better or worse you're going to have to go back into hibernation. We're only three days out, but we really haven't got the resources for it. If you look, the oxygen reserves are already declining."

"Convenient," she said, half teasing and half . . . well, embarrassed. Uncertain where she stood, or where she wanted to. She could see the oxygen gauge as well as he could; the atmospheric level was totally normal, and for all their exertions the tank reserve had declined by less than one percent. She technically *could* stay awake with him for the next three days and use up only maybe a third of their reserve, leaving more than enough margin to wake up the colonists during final approach. But at best that would be bad form, and at worst it could jeopardize lives, if any kind of off-nominal situation occurred. Whereas if she were safely tucked away in bear hibernation, the recycling system would be able to keep up, and they'd hang onto a *hundred* percent of their oxygen reserve.

And also avoid a lot of awkwardness.

So yeah, she let him Velcro her to the wall and pump her full of drugs.

"You *do* have a normal-sized dick," she told him as she started to drift off. "At least normal sized. Do I have good birthing hips?"

"What?"

"Good birthing hips. Good *birthing* hips."

And then, with seemingly no delay whatsoever, he was propping one of her eyes open and patting her a little too firmly on the cheek.

"Wake up."

"Nnngh."

"Not kidding. I need you to get up."

"Nnngh! I haven't even gone to sleep yet!"

"We're on approach, Alice. I need you to wake up the colonists."

"Oh. Oh. That was weird."

"Yeah, sometimes it's like that. Now come on, I need you."

When the formalities and grumbling were out of the way, she woke and peed and dressed and entered the bridge by the zero-gravity equivalent of stumbling blearily. Yes, she had work to do back in the passenger cabin, but first she wanted a quick look outside.

"That's it?" she said.

"Uh-huh," he answered without looking.

The gauges showed them still ninety-nine kilometers and 4.3 hours out from the station, but the Shade was the size of a dinner platter sitting right in front of you at the dinner table. And where it had seemed way too big from two Earths away, now it seemed too small. Was this what Colorado or half of Britain would look like, if you were a hundred kilometers above?

Near the center she could now make out a darker spot, through which no sunlight was visible at all, with a bright spot hovering in front of it.

"What am I looking at?"

Derek pointed. "*That's* the Hub section of the Shade,

which is totally opaque. *That's* the station, which is covered in lights. It's too small to actually see from here, but that's where it is."

"Huh."

"Look, you can come back here and gawk when the hibernation deck is taken care of, but those colonists need to be ready to leave the ship when we dock, or we're gonna get charged for their oxygen. I shit you not."

"Why?"

"Don't know. Take it up with accounting. Now . . ."

"Okay, okay."

Barely awake herself, Alice went back into the passenger cabin and studied the vital signs of all six women: B.Powell, P.Figueroa, J.Schmidt, M.Aag, N.Rostov, and S.Batra. All of them, regardless of their natural coloration, all had gray-blue skin and cyanotic lips and core temperatures of eight degrees Celsius—the exact air temperature of the passenger cabin itself, like the air inside a deep cave. They could easily be mistaken for corpses, if not for the LED monitors sitting next to their heads, showing nonzero blood pressure, and heart rates between five and ten beats per minute. That was a *lot* less than Derek's bear hibernation at roughly twenty bpm. When Derek was back here he looked basically alive, though perhaps comatose. Waking him up was a fifteen-minute procedure, and he was conscious for the last minute or two of that.

This was different. Alice hoped things were going to go smoothly here, but the medical professional in her disapproved of the cavalier way this very deep hibernation was being used. She knew it was used for cancer patients and heart patients, and she also knew that about five percent of the time, people really, actually didn't, wake up. That probably didn't apply to healthy volunteers, but still, "not lethal" was hardly the best starting point for something like this. And yet, these women had all agreed to it, along with pregnancy and other invasions, as part of the cost of getting to space. Hell, they probably would have agreed to it even if they *knew for a fact* that they had a five percent chance of not waking up.

With relief, Alice took the first step toward waking them all up, which was to turn the cabin temperature up to twenty-two degrees Celsius. Derek had pumped Alice full of thermoregulation agents, so her core temperature and even her extremities were theoretically fine, but she was sick of the cold tomb air back here. Sick of cold air against her skin! Of course, while it would only take a couple of minutes to warm up the air, the actual surfaces of the room would take longer, and the colonists' bodies, left to their own devices, could take many hours to reach even room temperature. They needed several different kinds of jump start, which Alice presently began.

She started by turning off the drip feed of hibernation drugs and replacing it with the revival mix. By itself that would also take hours to have any effect, since their bloodstreams were all moving so slowly. So next she turned on the bed heaters and cuff heaters, and started massaging the patients' legs—beginning with Maag and working her way through all of the others. Then she turned on the brain stimulators, located in the forehead strap of each woman, that would instruct their brains to instruct their bodies to warm up and come back to life.

Then she waited around for a little while, watching the vital signs creep up until the women began to look alive. Maag got there first; with her skin pinking up, she began to snore. From there, things started to happen more quickly, as the drugs were able to enter her system and work their own obscure magics. Alice removed and stowed everyone's goggles and hearing protectors, and then she shone a penlight into one of Maag's eyes, and noted a normal dilation response.

"Quit it," Maag said.

Then, a few seconds later, "Where am I?"

Maag's eyes were still closed, and she looked about ninety percent asleep, and still felt cold to the touch.

"You're coming out of hibernation," Alice told her, though she suspected Maag could neither process nor retain that information.

She busied herself with the other patients for a while, until Maag said, more clearly, "Am I falling?"

"You're in zero gravity, onboard the L.S.F. *Dandelion*."

"Am I tied up?"

"You're restrained to a surface, yes."

"I'm cold."

"Uh-huh. We need to warm your body up slowly, so we don't cause complications."

Maag was silent for several minutes, and then asked, "Where am I?" Still without opening her eyes.

"I'll come back in a few minutes," Alice said.

Pelu Figueroa had begun showing signs of life, and so had Bethy Powell, and Alice needed to adjust their feeds and turn off their neural stimulators, and meanwhile Maag had opened her eyes and was taking in the scene around her, trying to piece together what the hell was going on.

"Alice? Alice Kyeong?"

"That's right."

"Holy crap, am I thirsty."

Soon the place was erupting like a nursery school: "I'm cold!" "I'm thirsty!" "I need to pee!" Alice had her hands full dealing with all of it, coaching these confused human beings through the stages of the awakening process.

"Is there something around my head?"

"Yes, there's a strap. Do you want it loosened?"

"I want it off!"

The whole thing was similar enough to Maroon Beret field medicine to seem familiar, and yet different enough to feel like a real shit show for which she was not trained or prepared. It was no wonder Derek had wanted a copilot to handle this for him.

Alice couldn't release them all at once from their restraints, and Maag had already freed an arm and was using it to free her other arm, and was at risk of damaging equipment in her not-quite-there mental state, so Alice announced that she was going to release the women one at a time, and they would each need to wait their turn. That seemed to work, at least for the moment, and so she helped Maag free herself, and then she did the same for Pelu Figueroa.

"I need to change," Pelu said. "I feel like I've been in this underwear for way too long."

Alice knew the feeling. There were no laundry facilities onboard the ship, so during her awake times she had quickly used up both sets of her own space underwear, along with both pairs of socks, and she was forced to wash them in the lavatory sink and dry them on an air vent. The results were imperfect at best. Still, it was better than sleeping in a ditch, and she was running out of patience, so she told Pelu, "Wait until we get to Esley. Then you can shower *and* change."

Alice didn't know if that was true or not, but she could hope. At the Marriott Stars, each guest cabin had included a shower—a clear tube you closed over yourself, with a jet of water at one end and a sucking drain at the other. It had a filter somewhere inside it, so it kept recycling the same fifteen liters of water over and over again ("like a dishwasher," the pencil-mustached porter had said), and after about six minutes you pretty much stopped feeling like you were getting any cleaner. But it was still pretty good. Nothing like that had been available at Transit Point Station (she supposed they used washcloths instead), but ESL1 was a much bigger facility. Bigger even than the Marriott Stars.

While Pelu and Maag went back to use the bathroom, Alice freed Bethy and Jeanette, and then Nonna and Saira. Then she heated up six bulbs of coffee, told everyone to stay put in the passenger cabin and not screw around, and then finally, finally opened the hatches to the cockpit, went up into it, and closed the hatches behind her.

"Jesus," she said.

"Always a good time," Derek agreed.

More than three hours had passed, and in the *Dandelion*'s oversized rearview mirrors, Alice could no longer see the Sun or the edges of the Shade. Only the

blankness of the opaque Hub, and a complicated mess of
structures that Alice recognized as ESL1 Shade Station.
Like an oil refinery in a trailer park, covered in white and
orange floodlights, it hovered an indeterminate distance
from the Hub, and really quite close to *Dandelion*. The
navigation panel said the station was 1.5 kilometers away.

"Are we there?" Alice asked.

"Not quite. Another half hour."

"We could use the ACS thrusters," Alice suggested.
ACS stood for attitude control system, and referred to the
assortment of small chemical rocket nozzles distributed
around the ship's hull, to permit it to change orientations
in a controlled manner, or to make small adjustments in
speed or orbit. In theory, there should be more than
enough oomph in there to close this gap in a few minutes.

"Nah," Derek said. "I haven't touched ACS the whole
trip. Xenon does *not* come out of my pay, so I'm going to
use it all up."

Alice could grasp what he meant; there were four
separate ion thrusters on the aft of the ship, and by
adjusting the thrust levels between them, Derek was
slowly, carefully steering the ship. By manual control,
apparently.

"All the way into dock?" Alice asked. As a rule, she tried
not to be impressed by fancy flying, but it had never
occurred to her such a thing was even possible.

"Yes," he said, "all the way into dock."

He paused for a thoughtful moment and, without
taking his eyes off the radar display, added, "This ship is
probably going to be dismantled soon. These ion tugs
made sense when everything had to be lifted off the

Earth. A lot of sense. But there's no xenon in space, and with Clementine Cislunar selling rocket fuel . . . Hell, they're *delivering* rocket fuel to specific orbits, on demand. So yeah, it's only a matter of time till Iggy wants new ships."

"But you'll fly those, too, right? Chemical rockets, zoom zoom?"

"Yeah. I will. It won't be the same."

And that seemed to be all he wanted to say.

3.3
20 April

⟡

St. Joseph of Cupertino Monastery
Shoemaker-Faustini Plateau
Lunar South Polar Mineral Territories

My Dearest Father Bertram,

You have asked for an account of the arrival of our eight new brothers. "New" of course in the sense that they haven't previously dwelt with Saint Joseph upon the Lunar pole, not that we do not know them, for we lived together a year and more as you know upon the lava flows of Craters of the Moon National Monument, in Idaho, to prove our minds wouldn't snap under the strain of this, our lifelong exile from the boredoms of a planet already 3.5 billion years inhabited.

I miss you, Bert. I wish you were here to experience these things, requiring no narration save your own internal monologue. But as that's not the case, I relent and narrate for you.

On this particular morning there was some

uncertainty about the arrival time of the brothers' lander, for there is now enough traffic around Luna that Lunar Orbit Traffic Control (operated by Harvest Moon Industries) can call an "orbit hold" and make you go 'round again afore you burn your deorbit retros. Also there was work in need of doing, and since the buddy system requires we not go outside alone, Brother Puke was forced to join me, though he had little love for the task, and business of his own to attend indoors, and called me a pain in his neck, which was true and generous enough. For my own generosity, I declined to point out that from this day forward he'd be able to fob such duties off on someone junior, still excited to be here in any capacity.

Outdoors we went, to retrieve the stuff of life: water from a Harvest Moon autonomous truck, and methane and nitrogen from an Orlov Petrochemical autonomous lander. This first was a little clown car of a vehicle, barely larger than a bicycle trailer, loaded with two barrels of melted icy treasure hauled over from one of the man-tended but not full-time-staffed mining outposts. Call them moonbases Curly and Moe, in craters Shoemaker and Faustini, respective. When I think back on how I used to let the water tap run back on Earth (I nearly said "back home," but we both know that ain't correct), I shudder to think how much these two barrels cost His Holy, for all of that vast mineral wealth—worth more than gold and diamonds wrapped in cocaine—flows through these hands of mine and offends the oath of poverty I took with great conviction. To drain the barrels, I attached a pair of hoses from the outer wall of the main service hab: one to pump the water out, and one to replace it with pure oxygen ballast so the transfer didn't take forever and all the energy in the universe. Ironic that this *other* stuff of life should be the cheapest ballast we have for sacrifice, but water is not a compressible or expandable material, and must be displaced by something, and as we have noted, the Moon is forty-five percent oxygen by weight. It's the *hydrogen* that's precious here, of which water is only eleven percent, but this complaint you've heard before. Could I have used a sealed screw pump I'd've drained these tanks easily with no ballast at all, but that's a complaint Harvest Moon has also heard before. Apparently, these centrifugal peristaltic pumps are far easier to build and maintain in the Lunar environment, and do not vacuum-weld themselves into inoperative junk. And so, yes, I pumped oxygen into the barrels to replace the water, and let my offended oath go hang itself, for such is life.

It took near thirty minutes to drain the first tank, and another thirty to drain the second, and when that was done I hit the THANK YOU button and sent the little clown car back to its robotic masters at Curly or Moe. With Purcell's assistance I stowed the hoses and then set about the morning's second task.

Orlov Petro's methane comes with its own Lunar lander, a crab-shaped contraption roughly the size of a lumber cart, carrying three tanks of compressed methane—our source of both hydrogen and carbon for the CHON chow fabricator, the chemical synthesizer, and the drug printer—and three of nitrogen, which is not only raw material but also a preferred component of good breathing air, as an anitrogenic atmosphere raises the risk of fire and explosion and is really not great for the human body on a long-term basis; and also my nitrogen-fixing plants would starve, alas, for nitrogen is also fiercely costsome, being nearly ten times the price of the methane.

Brother Puke (or Purcell the Porpoise, if you prefer, for he sometimes laughs like one) helped me unwrench and unload the tanks from their secure holders and carry them to the service hab. We disconnected the corresponding empties and replaced them one by one with Orlov's fulls, carrying the empties back and securing them on the lander. For a nominal fee we could actually keep the lander and strip it for parts, or melt it down as raw material, for it's made of asteroid stuff and actually less valuable per kilogram than the consumables it transports. However, His Holy has purchased no such stripping or melting equipment for Saint Joe, nor any manufacturing of significance. Nor does he intend to, so far as I know, and so these landers would simply pile up as landfill. Instead, the crab retains a quantity of methane and oxygen sufficient to blast it back to Clementine. I set the timer for this (a good old-fashioned spring-loaded dial, like on a dishwasher when we were young), so that we would not be charged for keeping it, and so it would blast off at Vatican Midnight when we were all asleep.

I thought about scoring some marks on it with a screwdriver, for it has pondered me more than once whether *this same lander* cycles back and forth on our behalf, or whether there's a whole fleet of which we get a random pick each time. Harvest Moon buys this same methane and nitrogen from Orlov Petro, as does the Chinese base on Luna's opposite pole, so one does have to wonder how the logistics logic out. Transit Point Station and Marriott Stars are both Orlov customers as well, although one suspects they have no need of landers per se, and are thus likely on a different delivery route.

(Iggy the Rake makes his own gases, by the way, though not to sell, and Orlov buys his spaceship components and habitat modules from Renz Ventures. Danny Beseman buys from both and sells to no one, except dreams to the dreamers, which don't come cheap, although one supposes the exact same charge could be leveled against His Holy. The only difference, my love, is whether one dreams of dwelling in Heaven or upon the face of Mars, which is a kind of Heaven for unbelievers too savvy to upload to the Immortal Cloud—a scam which stirs me to rare anger, I'm afraid. At any rate, this monk would love sometime to chart what ends up where, and from what starting point, that all these trillions should so enrich just four men born of Earth.)

As luck would have it, our work was completed timely, for not two minutes after I set the launch dial there came upon the radio a voice, calling out, "Sierra Juliet Zero Niner on approach."

To which my correct reply is always, "Roger that, Zero Niner. Sierra Juliet Ground Actual requesting ETA."

The pilot, a Harvest Moon functionary, answered, "Sierra Juliet Zero Niner estimating touchdown in five minutes, twelve seconds."

Sierra Juliet is pilotspeak for Saint Joseph of Cupertino Monastery, as opposed to Sierra Lima, which abbrevs yon Shackleton Lunar Industrial Station, whose warnings we also get. Zero Niner meant this was the ninth inbound crewed flight to land this site, and also that the pilot was *cool*, as are they all. That nothing else was said meant that nothing else was expected, for all was nominal and good. More than mere courtesy, these exchanges warn the unwary to clear the drop zone, for a landing jet can kick up silent bullets of Lunar gravel with terrific kinetic energy, to travel sometimes many parabolic miles before impact.

In theory a General Spacesuit Heavy Rebreather is proof against such gravel impacts, but the better part of valor is to retreat somewhere safer, which in our case was the airlock. Unpressurized but with the outer hatch closed, it was fortress enough for this or any purpose, for in add to radiation it's designed to withstand the impact of stone soccer balls at interplanetary velocity.

The airlock offers three portholes facing three different directions, and without knowing precise where the lander would touch down, I chose one at random to crowd in front of, and Puke chose another, and we waited the couple of minutes until the lander appeared.

"Sierra Juliet Zero Niner on final," said the pilot. "Thirty seconds to touchdown."

"Sierra Juliet Ground Actual, roger that," I answered.

And there he was, dropping from the black sky like a wiffleball on a tongue of gray-white gas and then blasting, at what seemed the last possible moment, a sterner toot from his arse that did indeed kick up rocks. We couldn't hear them pinging off the hull of the airlock, but I felt the impact vibrations of several through my hands and feet. And then the lander was down, and Purcell ne'er did get a look.

"Sierra Juliet Zero Niner is down. Powering down. Sierra Juliet Zero Niner, engine power at zero," said the pilot.

"Roger that. We're coming outside," said I.

Out we went, Brother Purse and I, to greet our long lost. The pilot had already gotten up and thrown open his door, and came down the ladder first to show the others how it was proper done. I waved to him, and he waved back, then got out of the way of his passenger monks, who began to shuffle one by one down the ladder, bulky in their cladding and each carrying a ballooned-up duffel of personal crap.

"Welcome," I said to them, the rules of radio jargon being looser for feet on the ground than birds in the air. Various answers came back, until the pilot said, "Cut the chatter, people. Brother Michael, I have a schedule to keep, and I need someone to escort me to Shackleton."

"Roger, we can do that," I assured him, though it were exceeding inconvenient. By agreement and purchase, this lander would remain here at the monastery, a second and larger lifeboat for the evacuation of God's servants. In the event of dire emergency, it would allegedly truck nine Brothers back to Transit Point Station, though of course one hopes it stands there eternal, slowly outgassing whilst the monastery prospers. I do sometimes shiver to think this place may still be standing a millennium hence, steeped in long traditions hatched this very year, with ne'er an emergency God's own can't handle on site, for why else plant Saint Joseph's flag here at all?

It turned out the pilot's name was Eduardo Halladay, and I didn't know him previous, but Harvest Moon also follows the EVA buddy system, so he couldn't simply walk to Moonbase Larry on his own recognizance, nor could his escort walk back alone, so it was me and Purcell both who must accompany him, whilst Giancarlo donned a suit unassisted and came outside to help the Brothers in, for they'd been sealed in their General Spacesuits for an hour and more already.

I hugged them each in turn and bade them play Armstrong and Aldrin in the dust awhile, for the airlock holds only three bodies at once, and even when Geo got outside, it'd be four cycles in and four

cycles out to get all eight of them inside, which is
two hours of standing around.

I regretted the risk to Geo, compressing and
decompressing repeatedly like that, but he was the
only one who knew the mechanisms and procedures
of ingress; these newborns couldn't do it without
him. I regretted also the waste of water, for Geo
would be showering dust off his suit with the others
and then stepping back outside still damp, and the
sublimating vacuum would suck the moisture away
to infinity.

You have asked where water goes, in what ought to
be a closed system, and this is one answer, though not
a primary one. The habitat modules themselves are
thirsty, for truly anhydrous materials are unnatural,
and anything moon-made will drink a bit before it
settles down. We lose near half a barrel every time we
hook a new module up! Too, my slow winning of loam
and vegetation from the sterile Moon puts a lot of
water into other forms, as biological processes convert
it into lipids and hydrocarbons and acids amino, and
other assorted biomass. And yes, our suits and
modules leak. The grinding dust works into every seal
and joint, leaving gaps, leaving scratches through
which the odd molecule can worm its way out, and
though each Harvest Moon dwelling is guaranteed for
fifty years unmaintained, good practice calls for an
overhaul every ten. Even for a base as young as ours,
the loss of consumables is not only measurable, but
measurably increasing month by month. If we're to
stand a thousand years, we may *need* to build spare

parts ourselves, or rely on the equal longevity of Sir Larry's corporation.

Anon, we brought Pilot Eddie over to his peoples, and returned to find two monks still outdoors. The airlock, as I said, will only take three at a time, and so even relieving Brother Geo of airlock duty, still we needed fifteen minutes for Purcell and Duppler to go inside, and another fifteen for me and Ovid.

Outdoors alone with Ovid, I could sense nervous energy spilling off him in waves, and it made me consider how jaded I myself had already become to the novelty of this world. One hundred ten days in situ and already finding it so routine that I could forget, if only momentarily, that Brother Eggs, despite an hour and more on the surface already, was laying eyes upon all of this for the first time. I watched him play with his shadow, making a sort of puppet show of it. In another few hours the sun would begin slipping behind one of the low hills and cast the Valley of Saint Joe into twilight, but for now it was high enough to cast the ground into a bar code of hab shadows and the bright streaks betwixt 'em.

"You'll get used to all this," I told him.

"I hope not," he replied, but with no great emphasis or conviction. He sounded simultaneously exhausted and juiced, and that I could fully understand, for I'd felt it all myself these seven fortnights ago.

Monastic tradition discourages prattle, and radio safety rules discourage chatter, so Saint Joe's is a quieter place than even you might suppose, Bert-o, and so Ovid and I stood there in mostly silence for most of the next fifteen minutes, until finally the diode lamp outside the airlock switched from red to green, indicating the chamber within was fully evacuated, and one could safely open the outer hatch without the pressure of the air times the area of the hatch creating a force sufficient to tear one's arm out of its socket.

(One can imagine all sorts of safety interlocks that would make such an accident impossible, but in the end it's dire practice to introduce anything to a door that might ever keep it from opening when men need it open. There are even explosive bolts to take the thing off its hinges entire, should such be necessary at some point afuture.)

Eggs and I went inside, and closed the hatch behind us and, with gestures and by example, I bade him set down his duffel and sit on the bench.

"Twenty minutes?" he asked. I declined to answer, and bade him again to sit. Standing in Lunar gravity is no great chore, even with a Heavy Rebreather upon one's shoulders, but it is difficult to meditate or pray that way, and I find my de- and recompressions in the airlock not an inconvenience but an enforced peace to be sought and savored. Here's fifteen minutes where no tasks can possibly be performed, Bert, and there's no better time to clear the mind. Best acquaint Eggs with that from the outset.

The airlock has a pressure gauge inside of it, but I found I could gauge for myself the rise in air pressure by the deflation of Ovid's duffel. Airtight so that it might carry an atmosphere to protect whatever personals he'd brought to this new life, it slowly shrank from a tire-hard cylinder to a flaccid shrivel of rubberized fabric, like a life raft bleeding out on a beach. When our time of meditation was done, it seemed scarcely large enough to hold his belt and habit. Had I really brought so little myself, and most of it seed? I felt a pang of homesickness then, for all the things left behind, not only in abandoning Earth, but in the choice of monastic life itself, which we do not choose because it's easy, but rather because it ain't.

It being the time, I opened the inner hatch, stepped through it, beckoned him in behind me, drooping duffel and all. We showered away the dust of Lune, and then wrestled each other out of our bulky outer shells. The space underwear, contaminated through even briefest contact with the exterior of a freshly washed suit, also came off and went into the laundry lock. Finally we exited (or entered) into the station proper, where bustling activity forced us to dodge nude between our Brothers on the way to our cell (or module, if you prefer), for mine was now to be shared with Ovid. We dressed, and then joined the others in the module jokingly referred to as the Great Hall, which serves as both refectory and chapel, with benches enough to seat eleven Brothers, albeit barely, and upon the wall a cedar Jesus crucified and varnished with antiquity, from a vault of Vatican treasures to feel us wealthy at least in prayer. And beneath Jesus a camera and video screen which you have never seen, for these are how *we* see *you* when it's time for Mass, and oh how I wish that were not the only time or way to hear your voice. That and confessional, aye, about which more another time.

(When we've a full complement of twenty-five, Harvest Moon will have us equipped with a double-wide Barrel Vault that will serve as an actual Great Hall, for a thousand years God willing, and this room will be relegated to classroom space for those we educate, but that day is another two hundred in our future, which seems an eternity and then some.)

The meal, which had been printing on the CHON synthesizer all day long, from a program keyed in by Giancarlo that morning, and for which I'd been harvesting and lightly pickling vegetables all week, was bland and dull by what I hope will become the culinary standards herein, but sufficient to welcome our Terrestrial kin and to give them surcease and succor afore evening prayers and first sleep in what is, I can see through their eyes, quite spare and tight surround even by monastic standards.

But thus we learn not only to subsist and endure, but to build lives for ourselves whose example may, in God's name and Jesus' image, serve to inspire every soul who comes here afterward, to dwell upon the Moon.

I am, very yours and very truly,
Brother Michael Jablonski de la Lune

1.8
23 April

✧

ESL1 Shade Station
Earth-Sun Lagrange Point 1
Extracislunar Space

After all the expected rigamarole of docking and disembarking and greetings by members of the station crew, Alice found herself in a module that was practically made of windows. Big ones, bigger even than those of the view-at-your-own-risk observation lounge at the Marriott Stars.

In the room were a paunchy Caucasian man with streaks of gray in his beard, and a lanky half-Asian woman with long, red-brown hair, and bright blue eyes that couldn't possibly be natural. She was also paunchy! Correction: pregnant.

"Are you going to be okay here?" asked Derek, hovering by Alice's elbow. It was a vaguely corporate thing to say, having nothing to do with her being okay. Rather, it was a polite way of telling her that he had business elsewhere, and was going to deposit her and run.

"Fine," she said to him without turning. Her eyes were

on the man—Igbal Renz—and on the Earth hovering behind him like a white-and-blue racquetball.

He didn't look regal or wealthy or powerful. He looked like some fattish nerd, vaguely distracted and vaguely dissatisfied. She knew he'd made his money in something called Deep Belief Motion Control Networks, which had made possible all the robot waiters and butlers everyone seemed to be going nuts for these days. Space was something of a second career for him, albeit one he'd been throwing his energy behind for a decade and a half.

"Lot of windows," she said to him by way of greeting. She tended to greet new people brusquely, and this was doubly true if they held any sort of power over her, or thought they did. But the window thing was true, and worth remarking on, since windows in space were potentially very dangerous, and even the Marriott Stars had been cautious about them. It made her feel vulnerable, as if she were standing at the bottom of the deep ocean, in some sort of air-filled Christmas ornament. But really, she'd only said that out loud to buy herself a moment to size up this man, whom fate had decreed was her enemy.

She'd been sizing up ESL1 Shade Station itself through the windows and rearview mirrors of the *Dandelion* for the last several hours, and from the inside for the last several minutes as Derek brought her here. "Esley" was as different from Transit Point Station as TPS was from the Marriott Stars. First of all, almost everyone here was female. Other than Derek Hakkens and Igbal Renz, she'd only seen one dude, versus about fifteen women. (Luckiest dude in the world, he probably thought. Or maybe not; was a man surrounded and outnumbered by women any better off than a woman outnumbered by men?)

Second, only about half the people she'd seen were wearing coveralls. The rest were in a mix of track suits, yoga pants, stretchy posture shirts, sports bras and running shorts, and even just 3D-printed space underwear all by itself. The half-Asian woman beside Renz appeared to be wearing some sort of loose-fitting maternity pantsuit, complete with a floaty white cardigan that seemed about as impractical as humanly possible.

Renz himself, though, was unremarkable. He had on the same blue coveralls as Alice and Derek and all the other new arrivals. Although his beard was partly gray and his hairline was a bit receded, his hair was cut short in a not-quite-buzz cut that, while practical for zero gravity and probably done for him by a barber helmet, didn't particularly suit him. He looked like someone who spent about ten seconds a day worrying about his appearance.

There was something about his eyes, some intensity Alice couldn't quite pin down, but his posture was a lazy zero-gee slump. Not a fetal position, but also not like someone ready to leap up and kill a tiger. His right hand was fidgeting with something, though, a golf ball or something like that, and the deft movements of his fingers made Alice instantly cautious. There was something going on there.

"Windows? Really?" Renz asked her, with a funny mix of annoyance and amusement. His voice was higher and more gravelly than she would have expected. Without warning, he turned and hurled the golf ball at one of the windows, like a major league baseball player launching a fastball. It struck the window with a cracking noise that chilled Alice's blood, then it bounced away and commenced rebounding all over the room.

"Jesus!" Alice said, shielding her face and attempting to duck.

When the motion of the ball had mostly died down, Renz told her, "Thank you for your feedback."

"Jesus *fuck*," Alice elaborated. "What the fuck?"

"These plates are ten thousand layers of microlaminate diamond-sapphire-polycarbonate, manufactured right here on the station."

"From what?" Alice wanted to know.

"From near-Earth asteroids," he said, as though it should be obvious. That throw had tumbled him across the room, but he caught himself easily, never taking his eyes off of her. "It takes a shitload of power, but we've got about one million shitloads to burn. You have any other engineering advice?"

Alice didn't. Goddamn. If Renz's goal had been to jostle her out of her own head and into this room with him, here and now, he had most definitely succeeded.

"Interesting," Renz said, studying Alice. Studying Alice, who'd been trying to study him! "I thought you didn't scare easily. Pam, would you play the video file, please?"

The half-Asian woman—Pam—gestured with one of her hands, and suddenly all of the windows were opaque screens, and all playing the same video stream. It showed sky, cords, a human elbow, and some trashing billows of parachute fabric, and with a shock Alice realized it was the body cam footage from her in-air rescue of Florida Jones. She watched her parachute collapse as he landed on it, watched the two of them tangle in a mass of cloth and cords. Watched her hands cutting cords, tying cords, and pulling open the reserve chute, right at the last possible second. She watched the two of them falling through the trees. Her hand was out of sight when it drew the pistol, but the video clearly showed her aiming and firing and firing again. A human figure dropping in the sunlight-dappled shadows below. A human life ended forever, because of her. In self-preservation, yes, but she felt a stab of guilt about it now, perhaps more than she ever had before. She'd never had to watch this! The video ended, and looped back to the beginning again. The audio was off.

"You fired those shots with a broken hand?" Renz asked her.

"I thought this footage was classified," Alice answered, somewhat indignantly. It seemed, somehow, an invasion of her privacy.

"Freedom of Information Act," Renz said. "Our background checks are thorough, and when I heard about this incident, I had to know. I'm going to be honest with you: we need a *lot* more people like you up here. We've got all the smartyskirts we can handle—PhDs who cry when they break a nail—but nobody with this kind of ice water in their veins. Look at that! Look at you. That's where you break your hand, right there. Snap! See? But you don't even pause. You just assess what needs doing, and you do it. Like that. Like *that*. That's what we need up here. We need cool heads when accidents happen, which they do."

Alice wasn't quite sure how to interpret that. Clearly, Renz had little patience with incompetence, and she could definitely relate; in the Maroon Berets, incompetence of any kind could get a whole platoon killed. The same thing was probably true here as well, so "breaking a nail and crying about it" would definitely be something Alice would have a problem with—if such a thing had ever actually, literally happened. More likely it was metaphor or hyperbole, though, and there was no telling exactly what Renz actually meant. Did he have a problem with women? If so, then why was he talking up Alice's combat skills?

She was still digesting both the praise and the potential misogyny when Renz continued, "I originally wanted you for an astronaut, plain and simple. Lots of EVA duty, outside in a spacesuit. Calm-headed, like that. Hell, I *still* want that, but unfortunately the situation up here has changed. With the naval blockade and the attempt to sneak people onto our station, we're under new kinds of threat, and I think you have skills that apply there, as well. You spent some time with that woman, Dona Obata. What did you think about her?"

"I liked her," Alice answered crisply, as if to a superior officer. "She was polite and helpful."

"Did you suspect her of anything?"

"Not until the computer flagged her file," she said honestly. Always good if you could answer honestly. There was less chance of screwing up that way. "Before that, I never had reason to question her closely."

"And after?"

Alice nodded. "Yeah, I mean, there was something off

about her then. Her . . . cover was blown, I guess you'd say, but she didn't want to admit it. She was struggling in this weird way. I think she might have lost out on a big reward."

"What makes you say that?"

Alice did the zero-gee shrug. "There was just something off—something sleazy—about the way she was reacting. She was *angry*. Would someone on a government salary be angry, if she got caught and had to, you know, abort her mission?"

"Likely not," he agreed. "What do you think she was planning to do?"

"No idea," Alice said—again, honestly. "Or why, or who she was working for. She didn't exactly provide a lot of clues."

Pam asked, "Where did she learn to fly a space shuttle?"

Alice did a double take. "Excuse me?"

"It's gone," Pam said. "We've been trying to keep this quiet, but her shuttle disappeared. Transit Point tracked it for about thirty minutes, until they lost it behind the limb of the Earth. It never came back around."

"Jesus," Alice said. "Did it blow up?"

"No. There was no debris, no reentry plume. Transit Point would have seen those things. That shuttle *navigated out of there*. And it doesn't hold enough fuel to leave Earth orbit, so there are a limited number of places it could have ended up. Like, a really short list."

Alice thought furiously, then spoke: "What about NORAD? Or PCBH in Russia? Or the People's Liberation Air Force? They must have tracked it."

"Presumably," Pam agreed, "but they're not exactly sharing data with us. The shuttle's transponder was also disabled, *is* also disabled, or we'd've picked it up. We've got tracking satellites all over cislunar space. She went totally dark."

"Where did she learn to fly our ship?" Renz demanded, of no one in particular. "How did she even know that was something she'd need to know?"

Alice considered that. "She must've had help. Real-time help."

"What kind?"

"Someone on the other end of a radio."

"What kind of radio?"

Alice thought some more, and finally said, "Ultrawideband entangled. With line of sight it's got a range of, well, from surface of the Earth to a military communication satellite. How far is that?"

"Far enough," Renz confirmed. "And our sensors wouldn't be able to detect it?"

"No way. That's LPD/LPI signal, which stands for, I think, low probability of detection, low probability of intercept. It does have limited bandwidth, though. You can't send, like, video or anything, but it'll carry voices and text. Maybe a small number of low-resolution images."

Alice wasn't quite sure why she was divulging all this, except (a) it wasn't classified, (b) it didn't interfere with the goals of her mission, and (c) she was as perplexed as Igbal and Pam. What the silking fuck was Dona up to? And why? And for whom? It definitely did not suit the goals of Alice's mission to have a wild card like that in the deck.

"How small would this radio be?" Renz wanted to know.

"Oh, it could be pretty small. Size of a TV remote. It could *be* a TV remote."

"She didn't have a TV remote when her belongings were searched in Paramaribo, but your point is taken." Renz sighed. "There's no security staff at Transit Point. *You* threw her in that shuttle, am I right?"

"Me and Malagrite Aagesen, yes, but by then she wasn't resisting."

Renz mulled that over for a couple of seconds. Then: "More about Malagrite in a minute. Right now my problem is that we don't have any security personnel *here*, either. Our population is over thirty people now, and we all work hard and have access to drugs, and with bad actors attempting to interfere with us, it suddenly occurs to me and Pam that we're in a generally bad situation."

Alice successfully held back a snort at the mention of drugs, because really that was one of the main reasons she was here. Bad enough for a trillionaire to control the sunlight, but an *unstable druggie* trillionaire . . . But Renz was getting at something else, so she simply waited, blank-faced, for the punch line.

"I want to form a security team," Renz said, "and I want you to be the head of it."

Alice blinked. "What?"

"You, yes. We can bring up some professionals when conditions permit, but at this particular moment we're not getting anything or any*one* off of the Earth. The U.S. Navy is boarding and reflagging our ships in the Atlantic, and sailing them to Florida for storage. It's goddamn piracy.

At least they're letting the crews go, but, I mean, goddamn, right? Outrageous! It won't be such a problem once we get some factories and a refinery running in Suriname, but even that requires our workers sneaking some critical hardware past the blockade, in tourist luggage and whatnot. The Americans could shut it down anytime, and even if they don't, it'll be a year or more before we're fully operational down there. The other possibility is launching out of Liberia, but that's problematic for all kinds of reasons. Or we could revive our old sea launch platforms, but there's no reason to think the U.S. Navy won't just seize those, too. Point is, for right now we are definitely on our own up here, and we're going to need a sheriff. Quite frankly, Alice—can I call you Alice?"

She nodded once.

"Silk. Call me Igbal. Quite frankly, most of our people have never been in a fistfight, much less fallen out of the sky with guns blazing. We've got a lot of PhD smartyskirts here."

"As you said. And?"

"And you tell me. A lot of unexpected crap can happen in this business. I mean, it's *mostly* unexpected crap. That little emergency on the shuttle, with Rachael Lee barfing in her helmet, that was also you and Malagrite handling that, am I right?"

"Mostly her," Alice said.

"Right, well, if you had to pick a deputy, would it be her?"

Alice thought quickly. She was tempted to name Bethy Powell right away, but (a) on what grounds? On paper, they barely knew each other. And (b) things were suddenly going a little too well! She didn't trust a man like Igbal Renz to be that stupid. Was he *playing* her? Keeping his enemies close? Giving her enough rope to hang herself? Did it really not occur to him that Dona might not be the only bad actor in the mix? Alice was U.S. Air Force, for Christ's sake. Of course, so was Derek, and probably half the men down on Transit Point. And some of the other space pilots who were supposedly kicking around. Air Force people had always made solid astronauts.

Finally she answered: "First of all, I haven't said yes to anything. I know you're the boss and I'm the colonist, but just hold on a sec. Let me get my bearings. Second, assuming I agree to this, I'd need some time to figure out staffing. I don't even know what kind of threats we're talking about, here."

"Neither do we," said Pam. "That's the whole point. But it wouldn't be your only job, if that's what you're thinking."

When Alice didn't say anything to that, Igbal told her, "Take a day to think it over. If you don't want it, I'll give it to someone else. But I can't wait any longer than that. Fair enough?"

"Sure," Alice said. Because really, this might actually be the best possible thing for her. Then, sensing that she was dismissed, she tucked her flight bag, with its meager possessions, back under her arm and said, "Can someone show me to my cabin?"

"We call them apartments here," Pam said. "And yes, I'll take you."

❖❖❖

"We also have a shortage of medical personnel," Pam told her, when they were out in the hallway or connecting module or whatever they called it here.

Following along, Alice responded, "Not many doctors willing to sign away their wombs?"

When Pregnant Pam didn't immediately answer, she pressed further: "That bump of yours. Is it his? Igbal Renz's?"

"Yes."

"And there's not going to be anyone here to deliver it when it comes?"

Pam stopped and glared at her. "You're pretty bold for your first day. You want to let me do the talking?"

"Sure. Sorry."

"Have you ever delivered a baby?"

"No," Alice admitted, "but the Pararescuemen require a five-day course in obstetrics."

"Yeah, I know," Pam said. "It's one of the reasons I approved you for an Esley posting. But it's not the only reason. Are you dying for a shit-shower-and-shave, or have you got a few minutes?"

"I have a few minutes."

"Okay. What you're about to see falls strictly under the nondisclosure clauses of your contract. Can you keep your mouth shut?"

"I have a Top Secret clearance from the U.S. Air Force. I mean, *had*."

"Come with me, then."

Pam clearly didn't like Alice, although it was hard to say whether that was on general principle or her scintillating personality. On *both* of their scintillating personalities. But despite her disdain, Pam just as clearly needed something, and needed it badly. Was that something Alice could exploit?

God, that sounded so ghoulish. And yet, there it was: Alice was here to do a job. Probably an unpleasant one— probably one that Pam would truly hate her for—but in the meantime she had to win trust and find weaknesses, until she and Bethy figured out exactly what needed doing.

Pam changed direction and, after leading Alice through a lab and a kitchen and a hallway lined with doors that reminded her of the guest-room levels of the Marriott Stars, emerged into a comic-bookish chamber containing four transparent capsules—one occupied by an apparently nude, apparently hibernating human male. Except that the life signs monitor beside his head was reading all flatlines, and the capsule had insulation blankets duct-taped all over it, and there was frost on the inside of the clear plastic. Frost!

"What the fuck?" Alice both exclaimed and demanded.

"That's Hobie Prieto, one of Derek's pilot buddies."

"Is he dead?"

"He's hibernating."

"Jesus fuck," Alice said. "He's *frozen*."

"Nearly," Pam agreed. "He's packed full of proteins that inhibit crystallization, so his repair enzymes can stay in a fluid state. So, not really completely frozen. But his core temperature is minus two centigrade. If you dropped him on a concrete floor, he'd break."

"Jesus fuck," Alice said again. "How long has this been possible?"

"It may not be possible now," Pam said gravely. "We still need to wake him up, and confirm that he's healthy. And then . . ."

"And then?"

"And then I need you to put me in there."

Alice thought that one over for a second. The stonehearted part of her whispered that here was a perfect opportunity (again, *handed* to her) to get a problematic person out of the way. The medic in her whispered that it would be an interesting and educational process. But it was the simply human part of her that spoke: "I can't ethically do that. You're pregnant."

"I am," she agreed. "And that's the whole point. The future of humanity could be riding on this, and I can't ask anyone else to take the risk. And the longer we wait, the greater the risks, which means it needs to be now. Your crewmate, Rachael Lee, was supposed to be our backup obstetrician, but she's still under evaluation at TPS. Won't be here for several months, if at all. Which means it needs to be *you*."

Alice let that sink in for quite some time, and when she finally spoke it was the human part of her again, with a petty complaint: "Jesus Christ. Is there anyone in this place who doesn't want me for their fucking assistant?"

Alice's "apartment" smelled like a new car. Though smaller than her room at the Marriott Stars, it was about the size of an old minivan with all the seats ripped out, which was still pretty big by spaceship standards. It had its own private zero-gee bathroom, and a "bed" up against the wall to maximize space. There was room (though barely) for somersaults, as long as the inward-opening hatch was closed.

Instead, finally alone, Alice did a quick visual sweep for cameras. Even with quantum optics, there was a limit to how small a camera could be and still capture, store, and transmit intelligible images. That size was about half a millimeter, so it took her about twenty minutes to search the room, and another twenty to search it again.

When that was done, she dug out her "personal effects" and assembled her EMF detector. Disguised as a set of headphones, it plugged into the tablet computer she'd been using as a book reader for the past umpteen years, and would light up if it detected any electromagnetic field stronger than three volts per meter, whatever that meant. The room was of course full of electric fields (this was a space station, and it combined all the functions of an apartment complex, an ore refinery, a factory, and a huge electrical power substation), but by identifying and subtracting out the baseline fields, she was able to find the outlines of signal and power lines buried behind her walls. Other than the comm panel beside her dogged-shut hatch, she did not find any suspicious pinpoints that would mark a planted microphone or other sensor. And the comm panel was electrically dead.

Experimentally, she pressed the single button situated beneath the speaker.

"Hello?" she said into it.

"Yes?" replied an inhumanly deep voice.

"Who is this?" she asked.

"I am Lurch," the voice said, "the personal assistant."

"Oh," she said, and let go of the button. The wires in

the wall, which had lit up while the button was held down, went dead again. She swept the room a second time, still finding nothing. Of course, anything else that was currently switched off would register as null, so she briefly triggered an induction mode, to light up any wires at all, even in the off state. She did this very quickly, lest her own signals start raising suspicion. But that didn't pick anything up, either. The comm button appeared to be a physical switch, connecting physical wires to a distant computer somewhere. Which was okay with her; she just wouldn't press the button.

Finally, she sprayed every surface with "body spray" from a pump-action bottle that had cleared RzVz inspection. She didn't know exactly what was in it, but Dillon the CIA Guy had showed her how to use it during one of her ground-based training days, and apparently it would shut down certain kinds of microelectronics. Fortunately, there was no TV screen in here, or she might well have fried it.

"Regardless of any precautions," Dillon had told her, "you can always still be imaged by your near-field/far-field entanglement shadow. You can encase yourself in lead if you want, but the field shadow can never be completely hidden. Still, they won't be able to make out fine detail that way. It's not a popular imaging mode with Peeping Toms, for example."

So, reasonably confident she was unobserved, she assembled a pistol from her drinking straw and components of her hair clips, leg shaver, and the disk drive from her old-fashioned laptop. In training she had gotten to fire this weapon exactly five times, which was the number of shots she had available to her here on ESL1 Shade Station. "Make them count," Dillon had told her. "Or better yet, don't need them at all." It fired electromagnetically accelerated, pea-sized capsules of plastic birdshot pellets—"probably nonlethal, but you never know."

The gun actually did still look a bit like a shaver, which would still look weird if anyone (or any*thing* with see-through vision) spotted it in her pocket, but there was only so much she could do about that.

Finally, she unplugged the EMF detector and plugged in her wideband entangled.

In the texting app on her tablet, she pulled up a contact called TOMPKINS and tapped out the following message:

I am in position. Initial situation promising.

Expecting no reply, she turned the tablet off and put it away in a drawer, and then really did take a badly needed shower and an even more badly needed nap. Not a long one—Alice had long ago perfected the art of the catnap—but enough to get her brain in working order.

After that, she fished out the tablet again and typed up a message to Igbal Renz, accepting his offer and promising to select a deputy within a day or two. Pam had put Igbal's contact info into the tablet for her, so all she had to do was put his name at the top of the message and hit SEND.

She didn't expect a reply from Renz, either, but one came back almost immediately:

Excellent. You have run of the station, anywhere you like. Check back in with me in a few days.

Huh. Jesus. Was Renz *trying* to slit his own throat?

4.5
23 April

✧

Clementine Cislunar Fuel Depot
Earth-Moon Lagrange Point 1
Cislunar Space

Grigory had contacted Dona Obata through intermediaries of intermediaries—a murmured phrase, Russian mafia to Algerian mafia to Dona herself. A man like Grigory had friends all over the world, at all different levels of government and industry, and he had caught word about the deep-black-classified ESL1 interdict mission well before its participants had launched, and so, through layer upon layer of deniability, he'd put the question to her: "Are you amenable to parallel mission on freelance basis?"

And when the answer came back affirmative, he'd had his people slip her an entangled ultrawideband radio handset, disguised as an old smartphone. All subsequent contact—and there wasn't much—had been via that device.

So now, months later, when the two of them were lounging in bed together in the brand-new, matching

3D-printed pajamas she'd insisted on ordering, Grigory was surprised when she pulled out the device and said, in English, "The French government has tried to contact me."

"What?"

"My former employers."

"On that thing?"

"Yes."

He scratched his scalp. "Impossible. *I* gave you that. Is it same device? How is such a thing possible?"

He wasn't alarmed per se, but he was confused, and he didn't like it.

"Two-channel device," she said. "You and the French government wanted to communicate the same way. How everyone communicates today, yes? If they don't want to be overheard. The only difference is that you wanted a voice channel, and they wanted text. So, this handset is a clone of the device you gave me, and of the one they did. It doesn't look quite the same as either of the originals, but no one ever noticed. A black rectangle is a black rectangle. And anyway, carrying two similar devices would have looked suspicious."

"Tampering with the device we gave you looks suspicious," he said, though without any great conviction.

The problem with double agents was that they were demonstrably untrustworthy. Were they really working for you, or were they spies working against you, and *for* the people you had asked them to betray? But he'd worked with enough turncoats to realize they simply unmasked a basic truth: *anyone* could be working against him. Chances were, in an organization as large as Orlov

Petrochemical, he had many potential spies and saboteurs already embedded. It made sense to distrust Dona Obata in the same way it made sense to distrust everyone, and reality in general. How many men had gone to their graves unaware, at the hands of a close associate? Paranoia had a bad reputation, but in truth, he knew he could never be paranoid enough. He *would* be betrayed one of these days, and he probably wouldn't see it coming.

"I'm bringing this information to you," she said. "You're not *discovering* it; I'm *telling* you. French Intelligence. Contacting."

She showed him a screen covered in chat bubbles, containing cryptic French text. *"Bonne matinée oiseau chanteur. La fontaine est sèche. Ton oreille est chaude?"* Coded messages of some sort.

"What do they want?" he asked.

"They've figured out I'm here. They want to know if I'm safe, and able to function."

Function. That was an interesting word for it, Grigory thought. Function *how*, exactly?

"And are you?" he asked, trying on a menacing tone.

She sniffed. "I didn't have to tell you this. This is an opportunity. This is a direct channel to the highest levels of the French government."

"I have telephone and email," he told her. "I can call governments any time I please. Presidents take my call, my dear. What do I need with back channels?"

"We can plant false information," she said. "Turn our enemies against each other."

"Our enemies are already against each other. More than even you may know. What is to be gained by telling them anything? They *believe* you are here. They do not know it beyond doubt. You could be alive or dead. You could have slipped back to Earth on a landing body, or dropped to the surface of the Moon with a methane shipment. The shuttle that came here might have been empty; they might have murdered you at Transit Point, and sent the empty shuttle here to throw suspicion off themselves, and onto me. You see? Your former superiors *know* nothing, and that . . . ambiguity is more useful to us than any false information. These are treacherous, treacherous times, my dear. Much is at stake, and this makes people greedy and afraid. We *like* greedy and afraid, because these are handles to grab people with. So we tell them only that the tralphium will lower their energy costs and reduce pollution, and that Clementine is everyone's benefactor. Everyone's frightening, mysterious benefactor, whom they dare not cross. But if Clementine is unhappy, then Orlov Petrochemical is unhappy, and perhaps it won't be only the tralphium energy they lose. Perhaps even the deuterium can be shut off. I control *ten percent of global electricity*, and when the energy supply is controlled, people's hearts are controlled with it, or they freeze to death in the dark. They know this. Everyone knows this, or learns it quickly when circumstances explain it to them. My father turned off the gas supply to Europe many times, in order to educate them. They turned to solar, to wind, to liquefied natural gas from America, but this was never more than politics. They needed my father's natural gas pipelines, and so they did what was necessary, to keep him happy."

"Charming," she said, without disapproval.

He laughed. "Woman, you are not as afraid of me as you should be, nor as ashamed of yourself. And that is paradox, because I like you that way, unafraid and unashamed."

"That's not why I exist," she said, now finally seeming a bit annoyed with him. "For you to like or dislike. I'm not a fawning, fainting person, or a barnacle on your hull. People who have underestimated *me* in that way have often regretted it."

He considered that for a moment, then snorted, unconcerned. "How am I to interpret this? As threat?"

"No," she said calmly, "I don't threaten. If I meant you harm you'd be dead before your next breath. But now that you've seen my value, I will caution you: don't go thinking it's easily replaced."

At that, he simply smiled. "Are you saying the world is not overflowing with beautiful French African trained killers who also have head for business?"

"No more than it's overflowing with trillionaires." She paused, then added, "You know, I did try to come up with something better than liquor. I looked for gaps in your value chain, and I found nothing. You really do work every angle, don't you?"

"Of course. It would be quite difficult to accumulate one trillion anything without this. I had trillion rubles at the age of twenty-five. One trillion dollars and one trillion euros took much longer time, until I was past forty. People say I inherited my wealth, but my empire is *twenty times* larger than my father's. Twenty. And my father was very clever, very ruthless man."

"Mmm." She was quiet for a while after that, but eventually said, "When the American and the Kiwi take over Esley Shade Station, our supply of landing bodies could be compromised."

"Or at least delayed, yes. This thought has crossed through my mind."

"We do have two space shuttles on hand. Those could carry several weeks' worth of cargo apiece, if we save it up and land it less often."

"Indeed, and we have four lifeboats that could serve similar function."

She frowned. "Oh. Wow. Do you think that's a good idea?"

"Naturally not, since our own skins could be at risk if we do that—yours and mine. But we control the tralphium, no? I am thinking there will be public outcry on our behalf, if we tell tabloids we are planning to use even *one* of our lifeboats to bring safe, clean energy to the people of Earth, because Coalition countries have left us no other way. Governments fear this sort of outcry. This gives us leverage, either to pass our cargo ships through the blockade and get some launch vehicles to Suriname, or else to demand that an occupied Renz Ventures continue to sell us landing bodies. It hardly matters which; if we accomplish either, we hang onto our revenue stream and our leverage, both."

"Yes, well, if that's your plan, you have an America problem."

He paused, intrigued. Not many people spoke back to him in this manner, and the woman did seem to have good ideas. "How so?"

"You have, what, two power plants in North America? Neither of them on actual U.S. soil?"

"Correct. Go on."

"America leads the Coalition. That means America's basically in charge of the blockade, the embargo, and the raid on ESL1. It's America you need leverage over, and you haven't got it."

"No? America listens to the weeping of its allies."

"It doesn't. Certainly, it doesn't listen to the weeping of France. You said it yourself: our enemies work at cross-purposes to one another. You think an increase in European energy prices will bring the U.S. to the bargaining table? You know them better than that."

"All right, let us say you are correct. What solution do you propose?"

"France," she said. "France knows about the ESL1 raid, but is no longer in a position to benefit from it. In fact, they could conceivably benefit more from exposing it before it happens. That gives France leverage over the U.S. And you have leverage over France. More than you do over the U.S., at any rate."

"So, what, we politely ask Laurent Patenaude to politely ask Tina Tompkins to politely let an Orlov Petro ship through the blockade? In exchange for favorable electricity rates?"

"Yes. Exactly."

Orlov pursed his lips, thinking about that. It left a sour taste, certainly. In the long run, what he needed was to make *all* of them—America and Europe and Russia and China—irrelevant. It already rankled that he was at their mercy right now; would he compound it by groveling? But yes, that was what Magnus Orlov would have done. "Leave your feelings out of it," he'd counseled Grigory more than once. "Pay attention only to what you can quantify. If your reason for doing something, or not doing something, can't be expressed in numbers, then it's *erunda*. Nonsense."

Magnus had been sixty years old when his forty-year-old wife, Yelena, had finally (in his own words) "coughed up a legitimate male heir," and Magnus had died when Grigory was just twenty-five. That wasn't a long time to know one's father, particularly when he traveled all the time. But perhaps for that very reason, Grigory had always hung on Magnus' every word. It was only more recently, in his forties and fifties, that he'd begun to feel confident enough in his own judgment to go against that of his father. And right now, his judgment was telling him not to play a strong hand weakly.

"If America is target of this maneuver," he said, "why offer France any involvement at all? Why give them a chance to refuse, or play to their own agenda? I could simply email President Tompkins tomorrow morning, telling her, 'Orlov Petrochemical is friendly and will keep your secrets in space. And as friends, we ask for one ship per week to pass through your blockade, inspected to whatever degree you find necessary, and paying for the time of the inspectors, as necessary.' It's a velvet glove with an iron fist inside of it, and within the fist, a bribe. She would find such an offer difficult to ignore, and difficult to refuse."

"Oh," said Obata, blinking in surprise. "My. That *is* direct."

He nodded. "Indeed. And I will bet you one thousand rubles that she doesn't even take the bribe. There's no mechanism for the U.S. government to receive payment like that, and they cannot accept donations from foreign powers or foreign corporations, of which we are both."

Obata appeared to think that over for a while. Finally, she said, "Why an exemption to the blockade, rather than continued shipments from Renz Ventures? You're thinking RzVz may not survive the assault? Our orders were to capture it intact."

"*Your* orders," he corrected. "France's orders. Probably New Zealand's orders as well; I can't think why these would be different for either country. But the Americans always have a different standard for themselves than for their allies, hmm? There is good reason to believe your friend, Alice Kyeong, may be operating under a different directive entirely."

1.9
24 April

✧

ESL1 Shade Station
Earth-Sun Lagrange Point 1
Extracislunar Space

Venturing out into the station, Alice made a show of getting to know her own original crewmates a little better, while also familiarizing herself with the layout of the station. She talked for fifteen minutes with Jeanette Schmidt in a place called the "employee break room," which had a window and a Ping-Pong table and a little drink-bulb dispenser. She talked with Pelu Figueroa in the gym, one module down from the break room. She talked with Maag in the "galley," which was a dining area adjoining both a kitchen and something called the "Secondary Hab Corridor" or "Beta Corridor." She talked very briefly with Nonna Rostov, the nervous Russki, in "Gamma Corridor," where both of their apartments were located. Where *all* of the newcomer's apartments were located, in fact. The module was apparently brand-new, having been fabricated here at ESL1, installed and opened up over a period of a few days, and then left to outgas for a week before *Dandelion* finally arrived. That explained the new car smell, eh? And she talked with Saira Batra, the petite mathematician, in the docking module where they had first arrived, and where *Dandelion* was still attached, its docking hatch open to let the thing air out.

And then, with appearances properly kept up, she spent the better part of an hour talking to Bethy in every public place they could casually pass through, starting in Alpha Corridor and then gradually drifting through the station's other spaces. It wasn't immediately evident, but the modules of ESL1 Shade Station—some long and skinny, some short and wide, some fashioned into T and L shapes—formed three loops at three different orientations, so it was possible to get from anywhere to anywhere by several different routes. Alice made an effort to memorize these, so in an emergency—in *the* emergency she was here to cause—she'd know her way around. She and Bethy couldn't speak freely, of course, but they could speak in a fairly thin code. "How are things looking in a general sense?" Bethy asked at one point. They were in the hydroponics lab, where Bethy nominally worked, on the far side of the gymnasium where people tended not to wander very often. That wasn't public enough, though, so Alice turned them back around, through the gym and back toward the break room.

And she replied, "Better than you'd think! I haven't identified specific security issues, but with management on our side it shouldn't be difficult."

To which Bethy said, "Are you sure? Duckies, is anything that easy? Maybe you need a second opinion."

"Yours?"

"Yeah, if you like. I'm assigned to life support, but if you can do security in your spare time, I don't see why I can't help you out in mine."

The high pitch of Bethy's voice wasn't in any way abnormal, but it was at odds with her stocky-strong arms and legs and her callused hands, which in turn were at odds with her narrow waist and flared hips. Like a rhinoceros in a corset! And nearly everything Bethy said was rendered vaguely comical by her gung-ho Kiwi accent, so she left quite a first impression on people.

Even ignoring the Actual Mission and the months of zero-gee combat training, she was actually kind of perfect for the role of station security.

"I need to talk to some more people before officially taking anyone on," Alice told her.

"Gotta keep up appearances, eh?"

"Something like that. I'd stick with your normal routine for right now."

"Whatever that is," Bethy complained. "You get the feeling these people are just making it up as they go?"

"Definitely, yes. But making what up? There's some kind of grand plan unfolding here. There's method to this madness."

"Okay, Hamlet."

Alice stopped at that. "What?"

"Never mind. What are you doing today? Arresting drunks and writing parking tickets?"

"Me? No, I've got a date."

"Hmm. Really. Hunky Pilot Guy?"

"His name is Derek."

"Fluffy duckies, girl, you don't waste time."

Alice snorted. "You've been asleep. I've actually known the guy for months."

"Hmm. Good guy?"

"Yeah. I think so."

Bethy seemed to think that over. "Is there a, you know, operational benefit to the security team?"

"Depends what you mean," Alice said, then busted out laughing like a schoolgirl.

Bethy didn't like that. She didn't like it at all, and suddenly her dorky Kiwi self was replaced by somebody hard and cold that Alice had never met. "Don't compromise yourself. This *Security* business is serious, eh? Don't compromise *me*."

"Oh, lighten up," Alice said, rather surprising herself. "He's retired Air Force, like me. Loves the President. Yeah?"

"Irrelevant. Is he a friend of Security?"

"I don't know."

"Are *you* compromising *him*?"

This was getting a little close to their shared secrets, and Alice felt the need to rein it back. The two of them were drifting through the station, drifting from handrail to handrail in a not-very-purposeful manner that nevertheless looked perhaps a bit too polished for a pair of newcomers. Alice had her weeks aboard *Dandelion* as a partial excuse, but it wasn't like there'd actually been a lot of room to move around. It *was* nice to have space to roam; the loops and jumbles of ESL1 Station formed enough blind alleys to feel like there was also enough space to have a private conversation. But not *too* private.

Not this close to operational secrets. Even closed up in a private apartment, she wouldn't speak her secrets out loud.

"I don't know," Alice admitted. "Can we change the subject?"

"Find out," Bethy told her. "That *is* the subject."

When she finally went to look for Derek a few hours later, he wasn't easy to find. He was hanging out in the employee lounge, which was on the opposite side of the station from the galley, which was where people actually seemed to want to hang out. The break room was really just a T-shaped connecting module that led from Gamma Corridor on one side to, on the other, the station's small gymnasium and hydroponics lab, and also Egress Lock #2. But the break room had a little porthole window in it, and Derek was staring out of it, looking glumly at the Earth.

"Hey, flyboy. You okay?"

"I miss my sister and her kids," he said. "And my mom."

Alice nearly made some snide comment about momma's boys, but thought better of it.

"I miss blue skies," he continued. "Does that sound trite? It does to me."

"VR's not cutting it for you?" Alice asked.

She'd been told there was a full library of Earth environment simulations available, from ocean floors to mountaintops and everything in between. They also had "VR&R" (virtual reality rest and relaxation) at Transit Point Station and, weirdly, at the Marriott Stars. She didn't see why hotel guests fresh from the planet's surface would need that, so she'd supposed that was more for the benefit of the staff, going slowly stir crazy on their one-hundred-twenty-day duty rotations. Before the place had opened, guests were already booked out two years in advance, for zero-gee vacations ranging anywhere from twenty-four hours to three weeks, and it was expected to be hard duty for the hotel staff. In theory, the VR&R had also been available to all the military and intelligence personnel who'd commandeered the place, but Alice hadn't talked to anyone who'd actually used it. Their real lives were quite exciting enough.

But yes, with a proper VR rig you could stand in a sun-dappled forest with a cool breeze across your face. The high-end headgear could simulate hot desert breezes, too, or dry glacial ones, or swampy humidity. Feeling it against your eyes was somehow allegedly nearly as good as feeling it against your whole body. But that had sounded to her a lot like how vegetarians brag about their fake meat shit tasting as good as the real thing. Not really. First bite, maybe. But Alice had once gone a full month on kosher/vegan field rations, and was about ready to resort to cannibalism by the time she'd gotten back to an operating base. So yeah, VR probably got old quick.

Ignoring her, Derek said, "Since they took me off Earth-to-orbit shuttle duty, it's been two and a half years since I touched ground."

"Oh. Wow. That's a long time." Then, because she was supposed to be a colonist, "I guess that's all of us, though. Up here forever, going soft."

He snorted. "We're probably stronger than before we left. We land on Earth, I could kickbox the landing boss the minute we open the doors. That's not the problem. I mean, this place is growing fast—physically growing—but every component serves the master plan. Other than this Ping-Pong table, which doesn't really work in zero gee, by the way, there's not a lot of dumb relaxation bullshit here. It's depressing."

Alice could understand that. The gymnasium bubble on the Marriott Stars was expected to be one of its main attractions, but there was also an arboretum and a chapel and a restaurant. Would people take time out from their zero-gee vacations to eat steak, pray, and smell the roses? Marriott certainly seemed to think so.

"You could build something," she offered.

"Me? I'm just a dumb flyboy."

"Bowling alley? Puppet theater? An inflatable bubble wouldn't cost much."

"Tell it to Bigballs."

"You tell him."

He didn't say anything, and then it was super awkward for a moment. She could see he was too close to the problem, too limited in his thinking by the existing structures and rhythms of the station. Like a dutiful, rule-following Air Force pilot, he couldn't really conceive of disrupting the place for his own gratification. Soldiers tended to be more pragmatic; when assigned to a camp in the dead center of Nowheresville, they quickly set up makeshift games and wading pools and whatever else the available materials allowed them to come up with. Duct tape, trash bags, parachute cord and empty containers were the 3D printers of field deployment, used to create everything from couches to kites, barbecue grills to piñatas and bongs.

"Have a contest," she suggested. "Best use of a bubble module."

"Thanks, new girl."

"That's new head of security to you. Anyhow, are we going on your inspection pod?"

"Yeah. Let's get it over with. Going to be a tight fit, though."

What he meant by that, it turned out, was that Jeanette Schmidt was coming along with them. Alice tried to hide her surprise when she saw Jeanette waiting for them at the docking module, with her blonde hair untied and drifting around her, mermaid-style. Jeanette seemed surprised to see Alice as well, and Alice felt immediately annoyed with herself. Whoever said this was a date? *She* did. Not Derek.

Truthfully, she had imagined boning him silly when they were out alone in space again. Why not, right? And it had never even occurred to her that Derek might have something else in mind. That this pod ride was part of his actual job, and he had goals to accomplish and schedules to keep. Derp.

It might well be part of Jeanette's job as well. Wasn't she some kind of space resource expert or asteroid-mining expert or something? She seemed young for that, but then again Alice herself was not yet thirty, and the President of the United States had entrusted this potentially deadly mission to her.

Speaking of which, yes, Alice had her own job to do! Bethy was right; she *was* losing focus. Something about this place—this whole setup—was really distracting her somehow. But okay, this maintenance pod trip could provide her with good information about the Shade and the Station and their respective vulnerabilities. How would she take the place down? If worse came to worst, could she somehow just drop the whole thing into the Sun?

That thought made her shudder, for two reasons: first because she had calmly (if fleetingly) considered the cold-blooded murder of thirty innocent people. Second, because she had the vague sense that the physics didn't actually work that way, but she wasn't sure why. If the Shade was "hovering" on the pressure of sunlight, didn't that mean it could fall if the whole thing turned clear and the sunlight were allowed to pass through it? Pilot trainee or no, she realized she knew fuck all about orbital mechanics, and on the heels of that she recognized that the President had not sent her here to modify the orbits of things. She was here for petty violence, pure and simple. But yeah, where, and how, and against whom? Should she and Bethy simply put a round in the back of Igbal's head and then lock all the controls until the space marines arrived?

Again, the idea made her shudder. No. There was a better way, somewhere out there waiting to be found.

By way of greeting, Jeanette said, "I hear Dona stole that shuttle and hid it somewhere."

Alice responded with frustration and confusion she didn't have to fake. "You heard right." And then, before Jeanette could ask her next question she added: "I don't know how or why. It's super troubling, yeah?"

Jeanette nodded, her eyebrows cocked as high as they would go. "Little bit, yeah. Watch our backs around here. So, you're coming with us on today's inspection?"

She sounded disappointed.

"I need to understand the facility and its vulnerabilities," Alice told her without irony.

"Come on," Derek said wearily, opening a docking hatch and waving the two of them through. "You're going to have to share a seat belt."

Alice saw immediately what he meant: the pilot's seat was a kind of saddle, with weird stirrups and arm sleeves to hold him in place against what must be fairly moderate acceleration.

Behind that was something that looked for all the world like the back seat of a twentieth-century automobile: a bench of padded synthetic leather in weirdly tasteful burgundy and gray, with a padded backrest and an adjustable fabric belt buckled across it. She and Jeanette would fit in it together, but barely. The pod had big rearview mirrors on either side, much like the *Dandelion*, but the front of it was a single curved bubble of some thick, transparent material that was held to the aft hull with a ring of maybe twenty-four bolts. Alice felt a momentary flutter of panic, remembering there was *actually no air* out there, and realizing her whole existence depended on bolts and gaskets and whatnot.

But Jeanette was calmly gliding into the seat, and Derek was closing and dogging shut the hatch behind it, and Alice was supposedly fearless, with ice water in her veins, so she moved in beside Jeanette and buckled the two of them in.

"It's like a carnival ride," Jeanette said.

Except carnival rides didn't have pilots. What it was actually like was a "tuk-tuk" motorized rickshaw Alice had once ridden in Kaohsiung, right before the whole Taiwan thing went south. Driver in front, two passengers crammed in back, and not much feeling of safety. But she liked Jeanette, and didn't feel a need to be snitty, so all she said was, "Yeah."

Derek slapped on a headset, flipped a couple of physical switches, and started talking to the empty air. "Echo 2 requesting departure clearance. Affirmative. Affirmative. Filed eight hours ago. Correct. Two passengers, ID Alice Kyeong and Jeanette . . ."

"Schmidt," Jeanette supplied.

"Schmidt. Correct. Roger that."

There was a banging noise behind them that almost made Alice flinch.

"Roger, I show four docking clamps released. Roger that: Echo 2 on departure."

It took Alice a few seconds to realize they were moving. The acceleration was more substantial than the gnat-fart whisper of an ion engine, but still so gentle that she mainly felt it in her hair, which slowly pooled behind her on the headrest. With her ass belted firmly to the bench seat and her hips wedged between a bulkhead on the left and Jeanette on the right, her body didn't physically move. Nevertheless, in the portion of the rearview mirrors visible to her, she could make out the docking module falling slowly away from them, at roughly the velocity of a turtle. They were picking up speed, though: now walking speed, now running speed, now the speed of a bicycle. Now a car on the highway, and the station was shrinking behind them.

Out in front there was only the blankness of the ESL1

Shade, a dim, gray-black expanse, like flying over a desert at night, with a starry sky above it. Not twinkling. *The central Hub is opaque*, she reminded herself. But up ahead, the "horizon" of the Hub was bright, as though the desert were surrounded by a giant, ring-shaped city just out of view.

"You two okay back there?" Derek asked over his shoulder.

"Peachy," Jeanette confirmed.

"Echo 2," Alice said. "Figures you'd have a cool-ass call sign."

"Yeah," he said. "Call sign has to be cool, or what's the point? You must have used one, too. What was it?"

"Mockingbird."

He snorted. "Yeah, that figures."

"Who were you talking to, anyway?"

"Lurch. He handles traffic control, among other things."

"Oh. That's creepy."

Suddenly, the brightness rushed toward them, and the little inspection pod was bathed in light. Alice couldn't see the Sun itself—that was "under" them—but the Shade was now an expanse of glowing fabric, like a lampshade. Alice could see texture in it at many different scales: filaments crisscrossing with threads crisscrossing with cables, like a Halloween spiderweb on a fireplace screen on a linen tablecloth.

"Whoa," she said, abandoning her reserve for a moment.

"That's right," Jeanette chortled. "Pretty amazing actually being here, isn't it?"

"What is all that stuff?"

She was asking Derek, but it was Jeanette who answered, "Electrical wires. A square kilometer of Shade generates almost a hundred megawatts of power. Has to go somewhere."

"Jesus," Alice said, wondering why, for all her studying and all the briefings she'd sat through, she still had no idea what was going on up here. She knew the thing generated electricity, but she had never asked *why*. "What's it all for?"

Jeanette tossed her head. The acceleration had subsided, so her hair spun around her like a golden crown. "That's the trick, isn't it? People talk a lot about energy and how to get it. They don't talk as much about how to use it when you've got this much. The station is zone-refining space rocks by the shit ton, literally as fast as the gatherbots can haul them in. That basically means melting the rock in a linear fashion, like a little stripe of hot lava passing through it, while it's in a centrifuge. That tends to push different materials apart, so you get this rainbow of different materials you can literally just cut apart with a saw. It's very power-intensive, and so is the machinery that turns that material into products. RzVz is known for hab modules and spaceship parts, right? And the Shade itself. But most of what we're producing here are weavers and stitchers and more gatherbots, to *build* the shade. It's a very viral situation. But even all of that barely puts a dent in the available power! It still has to go somewhere. So there's a particle accelerator cranking out antimatter—specifically, antilithium antideuteride—to bank the excess energy until Igbal figures out what to do with it. Starship propellant or whatever. That's an inefficient storage process, but the energy density is phenomenal."

"How much antimatter?" Alice demanded, suddenly cold and hot at the same time.

"Almost a kilogram, I think."

"Jesus."

Alice knew fuck all about antimatter, just like she knew fuck all about everything else up here, but she knew the Air Force was deeply concerned about it in milligram quantities. A kilogram was, what, a million truck bombs, all in one little chunk?

"We're coming up on the first stitcher seam," Derek told them both. He pointed, and through the domed front of the pod Alice could see a discoloration in the Shade up ahead; a dark smudge surrounding a pinpoint of brightness. As it drew closer, it looked like a river of ants marching alongside a river of white-hot molten steel, and then it flashed by, underneath and behind them, and Alice caught a glimpse of what was actually down there: a rip in the fabric of the Shade, hundreds of meters long, surrounded by spidery robots. The size of pickup trucks, they were brightly illuminated by the sunlight spilling through the rip, and their arms were moving with a blurry speed that was somewhere between comical and creepy.

"You see that?" Derek said, apparently to Jeanette. "Once a tear is reported, the swarming behaviors kick in until a quorum is achieved. They've already arrested the spread, or else there'd be two swarms concentrated at the ends. Since they're spread out evenly, they must figure it's well in hand. Probably have it sealed up by the end of the day."

"Silk," Jeanette said, approvingly.

"I can slow down if you need a closer look at the next one."

"Thanks. That would be nice."

"I'm fine back here," Alice said, letting some of her annoyance leak through. Her body and mind had been calibrated for something altogether different from this. But if she rolled the tape back in her mind, she had to admit, Derek had never come close to asking her on a date. She'd had that conversation with herself! But with Jeanette here, Alice also had no opportunity to sound Derek out on the whole U.S. of A. thing—to see where he'd be standing if (actually, when) the government took control of this place. So that was two opportunities missed.

Sloppy. Alice was coming to terms with the fact that President Tompkins had been wrong about her. Maybe she did have ice water in her veins on a combat drop, but she was not a creature of nuance or deception, and she had a sense that here at ESL1 she was already running out of options and time.

But her comment went unanswered. Derek was in self-importantly busy flyboy mode, and Jeanette was absorbed in her own mission.

"What do humans even do around here?" Alice asked her.

"Not Shade maintenance," Jeanette said. "You'd need a million people, and what would they all eat? Nah. Wouldn't work."

"So why are we even out here in this pod? Don't these drones have video you can tap into?"

"They do," Derek said. "The beast with a million eyes.

We can even order a robotic flyover for particular sites if we need to."

"So what are we doing out here?"

"Same thing we're doing everywhere: big-picture stuff. Looking for issues nobody knows about yet. Machines don't innovate, they just do what they're told."

Spoken like a flyboy.

"How often do you do these inspections?"

"Me personally? Two or three times a year. Hobie Prieto does it more than I do, but I also inspect the sunny side, which he does not do. It's quite a bit more dangerous; if I had a problem, I'd have to cut right through the Shade to get back. Or go around the long way."

"Hmm. Hobie's the frozen guy?"

"Yeah." Derek sounded glum again. "Right now he's the frozen guy."

They changed course a few times, looking at the sites of two smaller rips, both swarming with stitcherbots, and it seemed to Alice that the Shade was a living creature of sorts, constantly repairing itself. Commanding cellular armies to the site of sensed injuries. Of course, the human body was not only constantly building and repairing itself, but also constantly dismantling. Thinning the bones when it thought they weren't needed, letting the eyesight deteriorate, letting the ends of the chromosomes wear away, ticktock. Humans were born to slowly die— something the Shade was presumably not. Why should it?

At the third site, moving much more slowly this time, they saw something new: a house-sized, jellyfish-looking thing passing cube-shaped blocks of shiny-black and shiny-silver material to the stitchers.

"Oh!" Jeanette said, clapping her hands, "that's a fillerbot! That's my job, Alice! Resource utilization. Look at that thing: right now all we're getting out of mined asteroids is five elements, two molecules, and 'slag.' We could be doing so much more. That's why I'm here."

"Every part of the buffalo?" she quipped.

Beneath a mane of floating gold, Jeanette made a frown that was somehow self-congratulatory. "Earth is a long way off, and right now our supply lines are shut. So yes."

"Okay," Alice said, suddenly hostile for some reason.

"What's that supposed to mean?"

"It means okay. Thank you for helping us use our resources efficiently."

"Well, you're welcome."

"Do I have to turn this thing around?" Derek said without looking back.

"We're playing nice," Jeanette assured him.

"Not sure this one knows how," Derek told her. "She's more of a shooter."

"Yeah," Jeanette agreed, nudging Alice with her shoulder. "You and that Kiwi girl, Bethy."

Alice froze. Just for a moment, but Jeanette felt it.

"What are you talking about?" she couldn't quite help asking.

Now Jeanette sounded almost gleeful: "Box of fluffy duckies? Seriously? That's a bad girl running nice girl software. You know what I'm talking about; I've seen you two in the hallway, practically holding hands."

"She's my first pick for deputy."

"Deputy what?" Jeanette laughed. Then, "Oh, don't worry, girl, your secrets are safe with me."

"Are they?"

"They are. Really. You can hold hands with whomever you want."

Well, Alice supposed it could be worse; she and Bethy *had* aroused suspicion. Of being lesbian lovers. Hell, there were worse cover stories for suspicious activity.

And because she was on really dangerous ground here, she simply shut her mouth and said nothing for nearly an hour, while the maintenance pod flung itself out to the rim of the Shade.

This gave her yet another sense of just how *big* a structure it was, because the speed indicator on Derek's instrument panel was consistently reading three hundred kph (relative to the Shade and the station, presumably), and yet they flew and flew over lampshade blankness, while Jeanette and Derek prattled about different types of sandwiches they liked, and then about ways of dressing up instant ramen noodles, and then about the Earthly merits of cooking on an electric stove, a gas stove, or in the microwave. They seemed to be having a good time of it, too.

"Microwave is your only option up here," Derek said, "although you can air fry them after they're cooked. Add some onions and turmeric powder and you're off to the races."

"Hmm. And you make the turmeric in the drug synthesizer?"

"That and the cayenne pepper, yes. You can also make

vinegar, but don't bother with soy sauce or sriracha. Anything made by controlled fermentation pretty much has to come from Earth."

"Unacceptable!" Jeanette said good-naturedly. "We should have beer and yogurt and kimchee up to the eyeballs!" Then: "Alice, isn't your, um, *friend* some sort of horticulturist?"

It took Alice a moment to rouse her voice into action, but finally she said, "I don't know, I think it's hydroponics."

"Yeah. Same thing. Would you ask her what seed stock we have?"

"I'm not her secretary."

"Ooh, still prickly. You're going to have to get used to confined spaces, you know."

Alice, who'd been crammed into all sorts of aircraft and boats and trailer-home barracks, and even a submarine once, said, "Noted." Then, feeling like she was doing a bad job as an undercover astronaut, added, "I'm sure it's an adjustment for all of us, in different ways."

Derek and Jeanette apparently considered that too obvious to answer. What Derek said instead was, "At present speed, we're about four minutes out from the rim. You can actually see it up ahead. See that line?"

"It's like the horizon's getting closer," Jeanette agreed.

"Right, well I'm going to flip us around and decelerate so you two can get a good look."

"Do we need to hold on?"

"If you like."

The maneuver was actually quite gentle, as was the deceleration that followed. Now they were flying backward, the glowing Shade scrolling past them the other way. Then everything was silent for a minute, until, without warning, light exploded all around them.

"*Fiat lux*," said Derek.

"Sunrise!" said Jeanette.

"Jesus," said Alice, shielding her eyes. Caught off guard yet again, damn it. But what did she think was going to happen?

"Hold on, I'm going to move us back inward a bit."

There was some groaning and thumping from the ACS motors. They drifted back into twilight, and spun facedown so that the inspection pod's bubble was facing directly toward the Shade.

"And there it is," Jeanette said.

Below, a machine like a combine harvester was sliding along the rim of the Shade and, well, *growing* it. It was crawling forward at maybe one meter per second, and in its wake was new shield material, glowing red-hot in a narrow line behind the machine and then cooling to a narrower line of opaque black and then, a few meters behind the machine, to a thready translucent material indistinguishable from the rest of the Shade.

"That's one of our weavers," Derek confirmed. "Igbal's big idea."

Alice took the bait. "*That's* his big idea?"

"There's a lot going on in that thing. It's a whole nanofactory in there, drawing power from the Shade, and material from that square hopper on top. Like Pac-Man in reverse. At its peak, the station was producing weavers at the rate of ten per month. Now it's about a third of that. Replacement level, basically. As of this morning, there are two hundred ninety-one of these operating."

Jeanette asked, "It uses a cubic-meter block of raw material every day?"

"Feed cubes, yes. Every three days, I think. And each cube equals just over a square kilometer of Shade, so altogether we're adding about twice the area of Manhattan every day. Those numbers might be out of date."

"Holy fucking shit," Alice said, with no particular emphasis.

"What?" said Derek and Jeanette, mildly and almost in synchrony. As if to say, what's surprising about that?

"It's . . . This is a lot. And it's all just swarm technology? Nobody really at the helm?"

"Moment to moment?" Derek asked.

"In general."

He shrugged. "Like any factory, I guess. Machines do the work. People are just there to look for anomalies."

"And do you find any?"

"Me? Not usually. I mean, one time a solar flare knocked out about a quarter of the bots, and I had to physically monitor the cleanup swarm. I was out here three days on that one."

"The Shade didn't act as a solar-wind barrier?" Jeanette asked.

"Oh, it did," he said. "Too well. We had charge dispersal surges all over the place, shorting everything out. Sandy Lincoln might know the details, but the energy involved was . . . pretty big."

"Huh. I haven't met Sandy."

"You will. She's all right. A little bookish, but nice."

Alice was annoyed to find that she was annoyed again,

at this whole situation. Neither Derek nor Jeanette seemed to find anything extraordinary about any of this, but Alice could see exactly why President Tompkins and the other Coalition leaders had been so freaked out. Given time, these people could *blot out the entire Sun* if they wanted to. They could refreeze the North Pole, bring back the glaciers, make it snow in Miami, and then freeze the whole fucking planet. And they really didn't give a shit.

"How much longer are we going to be out here?" she asked.

"What now?" Derek asked, sounding irritated with her change of tone.

"I need to pee," she answered. "And yes, I went before we left."

He sighed. "There's one of those portable things in the locker behind you. We can avert our eyes."

"No, I'm not doing that."

He sighed again. "Look, if I turn us around right now, we're an hour away at safe speed. But we've got five more weaver sites and two more rips on the roster. If I do a quick flyby, I could have you back in ninety minutes. Can you hold it that long?"

"Fine," she said tightly. And then, because none of this was actually Derek's fault, and because an hour would not affect the general fuckedness of the world one way or the other, she added, "I mean, yes. Thank you. I'm sorry to bother you about it."

"Not a thing," he assured her. And Jesus H. Christ, why did the fucker have to be so *nice*? Was it too much to ask, that the behavior of the world around her line up moment to moment with how she was feeling inside?

Momentarily fed up with pretense, she said, "You like a damsel in distress, don't you? How would you feel about saving the whole world?"

"Great," he said, matter-of-factly. "When do we start?"

To which Jeanette added, "It's what we're all here for, honey. Every one of us."

Later, from the privacy of her room, she searched again for signs of eavesdropping, and then dug out her tablet and texted the President: *Evaluating possible scenarios. Permission to recruit a retired Air Force captain to the cause?*

She waited for a response, wondering what the President might say. Yes? No? You're an idiot? A minute went by, and it occurred to her to wonder about the speed of light. Would it take more than a minute for her signal to reach the Earth? One more thing she didn't know. She waited another minute. Then five minutes. Then *ten* minutes. Still no answer.

Surely the signal had gotten there by now. Was the President even listening? Was Alice in any sort of communication at all?

Twenty minutes.

Thirty minutes.

Fuck.

5.3
24 April

✧

H.S.F. *Concordia*
Moored to Transit Point Station
Low Earth Orbit

"Harvest Moon just sent me their feasibility study," Miyuki said, pulling herself up into *Concordia*'s bridge.

Beseman, strapped into the copilot's chair and tapping at a bank of touchscreens, turned and looked at her. "Bad news?" he asked.

"Good, actually."

He visibly relaxed. "They can mine thorium?"

"From Imbrium basin, yes. It's a *long* drive from Shackleton, but they put a cost proposal together, and it's ... doable."

He sighed, looking unhappy again. "How doable?"

"Without disrupting our timeline? Fifty billion dollars. That's not fixed cost, either, so figure a hundred billion by the time we've dealt with all the overruns."

"Is it fixed *schedule*, at least?"

She nodded. "It is. I told them that part was nonnegotiable."

"Good. Okay. Good. But that means the cost of the LIFTR is actually just a fraction of the total cost to us, which is *not* good. Am I going to have to sell The Tunneling Company to pay for this?"

"We haven't run the numbers yet, but . . . probably, yes. I'm sorry about that."

He ran his fingers through his hair, and she could see him absorbing this new reality. Moving it to column "A" in his mind. "Well, it's one less headache to worry about, I suppose. Running *two* businesses from Mars would've been . . . Well, damn."

She knew The Tunneling Company meant a lot to him. He'd started it because one person too many had told him it wasn't possible to build a Hyperloop tunnel underneath the Rocky Mountains, from Denver to Grand Junction, and he figured he had the money not only to prove them wrong, but to turn a gigantic profit. It was his first really bold play as a trillionaire, and the last thing he did before setting his attention on outer space.

"I'm sorry, Dan," she said again.

"Yeah. Thanks. So it sounds like we definitely need to get rid of the tokamak reactor."

"We do, yes. Right now it's just taking up space."

"Okay. Any chance we can unload it on somebody? Orlov, maybe? Between the purchase price and the launch cost, we're probably half a billion in on that. I'd prefer not to just melt it down as scrap."

"I'll look into that," she said, "but there is another option."

"Hmm? Do tell."

She could see he was ready for any kind of good news

at this point—anything to soften the blow—and fortunately she had something he was going to like. "Remember that Magnasat proposal, to put an electromagnet at Mars Solar L1 to block the solar wind?"

Miyuki remembered it very well indeed, because one little satellite could supposedly cut, in half, the amount of radiation people would receive on the surface of Mars. Planetwide. She'd tried to push Beseman into looking at it more seriously two years ago, but at that time he didn't see the need. It was a column "C" item, when there was still a whole township to build. But as a way of repurposing equipment he'd already paid for . . .

"Didn't that require a really strong magnetic field?" he asked.

"Not really," she answered. "No stronger than an old-school MRI machine. The magnets in the tokamak are more than strong enough to do that same job. It'd be like a tower magnet for the whole planet at once. If we strip the shielding off, slap an ion engine on it for station keeping, and, I mean, also just to push it out there. Fuel the engine with oxygen ions instead of xenon, because we don't *have* any xenon, and can't get any for the foreseeable future. But yeah. I think we could probably do the whole thing with materials on hand, for under twenty mill."

For basically nothing, in other words. She watched his face, as the Magnasat moved from "C" to "A" back there behind his eyes.

"Wow. That's . . . Okay, let's look into that. But, uh, wasn't that also a terraforming proposal? Didn't it build up the atmosphere over time?"

"It does have that effect, yes, but the researchers who

proposed it were way off in their initial time estimates. Last I heard, based on the actual rates of outgassing from the Martian lithosphere, it would take about twenty-five million years to double the present atmosphere."

"Oh."

He'd looked excited for a moment there, and then let down for a moment, but that kind of thing was part of the daily roller coaster of running a business in outer space, so there was nothing all that unusual about it. Within a few seconds, she could see he was thinking the issue through in practical terms. He said, "Well, that's a little outside our time horizon, eh? And still not a big enough difference to matter. But it *sounds* good. It's an attractive idea, even just from a crew protection perspective. It blocks *half* the radiation? Am I remembering that correctly?"

"Not quite half," she confirmed. "I think it really was about the same as a tower magnet, which would be forty-five percent. That *would* save us from having to carry a tower magnet down there with us, and it would also protect us from ionizing radiation when we're outside of the township. So that's a double win."

With that word, "us," she was being a bit presumptuous; she was a leading candidate in the sponsorship race, with some of her substantial backing coming out of Beseman's own pocket. He was sponsoring her even though he'd promised not to play favorites, and even though he knew, for a fact, that if she got to Mars she would no longer be his assistant. She'd be starting a life of her own, on a brand-new planet. The yearning for it ached inside her, every minute of every day. But like anyone else in the competition, she *could* be displaced by a better-funded candidate. Only Dan and Carol Beseman were *guaranteed* a spot, and only because it was—ahem!—their ship.

But Beseman did seem to hold some genuine hope that Miyuki would make it, and it was apparently in that spirit that he said, "Put together a promo video, and see if you can't get your own followers to pay for this. Anything you raise, we'll tack onto your sponsorship total, and use it to show how ongoingly critical you are to the colonization effort."

She couldn't help smiling at that. "You've got your thumb on the scales, boss. Be careful that doesn't come back to bite us."

He shrugged, unrepentant and unimpressed. His relationship to Miyuki was necessarily a very close one, since she literally did half his thinking for him. She doubled his productivity, by letting him focus on the things that *only he* could do. She'd ended up as his personal assistant mostly by accident, because she'd been middle-managing some critical-path projects during the early design and build days for the Marriott Stars. Beseman tended to be a very hands-on leader, so anything on the critical path took up a lot of his attention, and so over a period of months he and Miyuki had ended up in the same room together almost every day, for anywhere from a few minutes to a few hours. He'd come to know and trust her enough that when Ara, his last assistant, had quit, he had ignored a hundred applicants to replace her and quite rudely asked Miyuki if she wanted the job.

And although the question was nominally insulting,

Miyuki had said yes immediately, without taking any time to think it over. It meant a substantial raise for her, and an upgrade to a jet set (and later, space set) lifestyle that would have seemed very glamorous to most people. She also knew, even before she'd answered, that it would mean she couldn't have a life of her own. She'd be on call 24/7, and within physical earshot of him for at least eight hours every day. She knew all this, and still she said yes, because she'd sensed—correctly!—that it would put her on a trajectory to Mars. That her one-in-a-thousand shot of making it there would rise to something more like one in a hundred. Maybe more. So she said yes, and although it was a hard road, it was the best road available to her, and she wouldn't regret the decision even if she *did* lose her spot to someone else. She had to take the chance. She *had* to.

Since that day, she'd been within earshot of him for almost more hours than she hadn't. She *always* traveled with him, unlike Carol Beseman, who frequently stayed home. Miyuki had occasionally mused to herself, that it would be easier in some ways if she and Beseman were also sleeping together. Lord knew, the job made it nearly impossible for her to sleep with anyone else! But he wasn't exactly her type, and anyway her self-esteem wouldn't let her sink that low, and the chance of losing Mars to a stupid love triangle was more than she could bear. In any case, Beseman did really seem to love his wife, and probably never wanted to find out what she might do if she caught him cheating. It could be the end of everything! The end of Mars, not just for her and him, but for everyone. But Miyuki would be lying if she said she didn't sometimes enjoy his company, even when they were busy and stressed, which was always. She hoped they'd be friends, in that magical future when she had her own life again.

Meanwhile, a company like Enterprise City never slept, and running it *while building* Concordia *and Antilympus Township* required literally superhuman effort. It required Beseman to delegate fiercely, to collect updates constantly, and to move his own physical self to the trouble spots, wherever they might be. Asia, Antarctica, low Earth orbit . . . they all blurred together in a haze of constant motion.

Carol Beseman (with whom Miyuki also hoped to be friends) took on quite a bit of responsibility herself. She was, among other things, in charge of Enterprise City's U.S. holdings, but by agreement she also had the household to run, so it was ready on a moment's notice to host dinner parties for politicians, billionaires, bureaucrats and celebrities. She had a staff of servants doing the heavy lifting, but still it took a lot of her time, as well it should, because the bigger Antilympus donors and sponsors and political allies needed that constant personal touch. It must be infuriating, Miyuki thought, to be at once a captain of industry, an astronaut in training, and somehow also a goddamn housewife, but that was perhaps *her* deal with the devil, for her chance to live on Mars. She and Beseman were also postponing the children Miyuki knew they both wanted—another thing that had to wait until they were all safely on Mars.

Truthfully, Miyuki had a similar deal with herself when it came to children and relationships. The pickings might be slim at Antilympus—just fifty men, period. But she dared to hope that one of them might just be the love of her life and the father of her children. And if not, well, then she would die alone *on Mars*, having accomplished more than most people ever would.

Did isolation bring people closer together? The colony *would* be isolated, in a way no group of people ever really had been—separated from Earth by enough distance that the speed of light became much more than a theoretical concern. Signals take anywhere from five minutes to forty-five minutes to make the round trip, depending on the positions of the planets. And of course when Mars was directly behind the Sun as seen from Earth (which happened for about twelve hours every twenty-six months), the delay was even longer, because you had to bounce your signal off a repeater at ESL5. That meant, among other things, that Beseman could *not* be physically present at trouble spots for Enterprise City or the Marriott Stars, or even the Earthly supply chains for *Concordia* and Antilympus. He was going to have to delegate even more aggressively to Earthly employees, and have a personal assistant or two *on Earth* to act as his eyes and ears and voice. Which would leave Miyuki, finally, free.

So literally her entire future hinged on her getting a spot at Antilympus, and even then she wouldn't have a real shot, if Beseman himself weren't one of her sponsors. Her *largest* sponsor, by a significant margin, and also by far her greatest proponent. It was an interesting question, whether his word *should* carry so much weight, but it absolutely did. And he did have his thumb on the scales, yes. He wanted her to have that future and that freedom, even if it meant someone else could not. Not in the first wave, anyway. So Beseman controlled her destiny, and she would do whatever it took to maximize her chances. Including letting him bend the rules a little on her behalf.

"It's delicate," he noted carefully, as if reading her mind. "If you're the one managing the optics of your own sponsorships, it could look like a conflict of interest. On the other hand, who else would you want doing that for you? People can see how important you are to the overall effort, and how hard it would be for me to get all of this done without someone like you. Without you, specifically. It may not fit some people's definition of fairness, but we can't please everyone, and nothing says we have to try. As long as the donations keep flowing, we don't *have* to be anything. We're the future of humanity, right here, and as long as we're consistent, nobody can tell us—tell *me*— what the rules should be. I believe in a better tomorrow, Miyuki, which *I'm* paying for, and which you've earned the right to be a part of. So to hell with what people think; we're doing this."

To which she offered an uncomfortable, "Um, thanks." What else could she say?

1.10
25 April

✦

ESL1 Shade Station
Earth-Sun Lagrange Point 1
Extracislunar Space

Alice found Igbal Renz in his overly windowed office, sitting in his chair behind his desk, building something in midair with a 3D pen.

"Knock knock," she said, because the hatch was open.

He looked up. "Ms. Kyeong. Alice. How we doing today?"

"I'm on the job," she said, "studying security issues, but I have questions for you. Lots of them. Your whole profile here . . . well, it's out of whack, isn't it? I mean, it's really panic city for all the major governments down there"— she waved vaguely at the Earth behind him—"looking up at you and wondering what you can *do* to them. You know that, right?"

He turned back to his work—some sort of circuit board, rendered in green and black and shiny-gold plastic.

"Control freaks," he said, his high, gravelly voice betraying no amusement.

"Yeah, well you're going to have to come clean with me. I need to understand what you're really up to, here."

"We," he said. "What *we're* up to. Yourself included."

She waved a hand in the air, impatient with him. "Fine. Fine. Can I come in?"

"Have a seat," he said, now fully focused on his work. The only chair in here was the one he was strapped into.

"What's that you're building?" she asked.

"Prototype."

"Prototype what?"

"It's a machine to ask me stupid questions, so the women around here don't have to."

He was being a dick, and he was her enemy, and she had a job to do that he was *not* going to like, but she actually laughed a little. God help her, she kind of liked the guy. His directness and focus were straight out of the Special Forces, but his pudgy body told a softer story, and she could also detect a nerdy sense of wonder about him, and a basic lack of self-awareness made him seem, at certain moments, almost childlike. Despite his depraved public image, in person he was basically a kid at Disneyland, loving the dream he was living. There was something authentic about it that she could, grudgingly, respect.

"Fuck off," she told him mildly.

He said, "I'm seeing if I can build computers using nothing but 3D-printed tunnel diodes. Right now all my gigahertz-range processors take six different materials and four different machines to build. I'm thinking I can do it with three and one, and free up some metals for a sexier use."

Sexier. Yeah. *There* was the depravity. Still childlike, somehow, but a lot less cute. She reminded herself that he was a drug addict, and a megalomaniac.

"Does it all come down to sex?" she asked. "Is that why you're doing all this?"

He snorted, still not looking up. "You read too many tabloids."

"Meaning what? How many women have you impregnated up here? How many are you planning to?"

Now he did look up. "With my own personal sperm? One."

"One?"

"You heard me."

"Pam?"

"She's my girlfriend, yes. My girlfriend of almost six years, if we're being nosy about it. She and I have an open relationship, but not *that* open. I don't keep harems. Shit. Are they still saying that?"

"Your own people are saying that."

He laughed. "Well that explains a lot. Shit. What do you think this is? I'm a *feminist*, Alice. Worldwide, my workforce is fifty-eight percent female. You think it's because I'm . . . Wow. So, what, you all came up here thinking I was going to . . . I mean, do you have any idea what that would do to the long-term plan? You think we can colonize space if everybody's half brothers and half sisters with each other? Holy moly. I need women who are willing to get pregnant, yes. Obviously. You load up a starship with people, they had better all be pregnant women! Anything else is a waste of mass budget. But from different fathers! From genetically diverse donor sperm!

Oh lordy, I can see I need a frank conversation with my PR people."

Alice's brain stopped working the moment he said "starship." Did she hear that correctly? Was this yet another big briefing she had somehow missed? Jeanette had mentioned something about antimatter starship fuel, but Alice thought it was just chatter. She'd thought Jeanette was speculating about some vague ambition of Igbal's. At *that* time, her brain had stopped at the word "antimatter," and its global security implications. But she could see it should have kept going. She should have followed up with more questions, different questions, instead of sulking about Derek Hakkens.

Better late than never, she asked, "What are you talking about? You're not seriously building a starship, are you?"

He pointed out the window above them, toward the Earth.

"You see that? That bright star hanging out there next to Antarctica? That's Alpha Centauri."

When she stared blankly back at him, he said, "You're an astronaut? Really? It's the closest star, Alice. Actually, it's the *three* closest stars, and there's a habitable planet out there. Mostly habitable. Proxima Centauri b, otherwise known as Renzworld. That's where we're going."

"Like, soon?"

"Eventually. Once we have an engine that can get us there in under twenty years. This is all highly proprietary information, by the way, Madame Sheriff. No blabbing."

All kinds of light bulbs went off in Alice's brain, and suddenly she didn't feel so stupid.

"That's why you're freezing people. That's why you're freezing *pregnant women*."

"Correct. Jesus Christ, Alice, what kind of Frankenstein shit did you think was happening up here? You actually believe the tabloids? Seriously? Dan Beseman's going to Mars, and he can have it. He can have it! Let his people name towns and hills and craters after themselves. My people—*our* people—can have their own planets. And they can terraform the shit out of 'em, with no U.N. Space Commission shaking a finger."

"'They'? You're not going with them?"

"Am I a pregnant woman? What did I just say? No, I'm not going, not on the first ship. It sounds like you think you're not, either. You said 'them,' not 'us.' But ultimately, that's why all of you are up here."

"I said 'them'? What are you, the grammar cartel?"

"Yeah. Yeah, I'm the grammar cartel. But you *are* a candidate for this mission, Alice. All you women are. You want to travel? See the sights? I can give you what no one else can. Crew selection has been a very gradual, ad hoc process, so for better or worse, you're going to have plenty of time to think about it. Unfortunately, our star drive research is progressing very slowly, and with many, many setbacks. But even if you decide not to go, or we decide not to send you, we're colonizing right here, too. This place"—he spread his arms, indicating the whole of the station—"belongs to us. The Lagrange point: ours. The Shade: ours. Mining, manufacturing, all under our control. This whole damn orbit belongs to us. The *future* belongs to us."

"Jesus, Igbal."

He looked at her for a thoughtful moment, scratching his beard and seeming a bit glum, then said, "Pam is going. With my baby inside her."

"What do you mean she's going?" The starship wasn't built yet. The starship *drive* wasn't *invented* yet. That was only possible if . . . if she got frozen now, and stayed that way until the mission launched. Whenever that might be. She said, "You're going to freeze her until then?"

His eyes were intense enough to be a little scary. "Last I heard, *you're* going to freeze her until then. Actually, you're going to freeze her, thaw her out, check her vital signs, make sure everything's working as intended, and then yes. Freeze her again, for as long as it takes. She'll wake up at Proxima."

"Jesus. Jesus Christ."

"I didn't get to Esley by thinking small. Nobody ever got anywhere by thinking small."

Alice clicked her tongue back and forth over her teeth, trying to wrap her brain around all this. Her brain limply refused.

"We're getting off track," she said. "I mean, I asked. Fair enough, I asked what you were up to, and now I know. But what I came here to talk to you about is, you're scaring people. You, personally, and it's a major security problem you don't really seem to grasp. People look at you, and they see someone who could *freeze the Earth*, or hold it hostage."

"For what?" he said, somehow managing to sound both amused and genuinely horrified. "To gain what?"

"More . . . power?"

He laughed. "Alice, in a totally literal sense, I've got

more power than I know what to do with. Terawatts of it! We generate as much electricity as North America, which is a lot of electricity, by the way. A lot! And let me tell you, there are *much* easier ways to destroy the world. Any space colony could drop rocks until the Earth cried uncle, and gave in to our demands. *You* could do it. Nothing they could do to stop you. They have some bullshit lasers, which they think will protect them, but against what? They can stop a rock weighing X-many tons. Fine, I'll just drop a bigger rock. Five X. Ten X. Or a thousand rocks at the same time, wrapped in stealth fabric. You think I can't? You think Sir Lawrence can't? You think *Grigory Orlov* can't?

"But *me*? Really? Think about it: What are my demands? I don't need money. I've got more disposable income than governments do! I don't need power or raw materials. What do we actually need up here? Just stuff from Earth. Let us ship some goddamn grapefruits and anchovies up here, and yes, maybe some Swiss femtosecond timing units. What's the difference? I want the blockade called off and the embargo dropped, but I had that already, two months ago. They could have just left us alone, and then we'd have *no* demands. It makes no sense.

"You know what they're really afraid of? The Coalition countries, the ITAR signatories? Precision! They don't give a shit if I freeze the world; they give a shit if I very slightly dim the sun over *America*, and focus a little extra sunlight on Outer Mongolia."

Alice felt her frown deepen. "Yeah, I was told you could do that."

"Of course I can do that. Do you know what a 2D binary Fresnel is? I can see by your face that you don't. That's fine. Point is, the Shade can *steer* light as well as block it. But it can't freeze the Earth. it just can't. Right now, as big as it is, the whole Shade only blocks only *zero point one percent* of the sunlight reaching the Earth. We'd need a shade *twenty times larger* to start a new ice age, and at the rate we're going, that would take a hundred years to build. Even then, the climate changes would be gradual. What you're talking about—freezing the whole world—would take centuries. Literally, centuries. You think governments care what happens in a hundred years? Seriously? You think any of the world's problems would exist right now if that were true?"

"You could move the Shade closer," she speculated. "That would block more sunlight."

"We could," he agreed with a little half laugh. "But that would also take years. It's a delicate sailing operation, and there's no way we'd ever get a chance to finish it. If they saw us moving it, they'd *really* freak out. That's not what they're worried about, either. They're toddlers, Alice. Greedy little toddlers. They care about reelection, taxes, and looking tough, in that order. It's stupid, but it's true. They don't give a shit about the future; they don't even think it's a real thing. It's just something that happens in movies. But *here in the present*, a zero point one percent shift in insolation—in sunlight hitting the ground—is more than enough to affect the weather. It's more than enough to affect crop yields and troop movements and maybe even steer a hurricane away from land. Or toward it! They look at me and see the God of Weather, and no way in hell are they going to make donations to *that* church. You see how petty? How stupid it is? Yes, I can sell rain and shine to the highest bidder if I want to. For chump change. For money I don't need. *That's* what scares them."

"Or antimatter," she said. "You could sell that. Or drop it on them."

"Or antimatter, yes. Real supervillain shit. But goddammit, why? I'm selling twenty million dollars a day worth of spaceship parts and hab modules, and another twenty million in raw ingots. I've got a billion-dollar sphere of gold in a fucking parking orbit in front of the Shade. A billion dollars! What am I supposed to do with that? It's a rounding error. It's a *rounding error*."

"It doesn't matter if you *should* scare them," she said. "It matters that you do. You're a druggie, for one thing."

"Breaking what law?" He looked at the circuit board in his hands, scoffed, and spun it hard against one of the windows. It shattered impressively, the shards tumbling off in every direction. "There! You see that? That's Earthly law. That's what their laws mean to the God of Weather."

"Wow. And you wonder why you have security problems."

Alice didn't know why she was bothering to lecture him. She didn't really know why she was having this conversation at all, or why she did anything really. Was she, like her mother, basically just crashing around in the world? Breaking things, making snide judgments, creating nothing of her own? Was it only the structure and discipline of the Air Force that had ever made her look like a functional person? It was an ugly thought, but perhaps more true than not. Best to get this business over with, somehow, soon, and get back to the Maroon Berets, where there was no gap between who she was and what other people needed her to be.

Thoughtful again, Igbal said, "DMT is a naturally occurring brain chemical. It induces euphoria, yes, but that's not why I take it."

Alice waited, not sure what to say, or how to exit the conversation without raising questions.

"Tribal drugs for contacting the spirit world have always contained DMT. The spirit world, okay? Contact with Beings of some kind. Since the dawn of time. It's also a component of near-death experiences, released by the brain when oxygen levels get too low. And what do people report, when they've come back from the brink? Contact. Contact with something they can't quite explain afterwards. Biochemistry research caught up with that in 1956, when a psychiatrist named Stephen Szára injected DMT into his own arm, and reported 'lights and sounds, Beings and infernal messages.' It's in the literature, Alice. That's a scientific fact.

"In the 1990s, the Beings were reported by about fifty percent of DMT users at dosages above sixty milligrams. By 2030, that proportion was up to seventy percent, and today it stands at seventy-eight. Why the increase? Why the thing itself, at all? About eight years ago, when I was living in San Francisco and *everybody* was vaping DMT, I got sick of hearing the same damn story from everyone I talked to. The Beings! The Beings! I reached a point in my life where that just sounded so improbable. Social trends are one thing, but a shared hallucination that lasts thousands of years, getting more and more specific the harder we look at it? Come on. *Come on.* So I asked myself, what if these Beings are real? What if they're fucking real, Alice, and they're in some neighboring dimension or some other part of the universe, and they're trying to contact us over some entangled channel that's flooded with decoherence noise? Wouldn't that be something?"

In zero gravity, the hairs on your arms are always standing up, so goose bumps don't really feel like anything except a vague sense of cold air brushing over the skin. So that's what Alice felt.

"Wouldn't that be worth investigating?" he asked her. "If we could find ways to quiet the environment, to keep the signal photons entangled long enough for our sensory neurons to interpret the . . . you know, meaning."

"By moving to outer space?"

"Bingo."

She digested that for a moment and then said, "You're crazy."

"Am I?" he waited, then waited some more, then said, "What's crazy? What does that even mean?" He barked out a strange little laugh. "The Beings aren't the only reason I'm here. They're not even the fourth biggest reason, as one quick look around will tell you. Can a crazy person do all this?"

"I don't know," Alice said, brusquely, because she felt like she had to say something.

He looked at her, then said, "Alpha Centauri is three stars. Proxima and Toliman, which we're going to colonize, and Rigil Kent, which we're going to shrink wrap. We'll build a Shade around the whole thing."

"What?"

"You heard me."

"Won't that take a thousand years?"

"Probably. A few hundred, at least."

"Why would you do that?"

"To build a really big battery. You reflect the star's heat back in on itself. The star expands. It expands enough, the fusion reactions shut down and it's just a really hot ball of gas. You extract energy from that—photovoltaic energy, just like here—and the energy is replaced because the star undergoes a little bit of fusion when it shrinks by that amount. It's ten to the forty-fourth joules of energy, wrapped up for our own personal use. We could, you know, send signals across the whole universe, or punch holes in spacetime straight through wherever the Beings are waiting. Or whatever. Whatever we want. Whatever we want, Alice."

She said nothing.

She said nothing again.

Holy fucking fucking fucking fucking fucking fuck.

President Tompkins was worried about this guy changing the *weather*? Alice was half tempted to murder him right here and now. Jesus!

And then another thought occurred to her. "You said 'we,' not 'they.'"

He laughed. "Now who's the grammar cartel?"

"You're going to live to see it, aren't you? You're going to freeze yourself for a thousand years."

"Um . . . Well, not exactly. That wouldn't work. Bodies absorb too much radiation damage in the crystalline state, and the cells aren't awake to repair it. No, I figure I can spend a year awake for every ten years frozen. Live to a hundred and fifty, biologically. That seems reasonable, right?"

Alice couldn't deny that. Life expectancy in rich countries was now close to a hundred, with fresh progress being made every year. When she stopped to think about it—which was rarely, but not never—she realized that when she got too old to jump out of airplanes, she'd need to find some other way to make a living for, oh, another *five decades* or so.

She said, "You're either crazy or . . ."

"Or what?"

Alice didn't have an answer.

"You let me worry about the drugs," he told her. "Let me worry about the starships and all that. Can you do that? You worry about being a medic, and an astronaut, and a security person, or sheriff or whatever. What should I be doing right now, securitywise?"

"I don't know," she admitted. Then, noncommittally, "It's a lot of new information."

Which was true. Her head was spinning with it, and she needed to sort out what it meant for her and Bethy and their mission.

"Well, maybe you could get back to me on that," he said, now snide again.

"Am I dismissed?"

"Yeah, get out of here. And close the hatch on your way out. I broke my damn diode board; I need some quiet."

3.4
25 April

St. Joseph of Cupertino Monastery
Shoemaker-Faustini Plateau
Lunar South Polar Mineral Territories

My Dearest Father Bertram,

I dreamed the Earth was seven peaches, and they were the protons and neutrons of a lithium atom whose S-orbitals spread all the way to Saturn. I awoke with tears in my eyes, my soul humming with an emotion for which I fear no name exists.

This morning a sudden and unpredicted spike in solar electron flux managed to blow a fuse in our radiation-blocking tower coil. Not the circuit breaker down here at the power transformer, mind you, but the actual fuse at the tower's pinnacle. In order to blow the fuse rather than the breaker, the surge must have exceeded four amperes for about ten seconds, or, more likely, more than forty amperes for less than one second.

I had to get up there and fix it, with Geo hovering

nervously on the ground, and someone from Shackleton came by to take the damaged part and some archived voltage data and figure out just what the boggle happened, because obviously that ain't how a tower magnet ought to die. The theory of Eldad Barzeley, Harvest Moon's chief solar radiation scientist, is that we were hit by a plasma toroid— basically an invisible smoke ring ejected by the sun and tumbling end over end to form a sphere—that was less than thirty meters across and moving at only about ten meters per second, but carrying so large a concentration of charge that were it to strike atmosphere it would manifest as a ball lightning the size of a house.

"Such events should be rare," he says, "but apparently not so rare that we don't need to account for them." Untangling the negatives, he means that they can probably upgrade the electromagnet's controller, either with a firmware update or else a whole replacement board, to account for at least this particular scenario, and perhaps a more general protection, so they said to expect someone to come by again in a few days to grade us up. We are, I remind you, beta testing every aspect of everything, and if the Sun is rolled across the sky by a dung beetle, as thought the Egyptians, or if it be a flaming chariot pulled by sky horses as thought the Greeks, and more than capable of melting a set of waxen wings in either case, it hardly matters, for even after all this time Ra retains his power to surprise us. Perhaps yon scarab isn't above punting us a little micro-sun every now and again, and perhaps the Moon is made of green cheese after all.

You have asked about rumors, and it's interesting, for I haven't heard the one that's piqued your curiosity, and I *have* heard another that apparently hasn't. To be more specific, no, an African woman in a stolen shuttle hasn't crash-landed here at the monastery, nor would I expect her to survive such an impact if she'd somehow managed it. Nor has any unscheduled landing taken place at Moonbase Larry, for we'd've heard on the radio a call to guard our flank against rocket-kicked projectiles. Further and more to the point, Larry's Boys are a chattering bunch, and if they'd seen this woman or knew of her whereabouts, I would not expect them long to keep the secret.

I can, of course, make use of the gray matter God hath given me and heave forth a speculation: she's with Grigory Orlov. Perhaps "with" in more sense than one, although here I admittedly let my more prurient interests in the world shine forth, without evidence, as celibate people are often wont to do. Surely everyone is copulating except me! At any rate, if she did not reenter Earth's atmosphere nor leave behind an expanding cloud of fuel and shuttle parts, then methinks she must still be in space, and the list of places to hide so large an accoutrement is not a long one. She could mayhap be among the Chinese, but this tickles me unlikely, for they make a great deal of their independence from all other nations and commerces. What gain would be seen by them in hosting a purloined ship and its purloiner? No, I think they'd throw her publicly in a Chinese jail for wasting e'en a moment of their time and a gram of their oxygen.

On the other hand, what's Orlov Petrochemical's interest? It depends why and from whom this woman fled, for Clementine to seem a refuge, but if she departed Transit Point as you say, then that would be a frying-pan-to-fire maneuver of the highest order for a woman on the run. Baron Grigory has less sense of humor than even *le Chinois*! But if she were one of his, then it makes more sense to this reporter, although I can't guess it any farther. One of his what? Doing what?

There is an idiom in Russian that translates perfectly into English: "The world is divided into the who and the whom." Grigory is definitely a who, so the question to my mind is whom he's whoming, and for what gain. And that's a question that rightly shudders my bones, for the Dark Horseman seems so capable of nefary that His Holy would do well to keep an eye, lest some of his hoped-for faithful be snatched instead into mortal sins of greed and wrath and pride and envy, and I think even a touch of gluttony, if still other rumors are believed.

So there. You have your girl, and grist for the mill of rumors in which you appear ensconced.

All the more surprising, then, that you haven't heard this next one, for the good people of Moonbase Larry let slip today that the largest of His Holy's secret benefactors funding this here Valley of

Saint Joe is none other than Sir Larry his own self. Which, after but a moment's reflection, makes sense, for he's of Irish stock and therefore Catholic in his bones, if not always in his heart. He needs a high-backed customer far more than he needs a billion dollars, and so he slips his petty cash roll from one pocket to another, and His Holy Himself stoops to kiss it along the way! What better validation for an off-world business than Heaven itself smiling down? Or up; I confess I'm not quite sure of the geometry from this vaunted vantage, for if God is in the clouds as we've long imagined, then we're seeing not up His robe but down the part of His hair, and that's a thought that takes some getting used to. Mayhap I'll imagine him in the clouds of Jupiter, and let my itchy soul rest a bit.

Now, repeating gossip is no monastic trait, and it's a sin I'll confess and atone right enough, but I have one more for your ear, and it's a doozy: Before arriving here, Brother Eggs somehow managed to get his hands on a set of space underwear with red and white stripes, like some oldey timey swimsuit one might see photographed beneath a straw barbershop hat and stood beside a giant-wheeled bicycle. As this violates both the letter and the spirit of our asceticism, both locally and in general, and present as well as past, I gratefully refer the matter to you for adjudication, and will abide by whatever instructions or counsel you see fit to bestow.

My love, I understand you (and seven additional

Brothers, aye) will *not* be with us in another month, but owing to a general state of disorder in cislunar space will be delayed by time unknown. I miss speaking with you one person to another, and also confessing my sins, for I confess here in writing that this place is too small for me to voice my most meaningful sins aloud. How private is the confessional video conference, albeit encrypted, if one's Brothers are always so close at hand? And while you may perform masses for us, for which we gratefully accept the switchboard connection to the divine, can the Eucharist truly be consecrated over radio waves? If God is merciful (which I do not doubt, for he sent his only son to intercede for our souls), he surely must accept these, our best efforts, as close enough for Heaven. And yet, one does not give up everything to be closer to Him and then feel one's soul aright with a distance in fact so great it takes one's prayers a second and a half to make the trip, or 2.7 seconds to bounce back refused.

I think you know that the word "abbot" derives from the Aramaic "*abbā*" and means, literally, "father," and in descent from the original Proto-Indo, where that word is "*pater*" or "paba," appears to have deleted its first plosive. Children and their mangling of words, am I wrong? This of course gives His Holy—our Latin *Papa*—a title older than yours, which I reckon fitting all in all, but also easier to hear over a noisy channel, which may say something about both the Protos and the Aram. In any case, this fatherlessness, or rather father-remoteness, is a real and distinct sensation for those of us who've tried to snuggle closer to the father of us all.

And so, ascetic even in our religiosity, we sip grape-flavored CHON drink tinctured with drug-printed ethanol, and nibble radio-blessed CHON starch wafers, and await the day, one hopes not too far in the future, when the Abba of St. Joe resides here among his wayward sons.

I remain, very yours and very truly,
Brother Michael Jablonski de la Lune

1.1
25 April

✦

ESL1 Shade Station
Earth-Sun Lagrange Point 1
Extracislunar Space

Back in her apartment, Alice saw she'd finally received a reply from President Tompkins:

Reqst apprvd 2 recruit local assist. Your rank breveted to Major (O4) for chain of cmd., duration of assignment. Authorized involuntary reactivation of Capt's commission, on pain of court-martial charge desrtn. Pls. inform name / serial no.?

Huh. Somehow, Alice had apparently jumped from Sergeant to Major in one giant leap. Was that all it took to make officer these days? Just travel a million kilometers from anywhere, and run out of ideas?

She replied:

Capt. Derek Hakkens USAF. That's all info I have at moment.

❖❖❖

This time, the reply came back within thirty seconds:

Roger that, Major. Bring him in.

Well. Was that a direct order from the President of the United States? It certainly looked like one. She'd been only half thinking when she made the request, but she felt a vague sense of guilt and foreboding about it now. Whatever was about to happen—whatever stupid thing was about to befall these people—Derek was now fully implicated.

Fuck. She really needed to be smarter about this. Maybe . . . maybe Derek could *help* her be smarter? With his smarmy flyboy precision, he was the exact opposite of impulsive. And he had survived the June Massacre over Coffee Patch, somehow ducking and evading through a sky filled with EMP drones. Clearly, he really did know how to improvise under duress. Either that or he was simply lucky, and did not happen to get painted by a Chinese drone radar on that fateful morning, but in any case he was a good and careful pilot, and caretaker of hibernating passengers. And he knew ESL1 Shade Station far better than she did.

But she'd be asking him to betray his friends and colleagues. Actually, she'd be *ordering* him to do that, and if he refused, well, he might never set foot on Earth again. Not in a Coalition country, anyway, not without being thrown into military prison for the rest of his life. That hardly seemed fair. And that was a strange thought all by itself, because "fairness" wasn't a concept that entered Alice's thinking very often. In war, some people were killed or maimed or disfigured, while others walked away without a blemish. Some came in as coddled officers who never saw gunfire up close, because they had good supportive parents who sent them to college and medical school. Hell, most people never went to war at all. Most people never shot anyone, or held a dying eighteen-year-old as he shuddered out his last breath, or watched their friends get blown out of the sky all around them.

Fuck.

President Tompkins had wanted an icy operative, and Alice was doing a poor job of being one, perhaps because she had no actual instructions to execute. Or targets. Not instructions or targets that were specific or made any sense. And yet, she was also unequipped for any sort of touchy-feely self-actualization-type crap. If there was a bloodless solution, she was the *last* person she would pick to identify it and carry it out. She felt like she was missing something here—maybe something really obvious—but knowing that did nothing to help her solve it.

Fuck!

And to top it all off, she was horny, because she'd walked out into the world this morning expecting to get laid and clear her head, and instead she'd been smooshed up against Jeanette Schmidt for four hours. And it occurred to her now, that if (or when) she did reactivate Derek's commission, he'd be in *her* chain of command, off-limits to her again and for *real* this time, on pain of court-martial for the both of them.

The obvious solution was to bone him one last time and *then* reactivate his commission, which seemed unethical on multiple levels, so the next most obvious solution was to keep her pants on until this job was complete.

Which did, actually, finally, give her an incentive to get the operation complete, and move it into the past.

Well, then. For the moment, all roads seemed to lead to Derek Hakkens.

"Lurch," she said, bracing herself on a grab bar and leaning on the comm button beside the hatch.

"Yes?" the machine voice answered from its little speaker.

"Where is Captain Hakkens?"

"Location blinded," Lurch replied. Meaning, Derek had asked the system not to report his whereabouts.

"Can you connect me to him, please?"

"Calls refused," Lurch replied, meaning Derek had taken himself fully offline for a while.

Sighing, she asked, "Where was his last reported location?"

"Apartment Alpha-six," Lurch answered.

"Is that his . . . Is that Derek Hakkens' apartment?"

"Yes."

"And when was that?"

"Eight minutes ago."

So then, Derek was in his quarters. Sometimes you just had to know the right questions to ask.

She let go of the comm button and opened her hatch, swinging it inward and then flipping around it into Gamma Corridor, and kicking off from a grab bar without bothering to close the hatch again behind her.

Derek's quarters were in the other residential cluster, so she flipped and kicked and soared and swung her way through the station, not caring if she showed off more zero-gee maneuvering skill than she was supposed to have right now. Gamma Corridor had a weird, flexible tube connecting it to Alpha Corridor, but the tube had several hard bends in it, and no handholds, and there was hard vacuum outside of it, and it all just seemed a bit sketchy to her. Instead she took the long way around, through Beta Corridor and a couple of laboratories. She passed women she didn't know yet except by sight, doing things she didn't have much clue about. Some had VR headsets on. Some were typing into tablet keyboards or whispering into microphones or peering into scientific instruments. One—Saira Batra, the mathematician from *Dandelion*—was diligently cleaning the wall (or floor) of Beta Corridor with a squirt bottle and a scrubby sponge.

"Hey," Alice said as she brushed by.

"Hi," Saira said back, not looking up from her work.

Finally Alice came to Derek's apartment—number Alpha-6—and rapped twice on the hatch with her knuckles. It was made of fairly thin steel, and rang like an old metal trash can lid.

For a few seconds, nothing happened. She knocked again. Again, nothing happened for a few seconds, but then she heard some rustling against the metal of the hatch, and then it swung inward, revealing Derek. His coverall was unzipped to the waist, revealing that bright orange space undershirt. His hair was messier than usual, and his lips looked red, almost as if he'd been . . . kissing someone.

"What?" he said, looking annoyed.

From inside, Jeanette Schmidt's voice said, "Is it Alice?"

"Yes," he answered. Then, to Alice: "Do you need something?"

"I need to talk to you. It's urgent."

"Right now?"

"It's urgent, yes."

"Come on inside," Jeanette's voice said. "Derek, invite her in." She sounded . . . nervous. Self-conscious. *Caught*.

Damn. It wasn't like Derek was Alice's boyfriend or anything, and she had *already resolved not to fuck him*. Not today. And yet, jealousy bloomed within her shriveled heart.

She couldn't stop herself from saying, "Damn it, Jeanette."

"Come in," Jeanette said. Then, more firmly, "Alice, please. Come on in."

Still looking annoyed, Derek nudged his body out of the way, making space for Alice to squeeze past him and into the apartment. But his irritation was giving way to . . . curiosity? Slightly smug curiosity? And in another moment, Alice could see why: Jeanette was hanging in midair dressed only in golden hair and gray space underpants.

Jesus. Jesus Christ. This wasn't the first time Alice had been invited into a threesome—Hell, it wasn't even the sixth. Over eight years among the Special Forces of every major service (including, once, the I-shit-you-not super-secret nuclear commandos of the U.S. Department of Energy), she'd heard just about every lewd suggestion it was possible to hear. But only ever half-sincere, and only ever from the men.

It's not like it had never occurred to Alice, to wonder what she'd do if the opportunity actually arose. This was, in many ways, the most sexually fluid decade in American history. But the opportunity never had arisen.

What she said was, "Jeanette? Goddammit. What makes you think . . ."

But the words trailed away, and she came inside, and let Derek close the hatch behind her.

Well, well.

In another wordless minute, her hands were on Jeanette's hips, and Derek's hands were on her coverall zipper, and Jeanette was saying, "Station full of women. You think I didn't think about that before . . . I might need you to show me . . . I might need you to . . ."

And Alice was saying, "I'm not really . . . This isn't actually . . ."

And Derek was saying, "Just relax. Take it slow. Just let it unfold."

And Alice was just taking Jeanette's breasts into her hands when the hatch swung open again, and a head covered in aquamarine hair was sticking in sideways.

"Derek?" said Maag. "Are you . . . Oh. Oh, wow. Excuse me! I didn't . . ."

Jeanette looked up, laughed nervously, and drawled, "Malagrite, your timing is simply amazing. You might as well come in."

To which Derek said, "Um, sure," and Maag said, "Are you serious?" And Jeanette said, "Why not? The more, the merrier."

And then the hatch was closing again, with Maag on this side of it, and all Alice could think to say was, "Oh, for fuck's sake."

And then, for quite some time, no one said anything at all.

6.1
25 April

✧

Airship *Lepidoptera*
West Antarctica
Earth

Lawrence stared morosely out the window, at the shadow of his airship on the paper-white, mirror-flat West Antarctic Ice Sheet below and behind him. It was an autumn afternoon here in Antarctica, so while the day was bright, the shadow lagged well behind the airship *Lepidoptera* itself, looking stretched out, more dragonfly than butterfly.

Lawrence Edgar Killian—*Sir* Lawrence Edgar Killian—would be the first to admit, he was accustomed to things going his way. Very accustomed. Too accustomed, perhaps. And yet, even trillionaires and Horsemen could have bad days, and this here was one of his.

Oh, his problems were first-world problems, to be sure. Gilded, diamond-encrusted problems! He'd wanted to gather up some close chums and skydive from the balcony of *Lepidoptera* onto the South Pole, and that had been kiboshed in pretty much every way the ki could bosh. His personal physician had caught wind of it and advised strongly against, saying, "Your heart has had enough nonsense for a man your age, Larry." And while he'd been more than ready to ignore that advice, his jump master had told him that even in heavy spacesuits they'd be risking amputation-class frostbite if they free-fell more than half a mile. Which, what was the point if they didn't? And then all but one of the chums had backed out in favor of other engagements, too full of their own lives to drop everything and indulge a septuagenarian on something like this. And even then Lawrence had been prepared to try it. Even then.

But the embargo and the blockade had somehow put all his threelium in the hands of Grigory Goddamn Orlov for the foreseeable future and then some, and that spelled curtains and mothballs for poor *Lepidoptera*, too heavy to float on normal helium.

And so, the craft *Popular Mechanics* had once called "perhaps the most fantastical vehicle real life has yet served up" was on its final voyage (or final for a long, long while) across Antarctica to Tierra del Fuego, where it would float into a rented airport hangar and, for the first time in almost six years, power down and sleep.

"Can't you run it on pure hydrogen?" one of the old chums had asked. "I hear it's not really that dangerous."

But Lawrence had looked into it, and the risks were horrendous. Specially designed hydrogen balloons could be piloted with relative safety—safe as skydiving, anyway—but for a craft of this type, this *unique* type— the ever-present risk of static electricity was a pin through the heart. And so *Lepidoptera* would be pinned to the

Earth, and by the time he could unpin it, he might just actually be too old for such things.

"Sir, your three o'clock is coming up," said Gill Davis, peeking around the gilded doorway into Lawrence's cabin, here at the aft of the airship's long gondola. His hand on the doorframe disturbed a pair of butterflies—a brushfoot and a swallowtail—that had been clinging to it. Their flight disturbed several others resting nearby, so that Davis seemed to have puffed into existence in a cloud of brightly colored wings.

"Right. Thank you," Lawrence said, glancing up for only a moment before returning his gaze to the airship's shadow trailing behind them.

"Are you all right?" Davis asked. He was a slight, servile, middle-aged man with truly impeccable manners. Truly impeccable. Would have made a perfect English butler, and some might say he *was* one, among other things. But there was concern in his voice.

"I will be," Lawrence assured him.

"You've been in here a long while. You should come have something to eat."

"I might do," Lawrence agreed. Then, just to sound less stuffy and disconnected, he asked, "How long until we reach the ocean?"

"I believe about twenty hours," Davis said, "although I can check with the crew if you like. We'll be crossing the Thiel mountain range a lot sooner, if you're pining for something to look at. And then it's the Ellsworth Mountains, and then we'll overfly the colony at Ciudad de Esperanza, and then the Ronne Ice Shelf. Then we reach the ocean, and run parallel to it toward the tip of South America."

"Hmm. I suppose I *am* pining for visual relief. This little adventure sounded more adventurous in principle than it turns out to be in practice, hmm? Just whiteness. Miles upon miles of blank whiteness, with only the occasional crevasse for our shadow to cross."

The crevasses were impressive in principle, too; blue-white cracks a mile deep, reaching probably all the way down to bedrock. But in practice they were just razor-thin squiggles on a white canvas, quickly vanished into the distance. To date, the only excitement along the way had been sixty hours ago—a storm they couldn't outrun and couldn't outclimb. *Lepidoptera* had to go to ground for that one, and wait it out for about five hours.

The ship's gas bag was roughly the size and shape of the old Goodyear Blimp, but with a much larger gondola slung beneath, and four brightly colored turbofans projecting out from the corners of that—the butterfly's wings. A *pregnant* butterfly that flew upside down, with its wings beneath its fat body, and impossibly beautiful for all that. How Lawrence loved this ship!

With little choice and little time, the crew had sat her down on the ice sheet, a mile and more above sea level, and they had all bundled into heavy coveralls and parkas and goggles and masks, and stood outside to watch as the bag deflated and, under the influence of carefully timed cable retractors, folded up like a paper map against the curve of the magnesium-alloy keel. The ship then looked like a fat-footed lizard carrying a quartered pickle on its back, and the crew threw mooring lines over it and affixed them to spikes they pounded into the ice with pneumatic hammers.

That gasbag was Mylar over Kevlar, coated on the inside with alternating layers of aluminum and glass many thousands of times thinner than a human hair, and on the outside with microstructured photonic crystal that shimmered in every conceivable color and pattern as winds and sunlight played across it. That bag remained, gram for gram, the most expensive aircraft component ever constructed, but though its gas transfusion rates were fantastically small, and although the lift gas was fifteen percent deuterium-depleted hydrogen and eighty-five percent threelium (the absolute lightest gas mix he could run without the aforementioned risk of fire and explosion), Lawrence still paid a billion a month to keep the thing inflated. A billion a month. It had seemed a playful, exuberant idea when he'd first thought of it, and some of the public seemed to agree, celebrating *Lepidoptera* as a wonder of the world when it finally took to the air. Iconic images of it had made the rounds: in the air over Paris, over London, over Mount Rushmore and the Grand Canyon, over Sydney and Tokyo and Kuala Lumpur. The world could be such a dreary place, and after Rosalyn had died, he'd just wanted to create something truly magical, and let it loose in the public eye.

But then the backlash had started. The tabloids had dismissed it as an obscenity in a world where a few children did still go hungry sometimes. And over time, year by year, more and more people seemed to agree, which did take some of the fun out of it. And seeing it huddled there on the ice, its bag folded, its fans angled against the rising wind, had taken another swipe out of the joy that this pride-and-joy contraption brought him.

It was slower and more fragile than an airplane or a helicopter, and colossally more expensive, and also vulnerable to the whims of weather, and of men like Orlov. Worse than that, it was *unappreciated* by, it seemed, even his close associates, who'd stopped coming 'round to ride on it with him.

Well, fine. So be it. He still had the Moon, did he not? No grander airship than that!

Davis said, "Shall I ask the crew if we can ascend to a higher altitude? It might afford a less monotonous view."

"Why not?" Lawrence said. "We've got to enjoy this trip while we still can."

"Indeed," Davis agreed. "I'll take my leave of you, for the moment, and consign you to your moping, but three o'clock is two minutes away. You have the address you're calling?"

"It's in my calendar," Lawrence assured him. "Along with the reminder. But thank you."

"Mmm-hmm!" Davis said, and disappeared in another cloud of butterflies.

Sighing, Lawrence turned on his teleconferencing system and clicked on the calendar reminder. He was a minute and a half early, but he wanted to get this over with. He believed in delivering bad news personally, and it was an ugly chore even at the best of times. He wanted it behind him.

The call went through, and his teleconferencing screen lit up, and in another few seconds he was looking across in full 3D at the control center of Shackleton Lunar Industrial Station. Fernanda Harb, the station commander, was standing there in her mustard-yellow jumpsuit, and beside her was Huntley Millar, the construction crew foreman, also in yellow, and Brother Michael Jablonski in a beige-and-brown monk's habit, his hands folded peaceably at his waist.

"Hello?" Lawrence said experimentally.

After a little under three seconds' speed-of-light delay, Fernanda smiled and said, "Lawrence, hello. Always a pleasure to hear from you."

"Not this time, I'm afraid," Lawrence told her. Then, "Brother Michael, I see you're dressed formally for the occasion. Egad, let me apologize profusely; when I scheduled the call I wasn't thinking about your personal logistics. What did you do, carry a clean, shrink-wrapped cassock and change in the airlock?"

After the same delay, Brother Michael smiled warmly and said, "It was more complicated than that, actually, but I thought it best not to meet you in my underwear. Please, sir, think nothing of it. After all these months, it's a fine occasion for me to meet your people as something other than spacesuits and radio voices."

"Well," said Lawrence, "you have my apologies nonetheless. Rosalyn and I always did our best to be godly people, and I fear without her to lift me up, my social graces have fallen. And other graces. She'd be very cross with me, if she knew I'd inconvenienced a man of God."

Brother Michael laughed at that. "A monk's raison d'être is to be inconvenienced, sir, and a Lunar monk doubly so. In any case it's helpful to see what you citizens do with the same basic modules we have at Saint Joe. I should have stopped by months ago to compare notes."

Lawrence grunted and nodded, not sure what else to

say. Brother Michael was an unassuming man, perhaps forty years old, clean-shaven and balding on top. Lawrence knew Michael Jablonski had a master's in divinity from Fuller and a master's in physical chemistry from MIT, and that he was temporarily in charge of the monastery, but knew almost nothing else about him, other than the fact he was Canadian. Lawrence had stopped by once when Michael and two other monks were training for their mission in the big water tank at Harvest Moon's Houston facility, but they'd been underwater in training spacesuits at the time, and everyone around them busy as bees. He hadn't stayed to chitchat.

What he finally said was, "I've never actually met a monk before. I'm afraid I don't know the protocol."

Brother Michael smiled and said, "You've met where I come from, sir. Imagine the annoyingly studious guy you went to college with, who wanted nothing more than to spend weekends in the library, learning everything and yet somehow taking a long, long time to graduate. Imagine also the annoyingly religious girl, who went not only to Sunday service but to twice-weekly Bible study, and also took classes in comparative religion and whatnot. Now imagine those two had a baby, who grew up only wanting to please them both, and the Lord."

Lawrence chuckled dryly. "That's you, is it?"

Michael spread his hands slightly, looking sheepish. "That's every monk in Saint Joe, I'm afraid. If we lived on Earth, there'd be nothing remarkable about us at all."

"I doubt that very much," Lawrence told him, "although your modesty is quite charming in this age and day. You've given a fair description not only of yourself but also of my son, Alan, although he doesn't live to please either parent as far as I've ever known. But his mother *was* pious, and his father—me—has a PhD. So you have that in common."

"Well then," said Michael, "that makes you even more a patriarch to us. If I may say so, sir, I'm quite impressed with that credential. How many PhDs go on to make a living wage, I wonder? Not many end up trillionaires, although I hear a fair number of plutocrats and *laboris generantii* have been known to buy a degree or two after the fact."

"*Generantii*, eh? I suppose some do," Lawrence allowed. "But not this one. Anyway, Brother Michael, it's a pleasure to meet you. Hello to you, too, Fernanda. And . . . Huntley, is it?"

"Good morning, sir," said Huntley Millar.

"Is it morning? I'm over the South Pole right now, where it's afternoon all day long."

"That sounds very romantic," said Fernanda.

"Not as much as you'd think," Lawrence grumbled. Then, ashamed of his greed and sloth and general ingratitude, added, "It's beautiful, but there isn't a soul in sight, and this vacuum-sealed window behind me would freeze my hand off if I held it there on the glass long enough. It's quite a deadly environment. Like yours, I suppose.

"Now, Michael, I assume you've figured out this isn't a social call. I'm sorry to tell you, your boss isn't coming on the next rocket, or rather if he is, I don't know when that will be. I can offer you my sincerest apologies about this, but the circumstances are very much beyond our control."

"I had heard this, yes," said Michael. "We try to cultivate some distance from the affairs of the world, but the big news gets through. We know about the blockade, and our dear abbot has already figured the implications, and made arrangements to remain for a time on Earth."

Lawrence grimaced at the mention of that word: abbot. He knew enough about monasteries to know that for one to operate without an abbot was a big deal in a bad way, and *he* was the one who'd insisted on having the three most qualified men go on ahead to prepare the way. Yes, and the eight most qualified after them, so Father Bertram Meagher needn't strain his back setting up a goddamn moonbase. It made him miss Rosalyn that much more, because she'd surely have insisted on a plan more pious, less space-man practical, and the St. Joseph of Cupertino Monastery would have its head in place already.

"We don't even know why the blockade is happening," he said, "which makes it impossible to know how long it will last. Believe me, it's a problem for all of us."

"I'd gathered," said Michael. "And since there's apparently nothing you did to bring it on, there's presumably nothing you can do to end it. Which means an apology is unnecessary and inappropriate, and I therefore gratefully decline to accept yours."

"We're looking at other launch options," Fernanda said, and it wasn't clear to Lawrence if she were speaking to him, or Michael, or both. "We think we can get access at most U.S. and Russian launch sites, but there's a substantial backlog, and their throughputs are quite low compared to Suriname. It's a lot of red tape, but we're working through it."

Lawrence nodded. It wasn't like the Surinamese were dumping rocket fuel in the ocean or working the launch pads with child labor, and yet they somehow got things done. There was a hustle-bustle about them that many other parts of the world simply lacked. Which was fine, as long as those other parts didn't use their military might to obliterate the advantage.

"It's going to be a while," he said to Michael, "No matter what. And whether or not you accept my apology or not, I *am* sorry this is happening. We were shipping, what, seven more people, in addition to Father Meagher? If you're shorthanded, we can try to share some personnel from Shackleton."

Fernanda looked alarmed at that, because she was also shorthanded, but Brother Michael quickly answered, "We're doing fine with what we have, sir. St. Joseph is intended, among other things, to serve as an educational institution, and some of the upcoming placements are in service of that goal. Right now we're still grubbing in the dirt, and won't miss a few eggheads or zealots more or fewer. Honestly, it's fine. There's a lot to figure out, and we're patient people by inclination and training."

"You're too kind," Lawrence said, meaning it. "Are you comfortable enough in your facilities? Are things going well, other than the obvious?"

"God is everywhere," Michael answered, somewhat cryptically. "He was on the Moon long before us, and will be here long after. He is the *entire universe*, peering back at us from every point and vantage. What can we possibly add to that kind of glory? Are you asking if the beds are comfortable? They are, and with the new, taller modules we no longer bang our heads on the ceiling. And the synthesizers all work, and so does the 3D printer. If this embargo *could* starve us out, it would only prove we were never adequate to the task of moon habitation in the first place. Sir, you have equipped us well, and I am content. Let the future bring whatever it may."

4.6
25 April

✧

Clementine Cislunar Fuel Depot
Earth-Moon Lagrange Point 1
Cislunar Space

Grigory found Dona Obata in what passed for the station's observation lounge: a grouping of four portholes on either side of the bay doors of the pressurized hangar, looking down at the crescent Earth. The night side of the planet was aglow with cities, so bright that they could be seen against the glare beside them—the daylit sliver of ocean and clouds. There were grab bars here, clustered around the windows, and a good deal of open space for acrobatics or just simply lounging around. In off hours and odd moments, most of the crew came down here to look at the continents rotating slowly, once per day, 323,050 kilometers straight below. And to watch the Sun's shadow creep more slowly across the spinning globe, completing a cycle every twenty-eight days.

On the station's opposite end was the gym, whose single porthole looked out on the Moon, but that had never enjoyed even a tenth as much tourism. The Moon was a lot less interesting to look at, and uninhabited across most of its face, and more importantly it was *not home*. Even among the elite of the elite of space workers, homesickness was a major health condition, for which medication was common, and for which staring downward was the only real relief. Grigory hadn't felt much of that himself—he owned seven homes on Earth, and he moved between them freely, and also between hotels in other cities. It had been that way for his entire life, since before he was old enough to speak, and so he'd never really developed a strong anchoring to any single location. He did miss his mother and sister sometimes, but it was easier to bring them to him, wherever he was, than to travel all the way to Minsk to see them. Minsk wasn't "home," either, and he didn't miss it.

But still, he knew the signs of homesickness when he saw them, and if he had to bet, he'd lay good money down that Obata, however hard she might seem and however hard she might *be*, was suffering from it now.

"What are you pining for?" he asked her, coming up from behind and grabbing a rail next to her.

"Africa," she said.

"Not Paris?"

She shook her head. "I never lived in Paris. For most of the time I was in *le Commandement des Opérations Spéciales*, I technically operated out of the Grenoble office, in the French Alps. But I was never there long enough to feel like I belonged. What I miss is Brazzaville, on the east bank of the Congo River, across from Gombe and Kinshasa."

"Democratic Republic of the Congo," he said, attempting warmth.

"No, *Republic* of the Congo, not *Democratic* Republic. It's two different countries." She sounded miffed, like this was a thing she was tired of explaining, and tired of being tired of.

"Ah. Forgive my ignorance, please. There are many countries in Africa, and I do business only with the northernmost and southernmost among them, ignoring the broad middle. This Brazzaville was your childhood home?"

She nodded. "A neighborhood called Poto-Poto, *almost* middle class. We had enough to eat, and shoes. And clothing and school uniforms and secondhand electronics. I had a normal childhood, I think, if such a thing exists. I paid attention in school, and I loved fishing, though I rarely got to do it."

"Mmm. It sounds nice. You left for good reason, though, I presume?"

Without looking away from the planet below her, she said, "I had the opportunity to attend college in France at no cost to my parents, and there I was recruited into *le Commandement des Opérations Spéciales* and offered E.U. citizenship. *Le Commandement* knew what they were doing—they suckered me right in, made me their own creation. I speak seven languages, did you know that? Not Russian very well, as you know. Not Italian or German very well, either, but I'm fluent in French, English, Kikongo and Swahili. I was also raised Catholic, which makes me a kind of specialist in the spy business, because it lets me navigate certain countries almost as an insider. Like being a diesel mechanic, instead of simply a mechanic. I know my way around Islam, too, enough to fool any casual inquiry. So even as a French citizen, most of the wet work I did . . . Do you know that term? Wet work?"

"Mmm," he acknowledged. "*Krovovaya rabota*, we say in Russia: blood work. Or dirty work, I suppose. *Gryaznaya rabota*. I suppose everyone calls it that."

"Yes. Everyone does. Anyway, all the *gryaznaya rabota* I did was in Western and Central Africa. Which is a very big place—bigger than Europe, and nearly as populous. It's true that I moved to Europe voluntarily, and then came to outer space voluntarily, and worked hard to be able to stay here. Don't mistake my meaning. But yes, I miss every centimeter of Africa."

"Smells? Birdsong? Particular kinds of trees and flowers?"

"Everything," she said. "I miss everything. I didn't feel it much at the Marriott Stars, but of course there you have the Earth turning right under you. It's not much different than being in an airplane; I mean, the ground looks like *the ground*. From here, you can't really see any details. it looks like a globe. I mean, when you can see it at all. It was a nearly full Earth when I got here, but now it's just this crescent. I don't think Africa's even down there right now; I think it's on the other side."

"It is," he confirmed. "Right now we are over western Pacific. Those lights you see are Japan and Australia. But Africa will be directly under us in twelve hours, if that helps."

"It doesn't, but that's all right. I'm an adult."

That word, adult, made Grigory think of his father, who had never really seen Grigory as one. Nor had Grigory particularly seen himself that way, until Magnus suddenly died one day and left Grigory no choice in the matter. He'd taken over the companies, using everything he'd learned at his father's elbow, and doing quite well, even if he *was* just playacting for those first few years. To Dona he said, "My father would tell you to ignore your feelings and do what is numerically best."

Still without turning to look at him, she nodded. "That worked out well for him, did it?"

"Yes. But I've done better by *not* ignoring mine. Feelings are *information*, from parts of ourselves that have been evolving for billions of years. Feelings sense danger and opportunity long before mathematics does. Ignore them at your peril, I say. We are optimized deep-learning networks, every one of us. Does it surprise you? That I have feelings? I think this homesickness is perhaps our brains telling us we're not very good yet at building homes in space."

Putting her face closer to the window, she fogged it with her breath and said, "Great. That's great, Orlov. You'd've made a fine chaplain."

He didn't know what to say to that, so instead he pressed on with the point he'd come down here to discuss:

"You should know that your friends, the American and the Kiwi, have arrived at ESL1. We've got people monitoring all the Renz Ventures news feeds, and they're reporting arrival of seven new crew members. Apparently an eighth one remained behind at Transit Point due to some kind of health concern. And you, of course, disappeared. They didn't mention that part, and the absence of comment tells me they're concerned, and confused."

"Okay."

"So. I need you to tell me when and how your friends will strike."

"They're not my friends," Dona said. "They were agents of competitor countries. Yes, I did know them well enough and like them well enough. They were colleagues, fellow operatives on a mission. But that would not have prevented me from doing to them whatever was necessary. It still doesn't. If they were *friends*, I couldn't act."

"Yes, fine," he said, annoyed by the distinction. By that terminology, he himself had no friends at all. He breathed in deeply through his nose, and then exhaled. The air in here smelled, somehow, like petroleum jelly and sand. "I still need you to tell me what they will do."

She shrugged. Still looking out the window, wiping the fogged glass with a sleeve of her uniform. "It was left up to our judgment. Our orders were to spend at least a few days figuring the place out, and then take control, decisively but with minimal loss of life, and minimal equipment damage. 'Bloodless' was a stated goal, though not an absolute requirement."

"Do they have weapons?"

Now she did turn and look at him. "Officially, no. And our belongings were analyzed at the launch center."

"But?"

"But anything can be a weapon. And the Americans in particular are good at disguising such things. They do love their guns."

He snorted. They did indeed. But this gave him the opportunity to ask something he'd been meaning to ask for days now: "Do *you* have a gun?"

Funny, he'd been nervous about asking her this. His heart fluttered when he spoke the words. And it was a strange thing, because he wasn't afraid of guns, and wasn't afraid of *her*. He supposed he was afraid that he might, after all, have to put her out the airlock for her trouble. It was a surprisingly upsetting thought, but yes, there it was. He apparently didn't want to lose her, this woman who showed no dismay when he spoke his mind. And that was a strange thing, too, but all right.

"Yes," she answered, without fear or embarrassment. "I do."

"A firearm?"

"Of a sort, yes."

He sighed. "Morozov searched your flight bag when you arrived, and he went over your shuttle in great detail over the next several days. I trust him as much as I trust anyone, and he assured me he found nothing suspicious."

"No," she agreed. "He wouldn't have."

"Are you carrying this weapon right now?"

"No," she said, "but I'll show it to you later. Three shots total; that's all it's got. I figured it was one for Bethy, one for Alice, one for Igbal Renz, and then people would start doing whatever I said. But I don't need a firearm to be dangerous, Grigory."

"I know it," he said. "Nor do I."

He pursed his lips, then, and nodded slowly. "Yes, please do show it to me. I think you are aware that some people here are also armed, and also trained killers. Perhaps your instincts can pick them out from the general population. Perhaps you think you can strike first, and neutralize them—neutralize *us*—but this would be difficult. Quite difficult. I personally would not like to find out how that skirmish goes. For you *or* for us."

It was her turn to nod. "I understand all that, yes. There are dangerous people here, yes. It's why *I'm* here. It's why I belong here. This is one of those cases where violence doesn't create any solutions. We're actually on the same side."

Stroking his chin, he said to her, "I know you got into my wall safe, Dona. Never mind how I know that, but you needn't bother denying it."

"I'm sorry," she said simply. "Force of habit."

He'd wiped the whole thing down the day she got here, inside and out, and yet a week later he'd found her fingerprints all over it, inside and out. No surprise; he'd half expected her to do it, and had given her plenty of opportunity. For some reason he hadn't bothered to clean the thing out, though, so her getting in there meant, among other things, that she'd seen *his* firearm, and the box of little shotgun shells it could fire. "Varmint load," the Americans called it. For killing rats and such. Perfect also for violence on board a space station, where their lack of penetrating power was an asset rather than a liability.

He told her, "You know, I understand. Truly. It's in your nature, and I *understood* your nature the moment we met. But you should know, people here have their habits as well, myself included. You are compromised in any number of ways. You may think you know this. You may even think you have some control over it, but you couldn't possibly know how all things work here. The danger you're in, every minute you draw breath. Habits that can be hard to break, yes? No matter the risk or cost. Violence solves nothing for *you*, but that does not mean it solves nothing for *me*, if you cross certain lines."

She laughed, wearily. "You always know the right thing to say. Such a charmer, this one."

"You think me rude? I have left you rope enough to hang yourself, and simply waited. That is kindness I do not lightly bestow."

"I do understand that, yes. *I'm* also not killing *you*." She held up her hands. "See?"

He sighed. This conversation wasn't going as intended. He supposed that was a good thing, a fine thing, that there was one person aboard this station who remained unimpressed by his wealth and power, unafraid of the violence he could command. One person with whom he must, apparently, behave genuinely, for she saw through him when he didn't. But at the end of the day, speaking without bluster was something at which he had no practice.

He touched his forehead, touched the grab rail in front of him, touched his hair—fidgeting like a schoolboy. "The world is every kind of poison, is it not? But in building *new* worlds, Dona, we must be careful what we bring with us, and what we leave behind. I have two daughters, did you know? By two different ex-wives. I have little contact with any of them. They don't fit into the cubbies of my life, so I pay them each a stipend, and otherwise think little about them. I thought perhaps you would want to be told that."

It seemed strange at times, that both of those lives were in the past. His life with Albina and Rada, and his life with Darya and Klara. Each had seemed, briefly, like a world unto itself, but they'd moved *so easily* into the past. They *belonged* there; they'd each gone badly and ended badly, in their own ways. And yet, at the time, each one had been his present and, seemingly, his future. The way things moved into the hungry past, inexorably and without comment, sometimes worried him, because he knew someday it would *all* be past, and he would be on his deathbed, with no future at all. And he knew—any idiot knew!—that meant he had to make the most of the present. To live every moment to its fullest. But what exactly did that mean? What did it prescribe? His role was a dangerous one, in a dangerous world. He could no more step away from it than he could step away from life itself. He'd made more than enough enemies, and if they sensed weakness, he was burnt. But still, one had to try.

"I don't know why I am telling you this," he said, "but I feel the urge to be known."

"Thank you for understanding," she said back to him, and it was such a strange thing to say, he couldn't tell if she was serious or sarcastic, or what she meant by it. It occurred to him that she was also nervous. Not about his power, not about his wealth. About *him*, Grigory, the authentic human being.

She turned back to the windows, and was silent for a while. Eventually, she said, "I've left plenty behind, to become what I am."

"You are speaking of more than just Africa?"

A pause. Then: "Speaking of myself. I left behind all the selves I could have been, if *le Commandement des Opérations Spéciales* hadn't put my life on rails, with no way to get off."

"Ah," he said, nodding, though she couldn't see it. "We

all leave selves behind, I think, to become new selves. And Africa was never a peaceful place, not in a million years of history. Never innocent, but I suppose *you* were, at one time. And now you're prepared to shoot your friends in back of the head, for money."

"You're an insightful man," she said, making it sound like something other than a compliment. "But it's not that little Poto-Poto girl I'm missing right now. Can't I just be homesick? Looking down at the world makes me realize there's nothing there for me to go back to. There *is* no Africa anymore. I mean, it's still a pile of shit. Still Africa in *that* way, but with all the same robots and drugs and 'content' as everywhere else. So much bullshit. I have enough money now, I could buy a villa there, with robot guards and a human butler, or human guards and a robot butler. But for what? The whole continent is drowning in bullshit, not even trying to be itself any longer. There need to be better places than that. If we're building things, we need to *build* better places than that."

Was that why she was here? Was that what Clementine represented to her? A *better place*? There were adventurers and escapists among the station's crew, to be sure, who loved the frontier and all it stood for. An escape from Earthly bullshit, yes. A chance to participate in the creation of a grand future. But space was also full of boring laborers, and boring followers, and its own kinds of bullshit. There *was* some freedom here for men like Grigory, but rather less for men like Morozov, and perhaps none at all for men like Daniel Epureanu, the Moldovan technician with whom Grigory had drunk and smoked and eaten caviar last month.

"There is bullshit in space, also," he told her. "In Russian, we say the world runs on *blat*, *ponty*, and *kompromat*. This translates, very approximately, as returned favors, status-seeking, and the dirt one digs up on one's enemies. There is precious little trading of favors in space, but *ponty* is all around us. Every man and woman here lords it over everyone beneath them. How could it be otherwise? My father lived for a time among the communists, who claimed to make all humans equal in rights and dignity. Hardly. Capitalism is at least more honest; your status is whatever you can grab from your fellow man. There is no wheedling for it, only grabbing by force or persuasion or by identifying a need. And there is *kompromat* up here as well. Your *kompromat* got you kicked out of Transit Point, and Igbal Renz has been targeted for death over his own, and rightly so. You think Esley Shade Station isn't as decadent as your poor, contaminated Africa?"

"Not for long, it isn't," she said darkly. "But you know, even Renz is trying to build something. I'm not sure exactly what, but I've studied the man. He's not just smoking DMT and blotting out the sun. He's up to something more . . . interesting than that."

"And the Americans can't stand it."

"No," she agreed. "They can't, and they're not alone in that. The French and the Kiwis and the Chinese can't stand it. It's a big light switch he's got his hands on, and they'll kill him for it. Like you said, these are treacherous times, even for trillionaires."

"Hmm."

"Even you."

"You think I don't know this? It's the air I breathe." Nervously, he reached out and put a hand on her shoulder. He said, "You and I have very little reason to trust each other."

"Correct," she agreed, her eyes on the dark world below.

"It would be foolish in the extreme, and so we both know better. But Dona, I'm going to propose we do it anyway. Fuck the world and its schemes. They say space has a way of changing people, and perhaps we can choose the manner of it, and build, as you say, better places within ourselves. If I reset my wall safe combination, will you stay out of it? Let us both have some secrets?"

She snorted, not turning. "Would you believe me if I said yes?"

"Let us say, I will do my best to believe you."

Now she did look over her shoulder at him, and there were weightless tears quivering in her eyes.

"Sadly, Grigory my darling, that may be the nicest thing anyone has ever said to me."

1.12
26 April

✧

ESL1 Shade Station
Earth-Sun Lagrange Point 1
Extracislunar Space

Alice had never been a big believer in the "walk of shame" following a questionable hookup. When you got right down to it, *all* of her hookups were questionable, and that was just her actual life, so whatever. And you couldn't "walk" in zero gravity anyway.

And yet, as she tried to drift inconspicuously back to her own apartment, she felt quite conspicuous indeed, as though she were marked head-to-foot in three sets of handprints, and Jesus Christ already, would these astronettes *quit looking at her*? She was on-mission. The *President of the United States* had told her to use sex to manipulate people. So why did it feel like both a betrayal of their trust *and* a step too far beyond her own comfort zone?

She wanted to get out of sight and sleep this off, but still she avoided the flexible shortcut tube between Gamma and Alpha Corridors, because the idea of it just squicked her out. Instead, she went back through the labs, back through Beta Corridor, back past Saira Batra, still quietly scrubbing the walls. Saira looked at her strangely. Finally, after what seemed like an hour, she made it back to her place, apartment Gamma-4. Opened the hatch. Went inside. Closed—

Bethy's uppercut slammed her in the solar plexus, knocking the wind out of her, and then Bethy's full mass was body-slamming her into the metal bulkhead, and the three millimeters of soft beige insulation coating the metal might as well have been asphalt, for all the cushioning it provided.

"Listen up, girl," Bethy hissed in her ear, "this isn't a goddamn summer camp, and you're not fourteen."

"Hi, Bethy," Alice said, her voice an embarrassing squeak.

"Fuck off," Bethy said. "I'm *this* close to putting you out the airlock and finishing the mission myself."

"I have new information," Alice said, through smooshed cheeks.

"Yeah? Let's hear it."

"Get off me."

Bethy didn't, so Alice repeated, "Get off, Bethy."

"Or what?" Bethy wanted to know. "You'll tell one of your little buddies? That wouldn't be smart."

And suddenly, with a sinking feeling, Alice realized Bethy wasn't on her side, either. No more than Dona Obata. No more than Sonya Kyeong. No more than anybody ever had been, in all twenty-nine years of her hard-fought existence.

Should she really be all that surprised?

"Who are you working for?" she asked. Then realized what a stupid question it was: Bethy had her pinned. Bethy was stronger and more aggressive. Bethy was firmly in control of the situation, and not about to relinquish that.

"That's a rude question, ducky. Why don't you let me do the asking?"

And that wasn't going to work for Alice at all, so she pulled the gun out of her pocket and jammed it into Bethy's ribs. Then realized it looked like a leg shaver.

Shit.

"What the fuck are you—"

Alice was as surprised as Bethy when she pulled the trigger. The gun barked and kicked, and suddenly all the lights were turning red and there were sirens blaring, and Lurch's voice was saying, "Explosion detected in Gamma-4. Explosion detected in Gamma-4. All personnel, seal bulkheads. All personnel, seal bulkheads. Damage control officers report to your stations. Damage control officers report to your stations."

Bethy let go of Alice and drifted away, holding her side.

"What did you do?" she asked. "Did you . . . did you *shoot* me? Oh my *God*, Alice." Jewels of blood were shimmering out from between her fingers, shining in the red emergency lights.

"I'll shoot you again," Alice warned.

The lights in the apartment slowly turned white again, and the sirens quieted but did not go silent. Apparently, they'd already made their point. Well, good, Alice did not want to be distracted right now.

"Who are *you* working for?" Bethy demanded.

"Mankind," Alice said, meaning it. She was *sick* of this.

Sick of people running their own strange games on her, when all she wanted to do was save the fucking world. Just that! Jesus!

But Bethy was quick; she lashed out with a kick, spinning the gun out of Alice's hand. It hit the wall, bounced back toward Bethy, who plucked it out of the air. But she was hurt, and the gun looked like a shaver, and she didn't know how to operate it, so she just brandished it vaguely.

"Stay here," Bethy said. "Please. I don't want to take you out."

"Give up," Alice suggested to her. "You're hurt."

"Nope."

Bethy opened the hatch and pulled herself out through the opening. This meant she had to let go of her side, which trailed droplets of blood in her wake.

Alice, who had seen her share of battle wounds, judged the injury serious but probably not fatal. Broken rib and a lacerated liver, maybe? The blood would clot before Bethy bled to death, but she'd be at risk for serious complications if she didn't get medical attention.

I did that, she thought. *I shot my teammate*.

She hurled herself after Bethy, and made it out into Gamma Corridor in time to see Bethy disappearing into the flexible tube that joined it to Alpha. Pelu Figueroa, the ultra-fit Argentinian, was out here as well, closing the hatch to her apartment.

"What happened to Bethy?" Pelu demanded.

"She's a government operative," Alice explained brusquely. "Do *not* let her back in here. Close this hatch behind me."

She then hurled herself into the tube, scrabbling along its dryer-vent surface, trying not to freak out as it flexed and twisted in her fingers. She rounded a blood-smeared corner, and then another, and then she was back in Alpha Corridor again. Still covered in three sets of handprints. She watched Bethy disappear into the docking module and slam the hatch behind her. There were rustling and banging noises on the other side of the hatch, and by the time Alice got to it, the handle wouldn't budge.

"Bethy!" she shouted.

This wasn't good. This really wasn't good, because the only stuff on the other side of the hatch were spaceships (*Dandelion* and two maintenance pods), a spacesuit gowning area, an egress lock, and one of the station's two airless, robotically tended manufactories. If Bethy was planning to steal *Dandelion*, it would maroon everyone here. Alice was pretty sure you couldn't get back to Earth in a maintenance pod. She was pretty sure the pods didn't have enough fuel for such a drastic orbit change, and she knew for a fact that they didn't have food or water or bathrooms or any fucking thing. Of course, ESL1 Shade Station's manufactories were probably capable of making another *Dandelion*, or better yet, one of the actual rocketships Derek was talking about, that could get to Earth and back in less than two weeks. But Bethy stealing a spaceship and escaping was actually the best possible scenario, here, because if Bethy wasn't headed back to Earth, then she was headed outside, for some nefarious purpose she'd never shared with Alice. And if these people were *lucky*, that might only mean damaging the giant electrical transformers or the telecommunications array. If they were *unlucky*, it could mean some devious sabotage of the Shade itself, or explosive decompression of the entire station, module by sealed module. Of course, Bethy couldn't have smuggled any serious explosives with her from Earth, or the RzVz ground teams and/or the Transit Point Station crew would have caught it. And while she might conceivably have managed to improvise some explosive devices here at Esley, she was caught by surprise at this moment, shot in the ribs by an erstwhile friend. Not prepared.

Ergo, whatever she was planning must not involve any equipment. Alice found that idea particularly chilling somehow. If Bethy shut off the magnetic containment on the antimatter storage, could she maybe vaporize the entire station, blow a city-sized hole in the Shade, and send the rest of it flailing and crumpling into a useless solar orbit? Just a giant wad of tissue-thin space junk to warn the other three Horsemen, and anyone else who dared to dream big. Jesus. Did Bethy know how to do that? Did *everyone but Alice* know how to do things like that?

Maybe it wasn't even that hard; these people weren't exactly security conscious. Maybe there was a big red DESTROY EVERYTHING switch hanging out in plain sight. If so, then Alice could be utterly fucked, along with everyone else on this station. Bethy had to be stopped. But how? Should Alice head for the other egress lock on the far side of the station, climb into a spacesuit, exit the station, find Bethy, and . . . What? Kill her? How? With what?

It truly sucked to feel so helpless, but what it really

meant was that she needed help. She'd never in her life needed it more! She turned—and Derek was there. His hair all messy, his lips all red, his coverall zipped only navel-high over a hairy torso bare of space underwear. He was barefoot, too, but he was here.

"What's happening?" he asked, not in an accusatory way, but just one crew member to another. *What's our emergency?*

In a rush, Alice said, "I'm not retired! I'm a brevet major in the U.S. Air Force, here on special assignment! Your commission is subject to involuntary reactivation right the fuck now, on orders from the President of the United States. I need your help!"

Derek stared at her for three full seconds. "What?"

"Air Force. You. Now. Bethy Powell is some kind of enemy agent, and she's on the other side of this hatch!"

"What?"

"Derek!"

"What . . . do you want me to do? I mean, do you have any proof? Of anything you're saying?"

Thinking for the both of them, she said, "No. Fuck you. We've got to suit up and get outside, right now. Come with me. Come on!"

She pushed and dragged him back toward the flexible tube. The other gowning area and egress lock were accessible through the employee break room, on the other side of Gamma Corridor.

"Governments are scared pissless of this place," she told him. "There's no telling what she might do. Assuming she's even working for a government."

Derek went into the tube ahead of her, not quite

willingly, and Alice followed close behind, saying, "I'm worried she's going for the antimatter."

"Oh. Fuck."

"Yeah. Move! Move! Can you get into a maintenance pod from the outside?"

"Um, maybe. If we blow the docking bolts . . ."

They spilled out into Gamma Corridor and swam toward and then through the breakroom.

"I thought you were just a medic," Derek protested.

"I am. Go! Go!"

When they got to the gowning area, they encountered a major obstacle, in that both their spacesuits were back at the other airlock. "Find something close," she said, rifling through the suit lockers. She found one that said S. LINCOLN on the breast, and "5" on the back, that looked to be about her size.

"These are all women's suits," he said.

"Find something, Derek." She struggled into the suit marked S. LINCOLN, hoping to God she wasn't forgetting a step and about to suffocate herself in the emptiness of space. She put the pants on first, then tried to slither up into the top half and realized the whole thing was too tight. She was still wearing her coverall! She stripped out of the spacesuit, and then the coverall, then slid the suit pants back over her shiny-slick space underwear. Much roomier. A little too roomy, but whatever; she got the top half on as well, and rotated the seals into place the way they had taught her at RzVz flight training. She'd never had to do it herself before; at Paramaribo there'd been a whole staff of assistants rushing her through the process. At Transit Point, they'd all been helping each other. Now, just her.

Meanwhile, Derek appeared to be struggling. He'd found an XL-type spacesuit—Jeanette Schmidt's—but it was XL in all the wrong ways. Wide through the hips and chest, not tall enough. He could fit himself into the pants and top, but he couldn't get them to mate at the waist. And his arms stuck out way too far. No way to fit a glove over that.

"No go," he said.

"Is there anything else?"

"I don't think so. You might have to go out there without me."

Alice found that idea way more terrifying than jumping out of an airplane with an oxygen mask and a gun, but it was about par for the course, so whatever.

"Okay," she said.

He shrugged back out of the suit top and, basically naked in wide-waisted spacesuit pants, helped her with the rest of her gowning operation. They were nearly finished when two women showed up. Their coveralls said S. DELAO and Y. MING. Both looked scared, which Alice found annoying.

"What?" she barked at them.

"We're the damage control party," said Delao.

"Great. Suit up and get out there. I need you to climb around to the other egress lock and unjam the hatch from inside."

"Who the hell are you?" Y. Ming demanded.

"I'm the new head of security, and I'm going to kick your face in if you speak to me like that again. Come on. We've got a saboteur out there."

"I'm not fighting any saboteur," said Delao.

To which Alice said, "Jesus, are you stupid? I'm asking you to open a fucking door. Derek and I will handle the saboteur."

"Who is it?" Ming asked.

"The Kiwi. Bethy." And then Derek slapped her helmet down and dogged it into place, and the sound insulation was really quite good. She could barely hear Ming's reply, and couldn't understand a word of it.

Then a voice rang out in her helmet: Igbal's. "What the hell is going on out there, Sandy?"

"This is Alice. I swiped Sandy's suit."

"Okay. What the hell is going on, *Alice*?"

"Saboteur, outside," she said. "Maybe headed for the antimatter. I'm going to need you to clear this channel and let the grown-ups talk."

Then, because that was rude and stupid even for her, she added, "I'll keep you posted as things are happening."

"Roger," he said. "I'll provide, what do you call, operational support as needed."

"Perfect," she said. Then, as she made her way into the egress lock: "Actually, do you have a location on Bethy Powell?"

"Hold on. Yeah, her suit is outside the station. She must have overridden the pre-breathe cycle, because the outer hatch is already open."

"Fuck."

Alice might not be much of an astronaut, but she was a hell of a sky-to-scuba diver; she knew all about decompression sickness. If you reduced pressure too quickly, you risked nitrogen bubbles in the bloodstream that could hit you like a liter of vodka and a fall down the stairs. In extreme cases you could outright die from it, with pink foam bleeding out of every orifice, but that mainly happened when swimming upward too quickly from deep water, with several atmospheres of pressure change over just a few minutes' time. When dropping unexpectedly from aircraft atmosphere (say, eight hundred millibars of normal air) to jump suit atmosphere (three hundred millibars of nearly pure oxygen), the risk was permanent disability via, as the Maroon Berets called it, "the bends, the chokes, and the staggers." It was really random, for reasons no one had ever understood, but if you screwed up enough and got unlucky enough and postponed treatment long enough, the joint pain and bone aches and flu-like malaise could dog you for the rest of your life. Alice knew a guy who'd Purple-Hearted out of the service in exactly that way.

If Bethy had cycled through the airlock in just a few minutes, then she was definitely at risk. And so was anyone following her out.

"This is a damage control situation," she told Ming and Delao, shouting a little to be heard through the helmet visor. "As soon as I'm out of the airlock, you need to get in and out of there as quickly as you can. No fucking around. Okay?"

The two women (currently shrugging out of their coveralls, revealing bright blue and bright paisley space underwear, respectively), nodded unhappily.

"Once you unstick that hatch and get Derek where he needs to be, come back outside again, quickly again, and wait for instructions. Okay? I know it's a risk, but the whole station is in danger."

They nodded again, miserably.

And then Derek was closing the inner hatch, leaving Alice alone in the egress lock.

"You all right?" Igbal asked her.

"Yep," she said, more or less meaning it. She was terrified, breathing faster than she'd like, and she had no idea what was going to happen or what she was going to do or whether she'd even be alive fifteen minutes from now. But for her that was pretty much a normal day at the office.

Igbal said, "I wasn't wrong about you, was I?"

"You were," Alice said. "But not like you think."

The airlock controls were pretty self-explanatory, so she shut off the air flow, overrode the pre-breathe and egress cycles, and turned on the vacuum pump. For thirty seconds or so, the air reverberated with a kind of mechanical slurping noise as it was pumped out of the chamber and into a storage tank somewhere. In an even bigger emergency, she could vent it directly to outer space, or even blow the explosive bolts on the outer hatch, but that would be wasteful, and she still hoped there was a future where that mattered.

As the air pressure dropped below four hundred millibars, the pump noises got noticeably quieter, not because the pump was shutting down, but because there wasn't as much air to carry the sound waves.

"Bethy can probably hear us," she said. "Can you cut her out of the channel?"

"Yeah, hang on. Lurch, would you please take Elizabeth Powell's spacesuit off the voice network?"

"Acknowledged," said a too-deep voice.

Take that, Bethy. Now you're alone.

Was she, though? During field engagements, if a lone operative fled on foot into the ocean, it meant only one thing: there was a submarine standing by to pick them up.

"Ig, where is Bethy now?"

"Floating free," Igbal answered. "She's activated her jets, heading for the Hub. Heading for the particle accelerator, actually."

"Fuck. That's not good."

"I agree."

"Hello?" said Derek's voice.

"Derek, where are you? Are you at the stuck hatch?"

"Close to it, yes. Alpha Corridor comm panel."

"Okay, stand by. Igbal, how much would you say that block of antimatter is worth?"

"That depends. Who's buying?"

"Let's say it's Cartel *vengadores*."

"Instead of a nuke? They could build a big nuke for about twenty billion dollars. Or a lot of little ones."

Fuck. Stealing an unguarded brick of antimatter would surely cost a lot less than that. Hell, subverting a government operative probably cost next to nothing, which made Alice wonder why *she'd* never been approached, the way Bethy and Dona clearly had. Too fucking honest? Too fucking stupid?

Operationally, it was better if Bethy were planning to steal the antimatter rather than simply igniting it in place. But not a lot better, because she'd want to cover her tracks, make the whole thing look like an accident. Leave no witnesses to report anything missing.

Alice could feel the spacesuit inflating around her as

the pressure dropped below two hundred millibars, then one hundred. But then it started to slow down, as the pump had a harder and harder time biting into anything. The lights dimmed, as if to show the air was no longer breathable. Alice found the control for her headlamps, and switched them on, turning the airlock chamber into a puppet show of light and shadows.

"Guys," she said, "I think there might be some sort of stealthed spaceship in our vicinity. Maybe not very large. Bethy's got to have some sort of an exit plan."

"Okay," Igbal said carefully. "I'll see what the *real* Sandy can pull up on sensors."

"Maybe nothing," Derek warned. Alice was inclined to agree. There wasn't much that could hide from high-end entangled radar, but regular navigation sensors were easily spoofed. That and a good coat of black paint could take you pretty far against the night sky. You could still track an aircraft by star occultation, but the Air Force rumor mill insisted true invisibility was also a thing, where light rays were bent all the way around an object, or recreated verbatim on the opposite surface. Alice had never seen it, but she had no reason to doubt it was possible.

"If Bethy gets to that ship," she said, "we're probably all dead. Hell, if she gets to the antimatter we could all be dead."

For example, if Bethy were a saboteur on a suicide mission, or a thief with less than perfect technique. Did Alice really want to wait around for that?

She said, "This is taking too long. I'm venting the airlock."

She did so, and with a little popping sensation the last

of the pressure fell away from her. The suit stiffened, like an old-fashioned air-pumped tire.

"I'm opening the outer hatch."

"If there's a ship," Igbal said while she did this, "it could also be listening. I'm going to encrypt the channel."

"Good idea," said Derek.

"We're suited up and ready to go," said Delao.

Okay, then. Outside the airlock was a cold, starry night, in the shadow of the Hub. Stepping out into it was actually much gentler than jumping out of an airplane.

She took a breath.

Looked around.

Drank in the wonder of it all. Above her: the stars, the full Earth and the full Moon behind it. Below: the station, the Shade, the Hub. She could even see Bethy, about a kilometer away, by the side-glare of Bethy's own headlamps. She hadn't thought to stealth herself and drift in the darkness. She was halfway to the Hub and a third of the way to the particle accelerator.

"I'm closing the hatch," Alice said, and did so, dogging it shut. Then she turned toward Bethy, let go of the handrail, and leaped out into the void with all her might.

Which was stupid, because her suit was equipped with jets. There was a two-nub controller on either pointer finger, so you could make a fist and steer with either thumb. She spent about ten seconds familiarizing herself with the controls, which were video-game easy. Then she somersaulted for fun, and engaged the jets for real. A speedometer in her helmet display ticked upward, and upward some more.

With gentle but relentless acceleration, she quickly

gained speed on Bethy; in just a few seconds, she could see the distance between them getting smaller. She gave it a few seconds more, all the way up to fifty kph, and then reverted to coasting, with just occasional steering pulses to keep herself from rotating too far off her motion vector.

When you were skydiving, you used the slipstream itself to rotate and steer your body. This was different, and yet weirdly not *that* different. Cruising at fifty kph felt really pretty normal to her—actually a bit on the lazy side. She was simply flying downward at an angle to form up with another skydiver, same as she'd done a thousand times before. Literally, a thousand!

"We're depressurizing," said Delao.

"Good," Alice told her. "Do it quickly." Then: "Igbal, what does the antimatter look like?"

"Used to be too small to see, but the last time I looked it was a softball-sized sphere. Growing one atom at a time, like a tree."

"What does it *look* like?"

"It's a soft, shiny metal, like tin. Spinning around in a magnetic vacuum bottle that looks like a gumball machine."

"Can you shut the accelerator off?"

"I already have."

"Okay. And these magnets that hold your softball, are they *permanent* magnets?"

"No, tunable electromagnets, very strong. Run by a little computer that keeps the sphere from approaching the walls."

"Huh. Okay, well, what happens if I hit your gumball machine really hard?"

"It's designed to withstand a fifty-thousand-gee impact."

"Meaning what?"

"Golf club, very hard, in exactly the right spot. I doubt you could do it."

"You *doubt* it? That's your fail-safe system? Jesus. What happens if the magnets fail?"

"They won't. They're fueled by trace annihilation events. The closer the sphere gets to the walls, the stronger the field gets. Thing puts out gamma rays, by the way, so I wouldn't handle it any longer than absolutely necessary."

"Ah. Great."

Bethy seemed to have realized she was being followed, probably because Alice's headlamps were clearly visible in her rearview mirrors. Her jets plumed to life for a few seconds, adding additional velocity. Alice matched it easily, and it suddenly occurred to her that Bethy had no great body of skydiving experience to fall back on. She'd jumped out of a plane maybe ten times in her life, so even though she'd spent three months kicking Alice's ass at the Marriott Stars, she was at a disadvantage now, and probably scared. Lit up like a runway at night, crawling along at a slug's pace, wobbling visibly as she fussed with the controls. Even flailing her arms a little, as though that would accomplish anything.

"Lurch," Alice said, "would you cut Bethy back into the voice channel, please?"

"Acknowledged," said Lurch.

"Bethy?"

No response.

"Sergeant Powell?"

Again, silence.

"I know you can hear me," Alice said. "You're *falling*, girl, and I'm right on top of you."

"Fuck off," Bethy said, finally.

"You're not getting away, you know. If you give up now, I'll send you back to Earth in hibernation, no questions asked. If you don't, I'm going to have to kill you."

"Stay out of it," Bethy said. "I've got your gun. I've got your *number*. How many times do I have to press your face against a wall before you understand that?"

"You're not getting out of here," Alice repeated. "Even if you get past me, whoever you're working for is most likely going to kill you. And everyone else here. Kind of people want a chunk of antimatter, you think they're squeamish about collateral damage? You think they keep promises to little Kiwi government girls?"

"Fuck off," Bethy said again. "You have literally no idea what you're talking about."

"Last chance," Alice said. "No? Lurch, cut Bethy out of the channel again, please."

"Acknowledged."

"We're opening the outer hatch," said Delao.

"Good. You know what to do."

Bethy added speed again, a dangerous amount of speed, and Alice realized that in order to catch up, she herself would now need to add more speed than she could safely bleed off before slamming into the particle accelerator.

Fuck.

"She's going to get there before I get to her."

"Uh oh," said Igbal.

"Yeah. What happens if that thing goes off? Will we all very definitely die?"

"Very definitely, yes," Igbal agreed. "That's one bad softball. I mean, normal antimatter doesn't actually convert to pure energy all that fast by itself. Surface reactions tend to drive it away from whatever it's reacting with, which makes it a lousy fuel. Skitters around like butter in a frying pan, spraying gamma rays every which way. That's why we made it antilithium antideuteride. That's, uh, basically H-bomb fuel. Once the reaction starts, a fusion explosion disperses an antimatter plasma that reacts instantly with everything it touches. Boom. We'd never even know what hit us."

"Ah. Great. I'll, uh, see what I can do."

A few seconds later, Delao's voice said, "We're outside. Our blood is probably fizzing like soda, but we're doing it. We're halfway to the south egress lock."

"Okay," Alice singsonged. "Thank you. Clear the channel, please."

Bethy seemed to know exactly where she was going. The particle accelerator looked like a kilometer-wide ring of end-to-end cargo containers, and she was headed for a wide spot—a building, basically—that was on the side of the ring closest to the station. Presently, Bethy jammed on her deceleration jets and started to slow down. Alice did likewise, judging the rate so that she'd hit the building—hit Bethy, basically—at a velocity she could safely absorb with her legs. Like jumping off the roof of a car instead of jumping off a three-story house.

Bethy struck the surface of the Hub, bounced away,

jetted back down to it, and grabbed hold of a grab bar—
one of many situated on and around the building. Then,
pulling herself hand over hand, she approached a red-and-
white-striped door, and activated some kind of control
next to it.

That's when Alice struck her, feet first.

Bethy slammed hard against the side of the building,
then bounced and tumbled away into space. Alice herself
bounced and tumbled in the opposite direction, but
corrected with her jets—they were not difficult to
operate, even in a dizzying spin.

Bethy flailed for a moment, apparently disoriented and
probably hurt even more than she already had been. Alice
came down on her back, octopussing around her with
arms and legs, freezing her in a spread-eagle splay. The
two of them joined as one object, tumbling vaguely and
also drifting slowly Earthward. Bethy struggled, gave up,
then started fishing around in a belly pouch.

"Lurch! Let me talk to her!"

Lurch, the sort of quick-on-the-uptake AI that was
comfortable acting on sparse information, understood her
meaning and said, "Acknowledged."

"Bethy! Stop it!"

"Get off me!"

"Bethy! Stop! It's over. It's over. You're not getting out
of here."

"One of us isn't," Bethy said, then reached behind her
to press Alice's gun against the faceplate of Alice's space
helmet.

"Wait! That's—"

Too late.

1.13
26 April

✦

ESL1 Shade Station
Earth-Sun Lagrange Point 1
Extracislunar Space

A phrase of Igbal's rang in Alice's mind: *ten thousand layers of micro blah blah diamond-sapphire polyschmolly*. That's what the windows in Igbal's office were made of, so no meteor—no matter how fast!—could penetrate.

That's probably what Alice's faceplate was made of, too, because Bethy's shot—whose impact was extremely loud inside the confines of a space helmet—bounced right off and tore through the much more delicate material of Bethy's right spacesuit glove.

Alice's suit radio came alive with screaming, as their two bodies separated. Bethy's arm fountained gray-white gas, along with jewels of freezing/boiling blood and little gobbets of bone and hamburger meat. Then the spraying stopped, the suit having inflated a tourniquet of some sort. Alice hadn't known it could do that.

The gun itself spun out of Bethy's hand and tumbled away into the night.

Fuck.

Launching herself off of Bethy's body, Alice flung herself in the direction of the gun, before she could lose sight of it in the gloom. Aside from her wits, it was her only weapon, and she wasn't about to lose track of it when she was deep in enemy territory. Her headlamps caught it as a series of flashes bright-dim-bright-dim as it tumbled away, so she jetted toward it. She still had her own actual mission to complete, and was dubious about her ability to do it alone (if Derek chose not to help her with Step Two) and unarmed (if she didn't catch that damned gun). She gave her jets a few pulses, closed the distance, and in another twenty seconds or so, caught it. Then turned herself around and jetted back toward—

Bethy had stopped screaming.

Bethy had *moved*.

When Alice had launched herself toward the gun, she'd inadvertently launched Bethy back in the general direction of the (now open) red-and-white doorway. Which she had then grabbed and somehow pulled herself through. Alice watched Bethy disappearing inside, into a space lit with a bright blue-white LED glow.

"For fuck's sake," she said. "Seriously, Bethy?"

Alice jetted toward the open doorway, and through it, into a white-walled chamber filled to bursting with gray pipes and orange and green bundles of cable. She crashed into Bethy's back again and grabbed for her again. But Bethy had caught sight of her in a rearview mirror, and even one-handed and twice-shot, she managed to anticipate and evade the octopus grab. Bethy squirmed like a snake—surprisingly flexible in her puffed-up spacesuit—and threw Alice hard against a conduit of some sort in a classic zedo move. No, not against a conduit; against the *goddamn antimatter containment vessel*. The gun went flying, again.

"Fuck!" Alice huffed, before Bethy threw a shoulder against her and drove the air out of her lungs.

Tactical error: Alice had the advantage in open vacuum, with nothing to push against and nothing to throw or pin against. In here, it was the same old story as at the Marriott Stars. Alice sucked at zedo, and Bethy did not. Period.

"You brought this on yourself," Bethy said, finding a handhold with her left arm and pulling the shoulder of her right one deeper into Alice's solar plexus. Beside Alice's head, a slightly irregular, silvery-gray spherical object glittered and spun, inside a thing like a trash-can-sized gumball machine. Great. Thing was probably spraying gamma rays directly in her face. Also, where was Bethy getting the energy for all this? Her hand was shredded, practically blown right off.

She'd seen this kind of thing before among injured Cartel heavies, and it usually meant methamphetamine or cocaine, or something even nastier and more modern that offered boundless energy and made pain irrelevant. Had Bethy brought it with her, or snuck some time on the drug printer? Had she anticipated a struggle all along? What a depressing thought! So much for ever being friends, with anyone, ever.

Also, Alice couldn't breathe. Fuck. *Fuck!* Alice *couldn't breathe*.

"Brought it on yourself," Bethy said again. "Sorry, I

really woulda left you alone. Your choice to have it like this."

But Alice still had a free hand. The angle wasn't great, but if Bethy weren't wearing a spacesuit, Alice could possibly have very awkwardly choked her with it, or slapped her on the side of the head. As it was, she had to settle for undoing the latch on Bethy's helmet.

Would have left you alone, too, girl. Would have sent you back to Earth.

The latch was ridiculously easy to operate—yet another security issue RzVz had never thought to worry about. You had to pinch the two spring-loaded scissor arms of the latch together with your thumb and middle finger, and then twist counterclockwise. It was basically impossible to do by accident, but also pretty difficult to stop someone else from doing on purpose.

"What are you—" Bethy paused, then screamed. Her good (left) hand let go of the grab rail and pawed at Alice's hand, but it was half a second too late. Her scream got louder and more shrill, then fell silent as her helmet popped off like a champagne cork.

Bethy's eyes widened in shock, then dilated in terror, then seemed to bulge and glaze over in an unnatural way. Alice could *see* the air whooshing out of her open mouth, still apparently trying to scream. Bethy blinked several times and then let go of Alice, let go of her grab rail. Alice thought for a moment that that was it, but instead Bethy bunched up her legs and then *launched* herself in the direction the helmet had flown. It was back there somewhere, behind pipes and wires, rattling around silently in the vacuum of space.

Alice, though surprised, was used to dealing with unexpected shit, so she simply grabbed Bethy's foot and messed up her trajectory.

The two of them spun together through the maze of machinery surrounding the antimatter core. Bethy thrashed and kicked, and then *really* kicked, and then fell still.

Alice waited to see if something else was going to happen.

She waited some more.

Their tangled bodies came to rest against one of the chamber's white walls.

Nothing happened.

"Jesus," she said.

She was actually a bit surprised to be alive, surprised to have beaten Bethy Powell in hand-to-hand combat. Surprised, really, to be in outer space at all, to have any of this happening to her at all. Life was funny, eh?

Then Derek's voice came over the radio: "Alice? Are you okay? I'm in the maintenance pod now, prepping for launch."

"I'm okay, yes," she answered, in a crisp military tone. "No injuries, no need of rescue. Local threat has been neutralized."

All of that was straight out of the Maroon Beret handbook. But then, as a mere human being, she added, "Bethy's dead." And for the first time since she was, like, twelve years old, Alice Kyeong began to cry.

1.14
26 April

✧

ESL1 Shade Station
Earth-Sun Lagrange Point 1
Extracislunar Space

Having cycled through the airlock's re-pressurization cycle fast enough to *squeeze* her eardrums and sinuses, Alice would have stomped her way into Igbal's office if such a thing were even remotely possible in zero gee. As it was, she flung herself into the room with an angry glare, wearing Sandy Lincoln's spacesuit minus the helmet. With her left hand she arrested her motion on a grab rail, while brandishing her leg shaver with the right one.

Igbal was belted into the seat behind his desk, like zero gravity wasn't a thing.

"Are you all right?" he asked her, with what sounded like genuine concern.

"No," she answered. "I just killed somebody I thought was my friend. Thanks to you, thanks to your crappy-joke security."

"I'm sorry," he said. "Thank you for saving us."

"Oh, shut up," she said. "This is a gun, and I'm not who you think I am, so stay in your fucking seat and listen to me."

"Okay," he said, surprised and a little unbalanced by that, but going with it. "What's on your mind?"

"I'm a major in the . . . Fuck. I *am* who you think, but I'm still in the Air Force. I'm an officer. I mean, I . . ."

"Take a breath," he said. "Take your time. You've been through a traumatic experience."

"It's not over yet. The trauma. I mean, fuck."

"Take a breath," he said again. "Are you going to shoot me?"

"No," she admitted, looking at the gun and then stuffing it in her belly pouch. "Fuck. I thought she was my friend. I thought we were at least on the same side. It's your fucking fault."

Gently, he said, "We know each other, Alice. Just talk to me. What's going on?"

"I was sent here to seize and secure this fucking place." She waved her arms, indicating everything around them, and also indicating how crazy it was. The assignment. The place. Alice herself, who could barely string two words together.

"By whom?"

"The President."

"Of the United States?"

"Yes. Tompkins. That one. They're terrified of you. They're *right* to be terrified! Jesus fuck, Igbal, you left a *kilogram of antimatter* behind an *unlocked door*."

"It *was* locked," he said. "It was. Locked."

"Really? Nice job. Really well done on that."

He spread his hands. "What do you want me to say? This is why I needed your help."

"Yeah, you sure did. Jesus. Now listen, if things don't go *aces* here, the next ship to hit your dock will be carrying a platoon of space marines. Or a nuke. Your fucking bullshit is over. Over."

She gestured to show it was over.

"Okay," he said, not arguing the point. "What are your orders?"

"My orders are classified," she told him.

"No, for us. What are *your* orders for *us*? You're here to seize and secure the place, fine, consider us seized and secured. It's the least we can do for you."

"What's that supposed to mean?"

Igbal sighed. "Let's start over. Why exactly were you sent here?"

"To prevent you from altering the Earth's climate."

"Really? Wow. Okay, I won't do that." He paused, then added, "I don't mean that in a flippant way. I *promise* I won't alter the Earth's climate. Or weather. Or, you know, crop yields and stuff."

Alice licked her lips and then spent a few seconds just breathing. She needed to get her shit together here. Funny, that she'd never once considered what to do once she was in control of the facility. Call the President and wait for instructions?

"You're already doing it," she said, "and you're a weird scary drug-addict pervert. To them, I mean."

"Not to you?"

"Jesus, Ig."

Pam appeared in the far doorway, the one leading in

here from Igbal's apartment at the end of Alpha Corridor.

"What the hell is going on here?" she demanded.

"We're surrendering," Igbal told her.

"What?"

"We're *surrendering*, Pam. The saboteur has been neutralized—thank you, Alice—and the U.S. Air Force is now commandeering this facility to prevent us meddling in the Earth's climate. Alice was just about to issue us orders from the President. Is that about right? Alice?"

"That's right," she said, struggling to calm herself and think. "Except the threat is *not* neutralized. Think about it: there's probably still a ship out there somewhere, and the antimatter core is *wide open*. I need you to send Delao and Ming over there to weld the door shut or something, just as a temporary measure. And I don't think the superpowers are going to let you have an entangled radar installation here, but for fuck's sake, set up some star sensors and quantum gravimeters, so you'll at least know if there's an *object* approaching. Burglar alarms. Strings and cans. Anything."

"I can build an entangled radar," Igbal said. "Pretty sure."

"Then do it. And meanwhile, *stop making the Shade bigger*. Jesus, you've already got more power than you know what to do with, and they *do not* want your help with global warming. It's the fucking . . . exponentialness of this place that really freaks them out. Every day bigger, every day more powerful. Just shut all the weavers down. Right now, right where they are."

"Okay," Igbal said, seeming to find that a reasonable

request. He waved at his desk, pulling up a keyboard, then started tapping instructions into it. "This could take a few minutes, but I'm listening."

"Do you have some proof?" Pam asked.

To which Alice replied, "We'll call the President in a minute. Meanwhile, can we also shut down antimatter production? Just as a temporary measure? I don't have any orders about that, but let's just turn down the crazy a few notches and give people a chance to calm down."

"Yeah, we can do that," Igbal said.

"And knock off the drugs," Alice said.

"What, really?"

"Yes, really. What are you, seventeen? Join AA or some shit. Have Pam design a rehab program. *I* don't care what you do on your own time, but President Tompkins certainly seems to. Give her what she wants, and she'll keep a leash on the space marines. Do we . . . do you understand what I'm saying, here? Dial *way* back on the crazy, in a visible way. It's your only hope of retaining control."

"I thought *you* were in control," Igbal said.

Just then, Derek and Jeanette appeared behind Alice, swimming toward her through Beta Corridor. Maag was close behind them, along with someone else Alice knew only by sight.

"What's happening?" Derek asked.

"Security matter," Alice said. "Best if you stay out of it for right now." She gestured at the hatch. "Can you . . . can we? Yeah, close the hatch, there. Right. Yup."

With a confused look on his face, Derek did as he was asked. There was a whole station full of people here who wanted (and probably deserved) to know what was going on, but Jesus. One thing at a goddamn time.

To Igbal, Alice said, "I don't know what the computer security situation looks like up here, but you're going to need to do a full IT review with top security experts."

"Our setup's not bad," he said. "It's pretty decent, actually."

Annoyed, she answered, "Imagine every bad actor on Earth, becoming aware of all the goodies up for grabs here. Right now you could be riddled with bugs and trapdoors and whatever the fuck. Deal with it."

"I will," Igbal promised.

"Regardless," Alice continued, "the superpowers are probably going to want steering authority over the Shade. I need you to set something like that up. Make them feel important, even if the actual controls are here."

He raised an eyebrow. "Whose side are you on?"

It was a good question. Wasn't she the President's asset? Should she give a damn about Igbal Renz and his plans? Why did she . . . why did she feel like helping him? Why did she feel like she was not only *his* only hope, but everyone's? Some huge swath of the future seemed to depend on her specific actions, right here and now. So what was it going to be?

"They don't know what they're doing," she told him. "They don't know what *you're* doing. You don't, either, but it's a different sort of . . . Just shut the fuck up, okay? Just play ball."

"Okay. Playing ball."

"Can you initiate a video phone call from here?"

"Of course."

"Good. Call the White House."

Soon, a giant video receptionist—animated but almost convincingly lifelike—appeared on the windows behind Igbal, blotting out the Earth. Female. Prim. Attractive but not sexy. Enthusiastic.

"Hello! This is the White House. How may I help you?"

Alice told the AI, "This is Brevet Major Alice Kyeong, on special assignment at Esley Shade Station. I need to speak with the President right away."

"I'm afraid that's not possible," the receptionist told her happily. "What is the nature of your concern?"

"Let me speak with a human," Alice said. "Immediately."

That was a request that, in most cases, legally had to be honored, but of course the thing just dumped her off on the lowest public call center employee in Bumfuck, Iowa. It took another minute to get his supervisor, and then another several to get *her* supervisor, and then finally a human being at the actual White House who, after hearing the summary of who Alice was, put her on hold.

"Not exactly the hotline," Igbal said.

"I have a private channel," Alice told him, "but it's text only. I think a video call is called for, is . . . I think now is the time for a face-to-face conversation."

Apparently, President Tompkins felt the same way; when she finally appeared on the screen, she had Vice President Vick Chambers at her elbow, and some middle-aged people Alice didn't recognize arranged behind them, photo-op-style.

Without even really thinking about it, Alice offered up a crisp salute.

"Major Kyeong," Tompkins said, returning the salute after a light-lag delay of eleven seconds. "I take it this is good news?"

"Mostly good," Alice confirmed, "although Sergeant Powell is dead."

After a delay, the President looked appropriately concerned. "What happened?"

Ugh. This was going to be a long, annoying conversation. Alice was full of pent-up energy, and waiting this long between replies was like swimming through honey.

"Sergeant Powell was turned," Alice said, "and she attempted to subvert the mission for the benefit of unknown parties. An altercation resulted."

"In a spacesuit? That must have been dicey. I'll expect a full report," Tompkins said.

"This *is* my report," Alice answered, unfazed by Tompkins' authority and really pretty fed up with the whole situation. "The station has been secured. Expansion of the Shade is being halted, and Mr. Renz here has agreed to cede control over its transparency functions. Its steering, I mean."

"To the U.N. Climate Bureau," Igbal added. "Or another qualified body designated by the U.N. I'm also going into drug rehab."

Tompkins looked him over thoughtfully, then nodded. "All right. I'm sorry to hear that, but it sounds like the right thing. The U.N. piece of it we can talk about, but three senior members of the U.N. Security Council are responsible for Major Kyeong being there. So it's a bit of a moot point. Major, what's your security situation?"

"Unknown," Alice said. "There may be a stealthed ship

in our vicinity. Capabilities unknown. We're circling the wagons and battening down some hatches. All hazardous materials are being secured, and we're monitoring the sky around us."

"Understood," said Tompkins. "Are the Shade controls secured?"

"I believe so."

"Well, that's the news I've been waiting for." Then, after a moment's reflection: "I'm sorry to say, until the situation reaches some kind of steady state, I'm going to need you to remain on-site at Esley to ensure compliance."

"Yes, ma'am," Alice replied. She didn't ask for how long, because of course Tompkins didn't have a fucking clue what was going on up here, and now that the crisis was maybe over she would simply take the credit and push the details off to functionaries. Same as any Air Force general, or really any leader Alice had ever heard of.

Tompkins asked, "What's the status of Captain Hakkens?"

"Never activated," Alice lied. "The whole thing blew up pretty quickly."

"Ah. Too bad. There could have been a medal in it for him. You'll be receiving a Distinguished Service, by the way."

"Whee," Alice said, unimpressed.

"We'll hold it for your return," Tompkins said, also unfazed. She was a Democrat from Illinois, long accustomed to dealing with ingrates and cranks. Then, on a more serious note, she said, "The Kiwis will expect the return of Sergeant Powell's body, along with some kind of explanation."

"If I had one, I'd give it to them," Alice said. "I don't know what her deal was."

"Hmm. All right. We'll see what we can find out at this end."

"And returning the body would be a lot easier if you guys would drop the fucking blockade. It's tight rations up here, ma'am, and that trip requires a bathtub full of xenon."

"Hmm. I'll take it under advisement. Watch your language, please."

"Sorry."

For a few seconds, nobody said anything. Then, with a smile, the President said, "Your country thanks you for your service, Major. Really. We owe you a great debt."

Again without thinking, Alice saluted. "Ma'am. It's my great pleasure to serve."

Tompkins returned the salute, then leaned on a button to hang up the call.

The Earth reappeared in the windows, full and bright as the day it was made.

"Well," said Igbal Renz, "by my count, that's twice you've saved us, in the space of half an hour. You're a hell of a sheriff. And hibernation medic, and whatever the hell else. Do you maybe want a job?"

5.3
28 April

✧

H.S.F. *Concordia*
Moored to Transit Point Station
Low Earth Orbit

When Tina Tompkins announced a "new cooperative agreement with Renz Ventures" that "puts U.S. Air Force personnel on-site at Esley Shade Station in an advisory capacity," nobody was much fooled by the careful wording of her speech—least of all Dan Beseman. It didn't help that on the very same day, Tompkins lifted the naval blockade of Suriname, and cut back sharply on the list of embargoed goods, or that an unfortunately timed "industrial accident" had claimed the life of an ESL1 staffer that same morning. Yeah, right.

Orlov Petrochemical and Clementine Cislunar Fuel Depot issued a joint statement to the effect that government interference in private enterprise was un-American and in opposition to multiple treaties and U.N. covenants. The terse statement stopped short of expressing solidarity with Renz Ventures in general or ESL1 in particular, and also stopped short of warning against any such action with regard to Clementine. But there was, Dan thought, an edge of menace to it nonetheless. It was a well-known fact that Orlov Petrochemical facilities had always been armed, and did not rely on national armies or governments for their safe functioning.

Lawrence Killian took a nearly opposite tack, saying in a personal statement issued by his public relations office, "Actions that affect the entire world should not be undertaken in a vacuum, so to speak. Igbal Renz's behavior has been worrying people for some time now, and it's gratifying to see some adult supervision brought into the mix. I have every confidence in the U.S. Air Force to steward this power as they have so many others, in the interest of peace and global security."

Dan Beseman, for his part, issued no statements and made no public comments, either for or against the U.S. action. He did, though, make an entry into his daily journal.

Dan was an extremely famous person already, and he expected to be remembered fondly by history even if his Mars colony somehow failed, so his journal, while private, was written with an eye toward future audiences for whom Dan was a long-dead historical figure. No matter how his thoughts might wander, he tried to steer clear of petty politics, or really anything that had no direct bearing on the colonization of space.

With regard to the blockade he had written,

> *The very governments that have declined to meet*
> *the demand of ordinary people for access to space,*
> *are now throwing muscle around to prevent private*

parties from doing it for them. This shameful demonstration is no doubt meant to intimidate, and it succeeds handily. Guess what, Horsemen: it's still Earth's decision whether you succeed or fail! But still, it makes an opposite point as well, that space-based enterprise must do its level utmost to cut these ties and dependencies, so people like Tompkins can only watch and ask, as opposed to dictate. I would rather face ten Orlovs than a single Tompkins, and if a colonized Mars can only speak to its parent as a beggar or a child, then we will have failed in one of the most important tasks history has ever set. Thus, with creativity and poise, we must make a world that can, as quickly as at all possible, stand tall and alone upon the face of eternity.

Now, faced with the reality that the U.S. military had infiltrated, attacked, and violently seized a privately owned space station, he thought long and hard about the implications (which were disturbing in the extreme), before writing:

I hope it's a matter of record, and infamy, that on this date, the U.S. Air Force killed a civilian while illegally seizing control of ESL1 Shade Station. At least, I presume it was illegal; I'm going to have our team look into it, with an eye toward filing a lawsuit for, at the very least, wrongful death. If not illegal, then the situation in space is even more precarious than it had seemed, with governments assuming the right to such piracy.

The lesson is, we simply cannot launch Concordia *soon enough. Until we're too far away to invade or harass, and until our critical supply lines pass over the countries of Earth rather than through them, we are similarly at risk of governmental bad actors.*

And the situation is even worse and even more troubling than that, because (reading between the lines) it appears to me that the attack on ESL1 was perpetrated from within, by active military posing as civilian recruits. Are such tactics limited to only Renz Ventures? I doubt it very much, given how very insistent the U.S. government has been about placing their own four handpicked individuals at Antilympus Township. Allegedly NASA personnel, but who can say what their actual orders might be? What they might actually be trained and willing to do on behalf of the U.S., and failing governments everywhere?

So, placing our own trust in these four NASA Feds would be insane. At best, they serve two masters, and at worst they serve only whoever their commander in chief happens to be when they land and de-hibernate. But what does it mean to distrust? Is it sufficient to set four or eight or twelve trusted people the task of watching over them, and tie up precious resources of time and human capital? Can such a small military be curtailed and overpowered by determined civilian overthrow? Or are the potential costs simply too exorbitant?

No, it seems to me that if people like Tompkins assume the right to conquer, then people like us should assume the right to keep Federal stooges in a state of hibernation, and ship them back unopened on the first rocket to Earth.

Is it fraud, to accept U.S. money under that pretense? Not, I think, if refusing the money merely shifts the mode of attack. We have the right to self-defense, and that has to include the right to strike first where the threat is clear. Certainly we have as much right to prevent interference as they have to interfere in the first place. It troubles me to think along these lines, but it does feel that our hand is being forced, in this and other matters.

The only reluctance I feel, aside from general unease at the necessity, is that any decisive action on our part may provoke an even larger and more decisive response. Just how long are America's arms? How long are Earth's? And why in God's name do they care what we're up to on a faraway planet, except to satisfy a deep-grained need for control?

This much I know: the sky is too vast to be owned, but we will carve out a piece of it for ourselves and ourselves alone, no matter what.

He was about to save the file, when it occurred to him that his cloud backups could well be under government surveillance. Then he was about to mark the file exempt from cloud backups, but it occurred to him that if his systems were compromised, that could be a surefire way to mark it for particular government scrutiny. Was he being too paranoid? Did the concept of "too paranoid" even make sense in the context of known villainy?

In the end, he simply backspaced over all the text, and exited the word processor without saving, and wrote the whole thing out longhand in a paper journal, like a goddamn caveman.

1.15
20 May

✧

ESL1 Shade Station
Earth-Sun Lagrange Point 1
Extracislunar Space

Over the next several weeks, Alice saw to security upgrades throughout the station. IT upgrades from world-class vendors, beamed up here a gigabyte at a time. Radar and other sensors, manufactured here on the station, with paranoid AIs monitoring them 24/7. And guns! She had one 3D-printed for herself from online blueprints that didn't look like a goddamn leg shaver, and she got one each for Derek and Igbal who, as the only unfrozen men currently onboard the station, felt left out without penis extenders of their own. She also got one for Maag, who had agreed to serve as interim deputy until someone more qualified could be recruited and trained and shipped up here. Alice also set up a crude but hopefully effective armed sentry robot on the roof of the antimatter containment building, that would fire on anyone or anything that approached without displaying a special bar code; and she installed 3D-printed facial recognition deadbolts on the two egress airlocks, so that strangers could get into the lock but not actually enter the station without assistance from someone inside. It was pretty basic stuff, but *so* much better than nothing.

Meanwhile, Pam was increasingly agitated about the fact that her pregnancy was advancing and the state of her hibernation technology was not.

"If I have the baby here, everything is ruined. I'll never get to Centauri."

"You want a planet named after you?" Alice joshed.

They were in the hibernation lab, surrounded by beeping, buzzing equipment. They'd been warming up Hobie Prieto for the last ninety minutes, and both of them were busy with their hands and minds, so the conversation progressed slowly and with frequent pauses.

Nevertheless, Pam glared back. "Don't trivialize this. I'd be stuck raising a kid for twenty years, *here*, when I should be there. I've earned the right to be *there*."

Alice didn't understand that. Raising a kid did sound hard, yes, but wouldn't it be a million times harder at Alpha Centauri, a decades-long journey away from everything Pam had ever known? Hell, with the speed-of-light round trip, if she called someone back home for parenting advice, the kid would be *nine years old* before an answer came back.

Alice had always figured if she ever had a kid, she would invite her mother to help her out for the first few months—maybe even the first few *years*—because she didn't expect a baby's father to stick around in her life. The men she wanted to sleep with tended not to be the sort of men who could be counted on for anything else!

And yeah, incompetent, chaotic help was better than no help at all. But "no help at all" was exactly what Pam could expect out there. Just a bunch of first-time mommies, thawed out alone in the wilderness.

But Alice had learned there was no point arguing with colonists.

"It's hard to explain," Pam admitted.

"Evidently."

"Are you saying you never thought about it? Being a Founding Mother of a whole civilization?"

Alice snorted. "I'm more of a second wave kind of gal. Or fifth. Or never. But I guess it's possible, maybe. Someday." She would first have to figure out what was in it for her, and whether it was worth the obvious sacrifices. That seemed unlikely, but her whole life seemed unlikely, so you never knew.

"Okay, we're going to start shocking the heart with some very gentle voltages," Pam said.

It made sense; Hobie was still as cold as a ham straight out of the fridge, but his tissues were almost fully thawed. The scanner showed that only the marrow in his long bones remained in a vitrified state, and she could see the last of that melting away while she watched.

"Four hundred volts," Pam said, touching a control on her tablet.

Nothing happened.

"No problem," Pam said. "Stepping up to five hundred volts."

She hit him again.

"Oh," said Alice, "that worked. I got a beat. Is it . . . wait, there's another one. Yes, we've got a sinus rhythm.

Thready and weak, but regular at . . . five beats per minute."

"Excellent."

That meant they could start active warming of the blood, and from there it was pretty much a normal dehibernation routine. It also meant Pam hadn't *killed* Hobie with the freezing process, which was probably a great relief to her Hippocratic oath.

"So what are you going to do?" Alice asked. "Really, actually. You wake up twenty, twenty-five years from now, pregnant and very far away. Everyone's giving birth, and you're, what, deploying gatherbots and setting up a factory? In your spare minutes between diaper changes, on a ship full of screaming babies? I'm not picturing this."

"It's never been done," Pam admitted.

"Yeah. So what if you fail?"

"We don't. I mean, we just don't. When Cortez landed his army on the shores of Mexico, he burned the ships, so there was no way out except through victory. They *had* to succeed. Not that he's a good role model, but the same thing happened on Pitcairn Island. The *Bounty* mutineers found the very remotest habitable rock, and marooned themselves there. And survived. Maybe they're not the best role models, either, but it's like that. It'll be like that for us. In the worst possible case, we actually *could* spend a few years refueling the ship and then return home. Or, I suppose, go back into suspension and await rescue by the second wave. But at that point, you'd have to wonder if you'd ever wake up again. That's what you choose instead of dying outright."

"Great, Pam. You're a hell of a salesman."

"You think we can't do it? Except for the starship itself, we could do it right now. Think about all the manufacturing technologies we've developed here. We start with a skeleton crew and a handful of machines. Gather the materials for more machines, build a Shade, build a *much nicer* station than this one . . . Even here, we don't really need the Earth, not really."

"Blood warmers are on," Alice said, changing the subject. "Leg squeezers are on. Electrolyte drip is on. Brain stimulator is on. Oh, *that* did something. He's warming up faster, like a tenth of a degree every . . . six seconds? So, about one degree per minute?"

"Good, good."

"Should I hit him with the epinephrine?"

"Hmm. The protocol is still a work in progress, but let's wait till he hits room temperature. Maybe fifteen minutes. See how that goes."

They waited in silence for a while, but Alice's curiosity continued to get the better of her, and she asked, "Do you plan to breastfeed?"

Pam didn't look up. "Huh? Oh, you know, probably. Or maybe one of us will be the designated dairy cow for several kids at once. We need to be very loose and flexible, about everything. Nobody said creating a new society is easy."

"Hmm."

That sounded a little pat to Alice. She could think of a hundred problems with that. Did Pam even care what Alice thought? Probably not.

More silence, and then more silence still.

She began to notice Hobie was warming up a little

faster. He was, in fact, shivering. His pulse was up to twenty-five bpm.

"Is that a good sign?" she asked. It certainly looked like one, although Hobie's long dreadlocks and very dark skin color made it hard to judge how well the blood was really circulating. He didn't look dead anymore, so that was something.

"I would say so," Pam allowed, "although we need to watch for cerebral rebound edema, which is a risk in patients waking up from deep hypothermic ischemia. I'm also seeing an uptick in neural activity."

She paused for a minute, and then said, "We're going to need to find a way to automate this process."

"We? You're going to be frozen. Are you saying *I* need to find a way? Because that's a little outside my realm."

"Actually," Pam said, "your old crewmate Rachael Lee is going to do that. She's been doing well at Transit Point Station, so we're going to bring her up in the next crew shipment. What's the status on Delta Corridor, by the way?"

"Ten furnished apartments, ready next week. Where are we going to install it? Right here?"

She pointed to a blank spot on the wall, where a plate could be removed and a hatch installed. The hibernation lab was one of two modules hanging off the gymnasium, and one of the few currently available on the station that offered room for expansion. The whole place had grown in a haphazard manner, one crazy module at a time, with no advance planning, and it seemed that was likely to continue for the foreseeable future.

"I suppose we'll have to," Pam said. "By which I mean,

I suppose *you'll* have to. As you say, if things go well here today, I'll be frozen by then."

"Yeah. Lucky you."

Pam waited another minute and then said, "Let's go ahead and hit him with the epinephrine, and also the vasopressin. Let's see what that does for him."

"Got it." Alice tapped the appropriate controls, adding a tenth of a milligram per minute of the one, and 0.03 of the other, to Hobie's drip. Enough to rouse his body's systems, without significantly raising the risk of cardiac arrest.

Almost instantly, the heartbeat sped up and got stronger.

"Shall we open the cryotube?" Alice asked. "I'd hate for him to wake up inside there."

"Go ahead."

Alice popped the latches and folded the clear, rubber-edged, oval-shaped cover aside on its pneumatic hinges, so it sat flush with the side of the tube.

Hobie's shivering intensified, almost as though he felt the room air swirling against his skin. His eyelids began to flutter.

"Should Derek be here?" Alice asked suddenly. "Aren't they friends?"

But before Pam could say anything, Hobie opened his eyes and locked gazes with Alice.

"Whoa. Who are you?" he asked, in a weak voice. His accent was Caribbean.

"Alice Kyeong. Air Force medic."

He struggled vaguely against his restraints. "What . . . Okay. How long was I out?"

"Sixty-five days," Pam answered. "Just relax. You're doing fine."

"It felt like two minutes," he said. Then, "Jesus, it's cold."

"Give it time," Pam said. "Your whole system is rebooting. It's a known process."

But what came next was decidedly off protocol. Hobie's eyes opened wide, and dilated massively, so he looked like a black-eyed corpse.

"I saw them!" he cried out, in a much stronger voice.

"Saw what?" Pam asked, looking mildly alarmed.

"Iggy's Beings! I saw them. They spoke to me! They *sang* to me. My God, they gave me a message!"

"Um," said Pam, not liking that.

So it was Alice who asked him, "What did they say?"

"To meet them," he said. "In the dark between the stars."

"Oh," said Alice. "Fuck."

And that, truth be told, was pretty much the last sane day of her life.

Appendix A

Dramatis Personae, in order of appearance

Alice Kyeong: Twenty-nine-year-old sergeant in the U.S. Air Force Pararescuemen. Sent undercover to ESL1 Shade Station.

Soon-ja (Sonya) Kyeong: Alice Kyeong's mother. Lives in Burning Man, NV.

Dona Obata: Twenty-eight-year-old operative from France's *Commandement des Opérations Spéciales*. Sent undercover to ESL1 Shade Station. Grew up in Brazzaville, Republic of the Congo. Posing as a space colonist. Allegedly has two siblings, both in Europe, and two living parents in Africa, although it might be a cover story.

Jeanette Schmidt: Twenty-five-year-old Near Earth Asteroid Resource Utilization expert from Texas, by way of Colorado. Traveling to ESL1 Shade Station as a legitimate colonist.

Christina "Tina" Tompkins: President of the United States, successor to President Yano.

Laurent Patenaude: President of France.

Igbal Renz: Founder and CEO of Renz Ventures. Inventor of Deep Belief Motion Control Networks. One of the Four Horsemen.

Pamela Rosenau: A medical doctor, and pregnant girlfriend of Igbal Renz. Red-brown hair, blue eyes, vaguely Asian features.

Elizabeth "Bethy" Powell: First Sergeant Bethy of the New Zealand Special Air Service. Sent undercover to ESL1 Shade Station. Posing as a hydroponics expert.

Malagrite Aagesen: RzVz space colonist, with aquamarine hair. Chemical engineer and manufacturing process specialist.

Rachael Lee: RzVz space colonist. Medical doctor. Initially left behind at Transit Point Station due to microgravity adaptation problems.

Brother Michael Jablonski: Senior monk and de facto leader of St. Joseph of Cupertino Monastery—one of the first wave of monks to settle there. Has a master's in divinity from Fuller and a master's in physical chemistry from MIT.

Brother "Geo" Giancarlo: Former Vatican astronomer, and resident of St. Joseph of Cupertino Monastery. A member of the first wave of monks to settle there.

Father Bertram Meagher: Abbott of St. Joseph of Cupertino Monastery. Has a master's in divinity from Fuller.

Grigory Orlov: Founder and CEO of Clementine Cislunar Fuel Depot. CEO of Orlov Petrochemical, founded by his father, Magnus Orlov. One of the Four Horsemen.

Daniel Florinovich Epureanu: Moldovan maintenance supervisor at Clementine Cislunar Fuel Depot.

Andrei Morozov: Station commander of Clementine Cislunar Fuel Depot.

Mikhail Voronin: Subcommander of Clementine Cislunar Fuel Depot.

Derek Hakkens: Pilot for Renz Ventures, based out of ESL1 Shade Station.

Charles Oliver: Commander of Transit Point Station.

Dong Nguyen: Worker and astronaut at Transit Point Station.

Nonna Rostov: RzVz colonist, a materials scientist from Eastern Russia. Amateur guitar player, somewhat nervous in zero gee.

Saira Batra: RzVz colonist and mathematician, with a PhD in Topological Transformation Group Theory. Short with frizzy hair.

Pelu Figueroa: Forty-year-old RzVz space colonist. Certified yoga instructor and weightlifting coach, very physically active and fit, with PhDs in mechanical engineering and astronomy.

Sandy Lincoln: Physicist and RzVz space colonist. Has a PhD in theoretical physics from MIT, and a master's in mechanical engineering from Purdue.

Yuehai Ming: RzVz astronaut and space colonist.

Sienna Delao: RzVz astronaut and space colonist, sometimes known as Dee.

Lek Szczepanski: An ethnically Polish worker at Clementine Cislunar Fuel Depot.

Brother "Puke" or "Porpoise" Purcell: Resident of St. Joseph of Cupertino Monastery. A member of the first wave of monks to settle there.

Eduardo Halladay: Space pilot for Harvest Moon Industries.

Brother "Fox" Ferris: Resident of St. Joseph of Cupertino Monastery. A member of the second wave of monks to settle there.

Brother "Bear" Bryant: Resident of St. Joseph of Cupertino Monastery. A member of the second wave of monks to settle there.

Brother "Huey" Hughart: Resident of St. Joseph of Cupertino Monastery. A member of the second wave of monks to settle there.

Brother "Dewey" Durm: Resident of St. Joseph of Cupertino Monastery. A member of the second wave of monks to settle there.

Brother "Dopey" Duppler: Resident of St. Joseph of Cupertino Monastery. A member of the second wave of monks to settle there.

Brother "Grumpy" Groppel: Resident of St. Joseph of Cupertino Monastery. A member of the second wave of monks to settle there.

Brother "Ham" Hamblin: Resident of St. Joseph of Cupertino Monastery. A member of the second wave of monks to settle there.

Brother "Eggs" Ovid: Resident of St. Joseph of Cupertino Monastery. A member of the second wave of monks to settle there.

Huntley Millar: EVA crew foreman at Shackleton Lunar Industrial Station (aka "Moonbase Larry").

Doctor Sergei Chernov: Physician onboard
   Clementine Cislunar Fuel Depot.

Dan Beseman: Founder and CEO of Enterprise City
   LLG, and owner of both the Mars colony ship H.S.F.
   Concordia and the soon-to-be-populated Mars base
   known as Antilympus Township. One of the Four
   Horsemen.

Howard Glass: Interviewer for *Mars Today*.

Oliver Wang: Mars colony applicant, bidding $4B for a
   janitorial job. CEO and founder of his own company,
   which he is selling to fund his Mars seat.

Carol Beseman: Wife of Dan Beseman, with a
   guaranteed spot in the Mars colony.

Hobie Prieto: RzVz pilot, originally from Jamaica, now
   resident at ESL1 Shade Station. First human to be
   placed in full-freeze hibernation.

Miyuki Ishibashi: Personal assistant to Dan Beseman,
   and Mars colony applicant.

Eldad Barzeley: Harvest Moon's chief solar radiation
   scientist.

Sir Lawrence Edgar Killian: Founder and CEO of
   Harvest Moon Industries, and a major financial
   backer of St. Joseph of Cupertino Monastery. One of
   the Four Horsemen.

Gill Davis: Personal assistant to Lawrence Edgar Killian.

Fernanda Harb: Commander of Shackleton Lunar Industrial Station.

Vick Chambers: Vice President of the United States of America.

Appendix B

Notes

Notes from Thread 1:
A number of ideas in this section, including the ESL1 Shade and the idea of "freezing" or "shrink-wrapping" stars, come from Dr. Gary E. Snyder, a noted aerospace consultant and longtime personal friend.

For information about low-thrust trajectories, I'm grateful to Stephanie J. Thomas of Princeton Satellite Systems.

The ESL1 Shade weighs roughly 2,000 kg per square kilometer, or 300,000 metric tons overall. Its total volume is about 150,000 cubic meters. If that same volume were arranged as a solid sphere, it would be 62 meters across. At 1% efficient photovoltaic conversion, the Shade provides 150 gigawatts of continuous electrical power, and blocks 0.1% of the sunlight reaching Earth.

Lithium deuteride (LiD) is a nuclear fuel used in hydrogen bombs that undergoes a vigorous exothermic reaction when heated to thermonuclear temperatures. Only a tiny fraction of its mass is converted to energy, but the explosion creates an expanding sphere of superheated lithium-deuterium plasma in which every individual atom is exposed. The antimatter version of this material is perhaps the most dangerous substance twenty-first-century technology could plausibly create, because it's not only capable of converting to pure energy upon contact with normal matter, but of doing so very rapidly.

The uniform for Transit Point Station is a red jumpsuit.

Notes for Thread 2:

The gamma mirror is another idea that originated with Gary Snyder.

For theoretical information about Mach-effect drives, I'm indebted to Professor Heidi Fearn of Cal State Fullerton, who is not responsible for my (deliberate) mangling of the concept in search of new physics for Sandy Lincoln to explore.

I have never taken DMT, but I am fascinated by the accounts of people who have, and particularly by how common it is for them to report contact with beings of some sort. So I thought: what if that were true?

The uniform for Renz Ventures/ESL1 Shade Station is a blue jumpsuit.

Notes for Thread 3:

Information about growing plants in Lunar soil comes in part from the August 2014 *PLOS One* article "Can Plants Grow on Mars and the Moon: A Growth Experiment on Mars and Moon Soil Simulants," by Wamelink *et al.*, with considerable additional assistance from Wikipedia and assorted plant catalogs.

Shackleton Lunar Industrial Station and St. Joseph of Cupertino Monastery are located near the Lunar south pole, at approximately 88 S, 70 E, on a 175-kilometer-wide strip of land connecting the Shoemaker crater with the Faustini crater.

Numerous details of life on the Moon are purely invented, or pieced together from the accounts of Apollo astronauts. Other details come from the excellent (though eclectic and sometimes disorganized) resources at Lunarpedia.org.

The uniform for St. Joseph of Cupertino Monastery is a traditional monk's habit.

Notes for Thread 4:

Composition of a typical carbonaceous chondrite asteroid is 3–20% nickel-iron, 0–20% water, 0–6% carbon, 0–0.5% nitrogen, and assorted minerals from which a certain amount of hydrogen and oxygen may be extracted, with effort. Since Clementine is in the business of selling fuel and breathing gases, target asteroids are chosen to maximize the presence of these materials, and minimize the amount of metal and dead rock. Nevertheless, the refining process generates a lot of slag, which is sold off as radiation-shielding material. The relative values of each material depend not only on how difficult they are to find and extract, but also how plentiful they are elsewhere in the solar system. For example, the Moon has large deposits of water ice (and therefore hydrogen and oxygen), but is notably deficient in carbon and nitrogen. These two elements are therefore among Clementine's most valuable exports, since shipping from Clementine is still cheaper than shipping from Earth. Since nitrogen is also a small minority component of the target asteroids, it is by far the most expensive substance Clementine sells.

The uniform for Clementine Cislunar Fuel Depot is gray spandex.

Notes for Thread 5:

I came up with the name Antilympus Township because Mt. Olympus is the highest point on Mars, and the lowest point on Mars is a crater that is, very approximately, on the opposite side of the planet from (i.e., antipodal to) Olympus. And because "township" is both a pun and a good way of describing its anticipated governance style. Sound reasoning, I thought, but I did this before realizing that National Geographic's TV drama *MARS* had already named its Mars colony Olympus Town. I wrestled with changing my own colony's name, but finally decided not to, because dang it, NatGeo's base has no reason to be called that. It isn't on Mt. Olympus, and it isn't a town. So, whatever.

Although "Antilympus crater" is a name I made up, the place itself is real, and is more than 8 kilometers below areoid, which really does give it the most Earthlike conditions anywhere on the planet. It's roughly 28 kilometers wide and reasonably flat on the bottom, so there's plenty of room for human settlements to form and sprawl. For anyone who'd like to find it on a map of Mars, it's located at 38.89169 S, 62.16064 E. The equivalent spot on Earth is in the southern Indian Ocean, east of Johannesburg and southeast of Madagascar.

Concordia crew members and Antilympus colonists wear two-piece tailored beige uniforms.

Notes for Thread 6:

Yes, Sir Lawrence could lift the airship *Lepidoptera* with pure hydrogen, if he were willing to risk Hindenburging it. He isn't. ^{3}He, or tralphium, has about 25% more lifting power than normal helium, and a mix of 5% deuterium-depleted hydrogen and 85% tralphium has about 30% more. For a gasbag volume of 5,500 cubic meters, this equates to an increased payload of 1,800 kg, or roughly the weight of a midsized SUV, circa 2020.

The uniform for Shackleton Lunar Industrial Station is a mustard-yellow jumpsuit.

Acknowledgments

As has happened before, this book would not exist without the constant nagging of my friend, Dr. Gary E. Snyder. I'm also extremely grateful to my wife, Evangeline, for forcing her way through early drafts of the manuscript. Other early readers include Pete Collins, Megan Richardson, Cully Salehi, and Wayne-Daniel Berard, who helped with details in their various areas of knowledge. Most of this book was actually written on commuter trains and park benches, using predictive typing in an email application with an on-screen smartphone keyboard, so I'd like to thank Samsung, Dallas Area Rapid Transit, and the City of Richardson, TX, for providing this critical infrastructure. Other sources of technical help are thanked in the Appendix, but I would like to extend particular thanks to David Brin for inviting me to a NASA Innovative Advanced Concepts conference, where the rough outlines of this story took shape over a period of about three days.

About the Author

Engineer/novelist/journalist/entrepreneur Wil McCarthy is a former contributing editor for *WIRED* magazine and science columnist for the SyFy channel. A lifetime member of the Science Fiction and Fantasy Writers of America, he has been nominated for the Nebula, Locus, Seiun, AnLab, Colorado Book, Theodore Sturgeon, and Philip K. Dick awards. His short fiction has graced the pages of *Analog, Asimov's, WIRED*, and *SF Age*, and his novels include the *New York Times* notable *Bloom*, Amazon.com "Best of Y2K" *The Collapsium* (a national bestseller), *To Crush the Moon*, and *Antediluvian*. He has also written for television, appeared on The History Channel and The Science Channel, and published nonfiction in half a dozen magazines.

Previously a flight controller for Lockheed Martin Space Launch Systems and later an engineering manager for Omnitech Robotics and founder/president/CTO of RavenBrick LLC, McCarthy holds patents of his own in seven countries, including twenty-nine issued U.S. patents in the field of nanostructured optical materials.